THOSE WHO FIGHT

THE LAST RECRUITS
BOOK TWO

K. N. MILDE

One More Chapter
a division of HarperCollins*Publishers*
1 London Bridge Street
London SE1 9GF
www.harpercollins.co.uk
HarperCollins*Publishers*
Macken House, 39/40 Mayor Street Upper,
Dublin 1, D01 C9W8, Ireland

This paperback edition 2026
1
First published in ebook by HarperCollins*Publishers* 2026

Copyright © K. N. Milde 2026
K. N. Milde asserts the moral right to be identified as the author of this work

A catalogue record of this book is available from the British Library

ISBN: 978-0-00-866525-8

This novel is entirely a work of fiction. The names, characters and incidents portrayed in it are the work of the author's imagination. Any resemblance to actual persons, living or dead, events or localities is entirely coincidental.

Printed and bound in the UK using 100% Renewable Electricity
by CPI Group (UK) Ltd

All rights reserved. No part of this publication may be reproduced, stored in a retrieval system, or transmitted, in any form or by any means, electronic, mechanical, photocopying, recording or otherwise, without the prior permission of the publishers.

Without limiting the exclusive rights of any author, contributor or the publisher of this publication, any unauthorised use of this publication to train generative artificial intelligence (AI) technologies is expressly prohibited. HarperCollins also exercise their rights under Article 4(3) of the Digital Single Market Directive 2019/790 and expressly reserve this publication from the text and data mining exception.

CONTENT WARNINGS
Violence, death, gore, PTSD, mentions of suicide and assault.

To Naila, who has been reading my stories since their handwritten era.

Where would any of us be without the friend who was there while the page was blank, torn, or crumpled?

PART ONE

ONE

TOMORROW IS HOMECOMING DAY.

Wild, considering just six months ago, all I wanted was to leave home. If you'd told six-months-ago me that she'd be amongst the top graduates of the Sector Protection Force, I'd have thought you were talking to my six-year-old self. You know, the me that wasn't yet disillusioned by SPORE and who wouldn't have preferred dying to becoming their brainwashed slave—sorry, I mean "sworn soldier."

But here I am.

A deep breath in. I slap a new magazine into my M4—my loyal companion throughout training—and come out of cover from behind the rough cement wall.

The crumbling hallway is swarming with infected: people turned cannibals by the NERV virus that spread about twenty years ago. I aim at one of the stumbling roamers, trap its head in my sights, and shoot. It falls on the floor, limp and motionless. My comrades take out the rest in seconds.

Some of us who survived Basic, like me, are still fifteen. Others have turned sixteen already. Big difference! No, really, every time someone gets to add a +1 to their age, it's a win.

"Clear!" Ryan, our squad leader, announces.

My squad is spread out around me, spanning the length of the corpse-littered hallway. Some faces more familiar than others. Cris turns to me from where he stands, a couple of meters ahead. Always checking on me. I give him a smile and a thumbs-up.

His hair is slightly longer than it was four months ago. He's sporting a wavy fringe that falls back and slightly to the sides. He also has a bit of stubble now, which makes him so deaddamn h—

"Your Honor, may we have a short recess?" Jose's voice to my left ends my distraction. She's quoting one of those lawyer movies she keeps forcing me to watch with her.

"We're almost done," I tell her. Just this floor.

Cris and Ryan are setting up charges to clear the path ahead, blocked by a double door.

Jose, who's been my partner and roommate throughout the second half of AIT, lets out an exaggerated sigh. She tucks a thick curl of dark hair behind her right ear, revealing the beauty mark under it. Her tired brown eyes find mine. "Feels like we've been going forever."

And she's right. We have been going forever.

Our last field-training exercise is to clear an entire street of infected. We started by establishing security and fire support outside, then lured infected out to the street, bombing as many as possible as they gathered in clusters. After that, we picked out the rest with our weapons. Once the street was clear, it was time for the assault sections —which my squad is part of—to clear the interior of the buildings. When we're done here, the street will be clear, and we can call it a day.

Tomorrow, after six months working as a Spore and four months in the Advanced Individual Training—AIT, I'll finally go back to Kadia. Tomorrow, I'll finally be free ... from Sgt. Orlov and the training radar, though those extra details ruin the fantasy.

But that's all the motivation I need to push through this one more time.

"Charges are set, everyone get ready!" Ryan declares as he runs back with Cris, keeping a safe distance between them and the door.

I hide behind the wall again; Jose does the same on my left.

Within five seconds, the charge goes off, and the muffled sounds on the other side of the door explode. A chorus of growls and moans as the infected burst into the hallway.

"Open fire!" Ryan orders.

I come out of cover and shoot the first infected I see. Following Ryan's lead, we move up, clearing the path and crossing to the next hallway.

Infected stumble out of every single room. Our lead team gets on the floor, kneeling, while Bravo Team stands behind us. None of our shots are wasted, but we're also taking out the infected slower than we were five hours ago. We're all exhausted, anticipating the end of this assignment.

"Hold!" Ryan orders when the last infected drops, and we all still, waiting in case more infected show up.

Ryan's been leading our squad for the past two months, since Sara was promoted early. He was the leader of the green platoon in Basic. There's a lot to admire about him. People like him make me think that maybe humanity does stand a chance after all, that it's only a matter of time before more Ryans and Saras and Crises make up most of SPORE, and we take out all the infected in the world.

But I'm not actually that optimistic.

We wait another moment, listening. Nothing. No growls or moans or footsteps or shuffling.

Ryan gets back on his feet. "Partner system. Clear the rooms!"

"Man, can this day be over already?" Evan from Bravo Team says. He's barely standing on his feet, sweat glistening on his face. "Ry, my man, let's call it. We're *basically* done."

"I really need a shower," his partner, Tristan, sighs. "I'm meeting my girl's parents tonight."

Everyone cheers at the news. I give Tristan a thumbs-up. He spent the first half of AIT flirting with this civilian we met at Vigor, before officially asking her out. Their love story gave everyone something more interesting to stick their nose in than my and Cris's pathetic flirting.

Evan punches Tristan's shoulder playfully. "Nicely done. Don't forget to send us wedding invites."

"All right, chop-chop, squad." Ryan's voice is a mix of authoritative and encouraging. "Alpha, take the rooms on the right. Bravo, left. Home stretch!"

Evan and Tristan straighten up with loud groans and join the rest of us as we respond, "Yes, sir!"

Cris goes with Ryan. I go with Jose, and head to the room on our right.

Nostalgia hits me as I walk into the suite's living area. The furniture's colors hide under layers of dust. Human remains and discarded clothes on the floor. Window walls look out on what I imagine used to be the prettiest, liveliest of views. Only now, it's nothing but abandoned buildings, blocked roads and bare stores.

Mom and I lived in a suite like this one. Well, ours was slightly smaller, and definitely a lot cleaner, but these days I can't help latching onto the smallest reminders of home. I can't wait to see Mom again, lie in my bed again, breathe Kadia's air again—even though Spheria's air is much more refreshing.

Jose and I check the bathrooms, the two bedrooms, and all the closets. Everything's clear. Jose's flipping through an old photo album she found on the couch. I come to a stop by the fireplace. The snow globe that sits on top of it has me frozen. Inside it is a tiny city covered in snow. I'm hit with a flash, distant yet close, a turtle snow globe on my desk. The spot it occupied is empty in the next flash, and I wish, more than anything, that I'd—

"Ashley?" Jose calls for me as she starts for the door. "Ready to keep moving?"

"Uh, yeah." I snap out of it and join her.

We head back out to check the next rooms, announcing "Clear" after each one, before we regroup with the rest of the squad in the hallway.

"All right, squad." Ryan grins. "I think that's it. We did it!"

Cheers resonate about the hallways. Jose jumps me with a hug that nearly throws me off-balance, but I let her have it.

"Great job, everyone!" Ryan exchanges a fist bump with Cris. "It's been an honor, working with all of you. Now let's head back so I can kick your butts one last time in Fight Street. Loser pays for everyone's dinner."

Various acknowledging responses ensue, bets and challenges and dares.

Jose wraps her arm around my shoulders and drags me alongside her. "I can't believe we're gonna be real soldiers tomorrow. We'll be *free*!"

Clearly, some people are more immersed in the fantasy than I am.

"They told us we'd be real soldiers when we graduated Basic," I say.

"Well, *you* are." Jose squeezes me. "That's why Sara was promoted early. Rodríguez did acknowledge you official Spores. That didn't mean you could skip the rest of training. Unless you're Sara, I guess."

I just nod.

A sudden scream erupts behind us. I turn to Ryan stumbling out of a room, an infected biting into his protective sleeve. Cris headshots it. It releases Ryan's arm and falls dead. Wrinkly skin. Gray hair. A camper, a type of infected that hides behind corners and waits for prey to pass by before it attacks.

"Oh, my God!" Jose gasps. "Ryan, are you okay?"

Cris hurries to inspect the inside of the room, and sure enough, more gunshots follow.

"What the hell?!" Ryan turns toward us, looking past me and Jose. "Why was there an infected in that room?"

I look over my shoulder to the shame-ridden Tristan and Evan. That room was on their side.

"You didn't check…" Ryan's voice drips with betrayal.

"Ryan, man, we're sorry," Tristan says.

"We're just tired." Evan scratches his cheek. "That was the only room we didn't check. Swear."

Ryan's lips press. "You didn't check…"

"Clear!" Cris comes out of the room. "Ryan, are you…" That question stays unfinished. Shock dissolves his tense features.

I recognize that look in a blink. Not a second wasted as I sprint toward Ryan.

"You didn't check." Ryan's voice drops to a devastated whisper. Hollow eyes fixed on his arm.

"Ryan." I stop in front of him and shake my assault pack off, setting it down beside me. "Let me see—"

"No!" He backs away, one hand wrapped around the spot that the infected had latched onto. "Don't come near me."

Jose gasps behind me as realization sets. The others panic. Cris tears up.

Ryan's hands fall to his sides in defeat. His terrified eyes scan our faces. He blocked the bite with his protective sleeve, but he didn't do it properly. Maybe because the infected took him by surprise. Maybe because he's tired, unable to focus. A quarter of the bite sunk outside of the protective sleeve and straight into the flesh. It's the smallest tear in his uniform, the tiniest drop of blood spilling out. But it's there, and it's all it takes. I can almost hear Sara's voice as she drilled it into me early in our training.

"We need to amputate it." I tell him what he already knows.

"I don't…" Ryan's body shakes, chest rising and falling quickly. "I don't want to."

It's not his choice.

"Cris," I breathe, and Cris grabs Ryan in a beat and forces him on the floor.

Ryan struggles and kicks and screams. Jose joins to help keep him down.

I get on my knees and dig through my assault pack for the equipment I need.

"No!" Ryan cries. "No, please. This can't be happening."

Cris pins him by the shoulders, Jose by the ankles.

"Ryan." I try to tie a tourniquet around his wiggling arm. "Stay still and let me do this."

"I don't wanna lose my arm. I can't—not now. Not when I'm about to—"

"I'm sorry," I murmur, my own voice growing shaky.

"Tristan!" His scream is guttural, soul-crushing. "Evan! Why did you do this? Why didn't you check?"

Neither Tristan nor Evan say a word. They both hang back, but their crying reaches me all the same. Rahul and Koji, the other two from Bravo Team, join us, sitting by Ryan's side, whispering comforting, soothing words to him. If only words could cure.

Once I tear open his sleeve and give him the numbing shot, I grab the surgical saw.

"I'm sorry," I repeat, taking a deep breath. But Ryan's not listening. Just crying, pleading for me to stop. "It's the only way to save you."

TWO

"MAN," Jose sighs as we take the stairs. Tristan and Evan carry Ryan on a stretcher ahead of us. Koji and Rahul are leading the way to exit the building. "Just when you think you're safe."

That's her first mistake: thinking we're ever truly safe. Come on, Jose, you know better.

"It just goes to show, you never know when your time might be up," Jose says. "You think we'd know this by now. But it never fails to take us by surprise."

I'm not surprised. Not really. Ryan is cool. A good leader. A skilled soldier. A kind person. But the infected couldn't care less about what or who you are. The only thing they care about is all the layers of fresh and delicious meat they get to tear off you.

The less gloomy side, because there is no real bright side here, is that Ryan survived. Unlike many others.

I look over my shoulder to Cris hanging in the back, far from the rest of us. Head low. Distracted. Lost.

"I wonder when I'll die." Jose rubs her chin.

"Don't think about it too much. It's all random." I leave her side and go to Cris. "Hey."

His face is grim with sorrow. "Hey."

I give his arm a light touch, then let my hand slip all the way down to his and take it in a light hold. Jose shoots us a quick, curious look, but continues without gracing us with one of her cheeky comments. I'm glad she can read the room sometimes.

Cris's gaze lingers briefly on my hand. His warm brown eyes meet mine. I hate seeing them so consumed by misery. "I really am cursed, aren't I?"

I hate his self-loathing even more. "No."

"Then why is it always my friends or partners?"

Distant memories from Basic hit me. Cris, sitting next to his friend, June, who'd lost both an arm and a leg. Cris, carrying his other friend, Sam, and bringing him to me to amputate his arm before the infection spread. Nathan, Cris's former partner, ripped to shreds by a pack of infected.

And now, Ryan.

So maybe the odds are stacked against me in this argument.

"All that time you spent teaching me how to shoot…" His jaw sets. "It's useless. Doesn't matter how good a shot I am now. Everyone around me always—"

"Tristan and Evan should have cleared the room, like they were ordered to," I argue. "It wasn't your fault."

"But I was there," he counters. "With Ryan. Right behind him. He told me he heard a noise. We were both going in to inspect the room, and out of nowhere this camper—"

"It could have been you," I cut him off. "It was pure chance that Ryan was attacked instead. *It wasn't your fault.*"

I have no right to invalidate Cris's guilt, because I battle my own on a daily basis. And yet, despite how torn up he is about this, I'm glad it was Ryan and not him.

Cris falls silent, probably too tired to keep arguing. But a little life returns to me when he squeezes my fingers. Gently. Tenderly. Desperately.

I hold his hand tight until we step outside. Can't be caught engaging in PDA.

The empty street echoes with distant, raspy moans.

"Please don't tell me—" Koji starts.

An infected shows up from behind one of the buildings to the left and charges at us. Jose shoots it. The moans don't stop, though.

"Wave spotted!" a voice comes through my earpiece. Leon from left-side security. "It's coming this way!"

Bite. Me.

"Oh, my God," Jose grumbles. "You've got to be kidding me. A wave? Now?"

"Stay alert!" Sgt. Orlov, our AIT drill instructor, runs up to us. "We've alerted the Horizon outpost; backup will be here shortly, but you'll take the brunt of it. Everyone, get in position! Form a defensive perimeter and hold your ground until backup arrives."

We've dealt with waves before. They've gotten more and more frequent over the past months, and the running theory is that the fugitives managed to get the sentient crawler to obey them and are now sending waves at Spheria to overwhelm our forces and weaken our defenses. Eventually, they'll be able to kick us while we're down.

Tristan and Evan hurriedly drop Ryan off at the Casualty Collection Point before regrouping with us.

Dealing with waves while at base is more manageable. Dealing with waves while we're in the outside, and the closest thing to a base is an outpost that's three kilometers away? Well, less manageable.

The first stragglers are easy to take out, but the real fight begins when the chasers arrive. Unlike roamers, chasers are—if the name doesn't give it away—fast. Fast and muscular and ten times more dangerous. They can jump and tackle and dodge, sometimes even more efficiently than us Spores.

To think we cleared this street just a few hours ago. As many of them as we shoot, more come. They manage to breach our line of defense and tackle someone from the Second Rifle Squad.

That marks the first victim. The second victim is the one that stupidly breaks rank to run toward the first one, hoping there's a chance to save them, only to get tackled by the next chaser. There'll be nothing left of those two, save for a few limbs and whatever chunks of their flesh will be stuck to infected teeth for a while.

I don't freeze like I used to anymore. Not in the middle of a fight anyway. But the aftermath? The second that last infected falls and the gunfire stops? The moment the guttural screams of the injured are the only thing you can hear? That's the worst part.

Around me, the street is littered. Corpses all over, some piled up, others scattered around. Half-eaten faces. Twitchy hands. And still, some aren't dead yet.

When it's time to sweep the area for those who are still breathing but won't make it—put a bullet or a knife in each one's head to make sure they don't turn, stop their suffering and give them the only peaceful death they can have—I don't feel like I'm in my own body anymore. I'm floating outside, watching everything from a bird's-eye view.

My throat clogs up as if someone stuffed it with stones and told me not to swallow them. I stand at the bloodied half-corpse of Tristan, his mouth ajar, the only noises he makes choked gurgles. His leg is twisted in an unnatural way and missing a good chunk of his thigh. The right side of his cheek is peeling and nearly falling off.

He looks at me, his throat moves up and down as thick, stuck breaths fight to come out of his mouth.

I try to swallow those stones, but they don't budge. My hands shake as I raise my weapon and point it at him.

The terror that bursts in his gaze spells out the words he can't utter. I lower my weapon and take out my combat knife instead, crouching beside him. His struggling stops, mouth closing. His eyes hold mine for only a few seconds before shutting. He's ready.

I'm not.

"I'm really sorry," I whisper as I place my free hand on one side of his head. His chest rises and falls fast. His body shakes. He *thought* he was ready. But he's terrified. I'm terrified, too. Both of us want this to be over, and there's nothing I can do except give him what he wants. I drive my knife into his skull just as he opens his eyes to look at me. All his shaking stops. His chest flattens. But he's still staring into my soul.

Regi's face consumes his for a beat. Her hollow, dead eyes haunting me.

Some of the stones in my throat drop to my stomach. They rip my insides as I sit still, looking away from Tristan's face, before I pull the knife out with a squelch as it drags against his brain.

I want to throw up.

Around me, the gurgling and gasping and struggling gradually subside, like someone is putting out candles one after the other. But for every voice that goes quiet in the street, another one gets louder in my head.

Since starting AIT, we've had a fair number of casualties. And every single time, it gets worse. Harder. More *impossible*.

There's something so wrong about killing people when you're the one tasked with saving lives.

How much longer will this go on? How much longer before I'm

the one lying on the ground with my guts spilling out, waiting for someone to end it all?

Four months. SPORE has been hunting down the Lotivan fugitives for four months, and they still haven't found Lori—the sentient crawler. The weapon that's supposed to save all of humanity and give us options we never had in twenty years since the outbreak. The option to communicate with the infected. Maybe even control them.

I thought that ... since *she* joined them, she'd make all the difference. Give it a week and they'll find the crawler. But nothing has really changed. Guess she's not that special after all.

"Ashley." Jose's voice behind me, her hand on my shoulder. "Come on, we gotta take the bodies with us. We're retreating."

THREE

CRIS, Jose and I are the designated drivers on the way back to the outpost. If we had any spirit left, we would've turned this into a race—like we did when we took off. Instead, the drive is quiet and gloomy. From the outpost, we get our rucks and take the choppers back to Spheria.

Ryan and the rest of the injured have been taken to the hospital. The dead—what remains of them—will be split between being sent to their home sectors or being buried here if they have no families.

We stand in rows, girls on one side, boys on the other.

Sgt. Orlov is at the end of the line, arms folded behind his back. "Such an unfortunate end to your training, but ultimately a necessary reminder of what your lives will be like every day. Real soldiers do not give in in the face of despair. They count each sacrifice, loss, and death, as a step forward for humanity, or even a leap. Real soldiers expect danger at every moment, even if—no, *especially* if the fight is already won, because that's when the battle begins. Real soldiers never underestimate their enemy, no matter how unintelligent they may seem. Remember this, if you want to live longer than your comrades."

None of us dare ask what will happen to Evan. Most likely he'll be discharged from SPORE and sent back home to do maintenance work, if not collect trash.

"Now, then." Sgt. Orlov walks down the line, handing out mail.

A rush of disappointment hits me when he walks past me without a glance.

Mom is on an assignment. Those are the only times she doesn't send me mail. Malhotra sometimes writes me in her stead, but I guess he's busy, too. Mom's work as a doctor barely allowed her rest, and ever since she became a field medic, well, she has even less time now. I'm glad she's managed to write me at all.

Cris gets one. He takes it with both anticipation and worry.

"Private Rey," Sgt. Orlov calls as soon as he hands out the last of the mail. "Private Brown. Come with me for a moment."

My blood goes cold and my eyes snap to Cris's across from me.

"Don't make me repeat myself," Sgt. Orlov says. "Follow me."

I hold a sigh. "Yes, sir," we both answer.

Jose leans in from my right and whispers, "Ooh, I wonder what this is about. I'm sure it has nothing at all to do with all the flirting—"

"Shut up." I swallow a lump and step out of the line. Jose's so annoying, but like, in the most endearing ways.

"Whatever happens, plead not guilty," Jose whisper-calls behind me and Cris. The rest of our platoon chimes in with various flavors of *you're in trouble* noises.

We follow Sgt. Orlov outside the barracks, until he stops under a lamp. The chill of fall overcomes me in seconds. I rub my hands together for warmth. The days are getting colder as we approach winter. Naked trees hold onto their last, dying leaves. I love all the nature in Spheria. All the color schemes the seasons go through. There isn't much of that in Kadia, so I'll definitely miss some things about living here.

"Privates," Sgt. Orlov starts, "both of you have filed, prior to your AIT completion, a request for reassignment to continue your service at your home sector in Kadia. Correct?"

Oh. Is that what it's about? Phew!

"Yes, sir," comes our urgent response.

I haven't seen Mom since my graduation ceremony, and I know Cris misses his parents and grandpa. Maybe his grandpa *more* than his parents, but still.

"Unfortunately," Sgt. Orlov continues. My chest instantly tightens. "Your requests have been declined."

"Declined?" Cris repeats. "Sir, what for?"

"Given the events earlier today," Sgt. Orlov answers, "Private

Herd, who was to be assigned to the Renegades, is no longer capable of serving. Your reassignment would be quite counterproductive, considering Kadia's thriving numbers. You will instead serve as part of Spheria's Special Operations Division, indefinitely, until further notice."

"But, sir," I argue, "if only Private Herd was assigned to the Renegades, how come *both* me and Cris are being transferred? Why not just one of us?"

"Because, Brown," Sgt. Orlov's stern eyes fixate on me, "you were going to be assigned to the Renegades regardless."

You've got to be kidding me.

"As of now you are both serving under the command of Lieutenant Zaid Mansur, effective immediately," he says.

Mansur? That's—

"These are dire times, and they call for desperate measures," Sgt. Orlov adds. It still doesn't soften the blow. "We had to promote some of your comrades early for these exact reasons."

I frown. "And what about our leave? We're supposed to be given leave for at least a week to visit family before our official assignment."

"Yes, unfortunately, due to recent losses on the battlefield, we are in need of as many active-duty soldiers as possible. You will be compensated in credits, and any plans for visiting family will have to be postponed."

"For how long?" Cris asks, voice wavering.

"Indefinitely," Orlov says.

Cris's thick brows knit together. Eyes darken. I know that look very well. He's not just sad about not going home. He's worried. The last mail he received was from his dad, when normally it was his grandpa who wrote him. But his grandpa's sick. He's been in the hospital for two weeks now. Cris was counting on our reassignment to go home and spend whatever time is left with him.

"Sir," I try, "can't Cris go? Can't you assign someone else in his stead?"

"Brown…" Sgt. Orlov exhales. "You already know these decisions aren't mine to make. I only relay them, and you obey them. Understood?"

"Yes, sir," Cris and I say, half-heartedly.

"Well then, I'm sure you have much to do before you relocate to your new station." Sgt. Orlov waves us off. "Dismissed."

I turn around and stomp off. Cris follows me.

I'm not surprised. Not at all. This is a fact that's been shoved down my throat over and over: I never get to do what I want. SPORE is a place we go to do what we're told, when we're told, how we're told. Freedom for us comes in one flavor: death, and it's usually delivered by the infected.

"Ash, wait up." Cris takes my hand and pulls me back. I nearly slam into him when I turn. "Look, I know you're upset. I'm upset, too."

"Really? Then I must have turned deaf, because I didn't hear you once try to argue our case—"

"*But...*" he cuts me off, "think about this for a minute. We're gonna be working with *the* Lieutenant Mansur. If that's not gonna look good on our résumés, I don't know what will."

I can't help a sneer. "You're excited about working under a man you've never met before?"

"I've never met him, but I've heard of him. Haytham used to tell me all about him. That's his uncle."

"Good for Haytham." I shrug. "Why should I care?"

"I get it. Unless they come up with a higher status than privileged, what difference does it make to you?" he deadpans. "I'm telling you it makes all the difference to *me*. It could change everything for my family. For Grandpa…"

Great. Now *I* feel like the jerk. "It's not about that—"

"Then what is it?"

"It's Colonel Sergei," I say. The woman in charge of Kadia. The one who made my mom into a field medic to punish me for trying to escape. Who threatened to get her "accidentally" killed if I ever tried anything again. "She promised to never let me set foot in Kadia again. There is no reason why they wouldn't let me serve in my home, unless she—"

"Then my request would have been approved," Cris interjects. "I really don't think this is about you."

"Yeah?" I fold my arms against my chest. "You don't think Captain Malhotra heard that Sergei declined my request, and decided to decline yours, too, so you can stay and keep an eye on me?"

Cris throws his head back with a defeated sigh. "This again."

Okay, I don't actually believe that, but I like teasing Cris about it every now and then.

Back when I first started training for SPORE, Cris's platoon assignment randomly changed, and he was then assigned to mine. He later confessed that Captain Malhotra, Dad's old friend, had intervened to make sure Cris was around me all the time, to try and keep me out of trouble after my failed escape attempt. It caused a rift between us for a while but ... now it's all dirt under the bridge, or whatever that saying is.

"So, what's with the letter you got?" I ask, changing the subject.

He tugs it out of his pocket and unfolds it. "It's from my dad. Grandpa's still sick but says he's getting better."

"That's *some* good news," I say.

"Yeah." He stuffs the letter back in his pocket. Worry lingers on his face for another second before his gaze locks on mine. "Look, this could be temporary. They might reconsider our requests a month or two from now. So, let's focus on the bright side."

"What bright side?" I roll my eyes in feigned exasperation, but the sudden sting of his warm fingers against my cold face makes my breath catch.

He strokes my cheek gently. I lean into his touch, half tempted to collapse onto him entirely. My stomach flips when I catch the mesmerizing brown of his eyes, illuminated by the warm light of the streetlamp behind me.

"We get to work together," he murmurs, the tiniest hint of a smirk curls his lips.

Well, bite me. He's got me there.

FOUR

DESPITE THE EARLIER TRAGEDIES AND the downer of news Cris and I received, everyone is headed to our favorite hangout to celebrate before saying goodbye tomorrow. Not that I'm in the mood to celebrate anything, but Jose insists on me coming—*it's my treat,* she says. *And we owe it to Ryan. He wanted us to celebrate.*

Ryan introduced us to the hangout on our first week of AIT. Vigor is located in the Fifth Sector—Spheria's residential section, due southeast. Like most of the shops here, it's run by civilians. A big, multistory building, it looks more modern than everything else in the suburban neighborhood.

Walking into Vigor is like walking into a utopia. Vibrant, colorful lights and beautiful music beats buzzing through the speakers. Soldiers in casual attire gathering in different spots to partake in endless activities. Restaurants and dining venues offering a wide selection of traditional dishes from around the world. Drinks that not only come in various flavors, but also textures.

We're greeted with cheering and clapping from the shop and restaurant owners. Streamers and balloons decorate the place—it's even more festive in here than it normally is.

My eyes scan one face after another, searching for a particular one. And disappointment gradually consumes me when I don't find her. Haze is probably on an assignment with her Engineering unit. She would have been here otherwise.

We bounced back faster than I anticipated, but I guess we both owe that to ten years of friendship. Not that we managed to mend everything, and there's still that occasional awkward moment where we're tiptoeing around one sensitive subject or the other (Will, my ex, being both), but ... we're friends. And some things were so much worse in my head than they were in reality. I hate that about my brain sometimes.

"Looks like we got ourselves a graduation party!" Jose grins and pulls me along by my arm.

Our first stop is the arcade machines, where we each get to play one round. Usually, this is how we determine who'll be paying for dinner on a given night, but tonight we play in Ryan's honor and nothing else. I used to suck at these, but I eventually got the hang of the controls, which then allowed me to compete against Ryan. He still holds the highest score. I never did manage to beat him.

Once Jose and I are finished with our turns, it's time for a break. We bump fists and take shoulder pats and greetings from almost everyone we walk by, until we settle at a table and sit.

"Good evening, girls!" Mr. Tooley, one of the restaurant owners, approaches our table with a tray of drinks.

"Hi Mr. Tooley!" we both greet him as he serves our drinks with a bearded grin, wrinkly eyes squinting in the process. A round of cheerful *thank you*s ensues.

"So, this is it, then?" He tucks the empty tray under his arm. "You two are off on your new adventures tomorrow?"

"Afraid so." Jose frowns. "I'm going back home to serve with the Hummingbirds platoon—which, dare I say, sounds *so* cool. And Ashley's... Well..." She looks at me expectantly.

"Renegades platoon," I tell him. "Spheria's Spec Ops Division."

"They're holding onto you a while longer, then?" Mr. Tooley gives me a sympathetic smile. He knows I was excited about going back home, same as Cris. "Know what? Your drinks are on the house," he offers. "Consider it a goodbye gift. Or a congratulations."

"Oh, no, you don't have to." I shake my head. "Jose already offered to pay."

"Ha ha." Jose kicks my foot under the table.

He laughs. "That's okay. She can pay next time."

"Thank you, Mr. Tooley." Jose smiles. "You're a lifesaver!"

"Before I forget, have you seen Egan?" he asks. "He offered to do the dishes today, after we close, but I haven't seen him."

Egan Kollin. That's Zack's alias—given to him to hide his identity from the general public. I'm surprised he hasn't randomly spawned beside me yet, considering how much he enjoys my company.

I scan the spots he usually frequents. One of the game booths. The secluded seating area further in the back. Nothing. "Likely his sergeant sprung some unexpected assignment on him."

"If you do see him," Mr. Tooley sighs. "Tell him those dishes will be waiting for him."

I give him half a salute, touching my hand to my forehead. "Yes, sir."

"I'll leave you girls be. Take care of yourselves, all right?"

"We'll do our best." I smile as he walks off.

My mouth waters at the large glass of strawberry and vanilla milkshake before me. Apparently, Mr. Tooley's daughter, Zoe, loved this one as well. She was one of the casualties in the Double Wave Attack. We caught him one too many times staring at her picture. Eventually, Jose embraced her nosiness and asked him about it.

Zack was there that time, and the guilt that cut through his face could have easily been mistaken for the sympathy the rest of us were offering. It's why he occasionally helps out here. I don't know if he'd ever tell Mr. Tooley the truth, or if Mr. Tooley could ever take it.

I take a long sip of the milkshake. "Well, gotta admit. This is one of the best things that came out of Spheria."

"This, and the fried rice Sara introduced us to," Jose says.

I try not to let the mention of Sara sour the taste of the milkshake in my mouth.

"Uh-oh." Jose raises her brows at me.

"What?" I furrow mine at her.

"You're making that face," Jose teases.

"What face?" I feign ignorance.

"The *I can't wait to see Sara tomorrow* face," Jose says, then lowers her voice to a whisper, "sarcasm."

"If I were you," I say, "I'd grab that milkshake before some inexplicable force knocks it off the table."

Jose snatches her glass in both hands, holding it protectively. "Is *that* why you're so upset?" She leans in, searching my eyes. "Because of Sara?"

"Nope." Yes. A little bit.

"It's been like months now," Jose says. "You've both had time to let things sit. I'm sure you guys will bounce back like nothing ever happened. And let's be real, Sara's a sweetheart. Like, genuinely, she's the human version of a cotton candy, almost sickeningly so. You can't stay mad at her forever."

"Okay, defense attorney," I stop her, "I think you've made your case."

"Oh, my God!!" Jose's voice vibrates with excitement. "I can't believe it happened!"

"Calm down." I look at her pointedly, though I can't help the tiniest of smiles at her reaction.

"I knew it! I knew one of these days you'd crack and quote one of those lines!" Jose throws herself against her chair, back of her hand slapped on her forehead. "I can die happy now."

"Anyway." I hold a finger up to Jose. "No more Sara talk. We're celebrating here."

"Yes, Your Honor." Jose nods and returns to her drink.

It's a few minutes of casual chatter before Jose gets bored of pestering me and moves on to Rahul and Koji instead.

I take the chance to greet some old comrades from Basic I haven't seen in a while. Luke and Haytham are in the middle of a darts match. And Luke is ... losing.

"Hey, guys," I greet them.

"Hey, Ashley." Haytham smiles. "Congratulations on graduating!"

"Thanks."

"Hey, Ash." Luke's voice is strained. "Give me one second. I'm trying to save my dignity."

"Sure." I stand back to give him room and enjoy the show.

Luke pours all of his focus on the dartboard across from him. Hand moving back and forth before he tosses the dart. Aaaand it flies straight to the wall.

"Dammit." Luke drops his hands to his sides. "I'll just go ahead and never show my face around here again."

"Don't be too harsh on yourself," Haytham comforts him. "You're making progress. You hit the wall and not someone's butt this time."

"That's not the compliment you think it is." Luke turns to me at last. "Ash, congrats on becoming official SPORE fodder. If you're as lucky as my darts, you'll miss death a few times before you hit the bullseye."

"Wow, someone challenging my pessimism for first spot? I can't have that!" I throw a light, playful punch at his arm. "How's guard duty treating you?"

He shakes his head sideways. Luke graduated a while ago—AIT for the Defense Division is shorter than ours. "Sometimes I think I regret not going Spec Ops. But then I see all the body bags that make it back, and the stats for the ones that don't, and I realize I actually made the smartest decision."

Can't argue with that.

We settle down on an empty couch. Soft music plays in the background. That's one of my favorite things about Vigor. The music. To think people used to listen to this stuff whenever they wanted. The first time we came here, Jose dragged me and Sara to dance until we were dripping with sweat and could no longer move a muscle. We passed out on one of the couches. Mr. Tooley woke us up before closing, then we dragged ourselves to the barracks.

"Where are you stationed these days?" I ask Luke.

"It's a fifty-fifty split between watchposts and gates." He pushes back a few sweaty strands of smooth, brown hair, relaxing into the couch, one arm sprawled on the headrest. I envy him. Even though I've spent so much time in the outside, nothing compares to standing atop a watchpost, at the edge of two worlds. "This week I'm at the northeastern gate, supervising outpost resupply trucks. People try to sneak more than they're supposed to way too often."

"Have you arrested anyone yet?" I peer at him.

"Nope." A quick shake of his head. "Don't have that level of authority yet."

I turn to Haytham next, who's wiping sweat off his brow and emptying the last of his water bottle. "How about you, Hayth?"

"Well." Haytham tosses the bottle into a nearby trashcan. Score. "I'm only a scientist in training, but I'm learning a lot."

"Any chance you'll be finding us a cure soon?" I tease. "That would save us a lot of trouble."

"I don't know about a cure." Haytham scratches the side of his stubbled face. "All the samples we have aren't quite ... ready."

"Wait..." I gasp. "You're actually working on a cure?"

Haytham jolts up and gestures for me to lower my voice. Oops. Thank God for the music drowning out our conversation. He leans forward. Behind the worry in his brown eyes, enthusiasm burns. "I'm not supposed to talk about this. But I trust you won't repeat it."

His voice lowers even more. "Yes, for the past four months, we've been trying."

I lean over the half-asleep Luke so I can whisper back, "Have you tested it yet?"

"Not on humans, which is probably why we're struggling to make progress." Haytham exhales. "Testing it on animals isn't ideal, because they don't react to the virus the way we do."

"How did you even manage to make a sample cure?" I ask.

The enthusiasm shifts to something more akin to guilt. "Melisa's ... blood has ... opened a lot of opportunities and new discoveries."

Melisa—the name throws a wrench in my heart—one of our comrades from Basic. The sweetest girl. The kindest soul. A flash of her lying on the floor, tackled by an Active. Its long, slimy tongue deep down her throat.

"Is she..." I swallow a lump. *Don't think about it.* "Is she still...?"

"Alive?" Haytham flinches as soon as the word comes out of his mouth. "Well, *alive*... Yes, she is."

I don't know if that makes me happy or disturbed. There is probably no point in me asking, either, but I ask anyway, "Can I see her?"

"I'm sorry, Ashley." Haytham frowns. "Our work in the labs is classified. I've shared too much already."

"It's fine," I say. "You don't have to talk about it."

"Thanks for understanding." Haytham stretches before standing. "I think I'll go grab some more water. Do you guys want anything?"

Both Luke and I decline, and Haytham nods and leaves us alone.

"So, you two hang out a lot?" I ask.

"Yeah, when we have time." Luke's drowsy eyes open to find mine. "And now I have a lot of time since ... you know."

No, I don't. "Since what?"

"You know," he repeats. "Since Sara and I..."

I just stare at him. Still don't know.

His brows quirk, as if saying: *are you messing with me right now?* "Sara and I broke up."

Oh.

"I ... didn't know. I'm sorry."

"I thought she'd have told you." Luke side-eyes me. Guess he doesn't know about me and Sara, either. "She broke up with me a couple months ago."

"Why?" I ask. "Did you fight or...?" *Did she just decide you were useless to her now?*

"No." Luke rests his head back. "It was really random. She said she's going through something and wants to deal with it alone."

"I see."

Going through something.

Can you just look at me, please? Sara's voice echoes in my ear. *Just look me in the eyes and tell me exactly how you feel.*

Angry, I said. *I feel angry. Disgusted. At the thought I ever even considered you a friend.*

The memory makes my head taut, as if my brain is being crushed.

"I need to use the bathroom." I get up, and don't waste a second to run there. A splash of cold water on my face, a few wet pats on my neck, another splash, then I close the tap.

When I look up, tired green eyes stare back at me in the mirror. A dull face I barely recognize. Six months ago, my pixie cut was an even split between brown roots and pink tips. Now, after a few trims with Haze's help, the brown is taking over. I don't know if I'll ever find a pink dye again. Or that I'll dye my hair if I do find one. Even without the pink being the predominant color, my hair still draws attention.

Nina told me it was weird. Nathan told me he liked it. I think Cris was more shocked about me chopping off ninety percent of my hair than he was about the color. Mom was equally horrified by both.

What happened to your hair? She gasped the first time. *Please tell me that's a temporary hair dye and not a permanent pink,* she almost cried the second time.

Technically, I said, *all hair dyes are temporary...*

Oh, Ashley... She shook her head.

Because the hair grows back...

What would Dad have thought? Would he have liked it? Hated it?

A long, deep breath, then I force myself out of the bathroom, but I'm still lightheaded. The crowded lounge is too swarmed with people. Laughing. Singing. Eating. Shouting. Playing. Dancing. A jumble of noises and bodies so indistinguishable it might as well be a wave of infected on a rampage.

And then a strangled cry reaches me. My gaze lands on none other than Tristan's girlfriend, falling to her knees in front of a sorry Koji and Rahul.

Tristan's gory face flashes before me. I feel so ... small. Stuck.

So out of breath, like someone's hands are wrapped tight around my neck and squeezing the life out of me. I'm frozen, for a long time, or at least it feels like a long time. Standing still, despite wanting so badly to run away. I'm simultaneously here and not. Simultaneously me and someone else. The smell of food turns to rust. The plates are filled with guts and chunks of flesh. The lights stop flashing all the pretty colors, save for red. Blood coats every surface. Every wall. Every person. I want to scream at everyone to open their eyes. Look around them. But I can't speak.

A sudden force pushes me forward.

Everything warps back to normal.

"Sorry!" a passerby says, running past me and toward the sobbing mess of the girl on the floor.

My heart *pound-pound-pounds* in my ears. I turn away and push through the wobbly bodies toward the exit, until I burst out the other side of the door.

A cold breeze slaps me. I gasp for air, bend over with my hands on my knees as I battle the urge to vomit.

Breathe, Sara's gentle voice whispers to me. And I breathe. *Focus on breathing. Focus on me. Focus on your feet. What you can see. What you can hear. Feel. Here, hold my hands.*

But she's not here and I can't hold her hands.

I leave Vigor behind to go to the training hall instead. Then the shooting range. Then the gym. Then the mini obstacle courses set up outside our barracks. Keep myself busy. Keep myself grounded. I don't give my brain the chance to wander places it shouldn't. I don't stop until sweat coats me like someone dumped a bucket of water over my head. Until my muscles are aching and I can barely stand on two shaky legs. Until Jose comes to find me and reminds me, I haven't even packed my stuff yet.

FIVE

"SO WILL YOU MISS ME?" Jose hasn't stopped asking since last night. "I mean, I'm sure I'm not as fun as Sara was, but I thought we were good roommates."

I stop in the middle of pulling my ruck from under my bed. Sara this, Sara that. Sara, Sara, Sara. Scratch the endearing part. Right now, Jose's just plain annoying.

"I'll rephrase the question," she says. "On a scale from zero to ten, how much will you miss me?"

I shrug as I give it a thought. I'm too tired and sleep-deprived for this. "Two?"

"Ouch." Jose winces. Was that too harsh? I can't really tell anymore. Sometimes I think Nina rubbed off on me without me realizing. "Objection. The honesty has hurt my feelings."

"Trust me, I wouldn't be doing you any favors by lying." I put on my ruck. "You may not be a lawyer, but you are a soldier, I'm sure you can take it."

"Like a bite to the neck." Jose fakes an exaggerated dying expression.

"I promise not to leave you to turn." As I walk past her, I make a pistol with my hand, point it at her head, and shoot.

"I'll miss you." She falls into me with a hug. I stiffen. "I know you like to pretend you don't care, but you're a softie on the inside. Also, you were the least noisy roommate I could have ever asked for."

That's wild, given how much Sara used to complain about my snoring.

Ugh. Now *I'm* thinking about Sara.

"I hope we see each other again." She pulls back. "Maybe I'll be here in Spheria while you're on break or something."

I try not to struggle out of the hug. "Sure. Maybe. It's a strangely small, big military base."

Jose releases me, as well as an exasperated sigh. "You could at least *try* to sound more genuine."

All I give her is a smile. "See you around, Jose."

"Seeya," she says, then returns to her room to grab her stuff.

Jose's nice. Well, maybe she's not. I've learned that living under the same roof as someone for a few months doesn't mean you get to know who they really are. She made an effort to be my friend, I'll say that. And I did enjoy watching all those lawyer movies with her, even if most of the terminology was lost on me. I just ... didn't want it to be more than that. I didn't want us to be more than temporary roommates. Temporary comrades. There is no point in dedicating a spot in my heart to someone new when I'll probably stumble across their remains someday soon.

I leave what has been my dorm for four months. A shared kitchen and bathroom with two small bedrooms. An improvement from the barracks in Basic, where I shared one room with all the girls in my platoon. By the end, though, only two of us remained.

I still have some time before we go, so I head to the Burial Grounds.

As I pass the big gates, a giant rock steals my attention. Not just a rock; the Pit's Memorial, where the names of soldiers who died during Eukson's fall are carved. My dad's among them.

I used to come here a lot, after my return from the Pit. I would sit by the rock and pretend like I was talking to Dad. It's the closest thing I have to a grave. His body was never recovered. I half consider going there again. But the truth is, I haven't been able to visit the memorial for a while now.

Because every time I look at it, I remember that day…

When I sat on the ground with my back to the rock and Sara came.

When we had that conversation we'd both been dreading for so long.

So I don't visit the memorial anymore. I walk straight to Nathan's grave.

I plop down on the ground—didn't even remember to bring flowers with me. Sigh.

That day ... when Nathan died, it's still burned in my brain. His agonized screams as the infected swarmed him. The terror on his face when he realized his fate was sealed.

He saved me. Gave his life for mine.

And when Nina arrived and saw her brother being ripped apart, the cry she let out was bone-chilling. I shudder remembering it.

At the time, I had no idea the two of them were part of the conspiracy. They were just Nina and Nathan, my friends.

And even now, I can't lie to myself.

I miss them so *deaddamn* much.

When I head back, buses line up outside the dorms while all the newly graduated soldiers say their heartfelt or casual goodbyes. Some of these buses will be headed to the Spec Ops HQ and barracks in the northeastern side of Spheria. Others will head to the helipads, where choppers wait to take people back to their home sectors. Or, in mine and Cris's case, the Renegades.

A yawn forces out of me. I cover my mouth with my hand and stretch as best I can with all the extra weight I'm carrying. My eyes sting and my head keeps buzzing.

"You sleep okay?" Cris pops up next to me, carrying his loaded ruck in one hand. How does he do that, honestly?

No. I don't remember the last time I slept okay. Or the last time I slept uninterrupted for longer than a couple hours. Or the last time I slept without nightmares. Or the last time I slept without waking up drenched in sweat and out of breath, in desperate need of a shower.

"How long do you think we'll last?" I ignore his question.

His thick brows arch over serious, gorgeous brown eyes. "Long enough to lose a few limbs, at least. *Maybe* then they'll send us home."

"Should've thought of that sooner, huh?"

"Plenty of opportunities to come, I'm sure." He nods toward a small troop carrier parked all the way to the right. "That's us."

I smile and nudge his elbow. "Let's go."

The APC stops by a roadblock.

A guard informs the driver about protesters blocking the way ahead.

There have been a lot of protests since the Pit Mission. As much as SPORE tried to keep things classified, word eventually got out that there were survivors in the Pit. Children, who had to live out there for five years. People rose up, demanding that Sears be exiled for the bombing of the Pit. Ironically, it's not even him who bombed it, but that's not public knowledge.

Then there is the second party protesting against Rodríguez for bringing in terrorists and letting them live freely amongst us. By "terrorists," they mean the Pit survivors, most of whom are ten years old or younger. The oldest, Zack, is sixteen.

It's not just Spheria. Protests are rising everywhere, even in Kadia. Mom mentioned that in one of her letters. It reminds me of the days leading up to the Pit's bombing.

Rodríguez tried to appease both parties by painting the Lotivan traitors, dubbed the "Conspirators," as the big villains, the masterminds behind the attacks, and the biggest threat we're facing today. It didn't really work, even after the public execution of Lotiva's former colonel alongside some of his goons.

The driver takes a different road, and we reach the helipads without more hurdles on the way. Unfortunately, no sign of Haze here, either. I thought maybe she'd be doing maintenance on some of the helicopters and I could say goodbye. I guess not.

Shortly after, Cris and I get on a chopper and take off toward the Renegades.

SIX

THE RENEGADES' Forward Operating Base—FOB—is all the way out north, a couple hundred kilometers from the Pit in what used to be a food-processing facility.

A big section of the parking lot has been converted to a landing zone. There's an armory right about the center, with a lineup of large containers, some soldiers stationed there. A building complex covered in moss and ivy and so much grime. Decontamination Stations and other mobile structures, with the signature SPORE colors, black and gold. They go well with the background of fall, which paints everything outside the FOB in that dirt-flavored yellow and orange, some red.

We jump out of the helicopter to the freezing, rotor-generated wind. Gloomy clouds hang above us. I miss Spheria already.

A tall, dark-skinned guy approaches us with prideful strides. His short, curly hair shaven on the sides in perfect symmetry. Wide shoulders and chest held high. If you placed confidence and this guy next to each other, you wouldn't be able to tell the difference.

"Hey!" A welcoming smile cracks his serious features as he shouts through the whirring rotors. "Privates Brown and Rey, right? Welcome aboard!"

"Thank you!" Cris shakes the guy's hand, and I do the same.

"Follow me!"

He leads us out of the helipads and toward the industrial building.

The whirring slowly fades into the background. The air smells like a mix of damp and burnt wood.

"Sergeant Stephen Weeks," the guy introduces himself. As prideful as his posture is, humbleness coats his deep voice. "I'm from Kadia, too."

"I thought you looked familiar," Cris says.

"Yeah..." I recognize that name. "Dr. Weeks—Monica—is that your mom?" She's a therapist—I never talked to her much but I'd run into her often.

"That's right." Stephen nods, then looks to Cris. "And Juan is your grandpa?"

"Yep, that's him," Cris confirms.

"Great man." Stephen grins. "He used to send me on errands occasionally. How's he doing?"

"He's been better," Cris says.

"I'm sorry to hear that." Stephen frowns. "I haven't seen him since I joined SPORE two years ago. Never been back to Kadia since."

"Why?" I say. "Did they not let you?"

Stephen shakes his head sideways. "I mostly didn't want to."

Wow. Must be nice to have your wants taken into consideration.

"Not even to see your mom?" I ask him. "I'm sure she misses you."

Stephen lets out an awkward chuckle at that. Okay. I guess he doesn't want to talk about it.

"How long have you been a Renegade?" Cris asks, changing the subject and giving me a subtle *just drop it* look.

"Founding member," Stephen says, "so four months, give or take."

"You guys don't seem to have made any significant progress in those four months," I say.

Now Cris gives me a *why would you say that?* Face.

I shrug.

Stephen sighs. "Yes. Well, we're doing our best. We have patrol units surveying the exterior perimeters of the sectors, and outposts expanding their zone of operations. But our biggest worry is that the fugitives may have an informant on the inside. This assignment is also admittedly ... complicated. Fighting humans isn't the same as fighting infected. It's trickier. Nastier." He's contemplative for a moment. "It's hard to kill people. That's not what we're trained to do. Much easier when the enemy is someone you can't reason with."

From what I know, the low-ranking Conspirators who were captured were either exiled or, more likely, executed.

"That said, we haven't been successful in trying to reason with them," Stephen adds. "They usually shoot on sight. More recently, they killed the riflemen you're replacing."

"We're really sorry for your loss," Cris says.

"They were shot by a sniper," Stephen says. "I managed to identify her as Nina Grant."

My heart stops.

"She was in your squad, wasn't she?" Stephen asks.

I ever so reluctantly answer, "Yeah."

"I hope, when the time comes, that you won't hesitate to take the shot. Because she definitely didn't."

A flash to the laundry room of our barracks in Basic, Nina's hand in mine. Her face wet with tears—her brother, Nathan, was dead. He left her all alone. That quiver in her voice tugged at my heart. The pain and the silent plea for someone to tell her everything would be okay. I tried to be that someone for her, and even though she betrayed us anyway, I don't think I'd be alive now if I hadn't gotten to her then.

That day in the Pit, when we stood in a dark hallway, weapons pointed at each other, she'd begged me to let her go, and I did. But that was then, and this is now. I don't know that she'd be willing to lower her weapon this time, or, honestly, I mine.

"Check it out," a guy with shoulder-length, wavy brown hair and tanned skin says to his friend. They're sitting on folding chairs by a burn barrel. "The newbies are here."

"Real helpful, Connor," Stephen tells him.

"Nice hair," Connor comments when I pass by. "Is it your natural color?"

I laugh dryly. "Never heard that one before."

"Connor, what is the matter with you?" His friend smacks him on the back of his head and gives me an apologetic smile.

"Don't mind him," Stephen says. "He likes to mess around. And don't be surprised if he gives you a dumb nickname."

"Noted," Cris says.

We enter the industrial building with Stephen through a warehouse, which has been converted to a DFAC—dining facility. One of the people sitting there waves for us to stop. A girl with blonde hair tied up in a clean ponytail, bangs covering her forehead. Round face and fierce, blue eyes. She gets up and walks to us.

"Lucille," Stephen starts. "These are our new riflemen…"

"Nice to meet you," Cris offers his hand, "I'm Private Rey—"

"Slow down, cowboy, we'll have plenty of time for introductions later." Lucille barely spares him a glance. Great first impression. "Listen, Stephen," her voice lowers to a whisper, "I was right about last night. They brought him here."

"Don't tell me…" Stephen's shoulders drop. "What's the general thinking?"

"Try again," Lucille says, tossing her ponytail back. "It's the lieutenant who convinced him."

"Should you guys be talking about this in front of us if you have to be so cryptic about it?" I interrupt.

"Yeah, sorry," Stephen says, "you'll probably find out sooner or—"

"So, you're Brown." The cold weather has nothing on the iciness in Lucille's eyes as they snap to mine. She's not that much taller than me, yet it feels like she's looking down on me from the top of a watchpost. "The lieutenant finally managed to get the full package in here. How nice." Something tells me that's not a compliment.

"Lucille," Stephen warns. "How about not?"

Her scornful, pretty eyes flutter with mild bother, then she goes back to pretending Cris and I are invisible. "I hear a new WARNORD's being issued, so we'll probably be deployed soon." A quick tap on his arm. "Come find me when you're done breaking them in."

"All right." Stephen's gaze lingers on her for a notable second as she walks off, then he nods for us to continue. "I'm really sorry if people don't leave the best first impressions. Lucille's a team leader, like me. She's brilliant. One of the toughest people I know. Everyone's just been so stressed. We got so close to capturing the crawler last time and then everything went downhill so fast."

"What did she mean by 'the full package?'" I ask.

"It's … not important," Stephen says. I don't believe him. "Like I said, everyone's stressed. Olivia, one of the riflemen we lost recently, was in her team. We're all mourning in our own way."

Well, I'm not one to judge people's ways of mourning. God knows mine were terrible.

We leave the DFAC and enter the processing section. The big, mostly open space bustles with life. Incoherent chatter mixed with the rumble of generators and the hum of electrical equipment. Most people are gathered by burn barrels placed all around. Others are running errands, carrying containers and boxes here and there, cleaning weapons, and even working out. Looks like they're using some of the conveyor belts as separators for the different sections. They also have tents set up inside, probably for some privacy. We head for one of those.

"Mirani," Stephen calls. "You in there?"

"Yes, sir!" a girl responds.

The flaps of the tent part and a head pokes out between them, covered in a scarf. Brown skin, oval face with a defined jaw, and green eyes.

"Oooh, hello!" The girl comes out of the tent with a bright, welcoming smile.

"This is Cristian Rey and Ashley Brown." Stephen gestures at us. "Our new riflemen."

"Welcome, welcome." The girl's voice is full of energy as she snaps into a salute. "Specialist Dalal Mirani at your service."

"Nice to meet you," Cris says. "And Cris is fine. No one calls me Cristian."

No one except for Zack, which Cris hates. A lot. It's kind of amusing.

"Think you can give Ashley a tour of her new room?" Stephen asks. "I'll show Cris to his."

"It would be my pleasure!" Dalal's way too excited about something so mundane.

"I'll see you later?" I say to Cris before he heads off.

He gives me a nod and a heart-melting smile. "Later."

I follow Dalal inside. There are already some girls here, sitting on cots and chatting. None of them look familiar, though. This place is slightly reminiscent of our barracks in Basic, except we had bunkbeds then.

"Now, I know, this place is huge so try not to get lost." Dalal leads me toward the left innermost corner. "You might think you don't have enough belongings to make this feel like home, but it's a lot smaller than it looks."

"Oh, I can see that." I stand by what I presume to be my cot, which is literally just that, a cot, plus a small metal chest for storage purposes. I set my ruck and bag down.

"So," she says, her tone so serious I almost believe her, "this is your lovely corner. Be sure to write down anything that's missing. Like shelfing, a chair, desk or whatever."

"Right." I nod.

"When you're done setting up," she says, "do come to the DFAC. I prepared a welcome meal for you and your friend."

"Thanks?"

"You'll love it!" Dalal says. "I'm the best cook in our entire platoon. No offense to the actual cooks here. Do you have any allergies? Because Olivia had a nut allergy."

I shake my head. "No allergies. I'm a vegetarian, though."

"Duly noted. Most of what I cook is vegetarian anyway." Dalal grins.

As I'm about to unpack, my portor—portable locator—vibrates on my wrist. It beeps with a notification for a mission briefing. I was added to the Renegades comm channel this morning, and looks like I have work already.

"Ah, guess that welcome meal has to wait." Dalal checks her own beeping portor. "So, are you excited to meet the rest of your platoon?"

SEVEN

NO.

I'm not excited to meet the rest of the platoon, and I'm especially less excited when I join everyone in the DFAC and see the one face I've been praying not to see.

Sara's eyes hold mine from where she stands to the right with some girls. Her dark, smooth hair touches her shoulders now, which gives the tips on the sides an upward curve. It sways when she looks away almost immediately.

On my first day in Spheria, when I stood in line with the rest of the recruits, Sara had looked at me the same way she just did. Back then, I didn't know what to make of it.

She was my partner and bunkmate. Then she became my friend. Then I found out she was the girl my dad died to save. More or less.

It was my fault, she said, *that he got bit. I was paralyzed. I could have helped him.*

Sara was eleven. She was helpless. She lost her mom. Dad did what he always did: protect people. And I ultimately did the same thing when I was in a similar situation. It wasn't this that made things sour between us. I could never fault Sara for any of it. Could never blame her.

It was what happened *after* she told me the story, long after we came back from the Pit. All the questions that remained unanswered. The things she'd done behind my back. Everything else she kept from me. How was I supposed to think our friendship was real, when so much of it was built on deception and secrets?

What *actually* frustrates me, though, more than Sara herself, is that beat my heart skips upon seeing her. The unwanted yet stubborn thought of *I really missed you* that crosses my mind. Have I mentioned that I hate my brain?

"Have you met Lieutenant Mansur before?" Dalal nods at a man talking to some of the sergeants.

"No," I say. "But he's related to my friend. He's his uncle."

"Oh, perfect!" Dalal grins. "So, if the lieutenant rejects my marriage proposal, I can count on you to set me up with your friend instead."

"Uh…" I eye her skeptically. "Well, my friend is kind of … the odd one out of the family. But sure, I can introduce you."

"Renegades!" Lt. Mansur stands facing us with whom I assume is his first sergeant to his right.

I guess he is objectively handsome. The kind that makes girls like Dalal and others around me squeal and follow his every move with heart eyes. Even Sara. Tall with a strong build. Dark, short hair, more wavy than curly like Haytham's. Defined brows. A neatly trimmed beard frames his jaw, and the light brown complexion of his skin makes his confident hazel eyes stand out.

"Before we dip into mission details," the lieutenant says, "let's take one last moment to remember those we lost on our last mission. Privates Olivia Bonner and Kent Newland were among the founding members of the Renegades. Without them, there would be fewer of us standing here today to remember their sacrifices."

Judging by how some of the soldiers around me are tearing up, I'm guessing Bonner and Newland were good people. Too bad I have zero emotional connection to either of them.

"May their dedication to our cause fuel our resolve. Let us never forget: though our struggles may be lonesome, humanity suffers together." The lieutenant salutes.

Wow, that's very cheery.

The rest of the platoon salutes back, so I do the same. Left arm folded behind my back, hand clenched in a fist. Right hand up, the tips of the fore and middle fingers touching the side of my forehead.

"On to less gloomy subjects. Today we also welcome our newest riflemen," Lt. Mansur carries on. "Fresh out of AIT, Private First Class

Ashley Brown, and Private First Class Cristian Rey, who will be part of the First Rifle Squad."

I stand uncomfortably as the crowd cheers and welcomes me and Cris. Some people start banging on the tables in a unified rhythm. Something tells me this is their traditional way of welcoming newcomers.

From where he stands with Stephen and some other guys, Cris shoots me a grin. He likes the attention way more than I do.

"All right, settle down everyone!" the platoon sergeant orders. Everyone quiets.

"A little introduction for the new members," Lt. Mansur resumes. "We, the Renegades, have been tasked with locating and capturing the Lotivan fugitives who managed to escape after the Pit Mission. More importantly, our top priority is to find and retrieve the sentient crawler that they stole. As you may know, the crawler possesses the ability to communicate with both infected and humans. Acquiring it would create opportunities that could change our future."

I was there when the Lotivan Spores kidnapped Lori. After we returned from the Pit, I was one of the people they interrogated to get as accurate a description of her as they could. Even more relevant is that she's Zack's sister.

"One of the patrol units has located a potential fugitive hideout," Lt. Mansur says. "We don't have exact numbers on the fugitives who might be hiding there, and it's also unclear if they're the same ones we encountered last time. But if they are, that means the crawler is with them. Your squad leaders will explain what each unit will be doing. Take thirty, and then we'll take off. May God protect and watch over us all. Ameen."

"I wish more people remembered God," Dalal breathes. "Maybe humanity wouldn't be suffering so much."

"So you think what's happening right now is God's punishment for people not remembering him?" I ask.

"No," she says. "I think what's happening right now is people suffering the consequences of selfish, immoral actions done by those who don't remember God. Or people, frankly."

I ... can't really say I've thought about God much before. Mostly in the sense that I kind of knew, from when I was a kid, that there is a God. But that was it. My parents weren't religious. I went to church with Haze a few times because, well, she's my friend and I didn't want to be alone. Cris still goes to church every Sunday, says it's one of the only nice things he got to do with his family, and that it brings him a sense of peace and relief.

Maybe I should consider going, too. I haven't been feeling much in the line of peace or relief these days.

"Anyway, that's not the only thing I like about lieutenant." Dalal continues her tangent. "He's one of the few commanding officers who actually care about their subordinates and *show* it. So good with keeping morale up. His units usually have the lowest death rates. You should be flattered to have been assigned here."

I think I still would have preferred going back home.

"Oh, also, something else I really like about him: he personally comes to greet every new soldier that joins his unit." Dalal nods toward the approaching lieutenant.

I snap to attention and turn to face him. "Sir."

"Private Brown." A charismatic smile stretches across the lieutenant's bearded face. "Welcome to the Renegades. I see you've already made Specialist Mirani's acquaintance."

"Yes, sir." I hold my salute.

"At ease, Private." His eyes search around for someone. "Where's our other newcomer?"

I wave at Cris to come over.

He gives the lieutenant a firm salute as soon as he joins us. "Lieutenant Mansur, sir. I'm honored to be part of the Renegades, sir."

"The honor is mine, Private." The lieutenant graces him with an even bigger grin. "I heard you two were top of your platoon. Not to mention, Survivors of the Pit."

Survivors of the Pit. We received medals for that. The last mission we went on before graduating Basic. The end of a journey not everyone made it through. My heart aches as Melisa's face flashes before my eyes. I bite my lip. Now's not the time.

"I look forward to seeing what the two of you can do," the lieutenant says.

Yeah, I look forward to that, too, because I still don't know why I'm here.

"I made sure to put you in a squad with some familiar faces," the lieutenant says. "I figured if I'm going to keep you from your families a while longer, the least I can do is keep you around old comrades."

I really wish you hadn't done that.

"Faces, sir?" Cris asks. "I've seen Specialist Jung already, but I can't say anyone else is…"

"Might want to look again, Rey." A most familiar authoritarian voice comes up behind us. Cris and I turn to none other than Sgt. Seidel—our drill instructor from Basic. Her dark brown hair's not in a bun like it used to be. It's a loose bob, almost reminiscent of Sara's hair in Basic, just without the bangs.

Her name patch reads: SSG Seidel. *Staff* Sergeant.

"Congratulations on the promotion, sir," I say.

"Thanks." She smiles. It looks weird. "Right back at ya."

Okay, I know Sgt. Seidel has always been significantly nicer than Orlov, but she's a lot nicer than I remember her being. I'm not sure if it's because she's not our drill sergeant anymore, so she can be a little more casual, or just because I got so used to Sgt. Orlov's harshness. Regardless, I'm happy to see her again.

Sgt. Seidel nods for us to come with her. "Let's introduce you to the rest of the squad and go over mission details."

"Yes, sir."

RENEGADE

RENEGADES PL...

- **HEADQUARTERS (5 PERSONNEL)**
  - 1LT. ZAID MANSUR — PLATOON LEADER
  - SFC. KRAIG PRATE — PLATOON SERGEANT
  - PFC. CLAUDINE ARIA — RTO*
  - SPC. LEIF SHEDDER — COMBAT MEDIC**
  - SPC. ELLIOT SLATE — FIRE SUPPORT RTO*

- **RIFLE S...**
  - **SEIDEL SQUAD (9 ENLISTED)**
    - SSG. LEA SEIDEL — SQUAD LEADER
    - **ALPHA TEAM**
      - SGT. LUCILLE DECKER — TEAM LEADER
      - SPC. DALAL MIRANI — AUTOMATIC RIFLEMAN
      - SPC. SARANG JUNG — GRENADIER
      - PFC. ASHLEY BROWN — RIFLEMAN
    - **BRA...**
  - **BRONS... (9 E...)**
      - SG...
      - AU...
      - SF...
      - F...

PLATOON

- WEAPONS SQUAD (9 ENLISTED)
  - REDFEARN SQUAD (9 ENLISTED)
  - SSG. CASSIE TATTER SQUAD LEADER
  - MEDIUM MACHINE GUN TEAM (X2)
    - 2 MACHINE GUNNERS
    - 2 ASSISTANT MACHINE GUNNERS

(partial boxes from left column, cut off): ...HEN WEEKS ...LEADER; ...CE LANG ...RIFLEMAN; ...OR BROOKS ...ADIER; ...TIAN REY ...EMAN

1LT: FIRST LIEUTENANT
SFC: SERGEANT FIRST CLASS
SSG: STAFF SERGEANT
SGT: SERGEANT
SPC: SPECIALIST
PFC: PRIVATE FIRST CLASS
RTO: RADIOTELEPHONE OPERATOR

* ATTACHED FROM COMMUNICATIONS DIVISION
** ATTACHED FROM MEDICAL DIVISION

EIGHT

WE GROUP up with the others at one of the dining tables. Turns out I've already met all of them, even if I'm a little hazy on their names. Except for ... well, Sara, who stands across from me, watching me watch her.

"Brown," Sgt. Seidel starts, "you're with Alpha Team, that's with Sergeant Decker." The blonde who was passive aggressive with me for no reason. "Specialist Mirani, and Specialist Jung."

Oh. Great. They've put me with Sara. God, please let me get eaten. The sooner the better.

"With your background in the medical field, you'll also be our combat lifesaver," she continues, then turns to Cris. "Rey, you're with Bravo Team, with Sergeant Weeks." A gesture to Stephen. Both he and Lucille look young for sergeants, but slightly older than the rest of us. Didn't Stephen say he became a SPORE about two years ago? So he must be around seventeen. "Specialist Brooks." A nod to the boy who commented on my hair earlier. His eyes are on me as he holds up a peace sign. "And Specialist Lang."

That's the one who smacked Connor's head for the comment. A wide nose occupies the center of his pale face. Short, dark hair with a side parting. He gives both me and Cris a smile that makes his nose stretch even wider.

"Nice to meet everyone. I look forward to working with you and getting to know you." Cris's tone is formal and professional.

Personally, I prefer his casual, smug, playful tone that he uses with me when we're alone. Much more charming.

When I don't say anything, Cris bumps my elbow.

"Same," I add, then shoot him a glare. *Happy?*

"Just to catch you up to speed, in case you're not aware of everything," Sgt. Seidel says. "We've managed to capture and interrogate most of the higher-ups in Lotiva who were behind the conspiracy."

Capture and interrogate doesn't begin to cover it. I was there for the execution of Lotiva's former colonel, Bjorn Edström. Up until soldiers started knocking chairs from underneath the prisoners' feet. Then I ran straight to the bathroom and spent about half an hour hunched over the toilet vomiting. I want to vomit again just thinking about it.

"We also interrogated the Pit survivors and their leader, Zackary Caves," Sgt. Seidel adds.

Zack was hospitalized for a while after our return from the Pit due to a stab wound. Once he recovered, he and some of his people who were of age started training for SPORE—not their choice, of course. The deal was: SPORE welcomes them in, provides the young kids with shelter, and in exchange, Zack and the others work for the force to earn their place and prove their loyalty. Not that long ago, Zack graduated Basic alongside Haze, and they're now in the midst of their AIT.

"We put together an inconclusive list of Lotivan fugitives and possible hideout locations, which we've been monitoring and investigating." She taps a map sprawled on the table. There are marked points, including our FOB and the Pit, other relevant markers, like outposts, patrol routes and more. The Xs are likely places they've already cleared. "The issue is, we don't know who all that died in the Pit are, and those who remain are split up. We have no clue which of these groups are in contact and which are not. We also don't know if the sentient crawler is staying with one specific group or being passed around."

That's a lot of things we don't know. Do we have any piece of concrete intel whatsoever?

"We've just identified what we think might be another fugitive hideout." Sgt. Seidel points at another spot on the map. "It's an auto-parts store located a couple kilometers from where we last encountered the fugitives. The recon unit reported suspicious infected activity." She opens a folder and displays a bunch of photos taken from a bird's eye view. "There's a larger concentration of infected than you'd find in a regular camp, which could mean our objective is there somewhere.

"We don't have an identified target. There are large containers and vehicle parts everywhere, in addition to the store itself. The fugitives could be hiding in any of these. Likely they also have infected placed as a trap inside the containers. Considering how our last encounter with them went, it's doubtful they managed to get the crawler to obey them completely. Caution is advised regardless."

"Sir," I say, "you're saying the fugitives *can't* use the infected?"

"Not efficiently, no," Sgt. Seidel replies.

"What about all the waves?" I ask. "Why have they become more frequent if it has nothing to do with the fugitives?"

"That, we're still trying to figure out," Sgt. Seidel says. "One more reason why we need that crawler."

"Okay," I say, "so let's say we kill the infected and find the fugitives, what then? Do we shoot on sight?"

Cris shifts uncomfortably on my side. We've killed more infected than we can count in our training. We also killed a fair number of humans during the Pit Mission. Except for Cris. He refused to shoot them. And no matter how good a shot he's become, I highly doubt he changed his mind about that. He still flinches every time we have to put down the fatal casualties. He'd wait until the very end, until they're actually gone—the second they start shaking—before he kills them. He really shouldn't have been assigned to the Renegades. They should have just let him go home.

"The lieutenant is very strict about taking a life without a life." Sgt. Seidel straightens. "But the fugitives haven't been receptive to any attempt to negotiate. They've attacked some of our field camps, stolen resources, and killed many of our comrades. Use your brains. If you can capture them alive so that we may get more intel from them, good. But I'd rather you shoot before they do."

"What if we can shoot to disarm instead?" Cris asks. "There is no need to kill them if we can just restrain them and take them by force. They're much more valuable to us alive than dead."

"Only if your life isn't on the line," Sgt. Seidel says. "The crawler is what's valuable to us here. The fugitives, not so much."

"Oftentimes, we don't have the choice." Stephen sounds sullen.

"And sometimes *we* don't give *them* the choice," Connor argues.

"Mmm, what a surprise." Lucille's flat tone indicates anything but surprise. "Connor siding with the enemy."

"How about siding with humans?" Connor protests, leaning over the table to catch her eye, but Lucille is more occupied with brushing imaginary dirt off her shoulder.

"Look around for a minute." She nods her head vaguely about the table and finally graces Connor with an unimpressed look. "What do you think *we* are? Aliens in disguise?"

"Save your bickering," Sgt. Seidel warns. Connor resorts to angrily staring at Lucille instead while she picks her nails. Okay. Guess I missed a few chapters of whatever's going on between them. "Now, Rey, Brown, here's a list of the known fugitives we're after." She lays out some ID photos across the table. "First, we have Vincent Hayes…"

But Nina's photo is all I see, and I'm fixed on it until…

"Brown?" Sgt. Seidel calls.

"Yes, sir."

"Go with Jung." She nods toward Sara. "Then meet us at the armory."

Go with her where? "Yes, sir," I respond anyway.

I follow Sara into the processing section while the others head outside. The walk is quiet, just the way I want it, and I pray in silence: *please don't start a conversation with me, please don't start a conversation with me, please don't—*

"So how are you doing?" Sara asks.

Bite me.

"I know you and Cris wanted to go back to Kadia." She offers a sympathetic smile. "I'm sorry it didn't work out."

Well, nothing ever works out, so.

"But we really need you here, too," she says.

How long is this walk going to be, exactly?

"Ash, please say something." She leans over, trying to catch my eyes. "I know we didn't leave things on a good note, but we're here now, we should talk—"

"Remember that time," I interrupt, dodging her gaze, "you told me that when you're not sure if you should stay mad at someone, you ask yourself if you'd still be angry at that person if they died the next day?"

"I…" Sara falters. "I remember."

"The answer is yes." It's a lie, but I hope she believes it. I'm not ready to deal with her yet. "I'd still hate you even if you died right this second, so don't bother. Just tell me where the hell we're going."

I catch her frown from the corner of my eye. A traitorous stab of guilt burrows in my chest.

"We're going to get Zack," she says.

NINE

SO ZACK IS HERE.

We go to the damp, cold basement, which has been converted to a mini "prison." A guard sits on a folding chair by a burn barrel, yawning. He quickly gets to his feet upon hearing the clack of our boots against concrete. After Sara discloses why we're here, he unlocks the door to what I think used to be a storage room, and lets us in.

"Would you look at this lovely surprise, Ashley and Sarang both here to see me personally." Zack sits on a sleeping bag, legs folded, a book in hand. A stupidly big smile slapped across his face. Messy waves of brown hair sticking to the sides. "Are you two working together again? That's right, because you just graduated AIT, didn't you, Ashley? Congratulations!"

"Uh... Thanks, Zack," I say, then quickly correct myself, "I mean, Egan."

"It's okay. Everyone here knows who I am. You can call me Zack." He closes the book, gently puts it aside, then pulls to his feet. He's taller than both me and Sara, though slightly shorter than Cris. Tan skin and intense, brown eyes. A small scar slashes the right side of his upper lip. "Well, then, to what do I owe this humbling honor? Because I thought I was brought here last night to be tossed out to the infected like you've been doing with all those Lotivans. But you gave me a room all to myself and everything."

Aside from the sleeping bag, there's a tray with empty bowls, utensils and some breadcrumbs, and a small window to the right—

enough for light to come through but not for someone his size to squeeze out of.

"It's about Lori," Sara answers. "We think we may know where she is."

Zack's bright expression disappears in a flash. His brows furrow. A bone-chilling darkness takes over his intense eyes, like a storm is brewing behind them. I'm staring at a completely different person from the one who was standing here a second ago.

"Lieutenant Mansur wants you to come along," Sara says.

"You found Lori?" Zack watches Sara as if he's studying the smallest of her moves.

"Potentially." Sara shifts her weight to one foot. "We're not sure. We didn't actually see her or any crawlers, but it's a possibility."

"You must be getting desperate, if you're finally seeking my help." He's very smug about it. "When I offered to be involved, it seemed like people would sooner feed me to the infected than work with me. Which was odd, because I thought the whole point of recruiting me was to have me as an asset on the battlefield. Where did this sudden trust come from?"

Zack graduated Basic with shiny scores, much to the displeasure of ... most who know who he is. Now he's training for Spec Ops, but he was often separated from our platoon. For someone who despises SPORE so passionately, he's pouring his heart into training. Probably why they've been hesitant about taking him along. Because out there, he'd be as much a threat as he'd be an ally.

"We *are* desperate," Sara admits. "Not to mention, Lieutenant Mansur actually wanted you to be involved from the start. It was Rodríguez who—"

"Yes, I know that," Zack cuts in. "So, what changed now?"

"What changed is we haven't been successful," Sara says. "Four months in, and we still didn't manage to get our hands on Lori. Lieutenant Mansur spoke with the general again. He convinced him that you're essential to this mission and that excluding you from it is what's been delaying our progress."

"Lori isn't an animal." Zack scowls at her. "If you're going out there thinking you can scare her into submission—"

"Zack, like I said, we don't even know if we'll find her there—" Sara holds up her hands, gesturing for him to slow "—and surely, if there is a way that we can bring her in peacefully, without using force, and without hurting anyone, there's no reason why we wouldn't."

"My apologies, Sarang, but I hope you can understand why I may not entirely believe that." Zack tilts his head to the side. "Even if *you* don't intend on hurting her, you don't speak for your commanding officers or your comrades."

"No, I don't," Sara agrees. "But what I can say is that you coming with us will definitely increase our chances of dealing with this as peacefully as possible."

"Zack," I start, and he turns to me. "You don't have to trust anyone, but at the very least, you might get to see your sister again. Isn't that enough?"

"Why, yes, Ashley." Zack smiles. "But I want you both to know, if even a single Spore points so much as a finger at Lori, it best be a spare finger."

"Great, so in the meantime," I say, "can we all pretend to get along?"

Sara gives me a non-lingering look.

"Sure," Zack says. "Anything for those lovely eyes of yours."

I almost choke on my spit. "W—I... *Don't* flirt with me."

He smiles like he couldn't be happier with himself. "I can't help it. You're too pretty not to flirt with."

My face is a boiling mess. "Do I need to remind you that fraternizing is forbidden?" Yes, I'm a hypocrite. But I don't really know how to deal with this. I'm not used to people flirting with me in a straightforward way, and I'm also not sure how to take it from Zack.

"I should think you of all people know how much I don't care about the rules," Zack says. So casual. So unbothered. "Just like I know you don't care about them all that much, either."

Sara clears her throat awkwardly. "We're supposed to be gearing up, like five minutes ago. Shall we?"

"Ladies first." Zack courteously gestures at me and Sara.

TEN

THE CHATTER DIES AS SOON as we show up at the armory.

Wary, judging eyes dart to Zack. Not-so-sneaky sneaky nudges and silent *look who's here* nods. Lucille, especially, watches him with silent scrutiny, until Stephen gently holds her arm and turns her attention to him.

Zack leans close to me. "I can already feel the ropes of friendship binding together and forming a lovely noose for my neck." He masks it well behind a big smile, but uneasiness clings to his gaze as it darts around.

"Caves." Sgt. Seidel steps in front of us. "You won't need any weapons for this mission. Put on your protective sleeve and bulletproof vest and wait."

"Oh?" Zack raises his brows. "Let me guess, I'll be assigned 'bodyguards?'"

"Yes, in fact." Sgt. Seidel nods to me. "Brown will be keeping an eye on you."

Uh... That's news to me.

Zack responds with a shrug. "I can't say I have any complaints about that."

Oh, boy. He's gonna keep doing this, isn't he?

"Brown." Sgt. Seidel gestures for me to follow her. "A word."

I walk with her a few feet away from the others.

"I want you to keep an eye on Private Caves." Her eyes are

following something behind me, and I don't need to look to know it's Zack. She meets my gaze. "Assuming we do find the sentient crawler, there's a chance Caves might take the opportunity to run away. We don't know what level of communication they had, but even a look from him might signal for her to attack or call on the other infected to assist."

"Sir, I doubt Zack would do anything like that, knowing that we have his people and they might suffer the consequences of his actions," I say.

"Better safe than sorry," she presses. "I'm not sure how welcoming the rest of your squad will be. You, on the other hand, played a big part in saving him and his people. He remembers that. Meaning, if there's anyone here who can gain even a little bit of his trust, it's you. If we want that crawler on our side, we need Caves there, too."

Is this why they brought me here instead of letting me go home? Because they think I'm the only competent babysitter they've got for Zack?

I hold back a sigh. Bite me and this deaddamn assignment. "Yes, sir."

Sgt. Seidel dismisses me. I join the others to gear up, then it's straight to the helipads. We're split across five helicopters, each squad on one, with Zack joining my squad. I make sure to take a seat away from Sara, which happens to be next to Dalal. Zack takes the one to my right. We strap in and put on our headsets so we can easily communicate during the flight. Five minutes later, we're in the air.

"So, Zack!" Specialist Lang's voice comes through my headset. He's sitting across from me and Zack. What was his name? Jayce? "You grew up in the outside, right? Me too."

Zack watches Jayce with the most offended look I've ever seen on him. "I didn't grow up in the outside." His voice sharp, jaw clenched. "I grew up in a sector called Eukson, or what you might know as the Pit. You know, the one that SPORE blew to pieces?"

Jayce's face falls. "I... Right. Sorry, I didn't mean—"

"Honestly, if people could think before they spoke, that would be amazing." Zack sighs. He just had to antagonize the one person trying to be nice to him, didn't he?

"You grew up in the outside?" I ask Jayce, merely to divert from the awkwardness. "How was it?"

A little life returns to Jayce's face. He dodges Zack's gaze and fixates on me. "It was different. That's the simplest way I can put it. Free but ... sometimes *too* free. My parents were among survivors of a fallen safe zone. They took off on a long journey to find a place they could defend with their limited means, and they ended up at this port in the Crimsonview shore, due northeast, Zone Thirteen. They called it the *Red Queen*, after the cruise ship they found on the dock."

"You lived on a ship? In a port?" I can't contain a gasp. "That sounds amazing."

"It was." Jayce smiles. "I do miss it a lot. What I remember of it, at least. The sunsets especially were gorgeous. Paints everything in this insane red hue. That's why it's called Crimsonview."

"Why did you leave?" I ask. If I had found a place like that in the outside, I wouldn't abandon it for anything.

"As nice as it was, it was also difficult," Jayce says. "Living on a ship is a good defense for when the infected come to the shore. But when it comes to staying alive—whatever resources we found there were running low. We had to venture out to look for more. Then other groups showed up, tried to take over. It wasn't sustainable in the long run. We needed stability. So, my parents and a few others decided to search for the sectors."

It's insane that, no matter where someone grew up, there'll always be people looking to escape.

"Did you all make it?" I ask. "To the sectors?"

Jayce shakes his head. "Of course not. I was more or less the only survivor. My parents taught me from a young age not to get too attached. To life. Living beings. I can't tell you how many people we lost while we lived out there. It was just the norm. Difficult, sure, but you accept it. You know it's coming, sooner or later. So you just enjoy the time you do have."

I can somewhat understand. Growing up in the sectors, we're pretty safe, all things considered. For most of our lives anyway. Come recruitment, we're suddenly plunged into a death field.

"I'm sorry your parents didn't make it, after all that," I say.

"They were trying to get me to safety, and they did." He sounds accepting, if a touch sad. "So, for all intents and purposes, they got what they wanted."

I guess that's one way to look at it.

The helicopter ride takes about thirty minutes.

We land in a rural area, a good distance from our destination so as not to alert the fugitives to our arrival. The rest of the journey will be on foot.

"Hey, Connor," Lucille calls as she hops out of the helicopter and hits the rooftop with a thud. "Excited to meet some old friends?"

Following behind her, Connor lets out an exaggerated laugh. "Totally. Assuming you're talking about the infected, of course."

"I'm sure we can get them there," Lucille teases.

Sara falls into step beside Lucille and bumps her elbow in a silent scolding.

I look to Dalal as we jump out, confused. "What are they talking about?"

Dalal pulls her headscarf slightly back so it's not consuming her entire forehead. She leans close, voice hushed. "Connor's a Lotivan."

I have to hold back a gasp. "What? Why would they let a Lotivan work with us after all that happened?"

"Because not all Lotivan soldiers were part of the conspiracy," Dalal says. "Connor's been interrogated over and over, his dorm and belongings searched multiple times. He even had to undergo multiple inspections every single day for like a whole month, before they decided he was clean. Unfortunately, not everyone here is excited to work with a Lotivan. Lucille gets on his case all the time."

"That sounds familiar." Zack's dry comment comes from behind us.

"They were in the same squad," Dalal says. "Lucille, Connor and Stephen. Before the Renegades, I mean. They had three Lotivans among them, Connor included. The other two were traitors. They killed Lucille's partner and three others. They almost killed her, too. She usually hides it under her bangs, but if you look closely, you can see the scar from the bullet that grazed her." Dalal points to the side of her forehead, near her brow. "Connor apparently tried to talk them out of it, but they wouldn't lower their weapons. Stephen showed up just in the nick of time and killed them."

That's pretty messed up. I'd heard about incidents like these before. SPORE lost about thirty percent of its force after the Pit Mission, and their numbers weren't exactly thriving in the first place.

I guess it makes sense they'd hire back some of the Lotivans who've been proven innocent. Even though I myself am having a hard time *not* being suspicious of Connor now.

"I feel bad for Connor, to be honest." Dalal frowns. "I heard they held his family hostage to threaten information out of him. Word is, they're still holding them hostage for that in-case scenario."

I keep a straight face as we come to a stop next to Connor, waiting for Lucille and Sara to get the rooftop door open.

"Pink hair, huh?" Connor flashes me a grin that carves a dimple into his right cheek. His half curly, half wavy hair dances in the wind. "Now that's a choice."

"No, it's like you said," I try to assume a casual tone, "my natural hair color."

Connor laughs. "Gotcha. For a second there I was worried you broke your funny bone."

"You know, that's not what funny bone actually—"

He gives me a look that tells me he knows. "So, we're cool then, Pinky?"

"A nickname already?" I raise my brows at him. "Did I leave that strong an impression?"

"That's what I'm good at." He shrugs. "Giving people useless nicknames they didn't ask for. You're Pinky. Dalal here is Scarfy—" at which she shrugs in defeat "—Lucille is Silly. Sara is Wispy. Jayce is Nosy. Stephen is Buzzy—"

"Buzzy for…?"

"Buzzcut."

Of course. "And Cris?" I nod to where he stands with Stephen, closer to the door. "You got a nickname for him yet?"

Connor studies Cris for a moment. "He looks like a Brawny."

That admittedly gets a giggle out of me. "Nailed it."

"I told you, it's what I'm good at."

"So how come Lucille's is different?" I ask.

Connor pauses, brows pinched. "What do you mean?"

"Silly," I say. "It's not based on looks like everyone else's."

"That," Connor nods, "is 'cause she wears her silliness on the outside."

I can't say I see it, but I did only just get here.

"Used to," he mumbles, and I barely catch it as the charge explodes and the metal door bursts open. "Good talk, Pinky."

Connor's hands drop to his weapon, and he starts toward the door. "Catch you later."

"Later."

Not that I'm the best at reading people or anything but ... he doesn't *sound* like a traitor.

Then again. I never thought Nathan would be a traitor, either.

ELEVEN

WE WALK IN A DOUBLE-WEDGE FORMATION, with our squad taking the lead.

Lucille takes point. Dalal follows behind her to the left, Sara to the right—and I'm at the rear of the team with Zack next to me. Given the urban terrain, we stick to a ten-meter distance between each person. Right behind our team are Sgt. Seidel, Lt. Mansur, and Pvt. Aria at the center of the formation; then Bravo team in a mirrored wedge formation behind them.

A few minutes later, we emerge from behind the trees to a perfect sideways view of the auto-parts store down the hill. The store building itself looks relatively safe. The backyard has rows and rows of old cars and containers forming blocks. And the wave—at least sixty infected—surrounds one section of the backyard with big shipping containers. A large concentration of them is focused on one container in particular. The rest are a little more spread out.

"Well, there's clearly something going on here," I say.

"Something," Zack joins in. "But not Lori."

I blink. "How would you know that? We haven't even explored the place yet to know where they might be hiding—"

"These infected aren't on guard duty," Zack says. "They're hunting."

"Are they?" Lucille intrudes. Brows arched in suspicion. "I'm sorry, are you telling me we've been looking for your sister all this time when *you* can telepathically communicate with the infected?"

Zack turns to her with an amused smile. "I don't need telepathy when my eyes work just fine." He nods his head toward the infected. "If they were guarding whoever was hiding here, they would be more spread out, focused on surveying the perimeters to prevent people from coming in. These infected are doing the opposite. They're surrounding the place tightly, to make sure whatever is in there doesn't get away. In other words: they've found food, and they're trying to get to it."

The one—or I guess, *one of the* perks of Zack having spent the past five years in ruin, surrounded by infected, is that he got the chance to observe them up close. Perhaps closer than any of our researchers had the chance to, in a variety of situations and conditions. He can read them better than anyone I've ever seen from one glance. I'm sure Lori had much to do with that.

"So, you're saying there are people stuck in here somewhere?" I ask.

"It could be people." Zack shrugs. "It could be a rat."

"I highly doubt all these infected are gathered here to feast on a rat," Sgt. Seidel says.

"You'd be surprised what starving people can throw a feast over," Zack says bitterly.

"You could also be lying," Lucille interjects.

"That's true." Zack nods. "I could be lying."

"Sir," I interrupt, before the two of them start throwing hands, and face Sgt. Seidel. "What if he's right? That would mean there is a chance it's not fugitives we're after. It could be some random survivors."

"Or a rat," Zack taunts.

Sgt. Seidel doesn't mind him. Her sharp eyes scan the infected for a few thoughtful seconds. "I guess this just turned from an ambush to a rescue. Everyone, hold your positions. I'll let the lieutenant know."

As Sgt. Seidel walks away, I turn to Zack. "Are you sure Lori can't be here?"

"Even if she was," Zack says, "clearly the people who have her couldn't get her to do what they wanted."

"So, you don't *actually* know?" I heave a tired breath.

He shrugs. "Maybe she's the one who called on the infected for help in the first place, and that's why there are so many of them."

"I knew it," Lucille sighs in exasperation, tossing her head back.

Zack watches with a prideful, amused smile.

I hate it. I hate Zack's mind games. I hate that he's as straightforward as he is dodgy.

"You might wanna consider toning down the sass." Cris towers over him. "At least when talking to your superiors."

"And why should I do that, Cristian?" Zack looks up at him. "I take issue with our superiors more than anyone else. It *is* them who decided to drop bombs on my home."

"Sergeant Seidel and Lieutenant Mansur had nothing to do with that," Cris argues.

"But they're part of the system," Zack says, "so they're still guilty by association."

"Wow." Lucille's smile is a cutting contrast to the grimness in her pointed stare. "When did you have the time to climb all the way up on that high horse? Bet the view's real nice, too. Can't tell the corpses of all the people you massacred apart from the dirt."

"I think there is a big difference between killing soldiers and killing civilians, wouldn't you agree?" Zack challenges. Not even a hint of remorse in his voice. "I only ever did the former. SPORE does both. Not my fault that half of its force is made up of kids these days."

"That doesn't change the fact that the ones you killed had nothing to do with what happened in Eukson," Lucille says. "But I guess there's no point asking if you blame the gun or the person pulling the trigger."

"Obviously, neither," Zack says. "Because, you see, before any shooting can take place, you need ammo."

Lucille flips her ponytail back. "Oh, the joys of working with a terrorist. Because working with traitors alone wasn't exciting enough."

"I'm *so* glad I'm not being unnecessarily dragged into a conversation I'm not even a part of, because I'm neither one of those things you just mentioned," Connor comments from the side.

Stephen, who's been silently watching all this time, finally walks up to Lucille, blocking Zack from her sight. He places a hand on her shoulder and gently pushes her back a few steps. He's always soft in the way he handles her. Is it because they're old comrades, or something else?

"Let's stay focused, why don't we?" he says. At least someone is being diplomatic. "We already have an enemy. No need to make more on *our* side."

"Sorry to break it to you, Sarge." Lucille doesn't let up, though. "But that wave already set camp."

"Maybe it camped because you antagonize every single person you don't agree with," Dalal says, frowning.

"You stick to the kitchen, hun." Lucille leans over to catch Dalal's eyes beside me. She's even more stubborn than I am. "Looks way better on you than talking down to your superior."

"I'm perfectly happy in the kitchen, and as I recall, you're perfectly happy eating everything I cook." Dalal keeps a calm tone, then adds an emphasized, "*sir*."

Wow. This ... squad clearly has a lot of issues to sort through. I just hope they work better as a team on the battlefield than they do outside it. Then again, they probably wouldn't have made it this long if they couldn't work together.

"Lucille." Now it's Sara's turn to speak up, joining Stephen. There's something about the way she leans in close to look Lucille in the eyes. Something about the way Lucille responds to it. Because her tense posture deflates in a beat.

Did they really have the time to get so close? In the span of ... what was it? Two months now since Sara joined the Renegades?

Though I guess she and I got close pretty fast, too. Almost as fast as we fell apart.

Sara has that about her. She knows how to approach people. Knows how to befriend them. Gain their trust. Manipulate them into being exactly what she wants them to be.

"Listen up, Renegades," Lt. Mansur's announcement steals our attention. Sgt. Seidel stands next to him with the other squad leaders. The chatter quiets in seconds. "It appears our initial suspicions may have been wrong. Infected activity suggests this is a typical wave, uninfluenced by human interference. Fugitives could still very well be hiding here, but before we can search the place, we'll have to secure it and clear the wave." He turns to the platoon medic. "How is that CCP looking?"

"CCP is fully set and operational, Lieutenant!" Specialist Shedder says.

"Good." The lieutenant nods. "Then it's time to initiate our assault. Security elements, move into position. Assault section and support, follow me!"

Lt. Mansur leads ours and the weapons squad toward the objective. Zack comes along as well, just in case.

The security element, which consists of the Second Rifle Squad under Sgt. Bronson's lead, splits to establish left and right-side security. They'll block off the objective and keep the infected concentrated in one area for more effective fire assault.

Once our section has advanced enough, the lieutenant signals for us to split. The platoon sergeant hangs back with the weapons squad as they set up their machine guns, while our squad moves up, sticking to the side of the auto parts store.

"Security elements in place," Private Aria, our radiotelephone operator, reports.

"Roger that," Lt. Mansur acknowledges.

And that's our cue to initiate the attack.

We learned a lot of things during AIT. Unlike dealing with aggro waves, which have to be taken out as quickly and aggressively as possible, taking out passive waves is different.

The grenadiers—Sara and Connor—load their grenade launchers with blood rounds, which are exactly what they sound like. On Sgt. Seidel's signal, they fire at two distinct spots, roughly four hundred meters away, in opposite directions. The rest of us get ready to aim.

The two explosions draw the infected's attention. But the main goal is to lure out the trackers. They're visually impaired, and rely on their sense of smell to find potential prey, following the nearest and freshest trail of blood. It's a matter of seconds before they break off from the group and start toward the blood-marked areas.

Luring the trackers alone isn't enough. They're normally followed by chasers—those are the real trouble, and the ones we have to eliminate first.

There are ... a lot of them.

While the trackers walk carefully, feeling their surroundings, the chasers hop on top of cars, jumping from one vehicle to the next, taking shortcuts as they follow the trackers. They're bigger, more muscular, and more alert.

"If you give me an M4, I can help," Zack says to Sgt. Seidel.

"Not a chance, Caves," she tells him.

"Call your shots," Lt. Mansur orders.

We call our shots, and at his signal, we shoot. The first batch of chasers drops dead in an instant, but the gunshots alert the rest of them still hiding in the wave.

And now they've spotted us.

TWELVE

THEIR GROWLS EAGER AND VICIOUS, the chasers alert the rest of the wave as they head the attack. We shoot them fast, and they dodge faster, drawing closer.

"Alpha, move right!" Lt. Mansur orders. "Bravo, go left! Spread out. Don't let them corner us!"

Sgt. Seidel breaks off with Bravo. My team and I move with the lieutenant, closer to the store building. Zack sticks behind me, Sara to my left. Lucille and Dalal ahead of us, standing behind a car and shooting.

The weapons squad up the hill provides covering fire when the bulk of the wave gets closer. The distant, echoey gunshots tell me security's picking off some of the infected on their end as well.

"Sir," Private Aria says, "Left-side is reporting a number of infected approaching from our nine."

And surely enough, growls come from further down the hill as a bunch of chasers runs out of the woods.

Bite me.

The gunfire must have drawn them here.

"Tell the fire support to focus on the new arrivals," Lt. Mansur says. "We'll handle this bunch."

"Yes, sir," Private Aria responds and proceeds to relay the order.

The shooting continues. The chasers go down slow. The closer they get, the trickier it becomes to pin them down. I jump on the roof of a car to get a better view. I catch one stubborn chaser in my sights as it hides behind a vehicle, waiting for the fire to slow before dashing forward.

Sara shoots an explosive round using her grenade launcher, which takes out a few of them in a cluster. The ones out of the explosion's radius come out with just a few scratches and continue toward us.

"You know," Zack says behind me and Sara. "It looks like you could really use an extra pair of hands with an M4. It just so happens that I have said pair of hands. If you give me a weapon, I'd be a complete package. How about that?"

"Or you could stay quiet and let us focus." Sara reloads her grenade launcher.

"Watch out!" Private Aria warns. "Multiple targets approaching from the roadside, on your three!"

I look to my right. *More* infected. Oh God.

"Brown, Jung," Lt. Mansur calls, "cover the road. Right-side security will assist you."

"Yes, sir," we acknowledge.

"Ash," Sara dashes for the building, "we can use the store for cover."

Good thinking. I follow her through a broken window inside the store. Zack tags along. At least he's not trying to break off or do anything crazy. We check the corners by sticking out our arms with the protective sleeves in case something tries to bite. And something does—Zack's struggling sounds come from my right as he tries to push a camper off of him, slamming it against a row of shelves and knocking the entire thing down. I hurry to him. He clears my way, and I shoot the camper in the head.

I hold a hand out to Zack and pull him up. "Stay close."

"Yes, sir," he says.

Sara's already taking cover behind the cash register, and I take mine behind one of the shelving units. Then we open fire. That successfully draws the infected's attention to us, which means they won't go for the rest of our squad. Security stationed on the rooftop of the building starts shooting as well and the concentrated firepower takes them out fast. We prioritize the chasers, of which, thankfully, there aren't that many, then move on to the roamers.

I empty my entire mag, then pull back. "Reloading!" I announce.

"I've got you covered," Sara says.

I slap a new magazine into my rifle then poke out of cover to resume shooting.

"Not to alarm you or anything," Zack says, "but I think we've got a problem." He's nodding behind me, toward the back of the building, where some chasers are running in our direction.

Well, crap.

We can't let them surround us.

"Help me block those windows," I tell Zack. "Sara, can you hold them off?"

"Don't take long," she says, voice strained.

Zack and I run to the back and start pushing the shelves to block the entry points. Unfortunately, one of the chasers manages to jump through from Zack's side before we block the last window.

"Get down!" I shout. Zack ducks and I shoot the chaser without wasting a second. "Come on, almost there." We get right back to it. He helps me push the shelving unit, and we block off that last window.

"Ash," Sara calls. "I could really use your help back here!"

A couple of roamers are entering the store through the broken glass walls while Sara's busy reloading. Crap.

I hurry to her and fire at those infected from the hip, blowing off one's kneecap and blasting the other one's chest. The first one loses its balance and the second one falls. Giving me plenty of time to finish them off.

"Thanks," Sara says, popping back out of cover.

The number of infected is surely thinning out—well, at least on the roadside. There's still some intense gunfire out in the back, where the rest of our squad is, but it's not as crazy as before. We're making progress.

It takes us about ten minutes of constant shooting and reloading before things fully calm down. No more infected marching down the road. Sara and I still, watching expectantly.

"Is that it?" I stand by the door, taking a closer look out.

"The others are still fighting." Sara comes up beside me. "But we have to have taken out most of them by now."

"I sure hope so," I breathe out.

"Hey." Sara smiles, nudging my elbow. "It's good to be back, partner."

The word *partner* sends a cold storm through me. I can't bring myself to return the smile. I just stare at Sara, frozen.

Her smile fades, slowly turning into a frown as she looks down.

I shake myself off and turn toward Zack. He's standing in place, hunched shoulders, staring at the blocked windows in the back. The gunfire and growls on the other side seep through the tiny openings.

I walk up to him. "Hey, what's up?"

"She would have picked up my scent by now." Zack swallows hard. "She would have told the infected to stop attacking."

Right. I almost forgot the main reason we're here. Lori.

"So, you were right," I say. "Lori's not here."

"Yeah." Zack doesn't sound too excited about being right. "I guess not."

"Let's regroup with the others," Sara says. "They probably need our help."

I nod and nudge Zack to come along. Sara takes the lead and jumps out one of the side windows we came in through earlier.

Piles of corpses litter the ground all around us. Blood paints everything from the ground, to the exterior walls, to the old, rusty vehicles. Only a few infected remain, and it doesn't take us long to focus all our efforts and take them out.

That silence that settles after is always so surreal.

Before we carry on with the objective, we take care of the injured while the fire-support squad establishes three-sixty security. From our squad, Jayce has sprained his ankle, and Lucille has fallen and cut her arm open on a piece of glass. I take care of both while the platoon's medic tends to the other injured.

Once we're done, the reserve starts moving casualties to the CCP, Zack is ordered to join them and remain on standby. The rest of us split into pairs to dive into the maze of vehicles in the backyard.

Now that we know it's unlikely we'll find Lori here, that only leaves two options: survivors or fugitives.

THIRTEEN

"SO," Cris starts as we walk side by side, weapons at the ready, "you're friends with Zack now?"

Even though Cris was the first to volunteer to stay and help evacuate the Pit Survivors with me, and I know for a fact he sympathizes with them, his problem with Zack is a little more personal. Zack directed the Double Wave Attack, where we lost many of our comrades. Sam, Cris's friend, could have easily been one of them. He ended up losing an arm. I was always acutely aware of Cris's eyes whenever Zack approached me in Vigor. How sharp they became. How scrutinizing. His protectiveness always made me all fuzzy on the inside.

"Is that jealousy I hear?" I tease. "Don't be so subtle."

"Jealousy?" He lets out a wry laugh. "Come on now, I have much higher standards for guys who would make me jealous."

"Do you?" I snort. "I'd love a list."

"'Never killed innocent people before' would be the first bullet point," Cris says. "See? He already doesn't check that list." He runs a hand through his beautiful hair and catches my eye from the corner of his. "I just think it'd be wiser not to get too close. Trust isn't a charity."

"What makes you think I trust him?" I tilt my head to the side, trying to catch both his eyes this time, just to confirm the absence of jealousy. He evades my gaze. "You know, Zack is just as justified in not trusting any of us as we are not trusting him."

"Only, *we* have a good reason not to," Cris argues.

"What would you have done if you had been in his shoes?" I counter. "If you were the one stuck in Eukson, helpless, abandoned, while your home got bombed to pieces?"

"And I sympathize," Cris says, defensive, "but that's exactly why I don't think it's wise to trust Zack. If I were him, I don't think I'd ever be able to forgive or forget what's been done. I would pretend, for as long as I needed, until I got what I wanted, and then I'd take the first chance I got to get the hell away from here. Or worse, kill everyone that ever wronged me."

"Is that really what *you* would do?" I raise my brows at him. "Or is it more what you think *Zack* would do?"

"Irrelevant." Cris's hold tightens on his weapon. "The point remains. He's dangerous."

And so are we.

The conversation is cut short when I spot dry blood on one of the shipping containers in the shape of a handprint. This is one of the containers the infected were swarming earlier. I stop by the door and take a breath.

"Hello?" I give the metal door a quick rap. "If you can hear me, you're safe. We killed all the infected."

No response.

"Are you in there?" I call again. "If you're injured, I can help you. I'm a medic."

Nothing.

Screw it. I gesture for Cris to open the container. He stands on the right-hand side of the door, removes the padlock under the lockbox then lifts up the door handles and twists them, disengaging the cams and keepers. He signals for me to get ready before opening the door.

A vile stench hits me before I can cover my face. I turn my head away, gagging. Cris backs up a few steps, retching.

Both hands back on my weapon, I dare a look into the dark container. Flashlight on with a quick flick, then I proceed in. A soldier sits inside with his shirt tied around his leg. I rush in, but one glance at his wide-eyed face confirms he's already dead. Has been for a while.

"Jesus," Cris's voice comes from behind me.

"He's dead." I lower my weapon.

"Did he bleed out?" Cris stands beside me.

"That, or the wound got infected." I turn away from the body.

I don't want to keep staring at it. A tap on my earpiece. "Brown here. We found a corpse. Likely fugitive. Male."

"Roger that," Sgt. Seidel's voice. "Mark the location, and we'll send someone to collect the body."

"All those infected we killed out there…" Cris pulls out a chemlight from one of his pouches, "were here for one dead person?"

I start back to the door. "Let's keep going. Maybe there's more."

"More bodies?" Cris drops the chemlight by the door as we head out.

"His leg looked pretty messed up," I say. "Can't imagine he managed to drag himself all the way to that container. And not to mention … someone would have had to lock him in from the outside."

"So, someone could still be here," Cris says, sounding hopeful.

"Maybe," I say. "Or they left him here and went to look for help or get some medicine, but they never made it back…"

A creak behind us. Cris and I come to an immediate halt and turn toward the noise, our weapons up.

"You heard that, right?" Cris says.

Before I answer, one of the container doors flings open and a rain of bullets shoots through it. Cris and I dodge. He hides behind the container to the left, I take cover behind a truck's front to the right.

I hold his eyes and signal for him to flank. He acknowledges with a nod and moves slowly to the other side of the container.

"We're not here to hurt you." I try to keep a calm voice.

Gunfire hits the side of the truck, I move slightly further to the right, and that's when I spot movement from behind another container. I drop to the ground seconds before the person shoots, and crawl under the truck. I open fire blindly if only to get them off me.

"Brown, we heard gunshots," Sgt. Seidel's voice says through my ear. "Sitrep?"

I tap my earpiece. "We're under attack. Spotted at least two fugitives. Both armed."

"Roger that, Private, on our way," Sgt. Seidel says.

More gunshots, but this time they're not in my direction.

I roll out from under the truck and shoot to my feet, pointing my M4 at the back of the fugitive. "Drop your weapon."

He freezes, though he keeps his weapon pointed where I assume Cris is hiding.

"This doesn't have to look bad," I say. "You mistook us for a couple of unnaturally chatty infected, right? But now that you got a second look, you know we're actually humans here to help you, and you lower your weapon and come with us freely."

The boy stands in place, body shaking. Maybe from fear, or exhaustion, or starvation. Maybe all three. How long has he been hiding here?

"We have food and water, first aid," I say. "If you or one of your friends is hurt, we can—"

The boy turns to me in a beat. And in that same beat I squeeze the trigger and shoot a hole through his head. He hits the ground with a thump.

I keep my hands tight on my weapon as I approach the body. His dingy uniform almost blends him with the dirt.

A wide-eyed Cris comes out of cover. "You killed him?"

"He was going to shoot me." I think, at least. He wouldn't have turned as fast as he did otherwise. He wouldn't have made sudden movements. He would have at least said something. Right? "This isn't the time. There's another one somewhere out here."

"You could have shot his arm or leg," Cris says. "Did you *have* to kill him?"

I don't know if I had to. I didn't stop to think about it. Sparing even a second of thought could have left me on the ground instead. I'm not out here to die.

You're not supposed to freeze, Regi's ghost voice still yells at me. *That's what gets you killed. That's what gets all of us killed.*

I bend down to inspect the corpse. His blue eyes are wide open, staring up into a distance no one else can see. Blood soaks the soil under his head, bits and pieces of his brain scattered around. Messy, clumpy dark hair frames his pale face. Cracked lips. He must have been real thirsty.

Stop—don't look at his face. It doesn't matter. He's gone.

A girl jumps out before us. I hold up my weapon and aim at her. Rage consumes her at the sight of the dead boy. I place a finger on the trigger, ready to pull—

"Wait!" Cris stands in front of me, holding one hand up and pushing his weapon to his side with the other. "Don't shoot, please."

"Cris?" What the hell is he doing?

"Please," he says. "We're not here to hurt you."

"That's rich, coming from the people who just killed my friend." The girl's voice is dry. Brown hair tied in a loose, messy ponytail. Cheeks sunken in. Dark circles under baggy eyes.

"We have a clear shot," Sgt. Seidel's voice in my ear. "If she doesn't stand down, we'll take her out."

"H-he tried to shoot us first," Cris says. What. The hell. Is he doing? "Please lower your weapon. Let's talk."

"There's a whole platoon here." I keep my weapon up, though take my finger off the trigger so that I don't accidentally shoot Cris. "Even if you manage to kill us both, the others will be here soon. I doubt you have enough ammo to take out everyone."

"Yeah?" the girl huffs, finger on the trigger of her handgun. "I'm willing to die trying."

"Cris!" I shout to warn him, only my body automatically jumps at him, pushing him out of the bullet's trajectory a second before the *pop*. We land hard on the ground.

Not a breath wasted. I roll around, seize the girl's head in my sights and shoot. A hole marks the center of her forehead. Blood explodes from the back of her head. Her body flops and sends up a cloud of dirt as it hits the ground.

My breathing is sharp. My blood runs hot. I turn behind me, almost hopelessly, and speed-crawl toward Cris lying flat on his stomach. "Cris? Are you okay?"

He breathes in, breathes out, and slowly turns around. I inspect him quickly for any wounds, but there's none. "Ash…"

"Oh, thank God." I breathe out. The wave of relief passes in a beat as frustration storms me. "What the hell were you thinking? You can't let your guard down when someone literally has their weapon on you."

"Ash…" He sits up. Terrified eyes fall from mine. "You're shot."

"No." I look down at my shirt. There's a hole in it. "I'm fine…"

"Medic!" Cris shouts as he reaches over to hold me. "We need a medic!"

"I'm okay," I assure him. I don't feel a thing. Save for tired. Really, really tired. Like that bullet somehow tore off the cap that kept all my exhaustion bottled in.

Cris helps me lie on my back, and my eyes are glued to his face the entire time. He holds my hand in his. So warm. Like it always is. "You're gonna be fine."

"I am fine—" A forced whimper escapes me when he applies pressure to where the supposed wound is and—bite me, *now* I feel the pain. It's like someone hit me with a punching bag and flung me across a whole building. My vision blurs, but I fight to keep my eyes on his face. He looks so cute when he's worried about me.

Closing footsteps and muffled shouts surround us.

Cris runs a hand over my forehead, pushing my hair back, keeping the other on my side.

My sleep-deprivation catches up to me, and I drift off to a long, comfortable sleep.

PART TWO

FOURTEEN

I WAKE up to soft whispering.

In ... Spanish?

I open my eyes to the same face I fell asleep to.

Cris leans over me with clasped hands, mumbling so sincerely, so ... passionately. It reminds me of when I found him in the hospital in Kadia, sitting by his sick grandpa. Only I'm on the receiving end this time.

"Are you..." My throat is dry and itchy. I try to clear it.

Cris's eyes snap to me. "Ash!"

"Were you—"

"You're awake!" He shoots to his feet in a blink and turns somewhere behind him. "Medic!"

"Wait..." I tell him, but the medic is already headed over and Cris is stepping aside.

Apparently, I've been out for two days, though my stiff muscles make it feel like weeks. My vest stopped the bullet from going in too deep and scrambling my insides beyond repair, though it left quite a bit of bruising—and a lot of pain. The sleep deprivation and exhaustion made everything more intense. All things considered, the damage was pretty minimal and I'm lucky to be alive.

Once the medic leaves, Cris helps me sit and drink some water, then he takes the chair by my cot.

Looking into his concerned eyes can heal a thousand bullet

wounds. "Were you praying for me?" I ask, smiling. "Before I woke up."

"What gave you that idea?" he teases, though that cute blush darkening his cheeks says everything. "I'm really happy to … hear your voice again and…" Relief laces his words. "I'm just glad you're okay."

"Me too," I say. "Glad you're okay, I mean."

It replays in my mind in an instant. Cris stepping between me and the fugitive. The girl's finger on the trigger. One gunshot later and we're both on the ground. I'd take a thousand bullets for him if it meant saving his life.

The glow in Cris's eyes dims. His gaze falls away from mine, as if in shame. "I'm really sorry."

"Don't do that." I shake my head at him. "Don't blame yourself. You wanted to do things peacefully, I get it."

His hands clutch into tight fists on his lap, pulling at the fabric of his pants. "When I saw her face, how scared she was, I … didn't wanna be the one—"

"We didn't have a choice." A reminder I probably need more than him.

Cris's face shuffles through endless conflicted emotions. It's clear there's more at the edge of his tongue.

"What is it?" I sit a little straighter, giving him my full attention.

"It's nothing," he says. "You're tired. I should let you get some rest."

"Cris." I reach for his hand. "I've been asleep for two days. I think that's enough rest." Yeah, sure, I could use more time to wake up, but I can't really fathom resting with that troubled look on his face. "Tell me what's on your mind."

He inhales a deep breath and meets my eyes with a hint of hopeful uncertainty. "It's just… What if we did have a choice?"

"She opened fire—"

"She had no reason to take our word for anything other than a lie. She was defending herself," Cris says. "I keep replaying it all in my head, and I just can't help but wonder … what if you *didn't* kill her friend?"

"Her friend was going to kill *you*," I argue.

"What if we incapacitated him?" he counters. "We could have captured him. Used him as a bargaining chip to get her to lower her weapon. We could have taken both of them alive. No one had to get hurt. Not you. Not them."

"There is no point wallowing about this." I shrug. Kinda regret urging him to talk about this now. I don't want to think about it. "What's done is done."

He frowns. "Look, Ash, I'm not trying to be ungrateful, because I am *really* grateful. You saved my life, and I wouldn't forgive myself if anything happened to you because of that... I just don't think I can—"

"We don't. Have. A choice," I repeat.

"Would you shoot Nina?" he fires back.

That question stuns me.

"If that girl in the auto-parts store had been Nina, would you have shot her?"

"Th-that's different," I stutter. "Nina's—"

"Your friend? Sure." He nods. "But why does that make her special? Those fugitives have friends, too. Families. Loved ones. They're all people. Just like Nina. Just like you and me."

Sure, but I can only spare so much space in my heart. "Cris, out there it's us or them. Out there, it's the people you love or the people they love." I don't even want to imagine a scenario where I have to decide between Nina and Cris, but... "If I have to choose between them and you, I choose you. I'll kill as many of them as I need to, to protect you."

A billion emotions flash through his face. His throat works up. I don't want to keep arguing about this.

"I..." I reach for his hand again, blushing. "I care about you."

That bullet may not have killed me, but the way his thumb brushes over my fingertips nearly does. "I care about you, too."

My heart almost leaps out of my chest.

See? That wasn't hard. What the hell have we been waiting for all this time? Why has it taken us so long to open up about how we really feel?

I mean, sure, Cris and I didn't get along much before, and yes, up until four months ago, I was still coping with the fact that I killed my ex, and two months before that, with the fact that he left me to die. But truth is, no one has ever looked at me the way Cris does—not even Will, and I dated him for a year.

Nope. Let's back track for a minute. No Will. This is a Will-free zone. There's just Cris.

Screw it. I'm not wasting any more time. I know he likes me, and he knows I like him. All that's left is to say it, so I collect my courage to do just that. "I li—"

Cris releases my hand and shoots up as if Sgt. Seidel just walked into the tent—she didn't. "I have to go."

I blink. "What?"

He rubs the back of his neck. "I should let you rest. And I need to … take care of some things."

"Oh." I try to get a read on his face. Is he feeling shy? Nervous? Did I make him uncomfortable? Or maybe he doesn't want to confess his feelings to me while I'm sitting in a cot. Maybe he wants this to be a little more special. A little more intimate.

"I'll see you around." He backs away, voice urgent and shaky. "Get well soon."

"Yeah…" I swallow. "You too—I mean… Yeah. Thanks."

In a matter of seconds, he's gone.

All the heat in my body turns freezing cold.

What the hell just happened?

FIFTEEN

I SPEND the next couple of days recovering and resting. The medic prescribes me some sleeping pills to take sparingly so as not to hinder my work performance.

The fugitives I ... killed had a map on them with some marked locations, and a few recon units were sent out to investigate, but many turned out to be dead ends. At least those of us injured get enough time to recuperate. Lucille with her cut arm and Jayce with his sprained ankle. The only downside is that I haven't been able to train or work out. I envy all the soldiers around the base doing laps or some form of strength or cardio workouts.

By dinner time, most of us gather in the DFAC.

My heart almost jumps to my throat when Cris walks in with Connor. I try to get his attention with a wave, but he only spares me a glance before returning to whatever conversation he's having with Connor.

We haven't really talked much since that day in the first-aid place. Every time I tried to find him, he was busy doing something or remembering something he had to do—or he was nowhere to be found.

Stephen takes a seat next to Lucille with a big sigh. "We just heard back from another recon unit. Place was empty. No traces. Again."

Everyone sighs and grumbles at the news.

Dalal fumbles with one end of her headscarf. "If only we captured them alive. Maybe we could have learned something."

That feels targeted.

"They tried to kill me and Cris," I remind her.

"Yes, and I'm sure that if you had the chance to resolve things peacefully, you would have taken it," Dalal says. "Personally, I've never killed any fugitives, and I don't plan to anytime soon."

"We don't have a choice," I repeat the same thing I said to Cris before. Don't know why I'm the one who has to remind everyone.

"I believe we humans have more choices than we think, at any given moment." Dalal's tone drops to a serious, solemn one. A startling contrast to her usual bubbly self. "At the end of the day that's what makes us different from infected, right? Our ability to control our actions, instead of operating purely on impulse and jumping the gun ... very literally in this case."

"Don't listen to her preachy sermons," Lucille says. "She treats every conversation like a Sunday service."

Dalal blinks. "You're thinking of Christians, first of all."

"You did the right thing," Lucille nods at me, "better you shoot the traitors before they shoot you."

"Also, I'm not *that* preachy." Dalal mumbles. "Am I that preachy?"

Jayce shakes his head *no* with a reassuring smile, while Connor waves his hand in a *just a little bit* gesture.

"You protected yourself, and your comrade. That's what matters," Stephen tells me. "You had to act fast."

"One might argue she acted *too* fast," Connor comments. He plasters on a smile when he looks at me. "Not that I'm judging or anything, Pinky. You fit right in with some of the snap-decision-makers here." Now he's side-eying Lucille, but she's not paying him any mind.

Gradual silence takes over the DFAC as soon as Zack joins us with his tray.

Lucille leans back against her chair with folded arms. "Oh, no," she fake-gasps, "did you lose your way to the terrorist dining table?" I've never heard anyone sound as condescending and aloof as Lucille.

"I don't think so." As if to spite her, Zack picks a seat facing her. "You're all here, aren't you?"

That actually gets a giggle out of a few people, and offended looks from everyone else.

Lucille lets out a hysterical laugh. "Boy, you got some mouth on you."

"As do you," Zack teases. "We should let our mouths hang out sometime, see how well they get along."

"Oh, please," Lucille sweetens her voice, "can my teeth tag along too? They'd *love* to meet your tongue."

"You know, with how red your face gets every time I'm around," Zack says, "I get the feeling you want to meet *all* of me."

Are they ... flirting or threatening each other? Judging by the awkward looks on everyone else's face, no one can tell.

"Hey, Zack," Jayce interrupts the intense staring contest between the two. Probably for the better. "Do you mind telling us a little bit about Lori? How ... it all happened?"

"Your overlords didn't share the details?" Zack mocks.

"Our 'overlords' don't know why the sentient crawler is sentient," Stephen answers. "But there must have been *something* that made it the way it is."

"*She*," Zack corrects, "was born like that."

"Born like that?" Dalal looks up from her tray with big eyes.

"My mother was pregnant," Zack explains. "She got bit, when the Tsunami hit. Lori got infected through her."

"So..." Jayce places his spoon down, his nose scrunched up. "You mean your sister..."

"She tore her way out," Zack finishes the sentence for him, and *clink-clink-clink* echoes through the DFAC as utensils drop. Gagging noises ensue. Scraping chairs. A few people abandon the tables. "I'm not a scientist. All I know is, when she came out, she didn't try to hurt me. She just clung to me, like she knew exactly who I was."

"I hope everyone is enjoying their food." Dalal sets her own spoon down, staring at her bowl in horror. "I spent so long cooking it. I would hate if all these bowls stayed full."

"I think it looks great." Zack stuffs a spoonful of soup into his mouth.

"How likely is it..." Stephen clears his throat, "that your sister would listen to anyone but you?"

"I don't know," Zack says. "She usually listened to those within her trusted circle, but didn't do things without running them by me first. Let's not fool ourselves, though. Those Lotivans can and will resort to any means to get Lori to obey them, if they're desperate enough. They'll torture her if they have to. Starve her. Threaten her. Lori's not immune to any of that."

"But let's say we do find it—*her*..." The hopefulness in Stephen's voice drains with every word. "You think she'll help us? You think all this, everything we're doing right now, will amount to something?"

Zack narrows his eyes. "Are you asking me if Lori will work for SPORE?"

"I'm asking you if Lori will help humanity," Stephen says. "Will she communicate with the infected on our behalf? Convince them to leave us be? Is that something she can do?"

"Beats me." Zack shrugs. "The whole saving humanity spiel isn't really my thing."

"It's not like we have a lot of options." Cris sounds sullen. "Either we get the sentient crawler to work on our side, or we continue fighting the same way we have been."

"Until humanity is wiped out," Connor adds.

There is a third option, and that is Melisa. If what Haytham said is true, maybe it's not so impossible to actually find a cure or vaccine.

But maybe getting Lori could also help with that. If she can communicate with the infected, that means she could communicate with Melisa, too. Right? Means that ... we can talk to her. Find out if she's still in there, somewhere, like she always believed the infected's past selves to be.

A sudden memory flash from that day in the Pit. Melisa's struggle to break free as the Active pinned her down. Its long, slimy tongue forcing its way into her mouth.

And now it's my turn to lose my appetite.

"You're all forgetting another option," Lucille says. "The more likely one, in my opinion. And that is the Tsunami *he'll* call on us as soon as he reunites with his sister."

Zack grins. "Now there's a thought."

"I'm curious, Lucille," I start, because honestly, she's starting to piss me off. "Do you feel this passionately about Eukson being bombed, too? You know, considering how many innocent people died that day?"

Lucille raises her brows at me. "What kind of a ridiculous question is that? Of course, I do. Frankly I don't know why Sears is even still here. He should have been exiled years ago."

Oh... So she *doesn't* know, and boy does that make me happy.

"You might be right," I nod. "If Sears had been the one who ordered the bombing."

Lucille eyes me like I'm spewing incomprehensible gibberish. "What are you on about?"

"It was Rodríguez," I say, and those words bring silence all over the DFAC. Sara, who's sitting next to Lucille, shoots me a stern look, like I shouldn't be saying this. I couldn't care less what she thinks. Part of the problem comes from all this lack of transparency. From all the lies we're fed every single day.

Everyone looks around in search of confirmation.

"Sears was the one in charge at the time—" Lucille says.

"Technically, he wasn't," I cut her off. "Rodríguez took over by force. Then he let Sears take the fall for the bombing because, what the hell, he was stepping down from his position anyway."

Lucille leans back in her chair with crossed arms. "And I'm supposed to just, what, take your word for it?"

"It's true." Sara lets out a resigned sigh. "Sears didn't order the bombing." Well, I wasn't expecting *her* to back me up, but then again, she never liked when I used to run my mouth about Sears.

All the doubtful looks on everyone slowly turn to conviction.

Lucille's jaw hardens. Her piercing gaze travels somewhere I can't follow. A slight shake of her head, and a disappointed smile. Then she picks herself up and leaves.

"I guess someone's not important enough to be privy to classified information," Zack comments with an all too smug a smile.

"Probably shouldn't mention this out loud," Stephen warns. "Doubt the general wants people finding out. And it might get…" he looks to me when he adds, "someone in trouble."

Zack's eyes meet mine, and the smugness dissipates into something reminiscent of gratitude. *Thank you,* he mouths.

I offer him a smile of my own. *You're welcome.*

SIXTEEN

I LEAVE a good distance between me and the DFAC before my mouth opens with heavy breaths. I hate how almost everything makes me on edge these days.

It's pretty cold out, even with my SPORE-issued jacket on, and I half want to go back inside and cozy up a bit. I clasp my hands around my mouth and blow into them.

"Ash?" Cris's voice startles me. "Sorry … I didn't mean to scare you."

I turn to him, slapping on a relaxed face. "You didn't."

"You okay?" he asks, eyeing my shaky hands. I guess he's not ignoring me now?

"Yep," I lie. "Just cold."

"Why are you outside, then?" He narrows suspicious eyes at me.

I shrug. "Needed some fresh air."

He doesn't look convinced and, well, I don't really care to convince him of anything right now. I want to ask him why he's been ignoring me all this time and why he's talking to me like nothing—

"Ashley," he says. "I think we should maybe talk … about us."

Oh.

Never mind. Thank God I didn't say anything. He must have been thinking about it—us. How to do this the right way. When to do it. Where.

I smile, a little life returning to me. "You know, I was starting to worry you were never going to ask me out."

"I... I'm..." His face falls. "I'm not."

I want to die. Oh, my God, I want to die. Please kill me, right now.

My smile vanishes. The cold in my cheeks melts away as heat fires through me in embarrassment. Why do I always have to get ahead of myself? Why?

"But, uh ... that's kind of what I wanted to talk about." He clears his throat. I can't even look at him straight. "We really shouldn't. It's kind of inappropriate. And not to mention prohibited."

Now that's ... jarring. Also, hypocritical. Also, what the hell?

"Really?" I dare look up, if only to try and study his face, read his mind.

"I just don't think it's a good idea," he says it so matter-of-factly it makes my heart feel like a block of ice.

I fold my arms, hoping to generate some warmth, hoping it makes me look indifferent. But my voice betrays me, and my words sell me out. "You didn't seem to think it was a bad idea to flirt with me every single day over the past four months."

"We were just messing around." He scratches the back of his neck. "Right? I mean ... at the end of the day, we both know this..." he nods between us, "wouldn't work."

"We do?" I flinch. Every word is like a hammer swinging down on that block of ice. I can almost hear it *crack*.

"It's just a distraction," he couldn't have said that more apathetically if he tried. "That's what it always was. But I think it's about time we took our jobs more seriously. Being here, working with the Renegades, under Lieutenant Mansur's lead... It doesn't make sense to risk jeopardizing our positions. At least, I don't want to jeopardize mine. I could be looking at an early promotion by the end of this, which ... I know doesn't really mean much to you, but it does to me."

"I see." My body is numb.

"Let's be real, you don't even like me that much." He's so confident about it, too. "Almost every conversation we have turns into an argument. That's fun and all, but it's not a solid basis for something serious, don't you think?"

I don't know what to say to that. I was prepared for a completely different conversation. But this? I don't even know how to begin to process it. How could I have felt so sure about us? About him? Was it really all in my head?

No. There's no way. I didn't imagine it. I can still feel that warm, gentle touch on my face. The way he stroked my cheek. That was real.

"What are you doing?" I try. My energy is drained, but I try. "You don't mean any of this. I know you don't. So what are you doing?"

"Ash…"

"Is it because of what happened?" I hold his eyes, searching for a *no* before I ask the rest of the question. "With those fugitives?"

His silence stretches for an eternity. His lips twitch, as though he's struggling to put on a smile and soften the blow he's about to deliver. My heart shatters before his answer comes. "I don't want death attached to my name. More than it already is."

Yeeeep. Figures.

"Maybe you think I'm a coward or an idiot. But killing isn't who I am. I don't want it to become who I am." No, why would he? He's always been self-righteous. "And I'd rather die doing the right thing, than live because I did the wrong thing."

Is this why he's been so distant? Because he can't stand looking at me? Because I'm a murderer? Like Zack?

"If you feel like your only choice is killing, I can't do anything about that," he says. I can't stomach the way he's looking at me. "But I don't want to be your excuse."

Even getting shot hurt less than this.

"Okay." I force the word out through a mangled breath.

"Look." God, please stop talking. "We're still … friends." I'm going to punch him. I swear I'm going to. "Comrades."

"You know what, *comrade*?" I snap. "We're done."

"Ash—"

Yep. There it is. *Punch.* Straight across his perfect, stupid jaw.

He flinches and backs away a few steps, pressing his fingers to his jaw. I hate the way his beautiful hair falls over his forehead when he looks at me with wide, baffled eyes. "What the hell?"

"You're a jerk." I shake my aching hand and stomp past him. As far away as my wobbly legs can carry me. As far away as I can get so he doesn't hear me choke on my tears.

It's okay. You're okay. You don't need Cris. You don't need Sara. You don't need anyone. You're fine. Everything's going to be fine.

I take in quick, sharp breaths, but that does very little to calm me. I want to collapse onto myself and scream my lungs out. I want to punch something until my fists are bloody. God, I wish I could close my eyes and open them again to find myself back in my room, in Kadia, lying on the floor, asleep, and none of this is real. All of this is a horrible, terrible, awful, miserable nightmare.

That doesn't happen, of course. I close my eyes and open them, and the only thing that changes is my vision, now blurred by unstoppable tears.

Then my portor beeps. Because why the hell wouldn't it?

But hey, if I'm lucky, maybe this is the assignment where I die.

SEVENTEEN

THAT ASSIGNMENT WASN'T IT. Nor was the one after that, or the one after that.

We waste about a month on useless assignments. Looking into suspected hideouts without finding anything concrete. Just traces suggesting someone *was* there but evidently left before we showed up. A waste of resources on nonexistent results.

"This is a corpse dump." Lucille kicks a rusty trashcan, sending it flying across the room and littering the already-dirty floor with more trash. "Clearly they're onto us. Someone's warning them so they can move before we arrive."

"But who could it be?" Dalal asks.

We're inside an office building, where we found what used to be a fugitive camp, completely abandoned. No trails. Just a bunch of infected, whose corpses are now decorating the hallways.

"Who could it be?" Sgt. Monty from Bronson's Bravo Team is the one who speaks up. He's one of many people who constantly give Zack dirty looks. "We know who it is, so why don't we save ourselves the trouble and put a bullet in his head right now?" He hops off the desk he's sitting on and stomps toward Zack, hand on his weapon.

I immediately step in front of Zack to shield him. Everyone else stands alert.

To my surprise, Lucille's the first one to block Monty's path. "The hell do you think you're doing, Monty?"

"What you don't have the guts to do," he barks at her. "We both know what he is. Only difference between us is that you don't want to get your pretty little hands dirty. Well, let me tell you something, sweetheart—"

She doesn't let him, though. Before Stephen or Connor even reach him, Lucille sends her knee straight into his crotch, and he falls at her feet in agony. Stephen and Connor are on him in the next beat. They pull him up and throw him toward the rest of his stunned squad.

Sara steps up beside Lucille. Cris, Jayce and Dalal stick by me and Zack.

"The difference between us," Lucille says to the frothing Monty, "is that only one of us will be packing to go home tonight."

"You—"

"Dude, stop." One of his comrades holds him back and drags him further away. "She's not the one you wanna mess with."

"That's right, I'm not," Lucille says. "But if you wanna try that again, be my guest. See if your hand will stay attached to the rest of you for long."

The air thickens with dark glares and silent threats. Another one of Monty's squadmates tries to throw a punch at Stephen, but Stephen blocks it with one hand and returns it with the other, landing it with a loud *crunch*.

Things don't get a chance to escalate further when Sgt. Seidel and Bronson return from whatever meeting they were having with HQ. They catch on quick to the hostility, what with Monty's and his friend's quiet whimpers and hateful stares. Sgt. Bronson escorts his squad outside, while Lucille and Stephen brief Sgt. Seidel.

I release a low breath, the tension in my muscles slowly easing up.

"Well, that was entertaining, wasn't it?" Zack leans against the wall with folded arms, a big, amused grin stretching across his face.

"Zack." I frown. "He was going to shoot you."

"Apparently not on Lucille's watch," Zack says, then adds a little loudly after Sgt. Seidel heads back out, "Aren't I just so lucky to have such strong and pretty bodyguards?"

Lucille pins him with a glare. "I'm starting to have regrets already."

I'm glad to see that despite the constant bickering, our squad does stick up for one another when it really matters. But Monty aside, someone else might try hurting Zack again, and they may not make as big a scene.

"You're worried about me?" Zack holds my eyes intently.

Yeah, I am, actually. And he should be worried about himself, too.

"That's sweet." He smiles. "But believe me, out of everyone here, no one watches my back more than I do. I only like surprises when I'm not on the receiving end."

I sigh. "Do you ever take anything seriously?"

"If you're this worried," he brushes a finger against my cheek, "feel free to bunk with me from now on."

I blush and smack his hand away lightly. His only response is a chuckle.

Just like Lucille said, Monty is discharged from the Renegades and sent home as soon as we return to the FOB. The lieutenant takes some time to lecture us about trust, teamwork, and more importantly, following orders. But it's clear not everyone—namely Monty's buddies—is very affected by the speech. Their faces spell it all out. *How could the lieutenant discharge a founding member to protect a terrorist? Why is he trusting someone who killed our own people?*

I guess the reason Lucille never got in trouble before is because the lieutenant knows everyone has their own opinions about Zack. But as long as they place the mission objective before their feelings, the way she does, there is nothing to worry about. Or at least, there shouldn't be.

In the end, the whole bunking with Zack idea wasn't totally crazy. The lieutenant orders our squad to take turns watching him, just in case. Connor and I are assigned first watch. We sit in the basement hallway by a burn barrel while Zack is in what he refers to as his "private quarters." He stays awake for a couple hours, chatting with us from behind the door, before going completely quiet.

"So." Connor leans back against his chair, rubbing his eyes. "Wispy told us you were the last person to see Nina. Or speak to her for that matter."

That takes me aback. I'm guessing he's not bringing this up just because Nina's a fugitive. "You knew her."

"I'd say I knew Nathan better than I knew Nina," Connor says. Then, with a silly voice, adds, "I guess in the end I didn't know either of them well enough." He takes in a breath. "How was she? When you last saw her. Was she injured?"

"She looked fine, given the circumstances." I shrug. "Plus, I thought Stephen was the one who last saw her. When she killed your comrades."

"He *thinks* he saw her. I didn't, so I can't confirm," Connor says. There is something about his voice, almost a sense of desperation. "You think she's okay out there?"

I ask myself that question almost every day. "Maybe. I don't know. Why are you asking *me*?"

"You're not in any kind of contact with her," he whispers conspiratorially, "even the secret type?"

"What? No." I gasp. "Why would you think that?"

"I don't know." Connor shrugs. "Thought I'd ask. You were friends—"

"No," I say. "I haven't spoken to Nina since the Pit, and I don't think it would be in my best interest to stay in contact with her given that she's a fugitive. Surely you don't need me to tell you that."

I don't know where all this questioning came from, or what to make of it. Is he asking because he's genuinely curious? Because he cares about Nina? Or is it more because someone asked him to? Is he trying to prove his loyalty to SPORE by getting me to spill any secrets I may hold?

I hate myself sometimes. I hate my lack of trust in people. I hate people.

"Relax, Pinky, no need to get so defensive." Connor holds up his hands in surrender. "I've got enough eyes on me as it is."

"Okay," I say. "Then maybe we should change the subject before someone overhears us and gets the wrong idea."

"All right, all right." Connor smiles. "New topic: what's it like being a Renegade so far?"

I shrug. "No thoughts. Honestly, I'm not even sure what I'm doing here."

"Wispy would disagree," Connor says.

"Yeah? Why's that?"

"Well, for one, she recommended you to the lieutenant," he says. "When we were discussing potential replacements for Olivia and Kent."

I blink at that. "Sara recommended me?"

He nods. "Yeah, she said you were probably the only person who could—"

"Of *course* she did." I scoff, my eyes rolling so hard they almost go into my skull. "She's still pulling crap like that. I can't believe her…"

"Okay, I'm getting the vibe that maybe I shouldn't have told you." Connor's nose scrunches up.

"No," I pull to my feet, "no, *thank you* for telling me. You have no idea how much I appreciate it."

"You're welcome?" Connor says.

I start down the hallway, toward the stairs.

"Where are you going?" Connor calls after me. "Hello? We're on watch duty?"

"Bathroom break," I toss back.

EIGHTEEN

UN-FRICKING-BELIEVABLE. And yet, totally believable.

The audacity of Sara telling me how sorry she was that I wasn't going home, when she's the reason behind it. It's as if I didn't have enough reasons to want to punch her teeth in already.

And there I was, starting to think that maybe there is a chance we can actually mend things. Thinking I actually missed her. God, I feel like such an idiot.

Who the hell does she think she is? I'm having the worst case of déjà vu right now.

You're looking at me like you either want to kiss me or punch me. Sara turned to meet my eyes, smiling. *Which is it?*

Do you have a preference? I teased, one arm around her shoulders while hers supported me by the waist and kept me upright. I'd slipped down a hill earlier and hurt my leg during a No Comms FTX. Couldn't walk by myself. I looked away from her, at the dirt path stretching ahead of us. *No, it's just... I've been thinking, it's kind of funny when you think about it. How things happened.*

What do you mean? she asked.

I mean that we randomly ended up in one platoon, I said. *One squad. Partners even. Don't you think it's funny? I'm not religious or anything, but it's almost like fate set it all up.*

But there was no hint of amusement on her face. Nothing but a look just like the one Ro gave me when I caught her stealing food from the cafeteria one time. Guilt-ridden and ashamed.

What? I nudged her.

Yeah, um ... about that. Sara's lips stretched into a nervous smile. *It actually wasn't random. I kind of ...* her shaky gaze danced over mine, *I kind of asked General Sears if he could arrange for us to be in the same platoon. Same squad. As partners.*

I came to a halt, wincing at putting too much pressure on my hurt leg. *That doesn't make sense. We were assigned together from the start.* Not like Cris, whose assignment suddenly changed after we'd already been split up. *We didn't even know each other's names then.*

Her silence struck me with instant flashes, from Recruitment Day, standing in line while this random girl with a short bob watched me. And again, when we were in the locker room. Then it clicked. I finally knew what those looks meant.

You already knew who I was ... I concluded, and she confirmed with a nod. *Was it because of the night of recruitment, when I tried to escape?*

No. Before that. She ran a grimy hand over her forehead, replacing all the sweat with dirt. *It was a few months after I came to Spheria. I'd asked Luke if he could get me updates about you, and with his dad's connections, it wasn't so hard. It helped that every Spore in Kadia knew who you were.*

Luke? Luke knew, too?

Hold on... My head felt heavy with a load of realizations. I freed myself from her to lean against a tree, so I could stare her directly in the face when I asked her, so I could see her expression. *You were spying on me? You had Spores spy on me? For five years?*

I... Sara frowned. *I know it sounds weird. It wasn't spying, I promise. It was just occasional updates about how ... you were doing. How you were dealing with everything.*

You mean my dad dying? Yeah, those weren't exactly the brightest years of my life, but apparently you already knew that. I sucked in a hard breath.

I just wanted to know more about you, she said. *I was hoping that I could meet you one day. Talk to you. And maybe ... become friends. I thought it might prepare me, in the future, to tell you everything.*

But it didn't, though, did it? I snapped. *You did all this, and in the end it had to come from Zack before you actually told me anything.*

Her shoulders sank. *It turned out harder than I thought it was going to be.*

Were you even going to tell me? If Zack hadn't said anything, did you actually plan on telling me yourself?

I ... want to say yes, Sara said. *And I can't tell you how many times I played the scenario in my head. But after I met you, and actually spoke to you ... I had no idea how I would go about it. The truth is I don't know if I would have told you.*

So just to get this straight, you used Luke to spy on me for five years, manipulated the recruitment process to make sure we ended up together—played nice with me, while pretending you had no idea who I was—all so that you'd have me right where you wanted me? And in the end, you didn't even want to tell me the truth? You did all that ... for what, exactly?

I just felt that ... if I could be your friend... If I could be there for you, one way or another, she said, *it was the least I could do, to honor him.*

And those words wrecked me.

The least she could do to honor him.

Oh, so I was what ... a charity case? Your atonement. My frustration couldn't have been louder. *'I'm so sorry I got your dad killed and broke you, here, let me fix you with my magical friendship glue?'*

Ash, I know how it sounds—

No, Sara, this isn't just about how it sounds, it's about what it is. My fists clenched at my sides. The burn in my eyes intensified. *I mean, we were good. Why the hell did you have to tell me all this now? Why couldn't you just laugh and say: yeah, fate's so deaddamn funny?*

The memory of it already has me choking.

Someone from Redfearn Squad points me to the warehouse, and there she is, with Lucille, sitting on one of the dining tables, laughing —Lucille is *laughing*. I didn't even think her face muscles could move like that. My body hits an invisible wall, and I freeze.

Sara's braiding Lucille's hair, and Lucille is holding what I think is a hand mirror and fixing her bangs. They have a bag of something next to them to snack on, and I don't think they've stopped talking, not for a second, to breathe.

Is Lucille Sara's new project, then? The next person she's going to tame? How much homework did she do on the Renegades before joining them? I'd give anything to learn what kind of dirt she dug up on Lucille.

Or could it be that ... they're friends because they actually get along? No secrets. No lies. No deception. It's all real.

All the rage boiling inside me simmers down to bitterness, then the bitterness into a sting. It takes seconds for my cheeks to soak in tears. I have no will to confront her. No strength to look her in the face. I turn on my heels and find myself a quiet corner to sit until I've run out of tears.

NINETEEN

WE GATHER in the DFAC for yet another useless briefing for another useless mission.

Morale's hanging by a thread, judging by the dull, tired faces on everyone. Slacked posture and concealed yawns.

"About two hours ago," Lt. Mansur starts, "the Hummingbirds platoon took off from Kadia on a search for medical resources, and ventured to Zone Zero to the northwest."

The Hummingbirds platoon. Where have I heard that before? Also, did he say Zone Zero? As in *Ground Zero*?

"On entering the science building, they reported a gas leak that caused asphyxiation upon inhalation—as well as chemical burns to exposed flesh wounds and organs, including the eyes and mouth. We know of at least two members who lost their eyesight due to exposure, and who suffocated to death before the rest of the platoon was alerted to wear their gas masks."

What in the world? That sounds even more horrifying than I would have imagined GZ to be.

"In addition," the lieutenant continues, "they came across an unidentified organic growth taking up the majority of the west side of the building. Our running theory is that whatever chemicals leaked in the science building may have had some undesirable effects on local plant life, which subsequently resulted in abnormal growth."

Killer gas *and* giant plants? Could this get any worse?

"The assault squads were ambushed by a wave shortly after

entering the building." Of course it could get worse. "They also noted unusual infected activity which they suspected might point to the presence of an Active or some other superior type of infected, such as the sentient crawler." Everyone straightens up, their interest piqued. "Unfortunately, we lost contact with the Hummingbirds about thirty minutes ago due to unexpected comm interference.

"Our objective is to head there, find any surviving Hummingbirds and rescue them," Lt. Mansur says. "Because of the potential threat of Actives, we expect there to be a concentrated number of infected, even though the Hummingbirds cleared the surrounding area before moving in. Considering the gas leak and its known side effects, we best get geared up accordingly. You'll have to wear your gas masks at all times. Our secondary objective is to find the source of the gas leak and, if possible, eliminate it. Spheria is sending a research team that will meet us at the objective. We suspect the source of the leak to be on the chemistry level of the building, which would be the fourth floor."

"Sir!" someone from Bronson Squad says, "why are we being sent to rescue the Hummingbirds? With all due respect, search and rescue isn't our job."

"Today it is." Lt. Mansur folds his arms behind him. "I've mentioned comm interference, and unusual infected activity. Both suggest that a group of fugitives may have taken refuge on campus. Finding them would be our third objective."

"Fugitives hiding in Ground Zero?" Dalal gasps to my right. "That's *bold*."

"Or stupid," Lucille comments from the seat across from me. "They probably don't even *know* it's Ground Zero."

"Who cares where you are if you have a super-powered crawler that can weaponize infected for you?" Connor leans back with his arms against the table. "I'd say it's more *smart* than it is stupid. Can you imagine how many infected there are in that university? If the fugitives can control them, they'll tear us apart in no time."

"All of that rests on the fact they managed to actually tame the crawler," Lucille challenges, turning to meet Connor's gaze, "which we don't know that they did."

"Our fourth objective, assuming the previous ones are successful," Lt. Mansur resumes, after he's done answering a few more questions, "is to look for any useful resources to bring back with us. Understood?"

"Yes, sir!" comes our unified response.

"Go get geared up and let's regroup at the helipads in fifteen."

We start toward the armory, and my eyes, as they tend to, drift to where Cris and Sara are—which is together. They've been hanging out a lot lately. Like, a lot. Doing chores around base. Going on early-morning runs. Staying up late to clean up the DFAC. Which doesn't matter because I'm not talking to either of them because they're both jerks.

But also, why are they hanging out together all the time? How could they possibly have so much to talk about? Other than their shared obsession with SPORE. And their shared breakups with me. And ... honestly the more I think about it, the more I realize how much they actually have in common. They probably have more to talk about than I ever did with both of them combined.

I don't like this realization.

Zack falls into step beside me, half blocking them from my view. "Hey, Ashley." He grins. "Looking pretty today."

Oh, dear God. Not this again.

"I literally look the same way I look every single day." Worse, probably. I didn't even brush my hair, just hurriedly combed my fingers through it.

"You look pretty every single day." Zack watches me with ... what I think is supposed to be his charming gaze. But it's like he's staring into my soul, and it creeps me out.

For some reason, though, that gets Cris's attention. His eyes snap to us. For half a second. But it counts. I want to stretch my arms all the way to him and land a punch across his stupid face. Much higher standards, he said? At least Zack's always been nice to me. Polite. Respectful.

"Say, would you like to have dinner with me, once we're back?" Zack asks.

My attention returns to Zack. I have to do a double-take. "Are you ... asking me on a date?"

He gives me a confident nod. "Absolutely I am."

Unexpected heat explodes in my face and spreads to the rest of me. Well, that's as upfront as you can be. He's bold, I'll give him that. And Cris does look like he's choking on his breath. Even Sara's glancing in our direction in disbelief. And if I'm being completely fair, Zack's not bad looking. Not one bit. I just ... never really looked at him that way because I was only ever looking that way at one person.

But I have eyes. I should use them more.

"You know what? Sounds great," I tell Zack, loud enough to make sure Cris hears it, too. "I'd love to have dinner with you."

Zack's eyes are big, as though he wasn't expecting that answer. At all. "You're ... serious?"

"Yeah." Hundred percent. I've sulked enough. I deserve to go on a date with someone I actually get along with. "It can't hurt to get to know each other a little more. Since we're gonna be working together for the foreseeable future. You know, build trust and all that."

"Or more." He winks. "Well, then, perfect. Let's do it!"

When we arrive at the armory, Zack stops by Sgt. Seidel to ask the same question he's been asking before every single assignment.

"Hey, Sergeant," he says, "do I get an M4 this time? Or at least a combat knife? You know, like a reward system. For every set of missions I behave myself, I gain access to one weapon for the next one."

"No." Sgt. Seidel deadpans, then nods for us both to move it.

Zack sighs and proceeds ahead. "Worth a shot anyway."

Sgt. Seidel gives me a *keep an eye on him* look, and I give her an affirming *that's all I've been doing since I got here* nod. But instead of following Zack, I stand frozen.

Because I just remembered why *Hummingbirds* sounded familiar.

"Sir." I turn back to Sgt. Seidel. "Do we have a list of names? Everyone who was with the Hummingbirds?"

She raises suspicious brows at me. "Are you asking about someone specific?"

"Uh..." I clear my throat. "Josefina Serrano. She was with me in AIT."

Sgt. Seidel holds up her portor and taps the screen a few times. I wait, heart in my throat, unsure whether or not I want to peek at her screen.

"Says here she's with the First Rifle Squad." Sgt. Seidel looks up from her portor to me. "She would have been among the assault unit that first entered the building."

"Do we know her status?" I can't hide the shakiness in my voice.

"She wasn't among the reported casualties," Sgt. Seidel says.

"So, she could still be alive." I wait for her to give me a thread of hope to hold onto. She doesn't.

"Is this going to be an issue?" She folds her arms behind her, stern brown eyes studying me. "Do you wish to be excluded from this mission?"

"No." I shake my head and swallow my uncertainty. "No. I just wanted to know."

"Well, then." Sgt. Seidel's rigid face spells it all out to me. *Don't get your hopes up.* "Move along."

"Yes, sir," I say, then proceed.

TWENTY

THE HIGHWATER UNIVERSITY OF SCIENCE AND TECHNOLOGY campus is almost as big as Kadia. *Almost*. It's like a whole city in and of itself. The architecture of the buildings is more beautiful than anything I've ever seen. So different from the buildings in Kadia and Spheria. These are more reminiscent of some of the pictures Will used to show me in the magazines he collected. They feel ... sophisticated.

Greenery covers the campus, sprouting from concrete and coating half the walls of the buildings that remain standing. There are trees with leaves of all colors: yellow, orange, brown, red and green. Big fences stretch out all around the perimeter. Lots of abandoned, rusty vehicles are lying about. Some of them have faded food pictures and big signs. Others look like either the buses we have in Spheria or like military vehicles. Statues and benches and dry water fountains decorate different areas.

Fewer infected roam the campus than I was expecting. They're scattered, moving so slow that they can't be anything other than roamers. Maybe a few trackers as well. They follow us as we fly over the buildings, but quickly fall behind.

I suck in a sharp breath, fiddling with my hands on my lap.

"You okay?" Sara, sitting beside me, asks.

I'm tapping a nervous foot when I stare her in the face and give her a firm, "Yes."

"You look stressed."

"I'm fine," I insist.

"So, what's up with the fences?" Cris asks.

"It's from the quarantine," Stephen says. "Back when the outbreak started, and Ground Zero was identified as the university, the government tried to quarantine it while they were simultaneously setting up safe zones to evacuate people to."

Oh, that's right. We did learn about that in our history lessons, I just never saw a quarantine zone before. This is where they locked people in ... and left them to die.

"We've come across places like this," Jayce chimes in. "During our travels. Quarantine zones were usually the places with the highest concentration of infected."

Trying to keep the virus in lockdown didn't work, but setting up safe zones did. The government tried to secure as many areas as possible before the virus hit them. It wasn't a hundred percent successful. In the end, only four safe zones made it, which became known as the sectors. This is excluding Spheria, of course.

What was it like? Being amidst all of this? Watching the world as you knew it come to an end? Seeing those fences go up? Being on one end of them or the other? As far as I've known it, those fences always existed. Humanity was always confined to the sectors. It couldn't have been easy ... giving up the rest of the world. All this land... *So much land.* People wouldn't have to be crammed into tiny living spaces. Hell, each family could have a whole house for itself even. But it's all just sitting here, rotting away.

"There it is..." Stephen gestures out of the door at a building.

A large blanket of infected corpses litters the place. Closer to the building, there are machine guns set up north and southwest—where the Fire Support squads were stationed. Their bodies are still there. Corpses on the two buildings nearest to the science building. More corpses close to what I think is the entrance. Further south, a decent distance from the fire-support setup, is what looks like a Casualty Collection Point. The Hummingbirds' choppers are in a fenced-in, overgrown field. On my map, it's marked as a sports field, and that's where we land.

The lieutenant and sergeants inspect the Hummingbirds' choppers, while the rest of us keep an eye on our surroundings.

"This place is so pretty." Dalal's eyes travel around with wonder and awe. "Subhanallah."

"Yeah," I agree. It steals my breath away even as I take in big inhales. Gorgeous and nerve-wracking at the same time. And to think this is where it all started.

"Pilot's dead," Sgt. Prate announces as he comes out of a chopper.

"Here, too." Sgt. Seidel hops out of a second one.

It turns out to be the case for all the pilots, some of whom were killed outside their helicopters, their bodies found across the field in the grass. All of them were shot.

"Fugitives, for certain." Sgt. Bronson pulls up to his feet from a crouched position after inspecting a ransacked resource crate.

"Has to be." Sgt. Redfearn nods, massaging his creased forehead. "They're getting bold."

"Comms are still down." Private Aria looks up from the Hummingbirds' laptop setup. "I'm unable to track any members of the Hummingbirds except the ones that are here in this field."

"Meaning the source of the interference is definitely in the science building or the surrounding areas," Sgt. Prate speculates. "Can you find it?"

"I can try," Aria says. "The comm jammers they use are very hard to counter. Without the Hum, the best I can do is give you estimations."

"Better than nothing." Sgt. Prate affirms with a nod.

The Hum. That's what the Conspirators used to keep their comm lines secure and undetectable by standard SPORE tech. I'm not entirely sure what it is, a software or server or something like that. During the assault on Lotiva, SPORE tried to gain access to the Hum so that they'd identify and track all the fugitives involved, but apparently there was a failsafe in place that erased the entire system. It's why SPORE is struggling to get a conclusive list on who was involved with the Conspirators.

"Renegades!" The lieutenant calls, and we all gather around him. "Here's what we're going to do. We're going to head to the objective in two teams. Bronson Squad, take a support unit with you. You'll do a ground break-in. Take the fuel and see if you can reach B2 and start up those generators."

Generators? Wait, why are we starting up the generators?

"Support unit," the lieutenant carries on, "you'll station outside, south of the building. Keep the path clear for Bronson Squad and watch the perimeter. Seidel Squad, Private Caves, and Private Aria, you're with me. We'll take a chopper and go in through the rooftop. Now, unless we manage to find and disable the source of interference, we won't be able to communicate with each other. Execute extra caution in case of Actives.

"I need a second support unit stationed on the rooftop to keep it clear for our evac if we need it, and you'll help the first unit with perimeter watch from higher ground. Redfearn Squad, you'll split up. One team stays here, the other one will be our security elements. Pick your buildings on the way. When the research team gets here, they'll wait until we've cleared the building before they move in. Sergeant Prate, I'm leaving you here to coordinate with the fire support and reserve. Everything clear?"

"Yes, sir!" we acknowledge.

"Get ready to move," the lieutenant says. "May God protect us all."

TWENTY-ONE

I WAIT while Sara and Lucille set up charges on the rooftop door.

Usually, I like being in high places, but with the seasons changing, high places start to get colder. It's chillier than I'd like it to be. I tap my feet on the floor to generate a little bit of warmth.

For now, my portor still functions. I can browse through the digital floor plan of the building that we downloaded before taking off. Each squad is also equipped with a printed copy for when our portors inevitably become obsolete.

We all have our gas masks on as well as ear protection. Once the door bursts open, we proceed in a tight wedge formation, using travelling overwatch to go down the stairs. My team takes point, behind us is the lieutenant with Sgt. Seidel, Zack, and Private Aria. At the rear is Bravo team, following the same formation.

Darkness blankets the inside of the Science Building. Some of the windows have metal shutters down. Others are painted in dust and barricaded with different objects, blocking daylight from coming through.

Our flashlights turn on as soon as we arrive at the first double door, leading into the fourth story. At Lt. Mansur's orders, Lucille and Dalal open the door and proceed, we follow after them.

A T-intersection greets us with silence, doors spanning to the walls left and right of us. No sign of that mysterious gas we've been told about. To our right, the hallway stretches to a dynamic corner, to our left, an L-intersection. The hallways themselves are littered with objects, cleaning carts, chairs, broken glass, and most notably, old human remains that have been reduced to skeletons in shabby clothes.

"Alpha, proceed left. Bravo, take right—see if you can circle around to meet us," Lt. Mansur orders. "Inspect each room."

We split up. Sgt. Seidel goes with Bravo. Lucille and Dalal lead our team. Sara and I follow them while Lt. Mansur sticks to the back with Aria and Zack. The rooms we inspect are mostly classrooms ranging in size, in addition to some labs with counters, chairs, empty flasks and various science equipment in different states—some of it sitting neatly on the counters and shelves as if no one touched it in years, and the rest of it broken into pieces and scattered all over the floor and surfaces.

The human remains are everywhere, some rooms have more than others. It makes me imagine the kinds of scenarios that must have taken place here. Maybe some of these rooms were used as cemeteries. The corpses that are missing parts of their bodies suggest that maybe they were torn to shreds by infected, which makes me imagine another scenario: people got locked up in these rooms with an infected and were brutally massacred.

No sign of Hummingbirds anywhere, though.

"Clear!" echoes about the hallways after each room is inspected. It's quieter in here than I'd like. Could mean there are campers hiding around corners. But so far, we haven't run into any.

I stay alert, though, haunted by what happened to Ryan.

Bravo regroups with us eventually as we make our way to the west side of the floor.

"No Hummingbirds or anything suggesting a gas leak," Sgt. Seidel informs us. "Elevator's three floors down, and the northeast staircase is blocked."

"There should be two more staircases," Lt. Mansur says, "one just ahead and another one northwest."

We finish clearing the floor. Not even a hint of a chemical explosion. The southwestern staircase is also blocked, and the northwestern one is only half-blocked, as if someone tried to clear it recently. Like everywhere else, there are remains on the stairs going down. How many people died here?

"Perhaps the next floor will tell us more," Lt. Mansur says. "Remember, there may be Actives. If you identify one, taking it out is top priority."

We acknowledge.

Identifying Actives is hard as hell.

Their intelligence allows them to mimic other types of infected and blend in with the crowd. During AIT, we ran into at least one Active that I know of, and I mistook it for a tracker. It wasn't until we started taking out the chasers during our Passive Wave Clearing drill that the Active announced its presence with a loud shriek. It sent the entire wave at us and called in backup from nearby blocks. We had some of the highest casualties that day.

"Sir," Private Aria says. "It appears we entered the range of the comm interference. We've lost contact with the reserve and rooftop party."

I check the screen of my portor. The map has turned blank. Signal lost.

We head down the stairs at the lieutenant's orders. As we reach the third floor, the air becomes increasingly misty. The stairs leading down to the second floor are blocked.

"This floor is supposed to be for biochemistry," Lt. Mansur says, "so it could still be our culprit."

Except it's not. It's more of the same as the fourth floor, with a layer of fog obstructing our vision. There are some cracks stretching along the floor, concentrated mostly on the west side and slowly decreasing to the point of disappearing on the east side. But we can't really identify anything that could have been the cause of a gas leak or toxic fog or whatever the hell this is supposed to be.

"How do we think this happened?" Dalal asks.

"It could be any number of things," Sgt. Seidel answers. "Chemicals stored improperly and in close proximity over an extended period of time. Could even be something that someone made and released intentionally, perhaps to try and find other means to kill infected."

"This gas can't be older than five years," Lt. Mansur adds. "The reports from the last mission to Ground Zero mentioned nothing of this sort. Something caused it between then and now."

And that something is not here, that much is clear.

"Even if we identify the source of it, how the hell are we supposed to clear it?" Connor says. "You think opening up some windows will do the trick?"

"That's what the research team will be here for," Sgt. Seidel says.

"We're here to eliminate the threat and locate any surviving Hummingbirds. Just mind that you don't confuse them for fugitives or vice versa."

The fugitives have previously stolen uniforms from other sectors to disguise themselves. Even the ones we found in the auto-parts store had Kadia's logo on them. So this is definitely going to be tricky.

"Let's keep moving," Lt. Mansur orders.

Most of the staircases are blocked save for the one due northeast, so that's the one we take to the second floor. The fog becomes notably thicker, so thick I miss a step and slip down the rest of the stairs until I hit a wall.

When I push to sit, a messed-up face looks at me from my right. I startle and push back, screaming. Bloodied eyes coated in a yellowish, pus-looking fluid. Mouth agape and dripping with a foamy white substance as well as blood.

Everyone behind me is alert, a hand yanks me back to my feet as the others point their weapons at the body on the floor.

Lucille steps toward the body. She pokes it with the tip of her boot. It doesn't move. "Dead." She crouches before it. "Hummingbird—Oh, God! What the hell is wrong with her face?"

Sgt. Seidel and Lt. Mansur approach the body to inspect it as well. I'm so thankful I can no longer see it through the fog, but the image itself still haunts me, making me shudder.

"Her gas mask's over there." Lt. Mansur nods to the corner of the landing. "She took it off."

"Looks like she was on her way up," Sgt. Seidel says. "Trying to run away, perhaps."

"That's not all." Lucille pulls back to her feet. "There's a gunshot wound at the base of her chin."

Silence as the realization sets in.

She killed herself.

"Must have been in agonizing pain." Sgt. Seidel sighs, shaking her head.

"Or she didn't think any rescue was coming," Zack comments, which causes a momentary awkward silence.

Lt. Mansur examines the body without touching it. "It does have the appearance of a chemical burn, but we can't be sure until we've identified the source. Maybe the research team will be able to do an autopsy as well. We're bringing all the deceased soldiers with us, regardless. They deserve a proper burial."

"Mark this location," Sgt. Seidel orders. "White chemlights will signal all the bodies we find. Once we've cleared the building, we'll come back to pick her up."

Dalal takes out a white chemlight and drops it by the body. She stands by it for an extended moment, murmuring something reminiscent of a prayer, then we proceed further down the stairs, and through the double door.

The fog now has a distinct yellow tint to it, thick and blinding.

"Stick close," Sgt. Seidel instructs. "If the infected show up, be careful with friendly fire. Use verbal cues to signal your positions to your comrades."

We move down a long, straight hallway. Clearing room by room. There's a considerable lack of remains here compared to before. We go until we reach a T-intersection. Bravo takes left, and we take right. The lieutenant hangs back with Sgt. Seidel, Zack and Aria.

The lack of infected is alarming. Isn't this supposed to be where it all started? Shouldn't we have run into infected already? That said, if there are Actives here, it's likely that the infected could be grouped somewhere, hiding, waiting for the perfect opportunity to strike. With how blind we are, there's a chance we could stumble upon them any second without knowing. That thought alone makes me feel like every wall has eyes. Every room is storing a group of infected, ready to jump us.

"Halt!" Lucille orders, and all four of us come to a stop.

My body tenses, I keep my finger close to the trigger, ready to shoot.

"I see something..." she says.

I squint, struggling to spot what she's talking about, but when I take a step closer, a vague shape manifests in the fog. It looks like a corpse, but as I stare longer, it looks more like ... a ... cord?

"It's not moving," Sara says. "We can try approaching?"

Lucille signals okay, and we proceed toward it. The closer we get, the more identifiable it becomes.

It's not a cord. It's ... a branch?

No. Not a branch either.

It's a tentacle.

TWENTY-TWO

IT'S NOT JUST the one.

The further we go, the more of these tentacles we see. On the floors, the walls—stretching all the way up to the ceiling.

"Ugh, gross!" I grimace. "What the hell are these things?"

"Nature takes over, I guess," Lucille says.

"I like nature better when it stays outside," Dalal says, "where it belongs."

"This is the growth," Lt. Mansur inspects the tentacle. His group joined us not that long ago. Aria went inside one of the rooms with Sgt. Seidel to look around. Bravo team hasn't returned yet.

This growth is purple in color with some yellow bulbs attached to it. Like fruit growing on a tree. Every now and again, the tentacles pulsate. A soft, yellow-ish light coursing through them, then vanishing.

Sara pokes one of the tentacles with her foot. Why she would do something like that is beyond me. "This looks organic?"

"Don't touch it, smarty-pants," Lucille tells her. "We don't know what it is or what it does. It could eat you alive for all we know."

"You *would* want it to eat me, wouldn't you?" Sara teases.

"I definitely wouldn't complain," Lucille teases back.

I hate this. I hate watching whatever the hell this is. This friendship. This ... *look at me, I've already replaced you* attitude. I hate it more than I hate these weird tentacles.

"It looks familiar." Zack's voice brings my attention back to the gross tentacles.

"Familiar?" Lucille turns to him. "You've seen this before?"

"Well," Zack says. "I don't know that I've seen *this* in particular, but I've seen something like it. In Eukson."

"Can you tell us more?" Lt. Mansur asks.

"We found a corpse," Zack explains. "Lori alerted me to it. It was hard to tell whether it was human or infected, but it looked like something was … devouring it? Absorbing it? There was this thing—this blob, sort of—covering its head, with tentacles sprouting from it. Nothing to this extreme. But Lori told me we had to get rid of it. She told me we had to burn it or it would become dangerous."

What the hell?

"Lieutenant," Pvt. Aria, who's coming out of a room to the right with Sgt. Seidel, calls, "that's the server room."

"How's it looking?" he asks.

"Some of the equipment looks pretty damaged, but some of it is still intact. There's a fifty-fifty chance all this will be for nothing. We won't know for sure until power is restored."

"What's all going to be for nothing?" Lucille asks.

I was wondering the same thing.

"East side's clear!" Stephen's voice as Bravo team returns, their footsteps echoing. "We found stairs. They're clear—"

"What the hell—" Cris comes to a stop in front of the growth.

"Holy Mother of infected," Connor gasps.

"Do we know what we're looking at?" Jayce tilts his head sideways, as if that would give him a better view.

"Sir," Sgt. Seidel says, "it might be wise to collect some samples, even without the research team. We don't know what we might encounter later."

"Very well." Lt. Mansur nods. "Alpha, Bravo, proceed ahead, make sure the rest of the floor is clear and see if you can find anything pertaining to our objectives. Seidel and I will stay here and get some samples to take with us. Aria, conduct a more thorough inspection on the equipment, see what we're working with."

"Yes, sir," we answer.

"And what do I do?" Zack asks. "Cross my fingers and pray for everyone's safety?"

"You can help us with the sample collection," Sgt. Seidel tells him.

Zack's displeasure is written all over his slouched posture, but he still responds with a casual "Yes, sir."

Our team takes the lead and Bravo tags closely behind us.

"Look," Dalal points up at the ceiling, where the tentacles are pushing to get through to the top floor.

"That explains those cracks," I say.

The rooms on this floor are full of these tentacles, different sizes, some thinner than others, most of them coming through holes in the floor.

"God," Dalal breathes. "It's a miracle this place is still standing."

"Guess it's coming from one of the floors below us," Lucille says. "I wonder if Bronson Squad found anything. Assuming they're still alive."

"Have a little more faith in our comrades," Stephen contests. "Sergeant Bronson is a competent leader."

"I'm sure the Hummingbirds thought the same about their squad leaders before they were all massacred here." Lucille's ever the pessimist. Or realist. Those two kinda go hand in hand most of the time.

"We don't know that they're *all* dead," Sara counters.

And I hope to God they're not. Jose's face flashes before my eyes. Our last exchange like a heavy weight in my chest.

Maybe Zack was onto something when he mentioned praying, because as soon as we turn the corner leading to a northern hallway, we find them.

Fresh remains, torn bodies, limbs and spilled guts—the uniforms confirm most of them are Hummingbirds, the others are infected with clear gunshot or stab wounds. I can't tell if any of these infected were Actives, though.

"Ae Allah," Dalal gasps.

"Man." Cris's shoulders fall. "This is awful."

I push past everyone and drop to my knees by the corpses, inspecting every uniform.

"Brown, what are you doing?" Lucille calls.

This one's not Jose. Neither is this one. Nor is the next one.

Much like the corpse we found earlier on the staircase, these ones are also covered in similar burn marks. But Hummingbirds aside, even the infected look different. Some of these bodies have pustules similar to those on the tentacles.

"They're all dead." Lucille's authoritarian voice is right behind me. Her hand on my shoulder, firm. "Stop touching them before you get yourself contaminated."

No Jose. I exhale in relief, but my stomach knots, dread creeping into every inch of me. Lucille squeezes my shoulder, and I stand again.

Everyone's watching me like I've lost my mind. Confused, unsure eyes behind their gas masks.

"What's up with you?" Lucille captures my eyes with mild worry.

"Nothing." I brush her off and step away from the corpses.

"There isn't enough of them here to account for everyone," Stephen says, as though reading my mind and trying to comfort me, give me a little hope.

"Sure, I bet we'll find more body parts on the floors below," Lucille claps back with the reality check I probably need.

Dalal takes out another white chemlight, breaks it before dropping it by the corpses and murmuring another prayer.

"Stephen." Lucille exhales. "Take your team, check out this hallway. The rest of us will keep going west."

He acknowledges and takes the lead down the northern hallway while we retrace our steps and resume west. No more Hummingbird bodies in any of the rooms. Besides the cracks and tentacles in the hallway, some cleaning carts and broken lab equipment. The stairs at the end of the hallway are clear though, so that should be our way down.

A pop echoes somewhere, coming from Bravo's location?

"Was that a gunshot?" Dalal asks.

More pops follow.

"Infected!" Stephen's muffled voice shouts.

"Move," Lucille orders us.

But as soon as we start back toward them, loud growls and screeches come from the staircase behind us.

We draw our weapons. Sara, Lucille and I with our M4s and Dalal with her M249, aiming in the direction of the staircase expectantly.

Lucille grabs a broomstick off of one of the cleaning carts and runs up. She slides it through the handlebars of the double door of the staircase. A second before a *bang bang bang* on the other side.

That should hold them for a little bit.

Gunfire in the northern hallway intensifies. Why now? Why all of a sudden are the infected coming?

Lucille leads us back. We're about to round the corner to join Stephen and the others when violent growls draw our attention all the way back east, toward the lieutenant and the others. More infected. Everyone except Zack is shooting at them.

"Lucille!" Stephen shouts. "We can handle it. Go help the lieutenant."

She hesitates for a blink but then complies. We bolt toward the lieutenant.

We shoot the infected as they pop up. Just like the corpses we found, these ones look all messed up and mutated. The pustules on them explode as our bullets pierce their bodies, releasing a yellow-ish mist and fluid that spatters on the floor. It's like popping a giant zit.

For every infected we shoot, about five more show up. The hallway quickly piles up with corpses.

"Bite me." I shoot another one. "Where did they all come from? Did anyone hear an Active shriek?"

"No," Dalal says.

They're all coming from the east. Some of them are wearing SPORE uniforms. Hummingbirds?

"If someone could toss me a weapon, I would greatly appreciate it." Zack's voice is strained. "But I see you have your hands pretty full right now."

"Oh, my God!" Pvt. Aria gasps. "That infected over there. It's Sergeant Gambol, from Bronson Squad."

As Lt. Mansur shoots him down, a daunting realization settles upon us.

Bronson Squad must have been wiped out.

"Not to alarm anyone," Zack says, "But that door back there looks like it's going to burst open just about—"

Something snaps.

"Now."

I look over my shoulder, straight down to the door that Lucille blocked as the infected pour out from the other side. Some of them split, running to where Bravo is, most of them run at us. Dammit. I start shooting at them. Sara then steps up before me and loads her grenade launcher. She fires an explosive round. It hits about twenty meters away and kills some of the infected within five meters of the explosion. The rest are either incapacitated or still running at us. That does lighten the load, though, and we're able to shoot them more efficiently.

"Say, Sarang," Zack's voice grows tenser by the second, "why don't you let me borrow your M4? You can detach the M320 from it. That way, we both have a weapon in our hands."

"Zack, not now," Sara grunts.

"Or I can just enjoy the show," he sighs in defeat and hangs back.

The floor starts shaking with us all of a sudden. A crack spreads across the tile beneath our feet.

"What the—"

Crap. The explosion... It must have...

"Move!" Sgt. Seidel shouts. "Move!!"

I tug a frozen Sara with me as we all fall back.

The floor collapses all through the west hallway, swallowing the infected with it.

TWENTY-THREE

SARA'S EYES widen with shock and worry as the two of us sit up. "I didn't think it was going to ... do that much damage."

"The structural integrity of the building was already compromised." I push to my feet and hold a hand to her.

She eyes it in silence, then takes it, allowing me to pull her up.

Some of the fallen infected moan as they try to crawl out from under the debris. The rest of them are crushed, body parts sticking out.

"Stephen!" Lucille steps up to the edge. The tremble in her voice unmissable as she shouts, "Connor?!"

No one responds.

It wasn't just Stephen and Connor on that side. It was also Jayce and—

"Cris..." My heart plunges to my stomach.

"Seidel," Lt. Mansur says. "You and Private Aria wait here for the power to come on."

Sgt. Seidel starts, as if she's about to protest, but swallows her words immediately in favor of a "Yes, sir."

"The rest of you," Lt. Mansur turns to us, "you're coming with me. We'll find a way to the first floor and try to locate Bravo Team and Bronson Squad... That's if anyone made it."

"I'm not going anywhere without a weapon," Zack contends. "You don't trust me. Fine. But you still need me. Tell me, exactly what use would I be to you if I'm dead?"

THOSE WHO FIGHT

He makes a solid argument.

Lt. Mansur exhales deeply. He walks over to one of the dead Spores and removes a sheathed combat knife off of him. He drops a white chemlight by the bodies before returning to Zack and holding the blade to him. "I hear your Close Quarters Battle skills are impeccable. This should be more than enough."

Zack snorts. He accepts the combat knife without complaint.

"Now," the lieutenant continues, "there's no way we'll get to the northwestern side from here. So, we'll have to go to the basement levels and make our way around. Here's hoping the staircases aren't blocked."

"Yes, sir," we acknowledge.

We head east, through a double door and into a hallway with several rooms. An Exit sign hangs above a door. This is where the infected were coming from—and aren't anymore. Did the floor collapsing have something to do with that?

Taking the stairs, we head past the first floor and straight down to B1. The door leading into that floor is an electrical one, though, and without power, we can't get through, so we continue to B2.

Following the same formation as before, we enter, our footsteps light and quick. It's dark as hell down here, but there's no fog as we go through the doors. The first room we find ourselves in is huge, with large machinery, pipes and pumps all over.

There's a door at the end, to the left, leading to a short hallway. The rooms there are nothing but storage. We round the corner and continue in a straight line toward the west side of the building.

A couple of hallways later, we're squeezing through pipelines, with our backs pressed to the wall. I'm surprised we haven't run into infected again, but I'm not going to complain.

The only staircase that would get us where we need it to is the northwestern one, and we're lucky enough to find it clear. As we make our way up, the fog slowly takes over again.

"The source has to be somewhere here," Dalal says. "Either the first floor or B1."

Lucille is practically running up the stairs, breaking formation as soon as we arrive at the first floor and pushing through the door.

"Decker!" Lt. Mansur calls after her, but she doesn't stop.

"Connor?" Lucille calls. "Stephen?"

We follow her into a wreck of a hallway. Infected corpses buried underneath debris. Some are still alive, crawling with missing or broken legs. Bloodstains, old and fresh, highlight the walls and floor. The strange growth is everywhere we turn. It's a living nightmare.

All the bodies on this side are infected. But that only makes me worry that the only reason there's no sign of Cris and the others is because they're buried under all the debris. I climb up the rubble to get to the other side of the hallway. Maybe they fell there?

"Ashley, what are you doing?" Sara calls.

"We have to find them." I reach up to one of those tentacles dangling above me and grab onto it. The pustules on it burst, releasing more of that yellow mist.

Aggressive growls explode ahead. An infected runs down the hallway across from me, headed straight for the mountain of debris. More of them follow soon. I let go of the tentacle and jump back down on the floor.

"Weapons at the ready." Lt. Mansur stands somewhere behind me.

The first infected's head pokes out from behind the debris, a dozen more follow.

"Open fire!" Lt. Mansur orders.

The yellow fog is highlighted with specks of light as our weapons pop.

Chasers. A lot of chasers. Too many chasers, in fact. Or maybe these are not chasers. If there is an Active here, which we have yet to identify, infected behavior changes. There's no difference between a camper and a chaser and a roamer. Point is: these infected are fast. Too fast. I end up opting for shooting at their legs to trip them rather than taking my sweet time lining up headshots. That buys enough time for the rest of my team to take out the infected. But more of them keep on coming.

"That's a lot of them!" Sara shouts in the back.

"Don't stop shooting!" Lt. Mansur says. "Take out every single one of them."

Their moans and growls are loud and echoey and hard to track, coming from almost every direction.

"Guys, check your six!" Dalal turns around and shoots a couple more infected running at us.

"Damn it!" Lucille curses. "They'll have us surrounded in seconds!"

"Over here!" a voice calls to our nine.

"Bronson!" Lt. Mansur says.

They're alive?

We walk back-to-back, shooting the infected as they come and following Sgt. Bronson's voice until we arrive at the double door he's standing behind.

Next to him is none other than—

"Stephen," Lucille gasps. "You're okay…"

"Come on." He pats her on the shoulder and nudges her to hurry.

Through the door, Sgt. Bronson leads us down the hallway while Stephen hangs back momentarily to block the path. I slow down to make sure he's okay and wait for him to catch up before resuming our run.

A side door bursts open ahead of us. An infected tackles Stephen and pins him against the floor. Stephen shoves his protective sleeve into the infected's mouth, but the infected doesn't bite it.

Just as I take aim, its mouth opens wide. Long, wiggly tongue slipping out and dripping with saliva.

A flash to the Pit hits me. Melisa straddled by an Active. Her choked cries as it slid its slimy tongue down her throat.

Regi's ghost voice yells at me. *You're not supposed to freeze.*

I pull the trigger. And *miss*. So, I run at the Active, grab it by the shirt and yank it off of Stephen. It's heavier than it looks, and I almost lose my balance and fall with it. Before it can lunge at me or Stephen again, I stab it in the head with my combat knife and push it off me. The corpse rolls and falls aside, limp.

Stephen sits up, breathing hard. He pushes himself to stand and helps me up with a firm hold around my hand. "I owe you one."

"Don't worry about it." I find my balance again and go to retrieve my knife.

The second I pull the blade out, the Active's jaw falls, making me stumble back. Its body isn't moving, but something slimy slips out through its mouth and slithers away. Fast.

It looks awfully similar to that thing I've seen before in Basic…

"What the hell?"

"I don't know." Stephen takes my arm and pulls me with him. "But we gotta keep moving."

We catch up to the others soon, fighting their fair share of infected. They manage to clear a path to the right, and we take it. Violent growls chase after us.

"Jung," Lt. Mansur calls, "get ready to blow them up!"

"Yes, sir," Sara says.

Sgt. Bronson leads us to a room where more soldiers are waiting for us—so not all of his squad was wiped out. We hurry inside, one by one. Sara is the last one at the door with someone from Bronson squad beside her. Both their grenade launchers at the ready. At the lieutenant's signal, they fire explosive rounds at the horde of infected coming at us.

Sara and the other soldier jump back, Lt. Mansur and Sgt. Bronson push the door closed and everyone backs away before the explosion rumbles the place. Some of the shrapnel pierces through the wood. Stephen, Zack, and others from Bronson Squad start pushing furniture to block the door.

Then we all stop to catch our breaths.

TWENTY-FOUR

"WHERE IS THE REST OF BRAVO?" Lucille asks Stephen.

He nods his head toward the furthermost corner of the room, where Jayce is lying on the floor, grunting and whimpering.

I rush toward him. "Let me see!"

"As soon as we fell, there was an infected on him..." Stephen struggles to get the words out. "I shot it but ... it was too late. It had already..."

There's a bandage around Jayce's arm, covering the bite. It's stained with blood and there's pus oozing from underneath it. Same on the other corpses we found.

It might already be too late but... "He needs amputation," I say.

"Which we can't do." Lt. Mansur crouches beside me. "Not here. Not now. Amputation requires exposing his flesh to the gas, which would worsen his condition."

I hesitate, but he's right. If we don't get Jayce out of here, there's no point in trying to save him.

"Lang, hang in there, son." Lt. Mansur gives his arm an encouraging pat.

All Jayce responds with is a whimper and a weak thumbs-up.

I stand up to look around the room for a particular face ... but I can't find it. "Where's Cris?"

"And Connor," Lucille adds.

"We..." Stephen starts, and my heart stops, "got separated. We were trying to pull Jayce out from underneath the rubble and then ...

these infected came at us. Cris and Connor fought them and then they lured them away to buy me time to get Jayce to safety. It was before I ran into Bronson Squad."

"Did you send someone to look for them?" I ask.

Stephen shakes his head. "We couldn't. The infected were everywhere."

A billion gory scenarios play in my head. My stomach flips.

"Sergeant Bronson..." Lt. Mansur walks up to the squad leader. "We didn't think any of you made it."

"We barely did," Sgt. Bronson says. "The stairs on the east side were no use, we couldn't get to the basement floor through there. And the entire west side of the floor was blocked with those ... strange plants. So we tried to clear a path through them. But as soon as we managed to breach it, the infected came pouring down on us out of nowhere. Lost half of the squad. But the good news is ... we found it." He gestures to a door on the side, and when he opens it, there's a small hole in the floor leading to the lower level, B1, into what looks like a computer room.

"How's it looking?" the lieutenant asks.

"Some of them are broken, but others are still in good-enough shape, they'll probably work," Sgt. Bronson says. "Only problem is, we still got no power."

"Yes." Lt. Mansur nods. "We'll have to do something to fix that."

"Wait a minute," Lucille interrupts. "What's going on? Why are we restoring power exactly? Shouldn't we focus on evacuating? I mean, clearly this place is done for. I doubt any Hummingbirds made it."

"Our work here hasn't even started," Lt. Mansur says. "We don't know that all the Hummingbirds are dead. Some could be hiding still. Even if they were dead, we still have to finish what the Hummingbirds started."

Silence, because yeah, we all pretty much figured it out by now— we were never told the *real* reason why we or the Hummingbirds came here.

"What did they start exactly?" Lucille asks. "Because I'm starting to think it had nothing to do with resources."

"Yes and no," Lt. Mansur says. "The Hummingbirds' objective was classified, and the general's orders were to keep it on a need-to-know basis."

Zack laughs. "Transparency just doesn't exist in the SPORE vocabulary, does it?"

"I don't know about everyone else." Lucille places a hand on her hip. "But I'd say we're past 'need' and verging on 'desperate' by now."

Lt. Mansur takes a deep inhale. "The Hummingbirds were here to collect data ... about the research that was being done here, as well as some tech."

"Tech?" Lucille says. "What kind of tech?"

"The kind that could increase our understanding of the virus and develop better weapons to fight it. The same kind that helped us develop the portors," he says, pointing to his portor. "The portable locator was a military project that the university was working on. Then the outbreak happened. The project was abandoned, until about five years ago, when we were able to send a unit here to recover some of the data on the project."

I'm guessing he's referring to the mission that General Sears led here.

"I thought the crawler was meant to be our ultimate weapon," Stephen says. "Isn't that what the Renegades were formed for?"

"We have no idea that we'll find that crawler," Lt. Mansur says. "We also have no idea that we'll find it alive, or that we'd be able to tame it. Not to mention," he turns to Zack for the next part, "we don't know that Caves wouldn't take off with it and turn it against us as soon as we find it."

"I can neither confirm nor deny that." Zack gives a very casual shrug. The kind I imagine is making Lucille grit her teeth so hard right now.

"We have to consider alternatives," Lt. Mansur continues. "We need to keep our options open."

Lucille exhales and shakes her head. "I can't believe you'd lie to us about something this big. We're in Ground *rotting* Zero for God's sake."

Are we really so surprised? The higher-ups have always kept things from us. There's no way the general would have placed his full trust in Zack and a strange infected that may not even be alive anymore.

"With all that's happened in Lotiva, and all the protests rising up, our political climate isn't looking so good," Lt. Mansur explains.

"Add to that, estimates suggest that Lotiva may not be a viable source of gas and energy for much longer. Meaning we'll need to do all we can now to prepare for that. Starting with getting the data in this building."

"Why didn't Sears get it the last time he came here?" Lucille asks.

"His unit only managed to get some, not everything," Lt. Mansur says. "This data we're after is encrypted. But now we believe we'll be able to bypass the encryption and access it."

"Where's this data?" Sara asks.

"In there." Lt. Mansur nods at the computers down that hole. "We just need to get at least one of them started."

"Hence the fuel for the generators." I nod as it all starts to make sense.

"Thankfully, we've managed to find a path to B2," Lt. Mansur says. "It shouldn't be a problem to get to the generators now. Provided that we're able to handle the infected."

"My squad and I are ready for your orders, Lieutenant." Sgt. Bronson stands straight with a firm salute.

"Here's how this is going to go." Lt. Mansur gestures for all of us to gather around. "We'll split into two teams. One will carry on the Hummingbirds' objective, and the other will look for survivors.

"Sergeant Bronson, you'll take two of your people and head to B2. I'll let you borrow Mirani so she can show you the way we took. Get those generators running for us."

"Yes, sir," Sgt. Bronson acknowledges.

"Seidel and Aria are waiting in the server room for us to get the power on. They'll need to join us in the computer room to begin the data transfer. Decker, Weeks, regroup with them. Once they get those servers running, you escort them here."

"Yes, sir," Stephen acknowledges.

Lucille, however, doesn't. "Sir, I'd prefer to stay and search for the others."

"Decker." Lt. Mansur's voice is sharp as he eyes Lucille. "You broke formation earlier and disregarded an order. I let it slide once. I won't let it slide a second time."

Her head drops. Her voice is more desperate than it is annoyed when she murmurs a low, "Yes, sir."

"Brown, Jung, and Caves—you're coming with me," the lieutenant continues. "We'll search for your missing comrades and any surviving

Hummingbirds. Once the power is back on, the electrical doors in B1 should open up. It'll make it easier for Bronson Squad to regroup with the others in the computer room. We'll retreat as soon as data transfer is complete."

"Sir," Sara starts, "and what do we do about this strange growth and the gas leak?"

"We'll keep looking," Lt. Mansur says. "Likely, the source of the gas leak is here on the first floor or on the level below us. But our priority is to get the power back on—"

"Jayce?" Stephen's panicked voice brings our attention to Jayce violently trembling on the floor. Stephen hurries to him, falls to his knees and tries to hold him still.

"He's turning." Lt. Mansur rushes toward them. "Weeks, we have to put him down, son."

Stephen stiffens at those words. Head shaking. Hand reaching hesitantly for his combat knife.

"Stephen." Lucille runs over to him, grabbing his shoulder. "I'll do it."

Stephen's voice breaks. "I'm sorry."

The lieutenant helps him to his feet and pulls him aside.

"It's fine. I got it." Lucille steps forward, taking out her combat knife.

I stand with Sara and Dalal, both of their sniffling muffled under their gas masks. I can't say I'm as emotional as either of them. I never got to know Jayce well, and I'm glad I didn't. But I still can't help a flash to Tristan's face. His haunting eyes as I drove the knife into his head.

It makes it all the more awful to watch Lucille suck in a deep breath, before pushing the blade into Jayce's skull.

His trembling ceases.

TWENTY-FIVE

UNFORTUNATELY, there's no time to mourn.

I give the hallway a quick scan as I turn around, shining my flashlight about. It's still hard to see anything with all the gas-mist surrounding us.

Other than the fog, the hallways are somehow clear, minus the corpses of infected we'd killed earlier. A few of them are standing idly about, unalerted, even as we walk toward them.

"What the hell is up with them?" I ask.

Is it because I killed that Active earlier? Did they just ... lose focus because they had no one to tell them what to do anymore? It's hard to think they can see or smell anything judging by the state of their eyes and noses. How did they find us before? How did they overwhelm us so fast?

"Let's be stealthy," Lt. Mansur says, and we switch our weapons for our combat knives, taking out the infected quietly.

I can only pray that Cris is hiding somewhere, safe, just unable to get in touch because of the comm interference. He's capable, strong, he's a better shot than he was during Basic. I trust him not to waste half of his magazine shooting walls before he can headshot an infected. But I can't help worrying about him. What if he ran into fugitives? What if he hesitated, the way he did last time, and tried to talk to them? What if they saw his hesitation and took advantage of it, shot him on the spot? What if they took him hostage? I shudder at the mere thought of it. That fight we had feels like such a minor insignificance now.

"Hey," Sara says to my right. "I know you're worried about him, but you've got to keep your head on straight right now."

"I'm not worried," I lie.

Sara lets out a soft sigh. I hate that she can still read me even without seeing my face.

I ignore her and turn to Zack beside me. "What do you make of the infected so far? You think Lori's here this time?"

"I don't know," Zack says. "But I'm leaning towards not."

Sgt. Bronson's team, Lucille and Stephen split up from us once we're back in the main hallway. They head for the stairs, and we head for one of the rooms where Stephen said Connor and Cris ran through a hole in the wall.

"The ceiling looks like it's going to collapse at any second," Lt. Mansur warns. "Watch your heads."

We go through a few rooms until we arrive at a mostly blocked area with the tiniest crawl space at the bottom. We try and clear some of it to expand the hole, then one by one, we go. I go first, slowly, and clear the other end before I can pull myself out. More dead infected and Spores—I can't tell if they're Hummingbirds or Renegades, but none look like Cris or Connor. I push to my feet, giving the place a quick sweep before I call, "Clear."

A distant echo catches my attention, coming from the east.

"Jung, go on," Lt. Mansur says.

It sounded like ... gunfire?

"You hear that?" I ask.

More distant pops.

Sara's almost through. "Is it them?"

"It has to be." I don't wait. I bolt into a sprint immediately.

"Ashley, wait!" Sara calls.

Her voice fades away. The growls and gunfire become louder, closer. Struggling noises. Thuds. The clacking of combat boots.

"Cris!" I shout. "Cris, is that you?"

My shouting helps some infected find me, so I welcome them with a rain of bullets. That is until my ammo runs out and I have no time to reload. This may not have been my best decision. I take out my combat knife instead.

I thank my thick combat boots for boosting the strength of my kicks, making the roamer lunging at me stumble back. I take a second to stab my knife into its head and another one to pull it out just as I duck away from a chaser attempting to jump me.

As soon as I shoot back up, another one is on me. I use my body weight—which has gone up slightly since I was introduced to Spheria's luxurious menus—to push the roamer against the wall, blocking it from biting my face using my protective sleeve. With my other hand, I stab the knife into its head, and duck once more when two chasers try to jump me, instead they jump each other. I try to use the chance to reload my weapon, but one of them is already up on its feet again and it lunges at me. I block it with my M4. Before I can figure out my next move, someone shoots the other chaser and yanks the one on me off.

Sara shoots it before it can get back up.

I stand still, breathing, watching the dead infected, before I look up to meet her eyes.

"Never go anywhere without a partner," she says. Echoing my dad's words.

I turn away from her and grab a new mag from my pouch, reloading my M4 just in time to welcome the next batch of infected. "Whatever happened to following orders?"

"Well, you suck at that, for one." Sara shoots the infected alongside me.

"That's funny because I look at it as me excelling at *not* following orders."

"Half full, half empty," she muses.

"Where are the others?" I ask. Lt. Mansur and Zack didn't follow us.

"The crawlspace collapsed," Sara says. "They'll try and find a way around."

"Okay, well, we have to keep going." I nod for her to come along. "Those gunshots were coming this way."

Just a few steps ahead, there are two corpses. One sprawled on the floor and the other pressed against a wall. Both female. Either Hummingbirds or Renegades from Bronson Squad. Their assault packs and weapons are missing. Just as long as it's not Cris, I don't care.

I approach carefully, and as I get a closer look at the corpses, something catches my attention. The body on the floor, the injury on the back of her head looks more like a bullet's entry wound. No teeth marks. I lower my weapon and bend over to turn her around, her face is all messed up where the exit wound is, bones sticking out of what little flesh remains on it. The name patch is missing for some reason, as is her gas mask, but I can still make out enough features.

The curly dark hair. The light brown skin. The beauty mark just under the right ear.

"J-Jose?" The second her name comes out of my mouth, bile rises up my throat. I fight hard to swallow it. My stomach churns. I can barely breathe, can barely stand. I place a hand on the wall for support, my legs shaky.

"Ash?" Sara comes closer. "Are you okay?"

My legs cave. I fall to my knees by Jose's body.

"Is that…?" Sara crouches beside me, a hand on my shoulder. "Josefina?"

My fists clench on my lap. What the hell happened? Who shot her? Was it friendly fire? Because of the fog? Or was it… Was it fugitives?

"I'm so sorry," Sara murmurs softly. "We should mark this place, so we can come back and take—"

"Shut up." I shake her hand off me and force myself to stand, as she does, and we stand face to face. "I don't need you to tell me what to do, and I especially don't need your pity or sympathy. Why is it so hard for you to leave me alone? How many times do I have to tell you?"

"I understand you're angry—"

"Damn right, I'm angry." I push her hard. She stumbles back. "She didn't deserve to go like that. She didn't…" I push her again.

Sara slams against the wall behind her, but she does nothing, says nothing. I hate the way she's looking at me. Like I'm fragile. Like I'm on the verge of breaking. Or worse, like I'm already broken. I don't need her to fix me. I don't need her—

More gunshots sound down the hallway. I forcibly dodge Jose and bolt into a sprint, Sara right behind me.

"Cris!" I have to find him, before whoever did that to Jose does it to him, too. If he runs into a fugitive, he's going to try to talk to them, and clearly they don't want to talk. They'll shoot him without a second thought, and I can't … I can't lose him.

There is a figure in the fog, shooting at the infected. As we approach, the figure turns toward us. Enough to distract them from an infected jumping from behind.

I shoot that infected off them, and with Sara's help, we kill the three remaining ones then continue on.

The shaky figure drags itself on the floor, away from the corpses, panting, gasping.

But it's not Cris or Connor.

It's a Hummingbird.

TWENTY-SIX

OR, at least, I assume she's a Hummingbird.

"Hey." Sara starts toward her. "Are you okay?"

I take hold of Sara's arm and pull her to a stop. She looks at me questioningly, but quickly catches on, hands ready on her M4, though she keeps it lowered.

I release her arm and point my weapon at the girl. "Identify yourself."

The girl sits still, watching us. "Specialist Tyra Markell with Kadia's Hummingbirds platoon."

I give the place a quick scan, in case anyone's hiding around the corner. This deaddamn fog is such an inconvenience.

"Are you ... rescue?" Her voice is shaky, dry. "They actually sent rescue?"

I want to believe her, truly. Her horror sounds genuine. And if it is, then I can't imagine what she must have been through—being stuck here for however long it took us to arrive, thinking no one's coming for her.

"What happened?" I nod behind us, indicating the hallway Sara and I came from. "Those two Hummingbirds back there. What happened to them? Did you see who killed them?"

The girl shakes her head. "No, I—"

"Don't lie."

"I'm not lying."

"You must have heard something," I insist.

"Yes, I heard *a lot* of things," Tyra claims. "But I wasn't with them. I don't know what happened to them. My guess is as good as yours. They ran into infected and—"

"It wasn't infected," I cut in. "They were shot."

"I don't. Know," Tyra repeats.

"Ashley," Sara whispers to me, placing a hand on my arm and urging me to lower my weapon. I don't. "I don't think she's one of them." Meaning, the fugitives, and I don't know how she can possibly be sure of that.

I shake her hand off my arm, keeping my weapon up.

Sara ignores me and starts toward Tyra. "Are you hurt?"

"I'm okay," Tyra says, then her voice cracks and she starts crying. "No, I'm not okay. I thought … I thought I would…"

"It's okay." Sara sits beside her, placing a hand on her back. "We're here now. We can help you."

"I heard some noise," Tyra weeps. "I thought that maybe … it was survivors from my platoon, looking for me. I … was hiding, and then I thought I should come out and try to meet up with them. But then the infected…"

"Yeah, that's all right, take a breath," Sara says.

"How did you survive?" I ask. "Every Hummingbird we ran into is very much not alive."

"Ashley," Sara scolds.

"They're all dead?" Tyra gasps. "Everyone?"

"We don't know that for sure," Sara reassures her. "But the ones we found so far … yeah."

"So why aren't you?" I ask the girl.

"I don't know. When the infected came, I was … paralyzed. I never saw infected like these before. There was an Active with them, too. Or at least I think it was an Active. We got separated on our way to the basement. Some of us tried to head back upstairs but … the place was falling apart. The stairs were blocked. I had no choice but to get back here. And then… Comms went down. I couldn't reach anyone. So I hid."

Well, some of what she said checks out.

"How many of you are here?" Tyra asks. "Is it just you two? Is everyone from your unit dead?"

"No," Sara says. "No. We're a whole platoon. We've had some casualties but … most of us are still here."

THOSE WHO FIGHT

I can't believe Sara's just answering her questions like that.

"What about your mission objective?" I ask, finally daring to approach so I can see her more clearly.

Tyra stares at me.

"Your *real* mission objective," I say. "We know you weren't really here for resources."

"Okay," Tyra breathes. "That doesn't mean the objective isn't still classified, and I'm not about to tell someone who wasn't in the briefing about our objective. If you know what it is, why don't *you* tell me?"

"Do you get what's happening right now?" I crouch before her, meeting her line of sight. "We need to make sure you really are a Hummingbird, and not one of *them*. And if we're gonna do that, you have to answer our questions."

"*Them*. The fugitives?" Tyra blinks. "How do I know *you're* not one of them?"

"How about names, huh, Ashley?" Sara tries. Her eyes scream at me to take it easy. "I'm Sara, and this is..." she gestures to me, "Ashley... We're both with the Renegades platoon."

"Renegades," Tyra repeats. "Yeah. I heard about you."

"Tyra," I say, "did you see anyone else here? Two guys from our platoon?"

"No, you're the first ones I ran into," she says.

"Did you find anything?" Sara asks. "Do you know where the source of the gas leak is? Maybe we can tell the others."

"There is no gas leak," Tyra says.

"What do you mean?" Sara asks.

But I know what she means. It just hadn't clicked earlier because everything was happening so fast. I didn't have time to think about it. *Actually* think about it. But now?

"It's the growth." I pull to stand, and gesture at the tentacles hugging the walls. When the pustules on the tentacles exploded earlier, they released gas. Like the gas that's been all around us this whole time. "The growth is causing the gas..."

We had it backwards.

"That's right," Tyra confirms. "It's what draws them toward us, too—you know, the infected. If you mess with it, they know. They can feel it or something. They just know and show up out of nowhere.

You can test it out right now, if you want. We have no shortage of tentacles in this place."

"No," Sara says, standing. She offers her hands to Tyra and brings her to her feet as well. "No, that makes sense. Explains a lot."

A rumble shakes the walls and floor, startling us. Objects around us rattle. Seconds later, lights flicker on. The ones in this hallway keep blinking. The hum of electricity courses through the place, beeps and clicks and buzzes coming from different directions. An electric door at the end of the hallway repeatedly glides open and closed. The mechanism must be broken.

"Oh, my God," Tyra gasps.

"They got the power back on," Sara exhales in relief.

"So, what do we do now?" Tyra says. "Do we retreat?"

"We can't retreat," I say. "We have to look for Cris and Connor."

"Okay. Maybe we can check if they *are* here somewhere," Tyra says. "There's a security room, just down the hallway. It's where I was hiding. If the power's back on, maybe the monitors still work. We can look for your friends."

Now there's a plan I like.

"Lead the way," I say.

TWENTY-SEVEN

WE WALK WITH CAREFUL STEPS, our weapons pointing here and there in anticipation of yet another sudden ambush by infected. We pass by empty classrooms of different sizes. They remind me of the ones in Kadia and Spheria—it's so strange how classrooms look the same everywhere. Everywhere I've been, at least. Walking down these hallways with the lights on doesn't make this place any less creepy. In fact, seeing the tentacles in all their detailed glory is much grosser. I wish the power would go out again.

Following Tyra's lead, we arrive at security without another encounter with the infected. I inspect the monitors while Sara searches the room. To my surprise, most of the monitors are still functional. Only problem is, not all the footage is visible. Some of the cameras have likely been destroyed, judging by the static. Others are obstructed by something, and I'll bet everything it's the giant tentacles all over the place. B1 is practically all unavailable.

On one of the B2 cameras, Sgt. Bronson and the others walk down a tentacle-free hallway. Whatever this growth is, judging by the footage availability (or lack thereof), B1 might be its source. In another screen, Lt. Mansur and Zack are fighting some infected. They're handling themselves fine, though, especially Zack with just the combat knife.

"Look." Sara picks up a small device from a crate full of many more. "These are past recordings."

"How do you know what they are?" I ask.

"Luke showed me some of this stuff before," she says. "But look at how they're titled. These are from before…"

"Before what?" Tyra asks.

"The outbreak," Sara says. "They must have brought these in here to inspect them. General Sears and the others, when they came here."

"And they just left them here?" I raise suspicious brows at that.

"I'm sure they took what they needed." Sara inspects the computer on the desk, looking for something. "Doesn't mean what they left behind isn't worth a look."

She plugs the device into the computer, then gestures for me to move aside while she messes with the keyboard and mouse. It opens up a page with a long list of files. Sara clicks on one of them. It starts playing a video. A recording from one of the cameras.

It's the hallway from this floor that we were in earlier, except … different. So different. There are no tentacles hugging the walls and floors. No holes or cracks. More importantly, no infected. Just people. People walking casually—no weapons on them or any protective gear. They're holding paper cups, books, bags, briefcases, files. Chatting, laughing. A janitor drags a cleaning cart in the back. Someone bumps into the person holding the cup and spills his drink all over his shirt. The girl who bumped into him apologizes, offers him a tissue. His friend just laughs at him. The janitor tiredly drags his cart over to where the drink spilled. The guy with the stained shirt smacks the back of his friend's head before walking off, disappearing into the edge of the screen. Is he going to the bathroom to wash up? Does he have a spare shirt or will he have to spend his day with stained clothes?

The footage cuts all of a sudden, and we're back to the screen where the list is.

"What happened?" I ask.

"I stopped it," Sara says.

"Why?" I ask.

"There was nothing important there. Maybe another one," she says.

Nothing important?

That was one of the most important things I've seen in my whole life. That was an actual glimpse into the world before the outbreak. Not like the movies Jose made me watch with her, where it's just people playing pretend. This was real. These were real people.

The first proof that the world before did exist. Not that I didn't believe Dad or Mom when they talked about it. But seeing it with my own eyes? After having walked through the aftermath of it all? It's something else. I want to take all these recordings and sit in front of a screen and watch them all day.

Sara scrolls down the list for a while until she finds something interesting enough.

This next footage is in a different location. On the top corner of the screen, it says B1. It looks like a lab room with a lot of capsules by the walls. The capsules have something inside them floating in liquid. I can't tell what it is. There's a man and woman in lab coats having a tense conversation. I don't know if they're students or researchers. They both look to the back of the room at the same time, as if something alerted them, then they run toward it and disappear into the edge of the screen. The recording continues.

"Where did they go?" I ask.

"Need a different angle," Sara says. She's about to close the video when one of the lab coats—the man—appears on the screen again, rushing back, covered in...

"Is that blood?" Tyra gasps.

Sara closes out of that one and opens another video. This one is in the same room but from a camera set by an electric door at the back of the room. It's closed. Then suddenly it opens and someone stumbles out of it, his hand on his bloody neck. The two people rush to his help. The woman yells something at the man, and the man hurries back. The woman puts pressure on the injured man's wound. A few seconds later, the other guy returns with a med kit.

"What happened?" I ask. "Sara, can you get footage from behind that door?"

"No." Sara shakes her head. "They must have kept the recording for that area separately. It must have been classified."

Back on the screen, the lab coats try to patch their friend up, but there is blood everywhere. Too much blood. The woman gets up and runs somewhere, probably to get help, while the guy stays, keeping pressure on the wound.

Then the guy in the lab coat starts shaking his friend, slapping his face. He moves his hand off the wound to perform chest compressions on him.

It works. His friend starts moving again—except ... he's not moving. His body is shaking violently. I'm hit with flashes of Melisa on the floor. He's having a seizure.

Everything stops for a moment. The guy in the lab coat sits still, covering his face in his bloody hands, mourning the loss of his friend.

Until his friend wakes up again. Something else. The guy in the lab coat barely gets a chance to react before his friend attacks him.

"This is it…" My breath catches. Eyes glued to the screen as the infected tears a giant piece of flesh off of the guy's face. Blood spattering everywhere. "This is Day Zero."

TWENTY-EIGHT

"THAT'S WHEN IT STARTED," I say.

"Maybe." Sara doesn't sound as invested as I am.

"Maybe?" I huff. "Didn't you see what I just saw?"

"They could have managed to contain it," Sara says, "for a while. And then something else happened. We don't really know."

"Hey, guys," Tyra calls. "Are those your friends?"

I look up to the screen she's pointing at. There are three boys. Although all are wearing gas masks, I recognize Cris leading the way down a hallway, weapon in hands, Connor is behind him, leaning on a third boy I can't identify.

"They're here!" My heart flutters. He's alive. Oh, thank God, he's alive.

"Who's that with them?" Sara leans closer to the monitors, inspecting the footage.

"Could be someone from Bronson Squad? Or a Hummingbird?" I look to Tyra for confirmation.

Tyra gives an uncertain shrug. "Hard to tell from here."

I look back at the screen. Connor and the boy with him have tripped on one of the tentacles and fallen. Cris comes to a halt, alert. Growls echo somewhere outside the security room. Heavy and fast footsteps run past us.

They must be headed toward Cris and the boys.

"Come on." I start toward the door. "We have to help them."

"Ashley! Goddammit, wait up!" Sara calls after me as I run out. Hers and Tyra's footsteps follow behind me.

I run down the hallway, following the growls of infected. There's some debris here and there, more cracks on the floor, but I don't let that stop me. I leap over the giant tentacles, step on the smaller ones, duck my head under the dangling ones. I follow the gunfire and moans until the footage I'd watched on the screen manifests before me. Not a second is wasted before I open fire on them.

Sara and Tyra are right behind me. They join in immediately. We're able to draw the attention of some of the infected toward us, lightening the load on Cris and the other boy. Connor seems too out of it to shoot. He's just sitting on the floor, leaning against the wall.

It doesn't take us long to kill all the infected, and I start toward the boys.

"Ashley, Sara ... you're both okay," Cris says. I can hear his smile.

"What's wrong with Connor?" Sara approaches behind me.

"Mild concussion. Slipped and fell while we were chased by infected earlier," Cris says.

"Hey there Pinky, Wispy." Connor tries to pick himself up, shooting me and Sara a peace sign. "And ... sorry I can't think of a nickname for your friend right now."

"So, who's that?" Cris gestures in Tyra's direction.

"Tyra," I say. "She's a Hummingbird." I nod to the boy in his company. "And what about him?"

"Also Hummingbird," Cris says. "I'm so glad we actually found survivors—"

"Wait, Hummingbird?" the boy interrupts, his eyes on Tyra. "Which squad? I don't recognize you..."

"You tell me," Tyra says. "Your voice doesn't sound familiar."

Silence as we all exchange wary looks with one another.

"She's not a Hummingbird!" the boy shouts. "She's a fugitive!"

"He's lying!" Tyra argues. "I was here with the others. I know my comrades, and he's not one of them."

"Okay, let's all calm down..." Cris holds his hands up.

"I'm not calming down," Tyra says. "He's a *fugitive!*"

I pull up my weapon and aim it at the boy.

"Whoa, whoa!" Cris steps up in front of him. "Ash, what the hell are you doing? Lower your weapon."

"He's lying," I say.

"How do you know that?" Cris holds his ground. "What if *she's* lying?"

"That's true, maybe *both* of them are lying." I keep my weapon up. "But he is *definitely* lying."

"Ash..." Cris's voice is low, calm. "Lower your weapon."

"I'm not lowering my weapon." I press, planting my feet harder. "You step aside, Cris."

Cris lets out a frustrated breath. "You're gonna do this now?"

"Step. Aside." My voice strains. Gaze shifts between Cris and the boy's silhouette behind him, anticipating sudden movements.

Cris shakes his head. "Ash, let's not make the same mistake again."

"What mistake?" I scoff. "Saving your life?"

"Killing people on a whim." His jaw hardens. The accusatory tone makes my chest tight. I can't believe he ever looked at me with so much tenderness before. Now those brown eyes are sharp daggers staring me down. "We can handle things peacefully."

"Tell that to Jose's mangled up face," I fire back. I swear if he doesn't step back, I'm going to shoot through him.

Cris does a double-take. "Jose...?"

"Okay, listen up, both of you." Sara steps up beside me, placing a hand on my arm, holding the other up to Cris, gesturing for us both to calm down. "At this point it's a 'he said, she said' debacle. There's a very easy solution here. We restrain them both and take them with us. HQ should have a conclusive list of the Hummingbirds. We just need to check which one of them isn't on it."

Yeah, screw that.

"What's her full name?" I ask, looking between Tyra and the boy, who's still hiding behind Cris. "Jose. What's her full name? If either of you is telling the truth, then you should have no problem—"

"Private First Class Josefina Serrano." Tyra doesn't skip a beat. "First Rifle Squad, Bravo Tea—"

And just like that, Connor jumps at the boy behind Cris, slapping his weapon out of his hold, making his shot miss Cris's head and pierce the wall instead. The boy throws the concussed Connor off him with ease, sending him stumbling on one of the tentacles. He scrambles up, leaving his weapon and running in the opposite direction.

I take off immediately after him, firing from the hip, miss. Damn it!

"Ash," Cris calls as I pass him by. He's helping Connor sit up.

"Take Connor and Tyra to the others. Computer room. They need medical attention." I don't spare him so much as a glance.

"Ashley, wait!" Sara runs after me. "I'm coming with you."

"We can't let him get away." I round the corner and fire again. Miss. It must have been him. The one who killed Jose and her partner.

He's about to round another corner but then doubles back quickly for a door, just as a bunch of infected show up. Sara and I shoot the bulk of them as we continue, then we push through the door and into an insanely large lecture hall. The boy is nowhere in sight.

"He's gotta be hiding here somewhere," I pant.

Sara signals for me to split off. I take the rows on the right, she takes left.

Some of the infected follow us inside, and we take them out in just a few headshots. The rest of them run past the door, their footsteps distancing. Did they really not see us go in here? Are they going for Cris and the others?

I grunt as I make my way down the rows of seats and desks, bending down to check under them. Nothing. Nothing. Nothing.

"There's something going on up ahead," Sara says, "by the teacher's desk."

I squint through the fog, keeping my hands firmly around my M4.

We approach the bottom of the hall. There's a thick tentacle piercing the floor. Thicker than both me and Sara combined. Pulsating. A shadow moves to my right. I open fire on it in a beat, but it dashes for a door and disappears behind it. I hurry after it, bust through the door, straight down a flight of stairs. Sara's footsteps follow me.

I hold up my weapon and try to line up a shot before firing at the fugitive. He ducks and I instead hit one of the giant tentacles. The pustules on it explode. The boy continues running, but I come to a forced stop when something drops from the ceiling and lands right before me.

That something shoots up and lets out a growl.

Thud-thud-thuds all around me. More bodies falling and rising.

Then the infected collectively take off after the fugitive.

TWENTY-NINE

IT'S like Sara and I don't exist.

The infected run straight past us, following the fugitive. It reminds me of that day in the subway tunnel, when Sara and I stood surrounded by crawlers, only for them to ignore us. That time, they were responding to the call of an Active.

Guttural screams echo down the tentacle-covered hallway, and I imagine the fugitive torn to shreds in seconds before his cries quiet.

"Ashley." Sara's voice is low and shaken. She gives me a quick pat on the shoulder then gestures for me to look up.

Our flashlights shine on a mess of bodies glued to the ceiling—not just the ceiling, no, even the walls. Infected. All around us are infected. They look the same as all the others we came across before, with the pustules on their skin.

"Oh, my God…" I gasp. "What the hell is going on here?"

"I don't know," Sara says. "I've never seen anything like this. They look like they're in some kind of stasis…"

"You can say that again." My breath catches. I can't even count how many of them there are.

"It's like a storage room," Sara says. "A storage room of infected."

"Now we know where all of those infected were coming from."

"Over there." Sara points with her flashlight somewhere to our right. "You see that?"

There's some strange light coming through a hole in the wall.

Carefully, we walk toward it, trying not to bump into the infected or tentacles, shimmying through invisible walls.

Miraculously, we make it to that light, and now we're close enough to see it's coming through a door rather than a hole. Sara carefully pulls the door open, just enough so we can squeeze through the other side.

That light intensifies. Pulsating.

We find ourselves inside a lab, but not just any lab. The broken capsules hiding behind the tentacles tell me this is the same room we saw in that recording. Or at least, a very similar one. All the tentacles in the room converge toward the direction of the glow, which stems from something at the back of the room. A bulbous growth fixed to a crumbling wall. And at the base of the bulb is … a skeletal corpse dressed in a SPORE uniform.

"What the hell?" I shudder at the sight. "This is the source of the growth?"

"Apparently." The shock in Sara's voice is evident.

"It looks like that body's been here a while," I note. "Could it be from that mission? The one that General Sears led?"

"It's possible." Sara nods.

I have no idea what the hell I'm looking at or what caused it, but it's both pretty and unsettling.

A spark of light travels through one of the tentacles overhead until it reaches the bulbous growth, and the growth throbs violently.

A hiss of compressed air releases behind us, then thud, thud, thud, as a number of infected drop from the ceiling to their feet. Sara and I turn, ready to shoot, but the infected don't come at us. They run in the opposite direction, toward the stairs.

"Someone must have triggered it somewhere," Sara guesses. "It's sending infected to attack them."

"We have to do something." I turn to face Sara. "If this is the source of the growth, maybe destroying it will … stop the infected?"

"That's a very weak maybe," Sara says. "If we mess with it, we might just make it worse. It's best if we get the lieutenant to have a look, or the research team."

"Zack said to destroy it, right?" I remind her. "Lori told him to burn it. You got your flame rounds for your grenade launcher."

"Sure but…" Sara shakes her head. "He also said the thing he found looked different. Not this extreme. It might be too late at this stage. I don't think we should mess with it before we know what we're dealing with. If we trigger it, then the infected will come after us. They'll rip us apart."

Those are all sound arguments, and yet something tells me letting this growth exist any longer is an even bigger mistake.

"Ash, let's head back. Regroup with the others."

"Sara," I plead, "we can't let this thing stay... All those Hummingbirds died ... because of it. The lieutenant and Sergeant Seidel already collected a sample, right? Maybe that'll be enough for the research team to study. And if not, well, then screw their research anyway. If people have to get killed for its sake."

Her face scrunches up in uncertainty. Doubtful eyes shift back and forth between me and the bulb. A low exhale of defeat as she meets my gaze. "Okay, we'll give it a shot, but get ready to bolt if this doesn't work."

I give her an assuring nod.

We back up toward the door, a safe distance from the bulbous growth. I reload my M4 with a fresh magazine while Sara loads up her grenade launcher with an incendiary round. At the count of three, we open fire at the pulsating core. The pustules pop one after the other, releasing more gas into the air, creating a thicker cloud that obstructs our vision. And with that, a chorus of growls begins.

Sara turns around; she leaves me to deal with the bulb while she loads an explosive round into her grenade launcher and fires it at the infected coming up behind us. I don't think it killed all of them, though, because their growls persist. I keep shooting at the bulb anyway.

"Ashley, look." Sara nods upward.

I do. The tentacles on the ceiling are wrinkling and shrinking, turning a dark gray.

"It's working?" My chest feels lighter. My finger on the trigger doesn't rest.

"I really, really hope so." Sara loads up another incendiary round and fires it.

We rip through the outer layers of the bulb, and the fire of the incendiary round makes the process faster, slowly but surely digging down to the skeletal corpse of the unluckiest Spore I've ever seen. The way its body is practically glued to the wall, skull cracked open and ... whatever this growth is, is sprouting from it. But it's working.

Only problem, though, is that as the tentacles shrink into basically nothing, chunks of the ceiling crumble, smashing the counters and lab equipment underneath.

"Okay, great," Sara deadpans, "now the place is falling apart."

"Yeah, we ... did not think that one through."

Sara lowers her weapon, slowly backing away. "I think we did enough damage to that thing."

"I totally agree." I nod, lowering my own M4.

"Come on!" She taps my arm, and we run back—not the same way, though, because surprise, surprise, it's blocked with debris and infected, so we bolt for one of the holes that's opened up in the now clear walls. Into a hallway, sprinting at top speed and narrowly escaping a very brutal burial procedure.

I practically fly the second I spot a door with a bright green sign above it that says Exit. With some brute force, we manage to get it open and explode into a parking garage.

"Go, go, go!" Sara shouts. "I see light, up there!"

Up a concrete ramp, we race against the building, dodging left and right. But then the dirt raining over us suddenly thickens. I look up at a piece of rubble falling at us. My first instinct is to throw myself at Sara, saving us both from being crushed.

I push myself up. There's a moment of acknowledgment when our eyes lock before I shift off of her. We both jump to our feet and continue running. There are some growls coming up behind us, but when I throw a glance over my shoulder, I'm pleased to see the infected aren't as good at dodging debris as we are.

Take that, suckers!

"God, I really hope the others are okay," I pant. Please tell me I didn't just bury our entire platoon here.

"Let's just focus on getting out of here," Sara says.

But the second we run out into the bright of day, a giant guy comes out from our right and slams Sara against a vehicle. I'm about to take aim but he swipes her in a chokehold and holds her against him, a combat knife in his other hand.

"What do we have here?" The big guy's face is hidden behind a gas mask, voice muffled. He presses the tip of his knife under Sara's chin. "A couple of lost little Sparkles."

I watch him through the sights of my M4. "Let her go."

"I don't think so." His knife sinks into her skin, but without drawing blood. "You drop your weapon or I'm going to draw a nice line down your friend's throat."

"You wanna bet? Your knife or my gun?" My hands shake but I try to keep a calm, confident voice. "Let her go."

"Hmm." The guy's hold tightens around Sara. She chokes. "And what happens when I let her go? Are you gonna let me walk away? Shoot me in the back?"

"Let's find out," I dare him.

"Let's not," another voice joins in behind me. A girl. I can't see her, but that voice… "Drop your weapon, Ashley."

The muzzle of a gun presses to the back of my head. "Nina…"

PART THREE

THIRTY

I LOWER my weapon and look over my shoulder.

There she is. Unrelenting brown eyes watch me behind a gas mask. Unkempt red hair tied in a messy bun, longer than I remember it. There's a guy behind her holding a shotgun—he's shorter, with dark, shoulder-length hair. Guess they got us outnumbered.

"*Ashley?*" the giant holding Sara says. "You know her?"

"Used to." Nina pushes her weapon harder against my skull. "Drop that M4. I won't say it a third time."

My lips press into a thin line, but I comply. I hold one hand up while I unsling my M4 with the other, then bend down and place it on the ground. I rise back to my feet with both hands held up.

Sara's shaky gaze holds mine. She doesn't struggle, though, nor does she say a word.

"Don," Nina says. God it's so strange hearing her voice after so long. I … missed her. "Grab that."

The shorter boy is the one that moves. He carefully reaches for my M4 with the tip of his boot, nudging it away from me before he swipes it in one hand and backs away.

"Now what?" The big guy keeps a tight hold on Sara. "Hug it out and walk in our separate ways?"

"No, Jed." Nina reaches to my front and removes my sheathed knife with a hard tug. "They're coming with us."

"Nina…" I swallow a lump and pray to God that Cris's way has even the tiniest bit of merit. "Look, we can just go. We won't tell anyone—"

"That's not true," Sara interjects. "Nina and these two are fugitives, criminals. Covering for them would be a crime."

"Yep," Nina says. "And *that* is exactly why we can't let you go."

I shake my head at Sara. Why? Why on earth did she decide that now is the time to start talking? Not only that, but make threats when someone has a knife to her throat?

There isn't even the smallest hint of regret in her eyes.

We're stripped of our portors, gas masks, weapons, and assault packs. Then they tie our hands behind our backs using rope.

"Nina," Jed says, "we should make a stop by that workshop we saw on the way. Might have what I need."

"Sure." Nina looks to me and Sara as she takes off her gas mask, revealing dirty, freckled cheeks and chapped lips. Her face is thinner—actually, her whole body is slimmer, barely filling the uniform she's wearing. Her brown eyes don't look as intimidating as they did from behind the gas mask. They're baggy and tired. Her voice, though, is still as biting as ever. "Time to put all those ruck marches to use."

We're led to one of the buildings on campus first—a small storage unit where three loaded rucks wait. Nina, Jed and Don take one each. Then we leave the campus and go through a forest, then through an abandoned street, where Sara and I are left with Don while Jed and Nina disappear for a while. When they return, we continue down through the sewers, which is where most of our journey takes place.

About halfway through, we make a stop to eat. Nina tasks Jed and Don with feeding us some snack bars while she digs through the loaded rucksacks.

"What are you looking for?" Don asks her.

"Doing a little reorganizing." Nina takes out a folded, empty rucksack from one of the full ones, then transfers a few things from the loaded rucks into it.

Jed clears his throat. His skin is tan, and he has a defined jawline and close-set eyes that make his face look a little too big. Short, disheveled, brown hair that reminds me a bit of Cris's at the start of Basic, though Jed's is even shorter and lighter in color. Of the three, he looks the healthiest, with his athletic build and way-above-average height. Even taller than Cris. "Seems unnecessary."

Nina turns to him with a familiar, pointed stare that's meant to intimidate, but it only ruffles butterflies in my stomach. "Jed, don't be a dimwit," she barks. "We leave this here," she shakes the rucksack in her hand, "in case."

"In case?" Don asks. His boyish face makes him look younger than he probably is. Round, innocent eyes. Curved, slightly bushy brows. Button nose and two beauty marks, one at the center of his right cheek, and the other near the left corner of his mouth. His skin is paler than Sara's, and even his lips are a little colorless.

"In case we need it," Nina clarifies. "Because if you haven't noticed, we've had a lot of in-cases lately."

"And, uh..." Jed says, "are we telling Vincent and the others about this in-case?"

"Contrary to Vincent's belief, he's not the boss of anyone." Nina stuffs the newly loaded ruck into a hollowed-out pipe and covers it up with some trash. "But, sure," she turns to Jed with an even more menacing glare, "you can tell him if you want."

We resume the walk. It's about twenty minutes before we stop at a ladder. Nina climbs it first, then knocks on the lid in a rhythm that's too specific to be random.

The lid lifts, and a girl looks down at us. "You're back!" She offers her hand to Nina and helps her climb out.

Jed frees my hands first so I can climb up while Don keeps his weapon on Sara. Once I'm out, Nina ties my hands again, then it's Sara's turn to climb up. Nina ties her hands immediately once she's out. Jed follows after, and Don last.

"Where's Cody?" the girl asks, inspecting the manhole. There's something familiar about her face, but I can't put my finger on it. Maybe I saw her picture on the files they showed us.

"Cody's gone," Nina says.

"Gone?" The girl turns to her. "Gone, like he ran away, or gone like he's dead?"

Nina exchanges an unsure look with Jed and Don.

"Did you even look for him?" the girl insists. "Or did you just leave him behind to save yourselves?"

"He's gone, Mia," Nina presses, voice sharp.

"And who are *they*?" Mia eyes me and Sara up and down. "Wait— you brought Sparkles in here?"

"Don't worry about it," Nina says.

"Nina..." Mia gives her a disapproving headshake. "Vincent is *not* gonna be happy about this."

I scan our surroundings. We're in a mostly empty parking lot, save for a few rusty, skeletal vehicles. A building to my left, its "modern" architecture slightly reminiscent of Vigor's. There's a boy on what seems like a makeshift watchpost. Judging by the flappy sleeve of his shirt, he's missing half an arm. A tall fence surrounds the entire place, and a small, locked metal door keeps the infected at bay. This is as secure as the outside can get. At least at first glance.

Mia takes out what looks like a radio from her pocket and holds it to her mouth. "Vincent," she says. "They're back."

Nothing comes in response, though.

Nina nods for me and Sara to follow as we walk across the parking lot and round the corner to what seems like the front yard. Jed, Don and Mia are behind us. A big gate to our right, barricaded—and to our left, what probably used to be the fanciest staircase leads up to the main entrance. A rusty, barely visible sign is fixed to the wall of the entrance: Highwater Police Department.

We take the stairs and enter through the broken doors of a vestibule into a spacious lobby. It's pretty dark in here, but the bit of daylight coming through the vestibule highlights the chipped walls covered in grime. The hardened dust glued to surfaces. Mysterious dirty spots made over time are integrated into the flooring, which I'm sure is hiding shiny marble underneath. There's some seating, a broken, wide window to the right that looks into a room of desks. A door across from us and more doors to our left.

Besides our footsteps, there's the echo of a continuous plop, and an approaching chorus of combat boots. Two more fugitives come out through the door in front of us, both armed, one with a shotgun and one with a handgun.

"W-what the hell is th-this?" one of the boys stutters. He has fair skin and short, blond hair.

"You brought Sparkles to our hideout?" the other boy says, panicked. He's slightly shorter than the blond, brown hair parted in the middle and bangs covering the sides of his forehead. "Nina, what were you thinking?"

"I don't think she was," Jed comments. "Looks like Nina's got a very soft spot for these two."

"Wait a minute." The brunet's eyes fix on me. "That's the girl you were watching, in the Pit."

Both of these boys look vaguely familiar. I think they were part of the group that showed up with Captain Hill in the Pit, the former commander of Lotiva's Spec Ops Division, who had been in contact with Zack and the survivors.

"You're the ones who took Lori," I say, hit by a flash from back then—that boy, the blond, he's the one who was carrying the unconscious Lori after they tranqed her.

"Im-pressive memory." The blond spares me one glance before turning to Nina again. "Now, a-answer me: why are they h-here?"

"For one," Nina folds her arms against her chest, "figured this might boost your plan's chances of success. You know, to have something to give in return for what you want to take."

"A-an exch-change?" The blond scowls. "I'm not d-doing trade with S-SPORE."

"And," Nina continues, "might be nice to diversify our intel sources. Just to cross-examine a few things. We've been a little too trigger happy, don't you think?"

"Right," he scoffs. "And after we've s-squeezed every drop of information we can out of th-them, what then? You're gonna k-kill them yourself? Do we feed them to the c-crawler?"

My eyes shoot knowingly to Sara's. Lori *is* here.

"See what I mean about trigger happy?" Nina sighs.

"That's i-ironic, coming from you, seeing as you killed more S-Sparkles than any of us co-combined," he says.

"It's not a competition, Vincent." Nina's hands fall to her sides. "But, thanks. I *am* better than you."

So this is Vincent. Doesn't look like he and Nina get along too well.

"Did you guys even get anything useful?" the brunet asks.

"Not enough," Jed says. "But yeah, we filled our rucks as much as we could."

"Mia," Vincent calls. "Why d-don't you help Jed s-sort through those resources and t-take inventory of our new stock?"

"Sure," Mia answers. She walks over to Nina, who hands her the ruck she's carrying. Jed takes Don's, and the two of them head off to a double door on our left.

"J-Justin," Vincent says to the brunet beside him. "G-Go back to the kennels."

Justin acknowledges with a nod, casts me and Sara a skeptical look, then heads back through the door he and Vincent came in by.

"Cody didn't m-make it, then?" Vincent asks.

Nina answers with a headshake. Cody. Is that the boy I chased to the basement?

A buzzing sound draws my attention to the portor strapped around Vincent's wrist. How the hell does he still have a functioning portor? None of the others have theirs on—that I've seen, at least. He and Nina exchange a knowing look before he leaves the lobby back through the same door Justin took. His muffled voice comes through briefly, as if he's talking to someone, but I can't make out anything before the sound fades away.

"So…" Don clears his throat. "What do we do with *them*?"

Nina turns to me and Sara with an ominous smile. "Let's show them to their private quarters, of course."

THIRTY-ONE

THE PRIVATE QUARTERS turn out to be holding cells. It's a good thing I've made the acquaintance before in Spheria.

"Nothing personal," Nina says while Don locks the door. She motions for me and Sara to turn around so they can undo our restraints through the bars. "I'm sure I would have gotten the same treatment had it been the other way. Possibly worse."

"So, what are you gonna do with us?" I stand with my back to the bars. As soon as my hands are free, I massage my sore wrists.

"That depends on you," Nina says. "Are you gonna be a problem?"

"Define problem." I turn to face her. "Because being on the run and kidnapping two soldiers is pretty problematic."

I still can't believe I'm actually looking at Nina right now. It feels like it's been ages and just yesterday that we went our separate ways.

"True." Nina leans close. Tired, yet ever so piercing eyes hold mine. The corner of her mouth lifts in a smirk. "So is letting a traitor escape when you had the chance to capture her."

I falter, and I can practically feel the burn of Sara's pointed stare. I never told anyone that I'd let Nina go that time. Just that she got away. I couldn't catch up to her.

"The others will come looking for us." Sara steps next to me. "Sooner or later, they'll be able to trace us."

Nina lifts her chin, looking past me to Sara. "That would require functioning portors with functioning trackers."

Of course, they messed with our portors. Always one step ahead, aren't you, Nina? None of us even suspected her of being a traitor in the first place. At least *I* didn't.

"Nina." I try to catch her eye again. "Why don't we talk about this? You have the crawler here, don't you? Lori?"

Nina doesn't answer that. She wets her dry lips with her tongue, restoring a tinge of their color.

"Look." I hold onto the bars, leaning close. I can't help the twist in my stomach, seeing her like this. And I don't want things to turn ugly. I don't want to have to fight her. "You've been on the run for how long now? Lost how many people? You're clearly running so low on resources you had to attack a SPORE platoon to save yourselves. All we want is the crawler, that's it. If you cooperate, if you surrender the crawler to us, SPORE will have no reason to keep going after you. They might even allow you to come back—"

"Come back where?" Nina scoffs, brows shooting up. "Lotiva? Who says we want to go back?"

"Okay, well, they can let you go wherever you want, then," I say.

"We can't promise that." And there Sara goes with another ill-timed contribution.

I throw my head back in exasperation. Why is she channeling her insufferable rule-stickler attitude now of all times?

"But what we can promise is that SPORE won't rest until they get that crawler," Sara continues. "There's only a handful of you left, and so many more of us."

I really should have punched her teeth in when I had the chance.

"So, you're threatening us." Nina furrows her brows.

"No!" I interrupt, shaking my head at Sara to *stop it*, then at Nina. "No, she's not. Listen, Nina, we just want this to end. We've had so many wave attacks in the past months. Things are getting worse. We're just trying to find a way to ... make things better."

"Better for who, exactly?" Nina takes a couple steps back.

"Does she even listen to you?" I ask. "All this time you had her, have you actually managed to use her? Has Lori been an asset to you in any way?"

"What, and you guys got it all figured out, then?" Nina's arms fold against her chest. "You're saying you know how to use her?"

"Not us," I say.

"Ashley," Sara warns. Give me a break.

"You mean her brother," Nina says.

How ... did they figure out that Zack and Lori are siblings? From what I know, Zack had tried to protect Lori as much as possible from Captain Hill, keep her abilities on the down-low. It doesn't make sense that he would have divulged their relationship to any of the Lotivans.

It's true, then? There *is* a spy? Didn't Nina say something before about diversifying their intel? Could it be that that's who Vincent was talking to before?

"And what does the general plan to do with the crawler?" Nina asks. "Upgrade his arsenal so he can save up on bombs when he decides the next sector has to go?"

"You're smart, Nina." Sara has never sounded more condescending, and it leaves me stunned. She's been hanging out with Lucille too much, if you ask me. "You know Lori's valuable to humankind. You know she could be the key to solving hundreds of our problems."

"Maybe I'm not that smart, then." Nina's lips press tight.

"Okay," I say, "so what are *you* going to do with Lori? Assuming you can do anything at all."

"Wouldn't you like to know?" Nina smirks. "You wanna know what I think? No one should have that crawler. It's a hip firing fest if I've ever seen one."

"Nina..." I can't tell what she's thinking or feeling. But she brought us here, and that has to mean something, right? "Please, just think about this for a minute."

The creak of a door. Footsteps. Another door. Then someone walks into the corridor of the holding cells.

"Nina, Don." It's Mia. I try to peek at her from behind the bars. "Vincent's calling a meeting."

Nina's eyes roll so hard they almost disappear into her skull. "Great."

"Did you ask them?" Mia whispers. "About Chloe?"

"Mia," Nina warns.

"But what if they know—"

"Let's not do this now," Nina says, voice stern.

Mia's lips purse. She watches me and Sara with something on the tip of her tongue, but then she turns on her heels and storms off with a huff.

"Who's Chloe?" I ask.

Nina turns back to us. "Enjoy your stay," she says, then she's off with Don.

THIRTY-TWO

SARA'S WATCHING me like she swallowed a bomb and is waiting for it to go off.

"What?" I demand.

She massages her creased forehead. If disappointment had an embodiment, it would be her face right now. "You let her get away?"

Oh, dear God.

"It doesn't matter." I shrug, backing toward the sad bench fixed to the wall and taking a much-needed seat.

"Yes, it does." Her shoulders fall. "She literally kidnapped us."

"She saved our lives." I give my sore kneecaps a rub. All the aching in my body is slowly coming to the surface. "If she hadn't shown up, who knows what those guys would've done to us?"

"If you hadn't let her go, those guys may not be alive now." Sara pins me with a scolding glare.

Okay, she wants to argue now? I can argue now. Matter of fact, bring it on.

"You know what, Sara? You're right." I hold my hands up in feigned defeat. "You're always right. I let Nina go, and it's my fault we're here right now. Next time I'll take a page out of your morally-correct decision-making book. Because you always know what the right thing to do is, don't you?"

Sara's frustration comes out in a low breath that ruffles the hair dangling in her face. "That's not—"

"Like manipulating everyone and everything around you so you can get through life without, God forbid, having to confront someone's inconvenient hard feelings." The words come out of my mouth like someone opened a floodgate. My hands drop to my lap, clenching into fists. "Like keeping secrets from me because you wouldn't want to break me with the truth any more than I already was, right?"

"Ash..." Sara pleads, head tilted to the side. Yeah, this isn't what she wanted to talk about. It's not what I wanted to talk about, either, but here we are.

"Like running away instead of owning up to your mistakes, because you're the mature one and I'm the dramatic one," I spit out. Bitter. Angry. But mostly, hurt.

Sara shrinks in her clothes. Gone is that scolding gaze, and in its place is a guilty, remorseful frown. "I didn't run away."

Liar.

"You didn't even want that promotion," I say. "We have a fight, and all of a sudden you change your mind and decide to take it, and then you're gone. That's not running away?"

"You're the one who told me to leave you alone." The accusation falls flat, like even she doesn't buy it.

"You wanted to know how I felt. I told you how I felt, and you couldn't take it, so you left. That was your choice," I say. "Also, I can't believe *you* recommended me to Lieutenant Mansur." I almost forgot about this. Almost. "I was going back home, and you just had to ruin that, too."

"Because..." Sara starts, then deflates, swallowing a lump.

"Because what?" I urge her. I would love to hear one good reason why she did that. Knowing full well it would turn the broken shards of our friendship to dust.

"It was supposed to be you," she blurts. "You're the one who was supposed to get that promotion in the first place. You're the one who was supposed to join the Renegades, not me."

"What are you talking about?" I squint. As far as our scores during training go, Sara's were always higher than mine, even if I did excel in certain areas.

"The only reason they wanted me there is because ... I'm from Eukson." Her posture sags and her eyes dodge mine. "Because they thought Zack would listen to me. That I could convince him to help us. That because we both grew up in the same sector, it'd be enough to earn his trust. But Zack doesn't trust me. He doesn't even like me. He thinks I betrayed our home. Our people."

Oh...

Okay, well, now I'm starting to see where this is going.

"And you know what? Sometimes I feel like I have." Sara looks up with a sorry smile. I've never seen her so defeated. "I don't know what the right thing to do or feel is. People hate Sears because they think he bombed Eukson. He didn't, though. I knew that. I couldn't hate him for that. And I saw what it did to Luke every time people made those snide remarks. Every time they threw him into the wringer because, hey, *your dad is atrocious and that must mean you are, too*."

I can't help a grimace. I still remember how uncomfortable Luke got when Haytham revealed his connection to Sears in front of our squad. How fast Nina jumped on it and teased him about it.

"I saw how much it hurt him, that he couldn't do anything about it," Sara continues. "He couldn't speak up against it or defend his dad, because his dad already accepted the blame."

Even if Sears was actually responsible, it wouldn't have been right to hold Luke accountable, too.

"And you can ask me if I hate Rodríguez for bombing my home, but the truth is? My home was already gone before that." Her soft voice cracks, and my heart cracks with it. "My whole world was already gone before those bombs dropped. And I was gone before I saw them drop."

I didn't forget the story she told me. She'd witnessed enough horrors that day, I don't think she needed to see more.

"But sometimes I think Zack is right." Her eyes look up at the ceiling as if searching for something. "I *should* be angry. I should do something with that anger. And I would ... if I could feel it to start with."

Sara's anger is rare, and even when it's there, it's tame, mild, unlike mine.

"I don't know who to be angry at," she admits. "Sears, because he didn't foresee that not killing his wife would have led to the doom of an entire population? Rodríguez, for scrambling to clean up a mess no one, including himself, was prepared for? Myself, for not being able to feel any anger whatsoever about it all? Unlike most people, even those who weren't there?"

I remember that time we were discussing the Pit, everyone from our squad in Basic. How Sara eventually snapped. That was the first time I saw her annoyed—pissed. After I learned her story, I thought that's why she reacted that way, but now ... I wonder. Was she frustrated at the fact that other people were angrier than she was?

"I kept pushing because I was indebted to your dad to do so." Yeah. She did a lot of things because she felt indebted to my dad. "He saved my life, and I swore I would never let his sacrifice be in vain."

I doubt my dad would have wanted that, though. I doubt he saved her to keep her in his eternal debt. Or to feel like his life was a trade for hers. He would have wanted her to live for her. Find her own purpose.

"I'm not compelled by this strong sense of justice to fight against what's wrong for what's right. But you..." Sara gestures with both hands in my direction, her smile persistent and sad. "Both you and your dad ... you helped Zack. You did what you believed was right. He was indebted to *you*. And if you'd been brought to the Renegades sooner, maybe Olivia and Kent would still be alive. Maybe Nina wouldn't have shot them, if she saw you there. Maybe she'd have lowered her weapon and been willing to listen."

That's a lot of maybes riding on my hypothetical presence with the Renegades.

"I took a promotion I should have never taken, and I took it for the wrong reasons," Sara admits. "I took it because I wanted to give you the space you wanted, but I made no concrete difference. Since I became a Renegade, nothing's changed. Except that we lost more people, and I'm *tired* of losing people, Ashley. Aren't you?"

"Is *that* why you broke up with Luke?" I ask. "Because you're tired of losing people?"

She falters. Probably because she didn't think I knew about that.

"You know," she says. "I understand you being angry at me for not telling you the truth sooner. Really, I understand. I understand you not being able to trust me because of all the things I did behind your back. I understand you questioning if our friendship was ever real. And I know you may not believe me if I said it was." Her breath hitches and my chest tightens. "But, God, is it really so hard for you to cut me some slack? That's the part that *really* hurts. That I'm so ... unforgivable. That you hold me on this perfect pedestal where, apparently, I can't make mistakes."

Every word makes me flinch. Every little shiver in her voice wrings my heart out.

"I'm not perfect. I never was. I never claimed to be or even tried to be." She takes a step forward, not once releasing my gaze. "I slip and I fall and I struggle to get back on my feet. Most times I can't do it alone. I held onto Luke for support too long, so long I was starting to drag him down with me. *That's* why I broke up with him."

My eyes fall away from her teary ones before they get infected, too.

"Funny thing? I *know* you don't actually hate me this much. You just wanted an excuse to let go. One less person to haunt you in your sleep. So, I guess that's just what we do. You let go, and I hold on."

She's right, and that makes me angrier.

THIRTY-THREE

SLEEPING in a cell is kind of nostalgic.

In all the worst ways. It's freezing in here. Nina gave us sleeping bags, which makes it more comfortable than sleeping straight on the floor. Sara even dragged her sleeping bag next to mine after she had enough of my teeth chattering. *So that we can generate more heat together,* she said. But I'm still so fricking cold. I could really use Cris's warm hands right now. On every inch of me.

Cris. What's he up to right now? Did the others make it out of that building? Go back to the FOB? Are they out here looking for us? Is Cris worried about me, at all? Does he think I'm dead?

What if *he's* dead? What if all of them are dead? What if Sara and I are the only ones who made it?

"Do you hear that?" Sara's voice almost startles me. She's awake?

"Hear what?" I turn around from facing the wall to look at her.

"Listen." She's lying on her back, looking at the ceiling. "Outside."

I listen. There are the moans of infected. Loud. Clear. In Spheria, you almost forget they exist with how far the fences tend to be from most buildings. But here, we're basically sharing a neighborhood with them.

I'm sure that's not what Sara meant, though, so I listen closely until I finally hear it. Distant whirring.

"It has to be them." Sara turns to me. "They're looking for us."

"Either that, or it's a scouting party," I speculate.

"Ash, we have to get out of here." She pulls herself out of the sleeping bag and sits. "We have to try and get Lori and make a run for it."

"Sara, we don't even know where they're keeping her."

"I'm guessing it's somewhere in the basement. They're probably taking shifts keeping an eye on her. We can try something. Trick the next person that comes here. You can distract Nina and I can—"

"I'm gonna stop you right there." I sit up, clinging to my sleeping bag because I'm not crazy like Sara. "I'm not tricking Nina, and you're not going to hurt her."

"You wanna try talking to her again?" Sara watches me skeptically.

"That's what you said, isn't it? Maybe Nina will listen to me." I hope she does.

The door at the end of the hallway opens, bringing silence between us.

"Good morning." Nina walks up to our cell. Her tone indicates it's been anything but a good morning. "You two are up early."

"It's cold." I hold the sleeping bag tighter. "Couldn't sleep."

"Yeah, sorry, I forgot to set you up with blankets and a radiator," Nina mocks.

Honestly, I just smile at that. I missed her snark. "You're up early, too. Are you here to catch up with some old friends?"

She snorts, then shakes her head. "You're funny."

"It's okay. I know you missed me," I tease. "I missed you, too."

Nina's lips twitch, but she doesn't let the smile fully curve them. "There's this helicopter that's been flying around outside. I'm sure you can both hear it."

"They're looking for us," Sara says.

"Exactly." Nina nods. "So we're crossing our fingers it leaves soon. They'll get tired of searching, eventually. It's a lot of precious gas being wasted on a couple low-ranking Sparkles who are probably dead and never to be found again."

"What if they don't leave, though?" Sara says. "What if they raid the place? Not sure you and your friends can handle an ambush right now."

"Then you'd make perfect hostages," Nina says. "Assuming the Sparkles care enough about you. You might just end up being collateral. Unless…"

"Unless?" I ask.

"You manage to convince the others of *your* plan."

———

"Absolutely not." Vincent paces back and forth at the front of the briefing room. "We are not c-c-cooperating with the enemy. After everything they did to us? Everyone they k-killed? You want to hand over the only thing that's kept us alive all this time on a s-silver platter?"

I have to say, his stutter really undermines him. He doesn't sound nearly as intimidating as he's trying to.

Everyone's spread out, sitting at the desks. Everyone except Justin, who I imagine is guarding Lori. They must be keeping her in the kennels. Nina's leaning against a desk in the front row, arms crossed. Sara and I are in the back, hands cuffed, with Jed watching us.

"Vincent makes a good point," the boy with the missing arm says. I don't know his name. "For all we know this could be a trap. We hand them the crawler, and then all of a sudden, we're ambushed by the Sparkles and captured. Or worse, killed on the spot."

"Also, we can't leave yet," Mia says. "Not without Chloe."

"Ugh, this again." Jed pinches the bridge of his nose. "Mia, we've been over this already. Chloe's not coming back. None of them are."

Mia shoots him a death glare. "You don't know that."

"If they were coming back, they would have already," Jed argues.

"It's your fault we got separated anyway." Mia's chair scrapes the floor as she shoots up. "If we go, they won't be able to find us."

"Mia, I'm sorry." Nina glances from over her shoulder. "But waiting around is just not worth the risk. We're wasting time."

"Wow." Now the glare is aimed at Nina. "You sure are eager to give up on your boyfriend, aren't you?"

Boyfriend? Nina has a boyfriend?

I look to Sara for confirmation. Her answer is a shrug.

Nina throws her head back, exhaling. "For the billionth time—"

"You know what? I don't care," Mia says. "You guys can leave if you want. I'm waiting for Chloe to come back." And out the room she stomps.

So far, this is going *great*.

"Vincent, man," Jed leans back against his chair, stretching his long legs out, "is it so crazy to let them have the deaddamn crawler?

What have *we* managed to do with it? The last time it called infected, they attacked us, too."

"I'm working on it," Vincent argues. "There's no b-button you can press to tame a crawler, and we've already c-come this far. What about you? How much progress d-did you make on that rotten car you're s-supposed to be fixing for us, huh?"

"You're fixing a car?" Sara leans over to find Jed's gaze.

Vincent curses under his breath, and everyone else in the room has varying disapproving expressions. I'm guessing he wasn't supposed to say that.

"I can help," Sara offers.

My eyes snap to her. *She can help?*

Nina pushes off from the desk and turns around. "Is that true?" She's asking *me*.

"Uh…" I'm really not sure. "We've had some driving lessons during AIT, but we're not really experts."

"I've had more practice than that," Sara claims. I try to scan her face for clues, but honestly, considering all the things she kept from me, I'd neither be surprised if this is true, nor shocked if it's not. "Before training. Luke and I used to work at the workshops, back when we were civilians."

"Even if she can actually help us with that," Don breaks his silence at last. He's done nothing but fiddle with his hands and balance his chair on two legs. "Do we even know where we're going? Crossing that bridge would still be risky."

"There are places, though," I blurt out.

Everyone looks at me.

"There's—was someone from our squad, Jayce. He lived in the outside."

"Ashley…" Sara gives me a warning look.

I ignore it. "He said there's this place in the northeast. Crimsonview, Zone Thirteen. It's called the *Red Queen* or something."

"What's the *Red Queen*?" Jed asks.

"It's a cruise ship," Nina answers.

"Wait, you know about it?" I ask.

Nina's quiet as everyone turns to her now. From the looks of it, even her friends didn't know about this. "It's where my parents were headed."

"Your parents?" I pause. "I thought you didn't—"

"Before they were killed," Nina adds. "By the Sparkles."

That catches me off guard. I don't know why I never really thought much about Nina's and Nathan's parents, and how they may have died. This is definitely not what I expected, though. I thought it would have been health issues or something like that.

"Your parents tried to escape?" I hope I'm not crossing a boundary by asking.

Nina nods. That tired look in her eyes dissipates in seconds. A spark of ... hope flashes through them. "Nathan and I were newborns, so we didn't know any of it. But one of their friends told us, when we were old enough. Nathan always wanted to go there. I didn't even believe it existed."

"Well, it does." I lean forward. "And likely there's still people there. Survivors. Or, hell, you could start your own survivor camp."

"With the kind of resources we have?" Nina scoffs. "We're better off getting rid of people than adding more."

"Well, point is, it's possible to make it out here." I hold her gaze firmly, encouraging. She's looked so miserable and exhausted since our encounter at the campus. I don't want her to lose the little touch of life that's returning to her at the thought of finding a place to call home. "And you're all trained, that's an advantage."

"I'll tell you this," Vincent interjects, stepping forward, "how about y-you fix the car for us, and then we'll see about giving you the c-crawler."

"Why don't I do you one better?" Sara challenges. "Show us the crawler, and then I'll consider fixing the car for you."

"Out of the question." Vincent shakes his head, slamming a fist on a desk for emphasis.

"Then I'm not doing a lick of work." Sara relaxes into her chair with a nonchalant shrug. "We haven't heard so much as a screech in all the time we've been here. How do we know you actually have her? We confirm first that you can fulfill your part of the deal, then we see what our options are."

Vincent smirks. "Fair enough. I'll g-give you five seconds. That should be plenty of time." His voice turns grim when he adds, "But if you try anything, I will shoot you. *Both* of you."

I believe him.

Jed undoes our handcuffs, then we follow Nina and Vincent out of the briefing room through a door to the right. We walk into an open office with cubicles then head down a short hallway leading south. The door to the basement is to the right. The staircase is long and cold. We pass through a double door and enter another hallway, so long and dark. Both Nina and Vincent flick their flashlights on and lead us toward a door on the left.

Vincent gives the door a knock. "Justin," he calls, "we're b-bringing the Sparkles in." Then opens the door.

It's a room full of cages stacked atop one another.

Justin shoots up from his chair, stunned, weapon tight in his hold. "Why?"

"They're offering to help us f-fix the car," Vincent explains, "in exchange for the c-crawler."

"Like ... we're gonna give it to them?" Justin's eyes pop. "Are you serious?"

"That depends on if they can fix that c-car first." Vincent gestures for us to come inside.

With Nina tagging along behind, he leads us further in, toward the backside of the room. And there Lori is. Inside one of the cages.

My heart drops to my stomach. I was starting to think we've been chasing air all this time but ... she's really here. Her face is way skinnier than I remember; cheeks sunken, skin framing the outlines of her bones. But she's alive. Her big eyes open wide upon seeing me. She grabs the bars of the cage with clawless hands and rattles it. Does she recognize me?

Vincent kicks the cage. "Back off!"

She shrinks and backs further into the cage. This is so unlike how I remember her from the Pit. Vicious and agile and aggressive.

"And you two," he tells me and Sara. "You stay r-right there. N-Not one step closer."

I hold my hands up defensively. To think we're this close. This close to having her. If I just knew Nina would back us up, Sara and I could take on Justin and Vincent, and we can—No. Stop it, Ashley. Don't do anything stupid. Let's think about this.

"Lori," I say.

"No!" Vincent stands in my face, blocking her from my view. "No t-talking to it—"

"I just want to tell her that Zack is okay—"

Lori responds to that with a shriek.

Vincent pushes me hard. I stumble back and slam into Sara in the process. "Get them out of here, n-now," he tells Nina, then stomps to the cage and kicks it until Lori quiets.

Nina lets out a sigh and gestures for me and Sara to leave with her, and I ever so reluctantly do. The door slams shut behind us.

CRAWLER

THIRTY-FOUR

"YOU AND VINCENT don't get along much, do you?" I ask Nina as we follow her, still in the basement.

"We clash," she says. "Like you and I clashed before."

Through a door, she takes us to a parking garage that's also part workshop, where Jed is already tampering with a vehicle.

Or, well, parts of a vehicle. It's all dismantled, though it vaguely resembles a pickup truck. There's some faded writing, spanning across the driver and passenger doors, that says Police in big letters. Next to it, a round, Highwater Police Department logo.

"This baby here is supposed to be our way out." Nina rests her elbow on the roof of the vehicle. "We've been trying to get it fixed, but we're missing some parts."

"Most roads are blocked. How do you intend on driving something this big around?" Sara asks. "I doubt it will take you that far before you hit a dead end and have to go on foot."

"Like you said, most roads are blocked. But not all of them," Nina says. "We got a map of all the roads that were cleared after the outbreak."

Jed wipes his hands on an old rag, then grabs a piece of paper off a workbench and walks over to us. "Here's a list of what we need." He holds it out to Sara. "We've been trying to salvage parts from some of the vehicles around the street. But I think our best shot is to find a vehicle like this one. I spotted two of them a couple blocks away from here, but there were infected there at the time, and we didn't really have much ammo to take them out. I'm thinking with our latest haul, that won't be a problem."

Sara reads through the list, her eyes narrowing by the second. "Tires, battery, fuel, piston rings, timing belt—and it goes on. So basically, you have nothing. What have you been doing all this time?"

"Figuring out the missing pieces, for one," Jed says. "Listen, I'm no expert, but my dad worked as a mechanic and I sort of picked up a few things from him. So I'm the closest we have to a mechanic here."

Sara walks past Jed and slides into the driver's seat, inspecting the interior of the car. "What the hell did you dismantle the dashboard for? You just gave yourself more work than you actually needed."

Jed swallows. His cheeks flush a darker shade. "'Kay, calm down. I think you've lectured me enough."

"Hardly." Sara gets out of the vehicle, exhaling.

"But it's still fixable, right?" Nina asks.

"As long as we find the stuff that's needed," Sara nods, "yeah, it's fixable. Just don't let Jed remove any more parts. If there's anything left to remove."

"Oh, lord," Jed sighs.

"All right, then." Nina smiles. "I guess we got ourselves a new mechanic."

"Why were you at the university anyway?" I hold the flashlight for Nina while she pops the hood of the vehicle open.

We're in the grocery store through which this police vehicle drove. It's stuck inside the wall, debris scattered around it.

Sara and Jed are taking a look at another one of these vehicles outside, just across the street. Mia is looking around the store for any other resources we can take. The others stayed at the station.

"Resource run," Nina says. "We were already out to scavenge. Almost went back empty-handed. But we saw those choppers fly by and figured it could be a good haul. Then Cody got lost, so we had to stick around longer than we planned to find him."

I try not to be so obvious when I ask, "How do you know he died?"

"I don't." Nina fights a strand of hair dangling in her face while she tries to pull the battery of the vehicle out. The stubborn strand keeps falling over her eye. "But it's a safe bet. We had no choice. We needed to bring those resources back with us."

"Your hair got long." I reach over with my free hand and tuck the strand behind her ear. There. "Ever considered trimming it?"

She side-eyes me. "Why? You don't like it?"

"Oh, no—uh, I think … it looks nice." Maybe I shouldn't talk to Nina about hair. We don't have the best track record discussing that particular topic. "Just maybe not the most practical."

"What would you recommend? Something like your haircut?" She pulls the battery out and then bends down to place it on the floor. "Want me to dye it a crazy color too? Like blue or purple?"

"Well, with your red hair, I think a blonde ombre would look cool. You know, like … a flame."

"Yeah?" She looks up at me from her crouched position, and this time she does cave to the smile tugging at the corners of her mouth. "I'll consider it."

I squint. "You're not gonna make fun of my hair? Or how I've basically kept the same hairstyle all this time?"

"Nope." Nina shakes her head. "If you hadn't, chances are I wouldn't have recognized you, and I'd have blown your brains out on the spot while you were threatening Jed."

"Wow, you've changed so much," I tease. "The Nina I remember would say she'd have no problem leaving me behind to die. She may have even found it exhilarating to shoot me in the head."

"Yeah, well." Nina rises to her feet, hands on her hips. Her voice lowers to a whisper, as if she doesn't even want me to hear it. "Maybe I missed you."

My stomach explodes with warm fuzziness at the confession. I crack a prideful grin. "I knew it."

Nina's timid gaze drops to her feet. "You should go see if Mia needs help. I'll check on Jed and Sara."

"Right. Okay." I give her a nod, then head off deeper into the store, following the low rattling and clattering sounds.

Mia is struggling to grab a toolbox from the top shelf of a rack. She's shorter than I am, and honestly that makes me a little happy.

"Hey." I walk over and grab the toolbox for her. "There you go."

She gives me an unsure look when I offer her the box, but she takes it anyway and sets it down to dig through it. "Thanks." Her eyes are still puffy from all the crying she did prior to us taking off.

She's still not sold on the whole fixing-up-a-car-and-driving-away plan, but she's helping anyway.

I kneel down in front of her. "So, Chloe. Is that...?"

"My sister." Mia's breath hitches. She shakes her head and continues digging through the toolbox with more intensity. I'm not sure she's actually looking for anything in there other than a distraction. "We were trying to find a working car, or parts to fix one up. It was Jed's idea to split up. Said we'd cover more ground, finish faster."

"How long ago was this?" I ask.

"I don't know." Mia squints, thoughtful. "Like a month. More? We had a rendezvous. They never showed up. We went looking for them, but we never found them. And we couldn't keep looking because we saw choppers flying around. We had to get away before they spotted us."

Over a month ago? And no one turned up? Yeah, the odds of their survival aren't so great.

"I know what you're thinking." Mia's pointed gaze shoots up to me. "Your friends are probably thinking the same thing about you and the other girl." She nods vaguely to where Sara is across the street. "But they'd be wrong. You're alive. Both of you. There is no reason why I should believe it's any different for Chloe."

Okay, that's actually a valid point.

"Hold on," Mia reaches into her pocket, "I have a—"

"You two." A panicked Nina hurries toward us. "Get to cover, quick. There's a wave passing by."

Crap.

Outside, Sara and Jed are hurrying to hide inside one of the buildings. Mia's quick to crawl to the next aisle and hide. Nina goes toward a stack of big boxes and I join her.

I sneak a peek from behind the boxes, through the windows of the grocery store. The infected walk across the street, slow. Judging by their build, most of them are roamers, with a few chasers sprinkled about, pausing momentarily to scan their surroundings before continuing.

Their moans aren't agitated, and even if there are trackers in the wave, I don't think any of us have a fresh scent of blood for them to follow.

We sit there until the moans are far, far away, then Nina gives us the signal to move out.

The second I walk out to the street a straggler jumps me. I stumble and fall to the ground. My hands grab at the infected's shoulders, trying to keep it at bay while it snaps its teeth at me with hungry eyes. Mia kicks it off of me and stabs it in the head with a knife. Nina takes my hand and pulls me to my feet.

The three of us still and look in the direction of the wave.

It doesn't seem like they heard.

I breathe out. "Sorry."

Sara and Jed come out from the building they were hiding in and join up with us. They've found some tires and a good engine, which Sara was able to scavenge for the necessary parts. According to them, the battery Nina and I found looks good, too.

We only fill half a canister of gas, though, but it's a good start, so we collect everything and start back. A quick detour on the way. We climb up a fire exit to the rooftop of a building. Nina motions for me to follow her to the ledge while the others sit down to have some snacks.

I rub my arms for some warmth. It's so cold up here.

Nina leans over the parapet with folded arms and nods ahead toward a long bridge, full of abandoned vehicles and brimming with infected. "That's the bridge we wanna cross. We were going to, but then a smartass took some of our resources and ran off, tried to cross it alone. The idiot didn't even make it halfway across before the infected spotted him. He hid inside one of those vehicles. And then minutes later, we heard a gunshot."

"A gunshot?" I ask.

"He killed himself," Nina clarifies. "His body's rotting in there. And the infected are all trying to break in so they can feast on him. He screwed us over in more than one way." Her throat works up. Hands clutched tight around her folded arms. There's worry in her voice and eyes. Hesitance. Uncertainty.

"You know, the first time I climbed a watchpost, I was six," I say, stepping closer to her. "And halfway through, I got so scared because I looked down and saw how high off the ground I was."

Nina turns to me, stray strands of hair dancing to the breeze.

"I was terrified of falling and hurting myself. I started crying. And my dad, he was there with me..." I can't help a small smile at the memory. "He told me, it's okay. He told me to look where I want to be, not where I'm scared to end up. So, I did like he said. I looked up to the top of the watchpost, and imagined myself right there. It took me a few seconds, but then I braced myself and kept climbing up. And I did it. It felt so impossible, but I did it. And I was … so proud of myself. So glad I didn't give up."

Nina's face softens.

"Maybe you can try it, too." I nudge her arm with mine and hold her gaze with a determined, encouraging one, nodding to the bridge. "Look where you want to be. Not where you're scared to end up."

She blushes. Her lips curl into a slow smile—that's twice I got her to smile today, and I'm even more proud of that than I was when I climbed the watchpost. She looks away from me and back in the direction of the bridge. "Thanks."

THIRTY-FIVE

WE GATHER outside the station in the back, where they've set up a fire and are heating up a mix of canned food in a cooking pot.

It's reminiscent of our field-training exercises, when we would build a campfire and set up tents and take turns with watch.

Although Sara and I aren't handcuffed anymore, we're unarmed. Jed and Mia sit close to us with their weapons, supposedly keeping an eye, but they've been busy bickering instead. I guess it's a good thing they don't perceive us as a threat? Well, most of them, that is. Vincent is still shooting us wary glances, but I get the feeling the others are more inclined to trust Nina's instincts than his, which is probably why they're relaxed around us.

"So, then, just to reiterate," says Alan, who I've found out is their medic—or was, until he lost his arm, so now he's training Don to help him, "the plan is to trigger the wave on the bridge, lead it to the station, Ashley and Sara contact SPORE for backup, and we take off with the car and cross the bridge while the wave is at the station?"

"We'll be fine with the crawler." Sara has her knees up to her chest, arms wrapped around her legs. "We can get her to communicate to the infected to stay still and not attack."

"What makes you so confident about getting her to listen to you?" Alan asks.

"We're actually not so confident." I sit cross-legged, hands clasped around my ankles. "But it's the best plan we've got, so…"

Alan squints. "It sounds suicidal."

"It is," Jed agrees. "But, hey, if it gives us a chance to get the hell out of here, I'm all for it."

"This is as good as ready," Don announces. "Everybody grab a bowl."

Once it's my turn, I hold my bowl out to Don and he pours me a ladle of soup. I stare at it, trying to decipher the ingredients. "Is there meat in this?"

"Nope," Don says. "Don't worry. Nina told me you're vegetarian."

"Oh." That takes me aback. Was not expecting Nina to have paid attention to my diet, let alone remember it after all this time. "Thanks." I take my bowl and sit again.

An awful realization hits me when I take that first spoonful. It tastes nothing like the food at Vigor. It's more reminiscent of the food in Kadia. Still, I have to eat.

"How much food do you have left?" Sara asks Nina as she brings her bowl and sits across from me.

"Not a lot." Nina shakes her head sideways. She sits next to me. "We're managing."

"Sara and I can give you our MREs," I say. "It's not much, but it should keep you going for a bit."

"Thanks for the thoughtful offer," Nina says. "We already took them."

Of course they did.

"I wouldn't go back if you offered me the world, but I miss Spheria's food," Mia says.

Everyone lets out noises of agreement, save for Nina. She never did get to try the food they give real soldiers. I bet she'd have loved the hangout. I wonder what her score would have been in Fight Street. She's usually very competitive.

"You guys ever been to Vigor?" I ask.

"Been?" Jed laughs. "Are you kidding me? We practically *lived* there during AIT."

"Right?" I say. "They have food from like, twenty countries or something."

"I miss the arcades," Alan says. "We used them to place bets over who's paying for dinner that night."

"Yeah, duh, what else are you gonna use them for?" Don chuckles.

"That's how they get us," Vincent breaks his silence. "They dangle fancy things in our faces that we didn't even know existed, get us hooked, then exploit us with this promise of a comfortable life to return to every time."

This is the first time Vincent's said something without stuttering once.

"Talk about being a massive downer." Jed smacks the back of Vincent's head playfully. "Come on, man. We're reminiscing. Don't turn this into a philosophical discussion about how all the good things are actually bad, and vice versa. Let us enjoy the lie every now and then. It's all we got."

"Reminiscing is pointless," Vincent says. "It makes you weak, and s-susceptible to deception." Well, that was short-lived. His gaze is on me and Sara, a warning to the others, before he gets up. "I'll go take some food to Justin. You guys enjoy your ... reminiscing."

Silence settles until Vincent disappears back inside, then the chatter resumes.

"How's Melisa doing?" Nina asks, and I think it's because she wants to divert the conversation so as not to sour the mood. Except, this is the worst topic she could have jumped to. I feel sick. "Did she join Comms like she wanted?"

"Melisa's dead," Sara says.

Nina's eyes pop. She looks to Sara, confused, shocked.

"She turned," Sara says. "She was attacked by an Active. In the Pit."

"Oh." Nina's head falls. She stares at the bowl in her hands with a frown. She and Melisa were partners. And even though they didn't get along all that much at first, always argued with one another, it's clear how devastated Nina is at the news. "Is anyone else…?"

I shake my head. "Luke and Haytham and Cris are okay. Cris is with our squad. Luke's with Defense, and Haytham's with Research."

"Good… That's good," Nina says. "Do you still go see Nathan's grave?"

"Yes," I say. "When I can. Yeah."

Nina nods. "I wish I could."

Yeah, I bet. Nina's cries from that night are still vivid in my ears. The way she screamed when all those infected surrounded him. The hollow look in her eyes after, when it was all over.

"We lost so many people since we left our homes," Don says.

"If the Sparkles weren't after us, we could have at least settled somewhere," Jed says. "I'm so tired of running all the time."

"I miss Mom," Don says.

"I miss Dad," Jed says.

"I miss both Mom and Dad," Mia sighs, wiping away a tear. "I wonder how they're doing. Chloe and I never told them that we were ... working for the colonel. Chloe said they'd be safer that way. They would have tried to do something otherwise, to protect us."

Naturally. I still remember what Mom tried to do on the night of recruitment. How she pretended like she had coerced me into escaping. It was all her idea. She was ready to take all of the blame, just so I didn't get exiled. God, I miss her so much. I miss home, even though Kadia's nowhere near as fancy or sophisticated as Spheria. Spheria's like a whole other world. Sometimes it feels so surreal. Like living in a fantasy. A lie. A false version of the real world.

It's not like sitting out here, eating bland food that was scraped together from old cans, enjoying the warmth of the fire against the freezing harsh weather, chatting about whatever.

Sure, we're more exposed to danger out here. The infected's growls are louder and more present. But there's also a sense of freedom. Liberty. Autonomy. Out here, the possibilities are endless.

And as I look at the people around me. At the way Don lightly punches Alan's healthy arm. The way Mia giggles softly at something Jed tells her. The way Nina smiles and shakes her head—I never thought I'd see Nina smiling again, after what happened to Nathan.

All of this reminds me of the days I spent in Basic, with my squad. When it was still whole. When we were all still together, a team.

I don't feel that same connection with my new squad. Not really.

But I guess I wasn't always close with my squad in Basic either, was I? No. In fact, I was actively trying to dodge friendship.

The same way I am now ... just for different reasons.

THIRTY-SIX

THE NEXT DAY, Sara and Jed get started on fixing up the car. Nina and I, despite having no clue what we're doing, assist them—while the others start getting ready for the upcoming journey, making passes through the entire station to see what useful things they may find.

"So, what's going on with you two?" Nina asks me when we take a break.

"Who?" I know who, I'm just stalling.

We're headed back upstairs, Jed and Sara are walking a good distance ahead of us.

"You and Sara," Nina says. "Doesn't seem like you get along like you used to."

Suddenly I miss when Nina hated me and wanted nothing to do with me. "Sure we do. We've never gotten along better."

She gives me a pointed side-eye. "It's none of my business, but surely whatever happened between you two couldn't have been worse than what happened between you and me, right?"

Objectively speaking, yeah, sure, I see her point. But at least Nina wasn't trying to hurt *me* specifically when she turned on us. Nina did what she did because she was coerced into it. Because she didn't have a choice. But no one forced Sara to deceive me. It was all her, and it's as personal as it gets.

"Hey, I have a question for you!" I not-so-subtly change the subject. "Do you know a Connor Brooks?"

Now Nina's pointedly *avoiding* my gaze. "Why?"

"He's in my new squad," I explain. "He asked me about you, said he used to be friends with Nathan."

"Yeah," Nina says. "He also used to be my boyfriend."

"He definitely left out that part." I gape at her. Now I'm very curious. "So, you broke up?"

"What do you think?" she deadpans.

"Right." I swallow. Okay, Ashley, tread very carefully around this subject. "Did you break up before you joined training?"

"You don't need to know."

"Okay, so if I see him again," I say, "should I not tell him that I saw you?"

Nina breathes out. "Ash, what do you want?"

"Nothing, I'm just … making conversation." I let out an awkward laugh. Between Connor and the boyfriend Mia mentioned, I really didn't think Nina was into, well, *relationships* as a whole. "He doesn't seem like your type."

"Oh." She turns to me with arched brows. "What do you think my type is?"

"I don't know," I say. "Do you even have one?"

She huffs. "This is stupid."

"There you go." I smile. "That's more like it."

Nina rolls her eyes. I bet she regrets not leaving me out there to die.

"What was your nickname?" I ask. "No, wait, let me guess. Was it Red? Freckles?"

A hint of amusement seeps into her at last. I take that as a win. "No. Connor doesn't give *superficial* nicknames to his girlfriends. Mine was Huffy."

Huh. Well, I can't say that doesn't fit her. It's actually spot on. That's funny, the only other person who has a non-superficial nickname like that is—

Lucille.

Oh.

Now I have more questions, but something tells me Nina's patience won't last through the first five, so I keep my mouth shut.

Jed and Sara go to get some water while Nina and I head to the training room, where they're keeping the resources. It also looks like where most of them sleep. At least, judging by all the sleeping bags and the rucksacks placed next to them, it is.

"Oh, thank God you're here!" Don shoots up from his chair where he sits by a storage closet. "I really need to pee. Can you keep watch for a minute?"

"Sure," Nina says. "We're just gonna see what our lunch options are."

Don gives a thumbs-up and hurries out the door.

Sara's and my gear is probably here. Maybe, if I'm sneaky enough, I can get my hands on a—Wait, nope. Why am I thinking about this? No. We have a plan. We'll stick to it. Nina wouldn't have brought me here if she didn't trust me.

I stand beside her, rubbing my hands together and blowing air into my palms while she undoes the locks to the storage closet.

"Still cold?" Nina shoots me a look from over her shoulder.

"It's freezing," I say. "How aren't *you* freezing?"

"You privileged people wouldn't last a week out here without the Sparkles keeping you fed and warm," she grumbles. "I got a sweater in my ruck. Go grab it."

"Which one is your ruck?"

"The one by the center window." She nods toward it.

"Thanks." I give her a smile and walk over to it. Kneeling down, I unzip the big pocket. Don't have to dig much. The crumpled sweater is right there, though as I pull it out, a few things fall out with it, mostly trash—I think. "You're so messy. You should clean up a little. Why do you have all these empty wrappers in here?"

"Duh, because you're not supposed to litter," Nina says.

I throw the sweater on. It smells like decades of unwashed sweat, but it's an extra layer of clothes so I'm not going to complain. I'm about to put back the stuff that fell out when I notice that one of them is a name patch. Not Nina's, though. The last name on it says Sanford. Another look inside the ruck, there's more.

I take them out, a whole handful, and flip through them. Most of them are covered in dry blood. "What are these?"

Nina leans over, glancing at me from behind the doorway of the storage closet. The frown pops on her face immediately. She walks back into the room with a few cans of food in her hands. "I took them off the Sparkles I…"

I finish that sentence in my head.

"Why are you collecting them?" I ask. "What are they? Trophies?"

"Not trophies." Nina sets the cans down on one of the desks and walks over to me. "Everyone deserves a proper burial, Ash. But we can't really do that. We can't just carry the dead with us to bury them. I figured the least I could do is ... take their name patches. Carry them with me. So there's someone who remembers them."

Huh. I never took Nina for the sentimental type, but I guess everyone copes with having blood on their hands differently. My preferred way is to forget it ever happened.

"Just put them back," she says.

And I probably should. I'm probably better off doing just that, but instead I continue flipping through them, reading all the names. I'm sure these don't cover everyone. Still, I look for the name I'm hoping not to find, until I find it.

My breath catches.

PFC. Serrano.

The rest of the patches fall from my hands. The dry bloodstains paint too vivid an image in my head. Half a face missing. The walls and floor colored in red. Bits and pieces of flesh scattered about. A gunshot entry wound at the back of the head.

"What's up?" Nina asks.

I look up to meet her eyes, but all I see is Jose's messed up face. Her lifeless corpse left in a lifeless place. Acid shoots up my throat.

"Ash, are you—?"

And before I know it, I jump Nina with a punch.

THIRTY-SEVEN

A JOLT of pain explodes through my knuckles. Nina stumbles back.

She steadies herself against the desk. "Ash, what the hell are you doing?"

"It was you?" I grab her by the collar, hook my right leg to hers and pull swiftly to knock her down, throwing my weight at her for extra force. We land on the wooden floor with a hard thud, and I'm quick to straddle her and wrap my hands around her neck. "You killed Jose?!"

Nina grabs my wrists, nails digging into my skin, trying to break my grasp. A few months back, she would have so easily tossed me around like a bag of dirty laundry. But she's weak, and I'm not. "You're gonna have to be … more specific than that."

"Ash, what are you doing?" Sara rushes into the room with Jed. She grabs me and pulls me off Nina by force, while Jed helps Nina to her feet. I try to break out of Sara's grasp, but she throws me behind her. "What is wrong with you?" She turns to me.

"She killed Jose!" I shout.

"So what?" The indifference in Sara's voice shocks me. "Nina also killed Olivia and Kent. You know, the two riflemen you and Cris replaced?"

That hits me like a slap in the face.

"She probably killed those Hummingbirds' pilots we found, too," Sara continues. "Jed and Don definitely helped her with that."

Jed watches us with a guilty look. He doesn't protest.

"The fugitives killed many of our comrades, starting from when we were in the Pit, but that didn't make you any less eager to work with Nina, did it?" Sara shakes her head. "Nothing is different now. Jose is another one of our many comrades they killed. Her life mattered as much as anyone else's. You don't decide whose life is worth getting angry over and whose isn't."

"Screw you, Sara. Jose was your friend, too."

"No. Screw *you*, Ashley," she says. "You wanted to team up with the enemy. We were doing that. Don't screw us over now just because you got a little emotional."

"Nina?" Mia comes rushing into the office, the others right behind her. Justin is the only one missing. "What's going on?"

Nina rubs her bruised face. "Nothing."

"Nothing?" Mia aims her weapon at me and Sara, wary. "Did they attack you?"

"Mia, put your weapon down," Nina says.

"What the hell?" Mia gasps. "They did attack you, didn't they? Why are you protecting them?"

"That's a good q-question, Mia," Vincent says. "*Why* are you p-protecting them? Especially *her*." He nods at me. "We both know what she did."

"Vince." Jed shakes his head at him. "Come on, man. We have a plan."

"Mia," Vincent ignores him, "can I borrow that photo of yours for a second?"

"Vincent, don't," Nina warns.

Mia hesitantly lowers her weapon and digs into her pocket, pulling out a torn, crumpled photo. Vincent takes it, then walks over to me.

"I'm hoping you have a good m-memory." Vincent holds the photo out to me and Sara. "But I can j-jog it for you, if not."

It's a photo of two girls. One is Mia, with her short brown bob. Her face looks fuller here, rounder. The other girl is slightly taller, brown hair in a tight ponytail, and … and I recognize her.

Add a few scratches on her face, some dirt, switch out her neat uniform with a dirty, ragged one, the clean ponytail with a few messy strands sticking out…

It's that girl.

From the auto-parts store.

"That's Chloe, Mia's s-sister." Vincent points. "Do you remember her?"

The girl who almost shot Cris.

The girl I shot to protect him.

"What about Henry and Oliver?" he adds. "Remember them?"

The boys that were there. The one I shot and the one who was already dead.

A sour taste burns my throat. I'm going to throw up.

"The Raven told me, weeks ago," Vincent says. I don't know who the Raven is. "That you k-killed both Chloe and Henry in cold blood."

In seconds, Mia's eyes fix on me with horror, rage and loathing. The resemblance is clear as day. She and Chloe are so alike. That's *why* Mia looks familiar.

My hands shake uncontrollably. I try so hard to keep my breathing as even as possible. But it's hitting me like a rapid sequence of gunfire.

I killed that girl.

No, she wasn't just a girl.

Chloe.

I killed Chloe. Chloe who had a sister waiting for her. Chloe who must have been doing everything she could to survive out there, so she could see Mia again. And I … made sure she wouldn't. And Henry… I look to Nina, the hidden pain in her eyes. Is that the supposed boyfriend Mia mentioned before? I killed him too. I killed both of them.

But I had to. I had no choice. Hell, they would've killed Cris—and me. Chloe shot me.

Just like Will shot me, and I killed him. To protect myself. It's not my fault. It's not like I wanted to kill them. Or did I? I didn't stop to think it through, or figure out what I wanted. I just acted. I had to act fast. I couldn't spare a second to think.

"I was going to t-tell you, Mia." Vincent turns to her now, while everyone else is quietly staring between him and me. Don looks uncertain, scared. Alan is eyeing me with almost as much disdain as Mia is right now. "But Nina talked me out of it. Said it'd be b-best to keep this from you, leave you with your naive h-hope."

Jed curses under his breath. Judging by his lack of shock, he probably knew, too. His hand falls from Nina's shoulder and reaches somewhere behind him.

"Well, now the rat's finally out of the d-dumpster." Vincent looks to Nina. "I thought I'd trust your judgment, but then you went and b-brought our friends' killer right into our hideout. Not only that, you want to give her the crawler that we've been r-risking our lives for months to keep."

Oh, no. This is all going to hell way too fast.

"Do you know what that makes you to us, Nina?" Vincent's hand settles on the sidearm holstered to his belt. "A traitor."

"Yeah." If only that hard stare Nina's giving him could kill. "The Sparkles labeled me that first."

"Guys," Don tries, "why don't we all calm down? Clearly there's bad blood on both sides here, but this doesn't have to get ugly."

Mia's weapon is back up in a beat. Shaky hands. Glistening eyes. Tears on the verge of falling. Within seconds, everyone draws out their weapons. Jed and Nina on one side. Vincent, Alan, and Mia on the other. Don's the only one, other than me and Sara, who's not holding a weapon.

"Guys." Don steps between the groups. "Please."

"Get out of the way, Don," Mia tells him with trembling lips, looking past him and straight at me.

Alan has his weapon aimed at me and Sara.

"Drop your weapons, Nina," Vincent says. "If you want to—"

Nina shoots a ruthless bullet through Alan's head.

THIRTY-EIGHT

IT GIVES me and Sara the chance to duck seconds before the room explodes in gunfire.

"We need to get to Lori," Sara tells me as we hide behind a desk. "Fast."

I take a peek from behind the flipped desk. Don is wrestling Mia on the floor, fighting her for her M4. She kicks him off her, but he clings to the weapon and manages to snatch it out of her hold. He tosses it across the room, and it lands close to me.

"Ash." Nina kicks it the rest of the distance. "Move it." She gestures to a door behind her and Jed. "We'll cover you."

I grab the M4 just before Mia stands back up and starts toward me. She comes to an instant halt when I point the weapon at her, but I can't even place my finger on the trigger. My whole body freezes. Chloe's face flashes before my eyes: haunting, resentful, terrified.

My chest shrinks. My breathing sharpens. My hands shake uncontrollably.

Nina comes out of cover ready to shoot, but Mia jumps out of her line of fire and joins up with Vincent. They both run out through the front door. Sara grabs my arm and pulls me with her toward the back door, while Nina hurriedly fetches Alan's weapon.

Jed and Don follow us.

"This is a mess." Don's on the verge of tears. "How did it come to this so fast?"

"Because Vincent never planned on letting them take the crawler, that's how," Nina says as she joins us. She holds the handgun she took off Alan to Sara.

"Nina," Sara accepts the handgun and does a quick check of the ammo, "how do we get to Lori from here?"

"There's only one staircase to the basement from the inside," Nina says. "The only other way would be through the garage door, from outside."

"We have to get there before they do," Sara says.

"So, let's split up," Nina says. "Jed, Don—you try and go through the garage. Sara, Ashley and I will go in through the basement."

"I don't want to kill them," Don cries. "We've been together for months. I don't want to kill them anymore than I want to kill you."

"They're going to kill *you* if you don't," Nina tells him.

"You shouldn't have shot Alan, Nina," Don tells her, and my mind flashes back to Cris scolding me for shooting that boy—Henry. "We could have talked things out."

"Not if you know Vincent," Nina says. She doesn't waste another second. She takes the lead. Sara and I go right behind her.

The second we come out of the break room to the main hall, bullets zoom past us. We scramble across to the other side, firing back from the hip.

Nina takes us through the hallway of the holding cells to the back of the building, and from there we cut through the evidence room, then come out straight into the hallway leading to the basement. We move quickly and carefully, checking our corners. Clear for now, though I can't tell if it's because they beat us to the basement or because they went outside. The lack of gunfire isn't reassuring either way.

Nina pushes the door slowly, its creak echoing through the empty stairwell.

Sara watches our backs while we proceed downstairs, plunging into darkness. Then through the next double door and into the stretch of a hallway. No one in sight.

"Something isn't right," Sara says. "Surely Justin heard all the noise?"

"He's probably hiding somewhere," Nina says. "Just cover our backs. Ash and I will check the kennels."

My grip on the M4 is still shaky. I don't know if I'm going to be able to shoot anyone, so I pray I don't have to.

Once again, Nina takes the lead. I take one side of the door and she takes the other, weapons at the ready, before she opens the door to the kennels. Silent darkness is all there is. Nina flicks on her flashlight and tosses it into the room to light up the place. Nothing happens. She barges in and I follow behind her.

The cage is empty. Justin's not here.

"Dammit," I curse. "Where the hell is he?"

Upon closer inspection of the cage, I spot a boxy device in there, with some kind of timer, fast approaching zero.

"Is that…"

"Ash!" Nina tackles me seconds before an explosion erupts, tossing us across the room and against a stack of cages.

I fight through a coughing fit and an agonizing pain in my head as I pick myself up.

"You have explosives?!" I bark at Nina beside me.

"Why's that a surprise?" She grabs onto one of the cages to help herself stand, her balance somewhat shaky. "Did you forget that time we exploded an entire street of buildings?"

Okay, to be fair, Zack gets credit for the Double Wave Attack more than anyone else. It's easy to forget he couldn't have done it in the first place without Lotiva.

The sound of a garage door opening. Nina and I take the back door into the garage and catch Sara sprinting after Justin, who has a motionless Lori strapped to his back.

"What's wrong with her?" I ask. "Tell me he didn't kill her…"

"No, likely just tranqed," Nina says.

We can't shoot him and risk hurting Lori in the process. Justin, however, opens fire at us randomly, sending us dodging to the sides. He makes it out through the garage, but Sara doesn't give the chase a break.

Nina and I join her once we've regained our balance.

A few infected are headed toward us. No doubt drawn by the shouting and gunfire and invited by the wide-open garage. No sign of Don anywhere. It's only Jed outside, coming from the right side where the main entrance is. He's an impressively fast runner, catches up with Sara in seconds, and the two of them keep going after Justin.

Then Vincent comes out of cover from behind a car and shoots. Jed tackles Sara to the ground, rolling them both behind another car for cover.

Nina opens fire at him but misses all of her shots. She doesn't even notice the infected coming from her left. I shoot it before it attacks her. Then I fire five consecutive shots at more of the infected surrounding the street.

Glad to know I don't freeze with the infected, too. Only problem is, they keep showing up. Justin's already caught up to Vincent and Mia and they're running away.

"Ash…" Nina takes a clumsy hold of my arm. "We gotta get back."

"But they're getting away—"

"Now," she grunts. "Before they surround us."

I turn to her, and that's when I see the trail of blood on the side of her head. Crap. "Nina?"

She collapses against me, and even though she's much skinnier than before, her weight still sends me stumbling back. I wrap my arms around her and plant my feet hard.

Sara's crouched beside Jed, who's slumped against the car with clenched teeth. He's keeping a tight hold around his arm, blood trickling between his fingers. Dammit.

Nina clutches my sweater with weak fingers, turning her head to the side before vomit bursts out of her mouth. Her legs cave, and as she falls, she drags me with her.

I hold her face in one hand, nudging her to look at me, but her head is so wobbly, she can't look at me straight. "You're gonna be okay." I hope—pray. Please let her be okay.

THIRTY-NINE

WE BRING Nina and Jed inside through the garage. Sara takes care of closing the door before the infected manage to get in, while Jed helps me, with his one healthy arm, drag Nina through the hallway and up the stairs.

"Don!" Jed shouts. "Don! We need help!"

"Where is he?" I ask.

"He didn't wanna fight them. I told him to stay back," Jed says, grunting. "Man, this hurts."

Don meets us halfway and helps me carry Nina so Jed can focus on walking and keeping pressure on his wound. We go back to the training room, where Alan's corpse is still on the floor, blood pooling under his head.

I lay Nina on her sleeping bag while Don goes to grab a medkit from the storage. She's not fully passed out, but she's not fully conscious either.

"Nina," I try anyway, holding a finger before her eyes and moving it from one side to the other. "Can you see how many fingers I'm holding up?"

She can barely follow my finger, and whatever it is she says, it comes out as a nonsensical jumble.

"I swear we had more things. Vincent and the others must have taken some resources. I don't know if this'll be enough." Don brings me the medkit and sits beside me. "Is she gonna be okay?"

"It's a concussion, most likely," I say. "She must have hit her head pretty hard because of the explosion."

I clean her wound with an alcohol pad, put some dressing on, then wrap a bandage around her head.

"I don't know how I would take care of them on my own," Don says. "Alan was our medic. He was teaching me stuff but…"

"Get her some water and keep an eye on her," I tell him as I move on to Jed.

Jed's sitting on the floor, leaning against the wall. I take out his sheathed combat knife and use it to tear open his sleeve, exposing the wound. The bleeding doesn't look too bad, and the bullet didn't go through.

"How does it feel?" I ask Jed.

"Like I was shot in the arm," he deadpans.

"Yeah, no kidding," I press my thumb lightly near the entry wound, and he winces. "How do you feel when you move your arm? Does it feel like it hit a bone?"

"How the hell am I supposed to know that?" Jed blinks. He sucks in quick, sharp breaths through his teeth. "It hurts. That's all I can tell you."

"Right." I borrow a flashlight from Don and use it to get a better look at the wound. I can kind of see the bullet. It didn't go too far in. "It *looks* like it only hit muscle."

Jed just stares at me. "I don't know what that means."

"Best to leave it in," I tell Jed. "Without proper equipment, trying to pull it out is likely gonna cause more damage right now."

"So, what?" His brows pinch when he looks at me again. "I'm just gonna be hanging around with a bullet in my arm?"

"Yes, more or less." I nod. There is no sugarcoating this. "If you're lucky, maybe your body will eventually push it out."

"That's disgusting." Jed grimaces.

I clean his wound as best I can and apply some dressing while he tries hard not to wince at every little thing I do.

"You're gonna have to keep the dressing and the wound clean and dry." I reach for a bandage next to wrap around his arm. "Take antibiotics. Get some rest. Don't do any heavy lifting or the sort."

"Does the heavy lifting in question include fixing one old vehicle in the garage?" Jed asks.

"Yeah, about that." Sara finally joins us, slightly out of breath.

"There was another explosive. Justin was probably trying to set it up but ran out of time. He did destroy the battery, though."

"Seriously?" Jed turns to look at her, wincing in the process. "Man—"

"Sara, can you please forget about the deaddamn car for one minute?" I turn to her with narrow eyes. "Right now, we need more medical resources."

"I already told you, this is all we got," Don says.

"No, it's not," I remind him. "Nina left some resources behind, didn't she? In the sewers? She probably left some medical supplies, too. It's not that far from here, and the route was relatively safe. You and Sara can go grab them quickly."

Don looks to Sara, uncertain.

"Okay," Sara answers. "I can do that. What else?"

"Should probably," I nod toward Alan's corpse, "see what he may have had on him and then … move the body elsewhere. If there are trackers with the infected outside, they're all gonna be drawn to the blood here. Meaning, they won't stop coming and soon they'll have the whole station surrounded. So, we'll need to get rid of them. See if we got any blood rounds, here or in that stash Nina left. It might be smart to fire a few away from here, give the infected a fresh trail to follow."

"Good idea." Sara nods. "Is that all?"

"Yeah, that's all," I say. "Just … be safe."

Sara gives me a nod. She takes care of looting Alan's body while Don prepares a few things for their journey, then they take off.

I sit by Nina, watching her closely. She's fully passed out now, and I'm sure that most of it is out of exhaustion and probably hunger.

Jed's lying on his side, wincing every now and then. "She'll be okay, right?"

"As long as her symptoms don't get worse," I say.

"But you're a medic, aren't you? You can look after her?" Jed asks.

"I'm not an official SPORE medic, no." I shake my head. "Trained with Mom, at the hospital in Kadia. She'd be a lot more help to her than I am."

But I know exactly what my mom would say if she were here. The same thing she always said. *You got it, honey. You don't even need my help anymore.*

"There's only so much you can do with the resources we got, anyway," Jed says. "I'm sure you're doing your best."

"How would you know?" I raise my brows at him. "You don't know me. You can't trust me like that. How do you know I'm not making it worse for her? Or that I didn't give her something to kill her in her sleep?"

"I doubt Nina risked her life to protect someone who'd kill her in her sleep," Jed says.

"Yeah, well... If she hadn't done that, she'd probably be fine right now."

"I'm sure she doesn't regret it," Jed says. "I don't care what Vincent or the Sparkles call us, Nina's one of the most loyal people I've ever met. She's loyal to the people that matter. The people she cares about. I can't tell you how many times she saved my life. Even Vincent wouldn't be alive without her. He was a team leader, before, but really Nina's been more of a leader to us than he's been."

I noticed. It's a little bit funny, considering how unsociable Nina used to be. I'm sure this was more out of necessity than anything. She couldn't survive out here all alone. She had to do the one thing she hated most: depend on people.

I reach over and tuck her loose hair behind her ear. Nathan would be proud of her. He'd be happy to know that she's still alive. Still fighting. That she kept going, even without him by her side.

"Which one was her boyfriend?" I ask. "Was it Henry? The one I…"

I don't really want to know. I don't want to know that I possibly killed the only person Nina opened her heart to. The one person she found comfort in while out here. I don't want to know that I'm the reason behind that tired, miserable face she was wearing when we met.

"I don't know that Nina would officially call him that, but … yeah." Jed nods. "She and Henry were close, from what I could tell anyway. You know Nina. She's very allergic to public displays of affection."

Yeah, but I guess not so allergic to affection itself.

FORTY

SARA AND DON come back without a scratch. As suspected, there were extra medical resources in the ruck they brought, and I keep them next to Nina, just in case. I leave Don with her and Jed so Sara and I can inspect everything else we have at our disposal.

"What are we gonna do?" Sara asks. "Vincent and the others could be anywhere now. We had our chance to get Lori and we lost it."

"Do you guys have any idea where Vincent might be headed?" I ask. "Can we track him?"

"Well, I don't think he'd be headed to our original destination," Jed says.

"He mentioned a place before," Don says. "A nuclear power plant... Right, Jed? Didn't the Raven say something about that for a rendezvous point?"

"Who the hell is the Raven?" I ask. That's the second time they used that name.

Don and Jed exchange a look.

"It's ... someone who's been in contact with us," Jed says. "From within. Giving us intel. Well, Vincent's the only one who ever spoke to this person. He's the only one with a portor that's still connected to the Hum."

"I thought the Hum was gone? Wiped out?"

"Yeah, it was," Jed says. "But not before they backed it up somewhere with someone."

"Do you know who it is?" Sara asks. "This Raven? Are they with the Renegades? Someone else?"

"Vincent didn't tell us much about who they are. Only that they don't want Rodríguez to get the crawler, and that's really all we needed to know."

So, Lucille was right after all. There is a traitor in our midst.

"Where is this power plant?" Sara asks.

"And if I tell you that, will you still help us fix the car?" Jed asks. "Or are you just gonna kill us all and run off? Would be very easy with Nina passed out, me with my arm and Don being a crybaby."

"I'm not a crybaby," Don protests, though his eyes are still red from all the tears.

Sara lets out a sigh. She goes quiet for a moment too long as her gaze flits to me, and I catch a hint of guilt in it. "There is a car," she says. "In that place we went to before. It was in relatively good shape. Battery seemed intact, too."

"Wait..." Jed leans forward. "That's not what you said when I ask—"

"I thought Ashley and I could use it," Sara confesses, wrapping an arm around herself. "If we managed to run away."

Of course she did.

"Anyway," Sara continues. "We can salvage that battery, probably, and replace the broken one."

"Probably?" Jed asks, doubtful.

"Yes, probably," Sara says. "Which is a lot better than unlikely."

"All right," Jed says. "Well, I can't go anywhere like this..."

"Why don't we get some rest for the day?" I say. "I don't see the point in going back out there right now, when we're all low energy."

"I'll see about making us something quick to eat," Don says.

"I think someone should still keep watch," Sara says. "I'll do a quick run around the station, make sure Vincent and the others didn't leave any more surprises for us."

"Let me come with you." Jed pulls to his feet.

"You're hurt." Sara frowns. "You should be resting."

"Yeah, well, I still have one healthy arm," Jed says. "I can handle a sidearm, and if you do run into infected, you'll need help."

"Not really, I'm very capable," Sara says.

"I'm coming, either way," Jed insists.

"What were you thinking anyway?" Sara's eyes narrow on him as they start. "Why would you—" A frustrated breath. "Why would you take a bullet for me? You should have dodged. I could have protected myself."

Jed shrugs, then winces immediately at the motion. "Guess I wasn't really thinking then."

"There." Don walks over to me with a couple cans. The ones Nina got out earlier. "Some bean soup would be nice. Keep us warm. I'll go get started on it. Are you gonna be okay alone?"

"Yeah." I nod. I guess no one wants to take a break, then. "I have to keep an eye on Nina."

"Okay." Don gives me a small, sad smile before heading off.

He eventually comes back with soup for everyone, though Sara decided to take first watch outside, so after forcing myself to finish my bowl and making sure Nina's sleeping soundly, I head out to take over for Sara so she can get some food in her, too. And because I desperately need some fresh air. I climb up the makeshift watchpost where she's at. The street's clear now. They managed to lure the infected away earlier when she and Don went out.

"Food is ready." I tell her. "You should go eat."

"Okay," Sara says, but she doesn't budge. She probably needed some alone time, too.

"I'm sorry I messed everything up," I say.

Sara turns around. "Things would have likely gone to hell sooner or later, if what Nina said about Vincent is true."

Yeah, I guess.

Still, I feel so stupid. Seeing Jose's name patch ... I couldn't control my anger. Her messed-up face flashes before me. I wish ... I wish I could picture her face before. I wish I wasn't stuck with all these ugly versions of my friends in my head. I wish I could remember them when they were still full of life.

I slide down to the floor and sit with my back to the railing, a hand clutched around my stomach. I don't know how long those beans are gonna stay inside. "At least she didn't turn," I murmur. "Jose, I mean. She always wondered how she'd die. Always said the worst way to go would be if ... she got tackled by infected and ripped apart. She always worried it would be a slow death. Painful."

"Yeah." Sara sits next to me, draping her arms over raised knees. "We should get some chocolate milkshake at Mr. Tooley's, in her memory."

I smile at the thought, but regret is quick to rip the smile off me. I wish I'd been honest with her, on our last day. I wish I'd told her that I'd miss her. A lot.

"How would you wanna die?" I absently start to lean against Sara, but catch myself before I rest my head on her shoulder. "Do you ever think about that?"

"I don't care how I die," she says, "as long as it's for a good reason."

"Like what?" I ask. "Turning yourself to bait and leading a wave of infected away from your comrades?"

She shrugs. "As long as it's for a good reason."

I can't help but roll my eyes. That's such a Sara answer.

"How would *you* wanna die?" she asks.

"I don't know." I shake my head. "I don't want to die."

"Yeah, well, it's too bad we don't really have a say in that," Sara sighs. "It's just a matter of time."

FORTY-ONE

I DON'T REMEMBER FALLING asleep on the watchpost, just that I told Sara to go get some rest, that I would take over for her, but when I wake up, I have a SPORE shirt draped over me and a nutrient bar beside me.

It's only when a shadow moves from the corner of my eye that I see Nina standing there, leaning against the railing.

"Nina!" I gasp, shooting to my feet immediately. "You're up. Why aren't you resting? You should be—"

"I'm fine," she says, looking at me from over her shoulder. "I can't even begin to count how many concussions I had over the past months. I'll live."

"That's actually worse. Repeated head injuries are nothing to take lightly—"

"I'm okay," she says. "Take a breath."

I take a breath, then let out a frustrated one in exchange.

"The others are passed out. Thought someone should be keeping an eye on the perimeter," she says. "Thanks for … you know, taking care of me and Jed."

"Yeah, no problem." I step toward the railing and stand beside her.

Nina looks at me, lips parted, though it takes a second before anything comes out. "You know… Sometimes I wonder why you let me go."

"Sometimes I wonder that, too," I confess. "But I know I don't regret it."

Her lips quiver. "Even though I killed your friend?"

"Nina, you *are* my friend."

"Right." Nina's face turns a shade warmer, like it always does when she's caught in the occasional vulnerable moment, and I've caught her in a few so far. She tucks her long bangs behind her ears, revealing that bruise on her cheek. The one from when I punched her.

I nod at it. "Does it hurt?"

"Just a bit. But it's a unique blush shade, so I'll say that." Nina snorts. "You sure like punching me, huh?"

It takes me a second to remember what she's referring to, but then it hits me. It happened twice before. Once during one of our assignments in Basic. She'd said something that pissed me off, and I punched her. Sara and Nathan pulled us away from each other before Sgt. Seidel got there. And the second time was in the Pit, when I found out she betrayed us.

That feels like it was years ago. Something I can actually laugh at now. And I do. "You kinda had it coming, every time, so…"

"I don't even remember what I said the first time," Nina says.

"Honestly, me neither," I admit.

She reaches into her pocket and digs out something—a name patch. Jose's. "Do you want to keep it? She was your friend."

She wasn't my friend, I want to say, because that's what I always said to Jose. To myself. But it's not true. It … couldn't be further from the truth.

"If you want to have it, there's no reason for me to keep it," she says. "I'm sure it would mean much more if someone who knew her had it."

I swallow a lump and take the name patch. "Thanks."

Did the others manage to recover her body? Or any of the bodies for that matter? Did they send her back home and give her a proper burial? Does she have a grave I can visit, or is this name patch all that's left of her? I don't know if I should hold onto it or give it to her family. I'm not sure how much they'll appreciate having a bloodsoaked name patch to remember her by.

"For what it's worth, I'm sorry." The sincerity in Nina's voice is undeniable. Her lips press together and eyes close, chin falling to her chest. "Look, Ash, it's … a complicated mess that we're in. Everyone's to blame and no one's to blame. You killed our people, we killed yours."

"Our people," I repeat. "Your people." The words taste sour in my mouth. "People. We killed ... people."

The iciness in my body makes me stiff. Just a few months ago, I couldn't even kill infected. Just a few months ago I froze because I saw too much humanity in the eyes of a tracker. Now ... I don't even blink when killing *humans*.

Cris was right. Who the hell have I let myself become? What the hell do I even stand for?

You're not supposed to freeze, Regi screams at me. *That's what gets you killed. That's what gets all of us killed.*

Stop it. Just stop it. Stop telling me that. I stopped freezing. I don't freeze anymore. I don't think anymore. I just kill. I'm a mindless, heartless, coldblooded killer. Just what SPORE wanted me to be. So stop it. What else do you want from me?

"You can't save everyone," Nina murmurs, scooting a little closer to me, until our arms touch. "But maybe that doesn't really mean much, coming from me. I already lost all my family, so it is what it is." A deep sigh. "Forbear and forgo."

I blink at those words, and turn to her, curious.

"What?" She side-eyes me.

"Nothing, just..." I shake my head. The memory is distant and yet so vivid. "Nathan said that before. On our first day in Spheria. Cris and I thought he meant to say 'forgive and forget.'"

"No." Nina snickers. "It's a Lotivan saying. Because you can't exactly forgive what happens there. You can't forget it, either. So you just have to forbear and forgo."

"Forbear and forgo," I repeat. It's ... not a bad saying.

A quiet moment passes.

"Hey, Ash, listen." She swallows. The warmth in her cheeks is echoed in the brown of her eyes as they try and evade mine. "You probably don't need me to say this but ... if you ever find yourself in trouble with the Sparkles for breaking a rule or two, and you start thinking you have nowhere to run, just remember that you do."

And now the warmth is spreading to my stomach. It's so surreal, hearing heartwarming words from Nina, but not surprising at all. I always knew she had a soft heart.

"Assuming we make it to the *Red Queen* in one piece," she says, "and assuming we can set camp there. You'll always have a place with me."

"Thanks." I smile. "And I hope you remember that not every Spore is bad. There are good people, too. Friends."

"I know." She furrows her brows. "That's why I'm telling *you* this."

I blush. Okay. It's definitely weird hearing Nina be nice.

"Come with me for a sec," she says. "I wanna give you something."

FORTY-TWO

THE FOLLOWING days are spent fixing up the car. With Nina back on her feet, we're able to venture out and retrieve the battery from the other police vehicle. We move stealthily between the station and the car, because an encounter with the infected is the last thing on our to-do list—*literally*.

Sara does most of the work, with Jed taking on the assistant role despite the injured arm. Turns out he's a very stubborn guy, so we leave him to it because three arms are definitely better than two. Nina, Don and I chip in when we're not busy looking for resources, scavenging the nearby areas and occasionally venturing further than is probably wise.

Nina says that when they get to the bridge, they might be able to retrieve the resources that one fugitive stole with him. So, there is that.

Don's out on the watchpost, and I'm just finishing up a patrol with Nina when the rumble of an engine reaches us. Not a second is wasted before we bolt for the basement.

As soon as we make it downstairs, we sprint down the hallway. Nina pushes the door to the garage and rushes in. "That sounds promising."

"Hell, yeah, it does!" Jed smacks the hood of the vehicle with a bright grin.

Sara smacks his hand once she comes out of the driver's seat. "Be gentle," she scolds. "We *just* brought her back to life."

"Sorry." Jed removes his hand from the hood. "Anyway, forget I ever called myself a mechanic. Sara here is an actual expert."

Sara wipes her dirty hands on an even dirtier cloth. "It's in decent shape, but we didn't find enough fuel so likely it won't be able to take you too far. The smart thing to do would be to make a stop somewhere to look for gas before it breaks down in the middle of nowhere and you're stuck with a wave or something."

"Right." Nina leans on one foot, arms crossed. "How long do you think it'll last?"

"I don't know," Sara says. "Twenty minutes. Half an hour, if we're pushing it."

Nina clicks her tongue. "That's not much at all."

"No, it's not." Jed agrees.

"Okay, we don't have much to pack," Nina says, "so we can probably take off in the morning—"

"Guys!" Don's voice comes through the radio strapped to Nina's waist. "Uh, I have some bad news. There was a wave passing by, and the infected may or may not have heard the engine because now they're all headed here."

I toss my head back. "You've got to be kidding me."

Nina pulls up the radio and holds it to her mouth. "How big is the wave?"

"Pretty big," Don says. "Like, more ammo than we can spare, big."

Sara slips back into the driver's seat and kills the engine. In a couple minutes, we're back upstairs and running out to the front yard of the station. No need to get on the watchpost to see it. The wave is visible from across the street. The stragglers are just a block away.

"Maybe they'll leave if we hide inside?" Sara suggests.

"I don't think that's just a wave," Nina says. "That's *the* wave. From the bridge."

"How do you know?" Sara asks.

"Been watching it for a while. I recognize some of these infected," Nina says.

"Okay," I say, "but if that's the wave from the bridge, that's a good thing. It means the bridge is clear. You can actually drive there. We can distract the infected, lure them away from the garage door and you can just go."

"What about you?" Nina turns to me. "Our original plan was that you'd have the crawler with you to help you fight. We don't have it anymore. This station is barricaded, but not foolproof. Enough of them show up, they're gonna break through."

"Well, we can contact our friends if you give us our portors back."

"No, your portors are useless within a two-kilometer radius because of the comm-jammer Mia set up. We didn't put it in the station just in case SPORE managed to locate the source of interference. With the wave here now, we can't get to it to disable it."

"Okay, uh…" I try to think of alternatives. "Yeah, I'm drawing a blank."

"Look, Nina," Jed says. "I hate to say it, but I think … I think we're better off letting *them* take the vehicle."

Them? Who's them?

Jed looks between me and Sara. "You can use it to get the wave's attention and lead it away from here. Once the road's cleared enough, we can get a move on and leave the station."

"He's not wrong," Sara says.

"We'd be smarter to cross the bridge on foot," Jed continues. "Less noisy. All the infected will follow the vehicle, and we get a chance to slip out quietly. Huh, Nina?"

Nina barely sits on it for a second. "Okay."

"Wait, really?" Jed leans back, wide-eyed. "You're not gonna argue with me? You usually do."

"Yeah, because *usually* all your ideas are dumb," Nina says. "I think you've been hanging around smart company enough that it rubbed off on you a little."

"All right, then, good." Jed laughs. "Not to mention, Sara worked really hard on that car. I think it'd be nice if she got to drive it for a while."

"Yeah, it's too bad she works for the enemy, or else you could've asked her out as a thank-you or something," Nina teases.

"What!?" Jed's cheeks darken. He stands with his mouth ajar, pointedly not looking at Sara. "That's not—what are you… *Nina*…"

Sara bites her lip to conceal an amused smile. I can't help a quiet chuckle myself. He is admittedly a little obvious.

"Okay. Back inside. Let's grab what we need." Nina takes the lead to the training room, straight to the storage unit.

Sara's and my weapons were apparently in that stash she'd left in the sewers, which tells me that she was planning on letting us go with our gear from the start.

She digs into a ruck and tugs out a couple of portors. She hands one of them to Sara, then opens up the map on mine and tags some coordinates on it before passing it to me. "This is likely where Vincent's headed."

I nod and strap the portor around my wrist before slinging my M4 over my shoulders.

"I put the trackers back yesterday," Nina explains. "As soon as you exit the jammer's radius, you'll be able to reconnect with your friends and call someone to pick you up."

"Got it." I nod.

Silence. Nina looks at me like there's something at the edge of her tongue.

"What?" I urge her.

"You should tell Connor that I'm alive and okay. Jed and Don, too," Nina says. "Vincent probably lied to him, told him that we died, or that you killed us. He was probably betting on that happening anyway."

"Wait... Hold on a minute—what?" It takes a second for it to sink in. "Connor's your contact? The Raven?"

"Yes, but he's not the one after Lori. Connor's getting his orders from someone else. Don't know who. It doesn't matter because Vincent doesn't plan on handing the crawler over to whoever is puppeteering Connor right now. He wants to keep it. He wants to convince Zack to join him, so they can raise an army of infected together and take down SPORE."

What? Zack? Vincent's after Zack?

I exchange a worried look with Sara, who's being awfully quiet. And to think Lucille was right all along, both about there being a traitor among us, and it being Connor. I see why Stephen called her brilliant.

"Why ... are you telling me this?" I swallow a hard lump. What am I supposed to do with this information other than report it to Sgt. Seidel or the lieutenant?

"Because I need you to tell him that he's putting his and his family's life at risk for nothing," Nina says. "If Vincent keeps the crawler and gets Zack on his side, Connor's gonna take the brunt of it. Whoever his contact is will think that Connor betrayed them. Or they'll see they have no use for him anymore and get rid of him to cover their tracks."

"And you think he'll listen to me? I barely know him. Sara worked with him longer."

"I don't care which one of you talks to him, just as long as you do it," Nina says.

"I thought you didn't want Rodríguez to get Lori," Sara says.

"I don't," Nina admits. "More importantly, I don't want Connor and his family to get hurt. So, talk to him."

I'm still unsure. What if he doesn't listen to either of us?

"Ash." Nina holds my eyes in a plea. "Promise me you'll talk to him and no one else. No one."

"Okay." I nod anyway. "I promise." To try, at least.

Then we're all just standing there, looking at each other.

"So, uh…" I clear my throat. "I guess this is goodbye."

"Don't make this sappy." Nina holds out a hand for me to shake. I don't. Instead, I hug her tightly. Her body tenses against mine for a second. Then, slowly, she relaxes and wraps her arms around me.

"It was good to see you again, Nina," I whisper against her shoulder, inhaling a handful of her messy hair. I'm going to miss her. So much. "Take care of yourself."

"You, too." Nina nuzzles her nose against my shoulder for another second before drawing back with a smile. Hers and Sara's goodbye is way less intimate, settling for a handshake.

"Thanks for patching me up," Jed says.

"And thank you for the food." Don smiles. "Even if … we kinda stole it."

"Good luck out there." I tell them.

A few acknowledging nods, then Sara looks at me.

"Ready?" she asks.

"As I'll ever be." I nod.

We grab our assault packs and head straight to the garage. Nina and the others will barricade the doors behind us in case some infected decide to hang back. We both toss our assault packs into the backseat. I slip into the driver's seat and Sara runs to the garage door. She rolls it up enough for her to fire an explosive round, then pushes it up enough for the car to get through. She runs back and slides into the passenger seat. Doors shut and locked. Then out of the garage I drive, straight up the ramp and to the road.

The big wave is finally here, gathering at the front of the station.

"Hey, guys!" I stick my head out the window and call while I simultaneously punch the horn. The infected turn toward us one by one. "How about a couple of tasty girls for lunch?"

The infected don't move, though, they just stand still, staring.

"That's weird," I say. "Why do you think they're—"

A shriek erupts all of a sudden, making me slip back inside the car, bumping my head in the process.

"Ouch." I rub the spot on my head.

"An Active?" Sara gasps.

Then the infected charge at us all at once.

That explains ... so much.

"Ash, hurry, drive!"

"Oh, man. That's not good." Hands back on the wheel, eyes on the road, I drive.

"Let me see if I can get rid of some." Sara reloads her grenade launcher then pokes out the window, firing an explosive round behind us.

"How's it looking?" I ask. "Are they all following us?"

"I think so," Sara says. "But it's gonna take a minute before the street's fully clear."

"Okay." I nod, silently praying that we didn't just leave Nina and the others stuck in the station with a wave.

Sara keeps on shooting, and I keep on driving.

PART FOUR

FORTY-THREE

WE DRIVE until we get to a dead end, a road blocked with a bunch of vehicles. I stop the car and we both take a moment to breathe.

I cross my arms over the steering wheel and rest my head between them, exhaling. "You think Nina and the boys made it?"

Sara pushes her windblown hair out of her face and throws her head back against the seat, breathing heavily. "I don't know." She brings up her portor. "It doesn't matter."

It doesn't matter? We just risked our lives to save them. That's all that matters. But I see she's back to pretending she doesn't care about a bunch of criminals.

God, I really, really hope this wasn't for nothing. I hope they made it across the bridge safely.

"Hello?" Sara holds her portor close to her mouth. "This is Specialist Jung and Private Brown, can anyone read me?"

We wait for approximately five seconds before there's some clicking on the other end.

"This is Private Aria with the Renegades platoon," our RTO responds. "Please repeat."

"Aria, this is Specialist Jung and Private Brown," Sara repeats. "Do you read us?"

"Affirmative, Jung," Aria says. "Please provide ID numbers for confirmation."

"S1695," Sara says, then looks to me expectantly.

"K0395," I say.

"Hold please," Aria says.

We hold for about two minutes, then a new voice comes through.

"Jung, Brown," it's Sgt. Seidel, "are you okay?"

"Sir!" Sara smiles. "Yes, we're okay. We just escaped a wave, but we're okay. We can send you coordinates to pick us up."

"It's them," Sgt. Seidel confirms.

Cheers and screams and celebratory whistling break on the other end. My chest flutters in excitement, and Sara meets my eyes with a grin of her own.

"Are you bitten?" Sgt. Seidel asks. "Does either of you need urgent medical attention?"

"No, sir, we just really need a shower right now," Sara says. I can't help a chuckle, matching the laughter on the other side.

"Roger that, Jung. Send those coordinates. We're on our way."

"Yes, sir," Sara answers.

"Finally!" I hold up a hand to her.

She high-fives me. "I can't wait to get home."

I lean back against the seat, inhaling deep breaths. I hate how excited I am about going back to base. But I missed Dalal's cooking, and the thought of getting to hold a bowl of her hot, spicy soup makes my mouth water. Also, getting to shower and use a toilet that works. Oh, and I can't wait to get out of these clothes and change into something cleaner and warmer. I want that SPORE sweatshirt so badly.

More importantly, I can't wait to see Cris again. And Zack. Honestly, even Lucille, and everyone else.

A wail breaks me out of the fantasy. My eyes snap to the side-view mirror, the reflection of a chaser hopping over a car and landing on the road, then charging straight toward us. More infected pop up. In front of and behind us.

"Bite me," I straighten up, hands on the steering wheel. "I think we accidentally brought some company with us."

Sara's brows knit together. "They must have heard the car."

"What do we do?" I turn to her.

"It'll still be a while before backup is here. We gotta hold them off till then." Sara looks around. "Let's get inside one of these buildings. Find a way to a rooftop."

"Good idea."

We abandon the car, and sprint to the sidewalk. The entrance of the first building we try to go into is blocked, so we run to the next one. Sara takes the lead. I follow her into what looks like an electronics store. Half-empty shelves holding broken and dust-eaten screens, laptops, and other devices I can't even begin to name.

"Ashley, check that door over there!" Sara points behind the cash register. "I'll keep an eye out."

"Roger." I run to the counter, jumping up and sliding across to the other side. I try to open the door, but it doesn't budge.

Behind me, Sara opens fire on the first batch of infected coming into the store.

I kick the door once, twice, three times. It does nothing. I take a few steps back and shoot around the handle until splinters fly all over and chunks of the door break off. Then I deliver one more kick, and it flings open.

"Sara!" I call for her, but the moment I rush in, a camper jumps me. I stumble back and fall against the counter. Luckily I'm fast enough to push my protective sleeve into his mouth before he gets the chance to clamp his teeth around my face. This one's heavy and big. I try to push it off of me, but I can't.

"Ash!" Sara's voice behind me before she sinks a knife into the camper's skull.

I throw his limp body off me just as more infected stumble out of the room I just opened. I'm starting to think that door was locked for a reason. I back-roll to the other side of the desk and land on shaky legs. I'm so tired. So hungry. So sleep-deprived. My aim is still top-notch, though, and the infected drop as soon as I open fire.

"We don't have enough ammo to take out all of them." Sara is shooting infected on her end as well, coming in through the entrance. "Once that room clears, we'll dodge and go in."

"Sara, I literally obliterated that door," I grunt. "Even if we do manage to get in, they'll follow us. And that's us blindly betting on there being a way upstairs through that door."

"There has to be," she says. "There's a second story to this building and the stairs are nowhere in sight where we are right now."

"Okay. I'm gonna trust you on this one. But if we die, it's your fault."

"Sure, I'll take the blame. Our chances are no better if we stay here, anyway."

Sara and I back away from the register and entrance, deeper into the store, leading the infected with us. Some of them—the chasers—

try to flank us using the aisles, and it quickly becomes a guessing game of where the next one will pop up from. All that extra shooting practice I did with Cris is coming in handy after all.

We dodge what we can and shoot what we must, until the infected stop pouring out of that room. Sara gives the signal and we both bolt to the left side of the store, running through the aisles and making our way back.

The chasers' growls erupt around us. A shelf collapses against me and I fall with it.

Sara comes to a halt, spinning toward me. Before she can reach me, a chaser jumps her and tackles her on the floor. I'm about to shoot it when a second chaser shows up and runs at me. I explode its knee with one shot and then its head with the next one. Sara's pushing the now-motionless chaser off her and rolling to the side. I shoot a third one before it jumps her from the right. Blood and brains spatter on the floor. Sara shoots the next chaser that shows up as I crawl out from underneath the shelf. Her hand stretches to me. I take it, and she pulls me to my feet.

We bolt straight for the cash register. I go in first, into a small hallway. Sara holds the door closed and I push a wide table against it, turning it around so that one end is to the door and the other to the wall. The infected are banging on the other side, but this should hold them off, at least for a while.

We continue down a long hallway of doors until we arrive at the end, where, to our right, we find the staircase.

"See!" Sara climbs them without missing a beat.

"Yeah, yeah, yeah," I gasp. "Let's save the 'I told you so' for later."

Sara arrives at the first floor and heads for the only door there is. Into what looks like an apartment. We close the door behind us.

Roamers stumble out of the rooms toward us, and Sara and I greet them with what bullets we can spare. As soon as everything inside quiets, we push a couch against the door, then stack the coffee table and some dining chairs on top of it.

I bend over, hands clasped over my knees, swallowing big gulps of air. "Oh, man. That was close."

"We should check the rest of the apartment." Sara breathes out.

I grumble in a low breath, but straighten up nonetheless. "All right."

FORTY-FOUR

THANKFULLY, the apartment isn't big, and we're able to sweep it in a couple of minutes. No more infected. We head back to the living area.

The banging outside has lessened. They probably realized they won't be getting through anytime soon.

"Thank God." I exhale, hands shaky, legs wobbly. I plop down on the floor to rest. "I can't believe we made it through that."

"I think we've survived worse." Sara grins, massaging her shoulder. She walks across the messy living area to a window, pops it open and sticks her head outside, sucking in deep breaths of the fresh, chilly air. "The others should be here soon."

I shiver slightly at the cool air against my hot, sweaty skin. Yeah, definitely can't wait to take a shower. I smell horrible. My muscles are aching. The faint throbbing in my head tells me I'm on the verge of a headache.

At the same time, this is all ... nostalgic. Familiar. To have Sara as my partner. To work together, just the two of us.

And, God, as much as I've been trying to ignore it. As much as I've been trying to deny it... I do miss this. I do miss *her*. So so much.

"I lied," I confess. Maybe it's the adrenaline or having seen Nina again—or maybe I'm simply getting over myself, because I can now admit that I was an idiot. "When I said ... that I'd still be angry at you even if you died."

Sara looks at me from over her shoulder, her eyes wide with

surprise—probably more at the fact I'm saying this than at the words themselves. But her lips curl into an easy smile. That genuine, sincere, forgiving smile that makes everything feel okay.

"I know," she says. "You say a lot of things you don't mean. I try not to take it personally, for the most part."

I don't know how she finds it in her to forgive so easily when I've held a grudge against her for months. "I'm so sorry I was being such a jerk," I say. There is so much I have to apologize for. So much I need to fix.

"It's okay." She turns to look out the window again. "I *did* mess up. I'm not going to pretend that your words didn't hurt me, but I'm not gonna stand here and pretend I didn't do anything wrong, either. There are a lot of things I could have handled better. You had all the right to be angry with me. All the right to question whether I was a real friend or not."

Okay, sure, but … I probably should have given her the benefit of the doubt. I probably shouldn't have said all the things I said. I don't know why my brain always jumps to the worst possible conclusion. I don't know why it's so hard to just … focus on the good, instead of only seeing the bad.

"We both messed up," I say. And maybe … that's where we should leave it.

"We both messed up." She rubs the crook of her neck, rolling her shoulder and inhaling deeply. "How much ammo do you have left?"

I check my pouches. "One mag. You?"

She reaches into her pouch and gets out a mag, tosses it to me.

I catch it. "Do you have enough?"

"Yeah." She rests a fist on the windowsill and takes in a strained breath.

Something's … not right.

"Sara?" I get up and start toward her.

"Wait!" She holds her hand up, gesturing for me to stop. "Stay right there." Her other hand, pressed tightly against her shoulder … is stained with blood.

"You're hurt." I start again. "Why didn't you say something? Let me take a look."

"No!" she snaps, and I come to a sudden halt. Sara faces me, taking a few steps back. "Please, just … stay away."

Wait.

"Is that—" My mouth dries. The words are tasteless as they come out. "Did you ... get bit?"

Her head falls. "I'm sorry."

My body stiffens. "No. There's no way—when did this even—how? Was it the chaser?"

"I should've been more careful," she whispers. "I should've used my protective sleeve. It's my fault. I'm so tired and—"

"No." I shake my head and step toward her. She backs away but I don't stop. "That's not possible. Let me see it."

"Ash, it's too late." She looks at me with tearful, pleading eyes. "This isn't something you can fix. It's not an arm or a leg that you can chop off and hope the infection doesn't spread."

"We should at least bandage it." My breath hitches. "Stop the bleeding, buy you enough time until—"

"Until what?" Her brows pinch. Voice drops in defeat. "I'm as good as dead. Stopping the bleeding won't change a thing."

"It will for me!" I beg. My eyes burn. "Sara ... I can't ... lose you. Not you."

"I'm sorry." Her lips quiver, grip tight around her shoulder. "But I don't want to hurt you. So please ... let's just make it quick."

Make it quick?

"No." A stone drops to the pit of my stomach. Acid builds up in my throat at the mere thought. "No. I'm not... Not killing you. I won't do it."

"If you don't do it," she says with a frustratingly casual shrug, "I will."

"No!" I lunge at her before I can think, snatch her M4, dismantle it, and throw it to the far end of the room. I toss mine as well, just in case she tries to take it, and block her way.

"Ash." She sniffles. "Please—"

"Shut up!" I yell at her. "I won't let you do this. I won't let you steal the time you—*we* have. I will tie you up if I have to, but I won't just sit by and let you take your own life."

She dodges my eyes and shrinks in her clothes. Her whole body shivers.

"You wanted me to hold on, right?" I hold my hands at my sides. "There it is. I'm holding on."

When I step toward her again, she steps back, but I don't care, I take her in a hug and hold her tight. She struggles for the first couple seconds, but then she gives up, arms snaking around me. Shaky hands clutch the back of my shirt, pulling at the fabric. Her face burrows in my shoulder. The sniffling turns into hiccupping and soon enough, muffled cries explode against me. I can't hold back my own any longer.

We sob for God knows how long before I force myself to break the hug so I can bandage her wound. Then we sit side by side on the floor, our backs to the wall, waiting for that helicopter to come.

"Do you remember," Sara murmurs, "when you, Cris and I snuck off to that empty watchpost to have dinner? Then the two of you started arguing for the billionth time that day?"

A smile curves my lips. I do remember. It was about a month into AIT, before everything went south between me and Sara.

"And I kept trying to soothe things between you, but neither of you was having it…"

Yeah, and we kept going until she finally snapped at us.

What the hell is wrong with you two today? I'm so exhausted on both your behalf, and all I did was listen to you fight all day. Jeez, at least take a five-minute break to catch your breaths. Or is it a whoever shuts up first is the loser *kind of day?*

Cris and I couldn't hold our laughter for one second, and God, the confusion on Sara's face was priceless.

"I'm still proud of myself for that," I admit. Cris and I wanted to see how long it would take to get her to snap at us for real. He said it would take two days, at least. I said I could get her to do it in less than a day. *I won.*

"I miss that," she inhales, "I miss us hanging out together. I miss Vigor. All those hours we spent at the arcades. How's my score in Fight Street looking these days? Am I still in fifth place?"

"No, you got dethroned by Rahul, actually."

"Unbelievable."

"Yeah, well, he had more time to practice. Ryan was still first place, though. No one managed to beat him."

Silence stretches too long, allowing the low whistle of the wind to dominate the air.

"Don't push the others away." Sara's voice is dry. "Lucille … has a lot to live up to. Expectations to meet. It's easier for her to keep a distance, so people believe she is what she's supposed to be."

I want to say I don't care. I don't care about Lucille right now or what she's been through. I don't care about the others, either. It doesn't matter. All that matters is here. All that matters is now. All that matters is *her*.

"Dalal is sweet," Sara continues. I don't want to listen to this goodbye speech. "Because she's really good at straining all the bitterness away and hiding it somewhere else. Stephen has his own scars, too. He had to stain his hands with the blood of his friends *to save* his friends, and he has to live with that for the rest of his life."

I hate listening to this. So much. I always wished I had a chance to say goodbye to Dad, but maybe it's a good thing I never did. Goodbyes suck. *This* sucks.

"Cris just wants to do what's right. Despite what he may have said to you, he still really cares about you." Stop. "More than he lets on. Your issue is that you're both too stubborn to admit it. You go about it in the worst way possible."

I press my lips tight, swallowing all the noises creeping up my throat.

"You'll have to talk to Connor yourself," she says.

"No," I shake my head. "He won't listen to me—"

"He will."

"How can you be so confident?"

"You have a good heart, Ashley." She rests her head on my shoulder. "I know you think it's a weakness but … I think that's your biggest strength. Because it means you'll always do what you believe is right. You'll always fight for it. No matter how difficult or impossible it might seem."

Don't cry. You've cried enough. Sara doesn't need tears now. She needs strength.

Her breathing slows. "I'm … so sleepy."

I rest my head against hers. "I'll take first watch."

"Thanks," she sighs. "Partner."

I sit still, feeling her body shift with the slight rise and fall of her chest. The burn in the back of my eyes intensifies. Numbness consumes me, inch by inch.

FORTY-FIVE

THIS CAN'T BE HAPPENING. It shouldn't be happening.

My mom and I... It's Sara's voice, but next to me, her lips aren't moving.

They're not moving until the walls around us disappear, replaced by an expanse of greenery, and I'm transported back in time. To that day Sara and I sat together, just like this, leaning against one another. The Pit's Memorial behind us. The cloudless blue sky above us. The heat of summer all around us.

... We worked the greenhouses... Like Zack and his parents. *It was just the two of us.* Because her dad died from cancer when she was still a toddler. *During the drought, we lost over fifty percent of the crops. And what was left...*

SPORE couldn't decide how to split it. They could split it evenly among everyone, but that meant there wouldn't be enough. Or, they could split it amongst the privileged and the soldiers instead.

The greenhouse workers didn't think it fair to give the fruit of their hard work to those who didn't earn it. That's when the protests started. My mom didn't join the protests, though. She didn't want to risk what little stability we had in our lives. And she didn't need to.

Because she was seeing a Spore, I remember; Sergeant Santiago. Sara wasn't sure if her mom was seeing him because she actually loved him, or because of everything she got out of it. The food and clothes and meds he would bring them. But he was the closest thing Sara had to a father, and every kid needs a father.

THOSE WHO FIGHT

Things got violent pretty quick. First the protestors vandalized the properties of the privileged to steal whatever they had. Then the Spores started arresting people. In retaliation, the protesters turned toward people ... like me and my mom. Those of us who were trying to keep our heads down.

They called them traitors for not fighting with them. If everyone united, they could overthrow SPORE in a heartbeat. But people were scared. Scared of what might happen if they *did* overthrow SPORE.

Some protesters caught Mom with Sergeant Santiago while he was sneaking her a crate of food. They beat them both up, took the food, then raided our home and took everything there.

And because the protesters assaulted Santiago, the Spores started beating them up in the streets, captured some of them and tortured them. Zack's dad was one of them. But that didn't stop the protests, it only gave people more reason to take things further.

They started killing the Spores. First, in secret. They'd drag them into an alley, steal their gear and weapons, then stab or shoot them.

And then the killing became more blatant. Gunfire, day and night, just outside their homes. Sara and her mom were always waiting for their turn.

The thing is, the day the Tsunami hit ... it was like any other day before it. Eukson was already in ruins. There were dead bodies everywhere. There were alarms going off nonstop. By the time we realized what happened, it was too late. Most of the soldiers were injured or dead. And those who weren't were too busy killing people to fight the infected.

When reinforcements came from other sectors, the Tsunami had already hit, and the infected had broken into Eukson.

The first time I saw an infected, I couldn't tell it apart from an angry protester. Until I saw it jump someone, rip the flesh off of them. My mom's friend was knocking on our door, calling for help, begging us to let her in. My mom told me not to, but I couldn't ignore her. Her daughter and I played together all the time. We were friends...

But as soon as Sara opened the door, an infected jumped the woman's back and tore a piece of flesh right off her neck. Sara froze. Didn't know what to do. Her mom came running. She pushed her out of the way just before that infected could jump her next.

It bit my mom instead. In the arm...

There was a long pause here. Sara took a moment to wipe away her tears. I wish I'd have reached over and wiped them myself.

Her mom had been keeping a knife on her since she was attacked, and she used it to kill the infected, then dragged the dying woman inside. The woman told them that she sent her daughter with her dad, that they were hiding the kids in the school and Sara's mom should take her there, too.

Before we left, though, Mom stabbed her friend in the head. Then she carried me and ran with me until she couldn't.

Her mom had lost too much blood, even after bandaging the arm. The infection was spreading. She was slipping away. There may have been a chance to save her at some point, but it was long past by then.

... So she asked me... Sara continued, *if I knew why she did what she did to her friend. And I said yes. Then she asked me...* Her breath hitched. *She asked me to do the same thing to her. And I said no. So she begged me to. I had to be strong, and being strong meant doing the hard things.*

She sat there and watched her mother die, and when she did, Sara stabbed her in the head like she asked her to. But after that, she didn't know what to do. She didn't think she could make it to the school. She didn't want to, either. So she just waited for an infected to find her, until one did.

I was ready for it to tear me apart, but someone killed it before it did. My heart thrummed in anticipation to hear what came next. *This soldier ran up to me. I thought he was going to shoot me, but he started inspecting me, like he couldn't tell if I was alive, hurt or bit. He was talking to me, but I wasn't really listening. Then he took my hand and made me run with him. I didn't know where he was taking me... Didn't really care, either. At the time, everything felt pointless: running, fighting, surviving... I couldn't find a single reason to do any of it...*

A feeling I'm all too familiar with.

But your dad... Sara said. *He was committed. He would run and fight and survive without tire. I'd never seen anyone as fierce as him. And I didn't think I could ever understand why anyone would fight the way he did. I didn't think there could possibly be any reason strong enough to have the will not to surrender.*

He took off his protective sleeve and gave it to her, showed her how to use it to protect herself. He gave her his combat knife, too, said it was better than the kitchen knife she had. She stood in the back while he cleared a path for them, but all the noise drew the infected toward them.

It all happened so fast. He was fighting one chaser in one moment, and the next there were three more on him. And I think he was operating on muscle memory. *Because he tried to block the bite. With his arm. Without his protective sleeve.*

Dad was bitten in the arm? I asked, and hope sparked inside me for some strange reason. But that's fixable. He just had to find someone to amputate his arm. Or he could have done it himself—

There was no one, Sara said. *He told me his partner had to be evacuated earlier, and that the Spores started retreating about an hour before. He couldn't go because he was stuck. And then he found me.*

Just like that, my hope died.

It was my fault; that he got bit. I was paralyzed. I could have helped him. I could have run at those infected and stabbed at least one of them. But I was just standing there, watching. I had all the time in the world to help him. But I didn't. He had another knife. Took it from one of the corpses, and still managed to kill the chasers. And then we ran.

Dad should have been looking for help. Every second counts. Leaving amputation any longer than five minutes after a bite is a shot in the dark.

We stopped after a while, she went on. *Found a spot to hide in and he ... he asked me to help him tie a tourniquet around his arm. Then he asked me to tie his hand to a pipe. I didn't know what he was doing. He asked me to look away, so I did. For a second. But then I turned back and I saw him pull out this long blade from his pack. I could tell he hesitated. I could tell he was wondering if it was too late. If ... at this point, he was better off keeping the arm so he could use it for the time he had left. But I think he had hope. I think he wanted to believe that it wasn't too late. So, he swung the machete down. I never heard a man scream like that in my life.*

Even now, my body shudders at the image.

I can't tell you I remember your dad's voice very well, but I do remember what he told me when I asked him why he did that, Sara said. *Why he saved me. He probably would have been fine if he'd left me behind. He told me he had a daughter just like me back home.*

That any time he had to fight the infected, any time an innocent life was at risk, he'd think about his little girl. How he wouldn't waste a second jumping in to save her life. He told her everyone is someone's little child. Everyone is someone's whole world. Everyone is worth saving.

I told him my mom was dead, I was no one to anyone, Sara said. *He told me to survive so that Mom's whole world does. Just like he fights so that his family's whole world survives.*

I couldn't hold back my tears then. I can't hold them back now.

So, we kept going. We found a working radio, because his had broken. And I remember he called for someone to come pick us up. We were to go on the rooftop and wait, and that's what we did. Sara's sniffle had me turning to her. Wet lines trailed her cheeks, glistening under the sunlight. *He told me he'd take me home. He told me your mom was a doctor, and she would take care of me. Told me you were a good kid, and you'd be my friend. That we'd be a family.*

I couldn't believe what I was hearing. For all intents and purposes, Dad wanted to come back. He *planned* to come back.

It was Sergeant Seidel who picked me up—of course, she wasn't a sergeant then. But for some reason, your dad refused to come with us. It was like he realized something. Or remembered something. I wasn't sure...

He told Seidel to go. He told her to go and get Sara to safety. That he'd call again when he was ready to be picked up. The first thing Sara did when she woke up in Kadia's hospital was ask about him, only to find out he never made it out. Soon after, Sara was taken to Spheria, and that was it.

The only known survivor of the Pit.

FORTY-SIX

WHIRRING rotors snap me back to reality. I'm back in the apartment, Sara's passed out against me. A helicopter flies outside. That must be them.

A couple of minutes later, voices echo on the other side of the door. Footsteps. Lots and lots of footsteps.

I turn to Sara. She's still breathing.

How many times will I watch my friends die?

"Over here!" a voice calls.

I slap a hand over my mouth.

Don't cry. Don't cry. Don't cry.

There has to be something I can do to stop this. Anything.

It can't have all been for nothing. Dad didn't fight and sweat and bleed for her that day just so I'd let her die today. He didn't give his life just so hers would be taken anyway. It's not fair.

There's still so much to talk about. So much to do. We're supposed to go to Vigor and get chocolate milkshakes in Jose's memory. I want to ask Sara if she still has that stupid snow globe somewhere and if I can still have it. I want us to visit the Pit's Memorial together, tell Dad that we made up and that we'll come see him more from now on. We're friends just like he wanted us to be. Family.

Please. God.

I want to hold on.

I don't know about a cure. All the samples we have aren't quite ... ready. Haytham's voice is a distant whisper. *We've been trying.*

A little switch of hope flips inside me. A spark of possibility.

Testing it on animals isn't ideal, because they don't react to the virus the way we do.

"It's not too late," I murmur, reaching for her with my hand, shaking her slightly. "Sara, it's not too late. There's a chance we can undo this."

Sara's eyes flutter open, heavy eyelids, tired face. I'm not sure she understands what I'm saying.

"Haytham told me they're working on a cure," I tell her. "They have samples ready, but they never got to test them on humans. They could try with you. They could help you—"

A charge explodes the door to the apartment. Cris is the first one through it, tossing aside the chairs and pushing the couch to clear the way. The rest of them follow. There are three new members with them, from the reserves squad, I think.

"Ash!" Cris lowers his weapon and hurries toward me. He has dark circles under his eyes, his face grim with worry. "Sara—"

"Please." I shoot to my feet. "You have to help her. We have to take her back to Spheria, now."

"Brown." Sgt. Seidel, eyeing Sara warily, walks toward us. Lt. Mansur beside her with an all-knowing look. "What kind of injury is that?"

"There is a cure," I blurt before I can stop myself. "It's not too late. If we take her back now, we can save her."

"Hold on..." Cris's brows arch. "She was bit?"

"What?" Lucille gasps. She pushes past Cris and walks up to us. "Sara? No way..."

One of the new guys points his rifle in Sara's direction.

I stand in the middle, shielding her from his weapon.

"Stand down, Grayson." Lt. Mansur's voice is calm.

Grayson looks unsure, but lowers his weapon.

"Private," Sgt. Seidel walks toward me, "step aside."

"No." I hold my ground, even if my whole body is shaking. "You have to listen to me. We can save her. We have a chance."

"With how she's looking, I doubt it." Sgt. Seidel shakes her head. "You've learned this from the very start of your training. Unless the bite is on a limb that we can amputate, the infection is definite."

"She hasn't turned yet," I argue. "She still has time. It could be hours—"

"It could be seconds—"

"But we have a chance to save her," I plead. "Ask the researchers in the lab. They have samples ready. If even one of them works, we could save Sara's life. We can't just ... *decide* that someone's life has ended without even trying to save it."

Sgt. Seidel gives me a stern look. "Brown, step aside."

"Please—"

"Ashley." Lt. Mansur is much gentler, much calmer. He holds a hand up in a peaceful gesture, and keeps his weapon lowered. "Why don't I take a look at her?"

I hesitate. "You're going to kill her."

"I just want to examine her wound," he claims, but I don't believe him.

"Rey." Sgt. Seidel looks to Cris. "Escort Private Brown back to the choppers."

Cris's lips part, a protest at the edge of his mouth, but he doesn't voice it. He steps toward me and takes my arm in a tender hold, nudging me to come along.

"No..." I pull my arm back, but he grabs it, firmly now, and drags me with him with basically no effort. It doesn't help that I'm so drained. "No. Please—"

"Ash," he whispers, grabbing my other arm. His touch softens, and he uses his body instead to gently push me along. "I'm sorry."

I try to fight him anyway, watching from behind the barrier of his shoulders as Lt. Mansur crouches before Sara, inspecting her wound. Sgt. Seidel sits beside him. I can't see their faces, but I can feel the grim air surrounding them all the same.

"Sir," Sgt. Seidel says, "I'll take care of it."

"No! Wait, please!" I struggle in Cris's grasp. When he doesn't let go, I stomp on his foot, and as he slouches in pain, I headbutt him. He releases me, wincing, but before I can run to Sara, Lucille blocks my path.

"Don't make this more difficult than it already is, Brown." She places a firm hand on my shoulder. The ice in her gaze is more like a thin, fragile layer than a thick, hard block.

"Mirani, Brooks," Lt. Mansur calls as he stands up. "Restrain Specialist Jung and take her to the choppers."

"Sir..." Sgt. Seidel's brows furrow. "Are you sure about this?"

"It's an order," Lt. Mansur says. "I'd like to hear more about this cure."

A breath escapes me. I feel as though a whole mountain has just lifted off me.

They're not going to kill her.

They're actually listening to me.

I don't know if Lt. Mansur believes what I said about the cure, but at the very least he's listening to me.

As a precaution, I'm cuffed as soon as we make it to the choppers. And while the others have their eyes on Sara, I nudge Cris and whisper a silent request in his ear. He gives me a skeptical look, but doesn't ask questions. Instead, he discreetly opens my assault pack, retrieves something from it, and stuffs it in one of his pouches. I thank him with a faint smile.

When we take off, I absently answer all the questions they ask me, about where we've been all this time, how we survived, and what happened with the infected that attacked us.

I leave out the part about meeting Nina and the fugitives and helping them relocate before SPORE's arrival. For obvious reasons.

Sara passes out completely about halfway through the ride, and everyone watches her intently, looking out for the smallest of twitches, the faintest of sighs, expecting her body to go limp at any instant before rocking back to life.

But none of that happens.

She sleeps soundly the whole time.

FORTY-SEVEN

I TAKE a second IBT when we arrive, the first one was before takeoff.

The device blips green. Clear.

Things don't go as smoothly with Sara, though, and the lieutenant argues with the medics for two whole minutes before he convinces them to step back.

My handcuffs are removed so I can go through the decontamination station, where I take off my dirty clothes, toss them in a bin, get sprayed with chemicals, then put on new clothes. A long-sleeved SPORE sweatshirt and a pair of sweatpants. A quick medical exam at the first aid station to patch any superficial wounds. Once I'm done, Sgt. Seidel is waiting for me with Cris.

"Rey will escort you to the Spec Ops HQ," she says. "You'll stay in a waiting room until further notice, understood?"

"Yes, sir," Cris answers, but he's not the one she was asking.

Sgt. Seidel looks at me expectantly.

"Yes, sir," I say.

Cris nods at me, and I follow him out of the helipads. No sign of Sara anywhere. They must have already taken her to the lab.

We go to the Spec Ops HQ, and once the guards clear one of the waiting rooms, they lock us in.

"Do you want water?" Cris stands behind me while I stare at the wall. "Food?"

I shake my head. No appetite. Can't think about food right now.

"Did the medics tend to everything?" he asks. "You feeling okay?"

He couldn't have asked me a worse question.

"Ash," he says, and the contrast in his tone between now and the last time we spoke is jarring. He sounds soft, caring, like he used to, before he said all those hurtful things to me. "I'm ... so glad you're okay." His shadow shifts on the wall in front of me. His hand reaching, then pulling back. "All that time you were gone, I thought—"

That I was dead. Gone. Forever. Yeah, I bet. Is that where those dark circles came from?

He takes my arm in the gentlest hold and turns me around to face him, but I can't bring myself to look up. I stare at his chest rising and falling. "I'm sorry about Sara. I'm sorry we didn't get there in time. We were looking for you everywhere. We swept the entire campus. We looked in the surrounding areas too..."

Yeah. That must have been them, that day. Their helicopter flying near the police station. To think they were so close.

"We did everything we could. But your trail had gone cold..." Cris sucks in a strained breath, as though he's reliving all of it in the span of a second. "That's not important now. You're alive. You're here. That's all I care about."

I should be happy to hear that, right? I'm all he cares about. I'm all that matters to him. I wish I could feel anything other than numbness right now.

"What I said to you that day..." His free hand takes my other arm, pulling me a step closer. "I didn't mean it."

But he was right. Even if he didn't mean it, he was right.

"I don't want people to die, whether that's *because* of me or *for* me. I don't want *you* to die." Desperation laces his every word. "All I ever wanted was for you to be safe. I didn't want you to take another bullet for me and not make it next time. I didn't want you to throw yourself at danger just because I couldn't..."

I know. He doesn't have to tell me. Doesn't have to explain anything to me. Because I've been doing the same thing, too, pushing everyone away so that I wouldn't lose another piece of me when they're gone. Sara was right. Like she always is.

The exhale he lets out next is coated in guilt and frustration. His hands leave my arms to hold my face, forcing me to look up, and God I missed his warmth so much. But even more so, I missed looking into the brown of his eyes. "I didn't think I'd see you again, and I can't tell you..." He pulls me even closer, his forehead pressing to mine, warm breath blowing against my face. "How happy I am that I get to look at your face one more time. That I get to hold you..."

"Please do," I whisper. "Hold me."

He pulls me in a tight embrace. His arms encapsulate me, locking me in as if the slightest shift in the air could steal me away. I nuzzle my face deep in his chest, feeling the thumping of his heart, taking in his scent and drowning in sweet reminders of home. My hands clutch his sides, nails digging into the sweatshirt. I want to stay like this forever. In this little bubble he made just for us. Where I'm safe. Where I belong. Where nothing could ever hurt me.

The lock clicks and the door opens. Cris and I jump away from each other as Sgt. Seidel walks in. I'm pretty sure she didn't miss a beat of what was happening. But she doesn't comment on it.

"Rey," Sgt. Seidel says. "Give me a moment with Brown."

"Yes, sir." He shoots me one last glance, then walks off and leaves the room, shutting the door behind him.

"Is Sara gonna be okay?" I sniffle. "Are they giving her the cure?"

Sgt. Seidel looks down. "They said there is no cure—"

"That's a lie!" My voice chokes. "Haytham told me himself, they're working on a cure—"

"They have untested samples of a cure." Sgt. Seidel folds her arms behind her, back straight. How can she keep such composure while I'm over here breaking into pieces? "With no guarantee whatsoever that they'll actually work."

"But there is a chance," I counter. My heart pounds against the constricting walls of my chest, as if it's looking for an escape. "There is a chance they'll work, and there is no reason for us not to take that chance."

"Brown, do you have any idea what you did?" Sgt. Seidel doesn't shout, but the weight of her voice thunders through the place all the same. "Blurting out in the open that there is a cure."

"I..." No. I wasn't thinking about that, I was just thinking about saving my friend.

"Do you know what that does?" Her gaze is pointed and grim. "Giving people that kind of hope?"

This conversation feels all too familiar. It reminds me of what

Colonel Sergei told me on the night I tried to escape. About the impact my actions would have on the people of the sector. Ironically, I care even less about that now than I did then.

"Do you know how many people your teammates lost? Do you know how many they'll continue to lose?" I've never seen Sgt. Seidel so ... disappointed. "So for you to plant this thought in their heads. That there is a way to end all this suffering. A way to save the lives we can't save. When there actually isn't..."

My throat tightens. I really wasn't thinking about that. I didn't care what it meant to the others. At all.

"What do you think that'll do to us?" Her brows lift. "To the team?"

"Sir ... I..."

"Trust is all we've got going for us, it's keeping us hanging by a thread," she says. "We've already suffered so much after Lotiva's betrayal. When people start thinking that their comrades are keeping things from them. Things as valuable as a cure. Trust is destroyed. People turn on each other for less. Why in the world do you think the work in the labs is classified?"

Bite me. I mentioned Haytham. I shouldn't have. I don't want him to get in trouble—

"You can't come out and tell people you have answers without concrete proof," Sgt. Seidel scolds. "Now, I've ordered everyone in the squad to remain silent, and not mention a word of it to anyone, no matter who they are. But it's enough that they know about this now. I can't control what they do when no one's looking. If one of them breathes a syllable of a cure to someone, well, then you may as well have caused the downfall of SPORE, and all of humanity."

"Sir," I try. "What I said about Haytham—"

"Oh, he's in his fair share of trouble right now, spilling classified information so carelessly..."

"He didn't tell me," I lie. "I just ... overheard a conversation he was having with one of his colleagues. He didn't say anything to me, I promise."

"He already admitted that he did," Sgt. Seidel says.

Crap.

"I appreciate you sticking up for your friend, but that's exactly the kind of bond you just destroyed for others."

"Is … Sara going to make it, at least?"

"We don't know. The lieutenant is currently with the research team, waiting to see what happens." Sgt. Seidel lets out a long, tired breath, head shaking. "But do you think it's worth it, Brown? Saving one person's life, and dooming everyone else's?"

The objective answer would be no. I know that. My brain understands it, but I'm more than just a brain. I'm a human. I have feelings. I have a heart, and my heart couldn't care less about everyone else.

"We've been looking for you," Seidel says, "over the course of the past week. We'd managed to find the comm jammer in the campus and Private Aria disabled it, but we couldn't trace yours or Jung's portors."

Thanks to Nina and her group disabling our trackers.

"Care to fill me in on what you've been up to?" Seidel asks. "Where were you? Why were you untraceable for a stretch of time? How did you manage to contact us again?"

Figures there's going to be an interrogation. Do I want to tell her about Nina and the others? Do I leave that out? I don't know if they're safe at this point. What if they're not? What if they need help?

"Brown," Sgt. Seidel presses, "I'm going to need an answer, and seeing the condition your partner's in, I'm afraid you're the only one who can give me said answer."

Maybe if I leave out some details.

"We were captured," I say, "by some fugitives."

"Go on." She nods.

"They took our portors and disabled the trackers," I explain.

"And they didn't kill you, why?"

"They thought they could use us." I shrug. "They were struggling with resources so they figured we must know some places they could hit up to find what they need."

"How did you get away?"

"We ran away," I lie.

Seidel's lips purse. "With all your equipment."

"We stole it back." I'm not even trying to sound convincing.

Seidel sighs. "And they didn't try to chase after you? Nothing?"

"Uh…" I evade her eyes. "There were infected. They had to fight them instead."

"Brown." Seidel pinches the bridge of her nose. "I can't help you if you don't want to help yourself. Either you tell me what really happened, or be prepared to face consequences. With your track record, I'm sure you understand things won't exactly go in your favor."

My track record. She means my escape attempt. It's true. She has every reason to believe I tried to run away again. But Sara? What about Sara?

"Surely you don't need me to tell you what's at stake here—"

"I know where Lori is," I say. "And I know who has her."

Sgt. Seidel's eyes widen. "What?"

It's been long enough now that Nina and her group are probably far away and safe. And right now, I need this leverage.

"Where?" Sgt. Seidel asks.

"Let Haytham go and I'll tell you."

She glares. "That's not how that works."

"It's either how it works, or it doesn't work at all," I challenge.

"You've already put us in an awkward position with what just happened with Jung," Sgt. Seidel argues. "You're in no position to be making demands, and withholding crucial information like this from us will not end well for you. I'm warning you, Brown. You don't want to go down this route."

"I don't want to," I say. "But I will."

She's quiet. Considering. "How do I know you're telling the truth? Maybe you're just making things up to get off the hook."

"You're more than welcome to keep me in jail until you verify," I say. "Only, I'm not saying anything until you let Haytham go. And when you do confirm, you can't keep me in jail, because you need me. That's why Lieutenant Mansur assigned me to his platoon, isn't it? You didn't let Zack join you until I graduated AIT. Because I'm the only one Zack even remotely trusts. I don't imagine he'll be so cooperative when he hears that I've been captured. And I'm sure you wouldn't risk that, now that we're so close, just because I temporarily held back a little information."

The disappointment on Sgt. Seidel's face is immeasurable. "I don't know what I was expecting from someone who was a fugitive herself."

"Well, how does that part of the vow go again?" I tap a finger on my chin, feigning thoughtfulness. "*I am the shoulder. Lifting my partner.*

THOSE WHO FIGHT

You can't make me vow on my life to help my friends, and then expect me not to."

"Very well," she exhales. "Is that all?"

No. It's not. But I made a promise to Nina. Lori's location will have to do.

"That's all."

TYPES OF BITES

LETHAL AREA
- BITES IN THIS AREA ARE FATAL.
- AMPUTATION NOT POSSIBLE.
- EUTHANASIA REQUIRED.

LOW-RISK AREA
- BITES IN THIS AREA ARE NON-FATAL.
- AMPUTATION POSSIBLE.
- HIGH CHANCE OF SURVIVAL.

HIGH-RISK AREA
- BITES IN THIS AREA ARE POTENTIALLY FATAL.
- AMPUTATION POSSIBLE.
- MEDIUM TO LOW CHANCE OF SURVIVAL.

FORTY-EIGHT

THIS ISN'T my first time in jail. Nor my second. Nor my third.

Except, maybe this "cell" isn't as bad as the others I've been in. Guess being an official member of SPORE comes with a jail experience upgrade.

I sit on the floor, leaning against the wall. The clock across from me ticks and ticks and ticks, until the ticking almost drives me insane.

Two hours pass since our arrival. Three since Sara was bit. That's plenty of time for the infection to take over. And plenty of time to stop it, too, if the cure works.

I try my best not to fall asleep, even though I'm drained. Any second now, Sgt. Seidel could be back with some news. Any minute now.

Still, I doze off, until the creak of a door forces me awake. A familiar face walks in.

"Haytham!" I stand up immediately, giving myself a headrush in the process.

"Hey, Ashley." He puts on a sad smile. "Sergeant Seidel will be here in a minute. I think she got a call."

I walk up to him. "I'm so sorry. I'm really sorry for getting you in trouble. Everything happened so fast, and I was saying anything to convince them—"

"It's okay." Haytham waves his hands dismissively. "It's my fault for revealing classified info. I don't think they would have let me go if I wasn't who I am. They probably would have discharged me."

The tiniest tinge of relief courses through me. "So, you still get to work at the lab?"

"I've been suspended," he says. "For a month."

Bite me.

"I'm sorry." His head droops, fists clutching around his pants legs. "I don't know why I told you what I did. I guess I was excited about the work we were doing, I wanted someone to share it with, even if it wasn't significant progress. But now I feel like it's my fault. I planted this idea in your head. Gave you hope where there is none…"

"What are you saying?" My head tilts. I try to catch his eye, but he won't look at me. "You said you had a cure—"

"Samples," he corrects. "I said we had samples of a cure, that we tested on animals, and none of our results looked promising."

"But the results could change if tested on humans," I say. "You said it yourself. The animals don't react the same way we do."

"Yeah." Haytham's eyes close. "I did say that."

"Haytham," I plead. "What happened to Sara?"

"I don't know." The words come out so stiff. So robotic. Like someone pushed a button and played a prerecorded message. "I only saw her in passing when they were bringing her in. She didn't look so good. But that's all I know. I'm sure Sergeant Seidel will tell you more when she finds out."

"Haytham…" I try to reach for his arm, but he backs up quickly, stretching the distance between us.

"I'm sorry." He turns around, and heads straight for the door.

Sgt. Seidel comes in just as he walks out. She closes the door behind her and stands facing me. "Thought you might wanna see him for yourself," she says, "just in case you decided to stall a little longer. Now, the crawler. Where is it?"

I take in a deep breath. Release. Don't screw this up, Ashley. Just play nice. "She's with a group of fugitives, north of Kadia."

"How do you know?" Sgt. Seidel asks.

"A friend told me," I say. "A friend with whom I share the kind of bond I destroyed for everyone else."

A knowing look settles in her eyes. "I take it Grant's alive."

I don't comment. "Thank you for releasing Haytham."

"You didn't give me a choice." Sgt. Seidel steps up toward me, holding her portor to me. "I want you to pinpoint the exact location of the crawler."

I use my own portor to send her the coordinates Nina tagged on it. Her portor beeps upon receipt. She inspects it.

"This is where they were headed, to meet up with someone," I explain.

"Who?"

"I don't know." It's the truth. Even they didn't know.

"And what about the fugitives?" she asks. "You said you know who has her. Can you identify them?"

"Yes." I nod. "There's three of them. Vincent, Mia and Justin."

Sgt. Seidel browses through a list of names on her portor. She taps, swipes, taps, swipes, taps, swipes, then holds up her portor to me again to show me the profiles of the three. "Is that them?"

It's their faces, albeit cleaner, a bit fuller, but it's them. "Yes."

Sgt. Seidel nods, taps a few more times on her portor. "Very well."

"Sir…" This next part, I'm not so sure about sharing but … I think a warning is necessary. "Can you please keep the coordinates confidential?"

"Confidential?" Sgt. Seidel raises her brows at that.

"Don't tell the squads just yet," I say. "Don't send a scouting party from Spheria or the Renegades."

"Brown." Her eyes narrow at me, skeptical, scrutinizing. "Do you know something?"

"I just think…" Don't screw up. Don't say more than you need to. "We should play it safe this time. Extra safe. Kadia's closer to those coordinates. Send a recon unit from there."

Sgt. Seidel's jaw hardens. "If you know something, you have to tell me."

"I don't know anything," I lie. "Please. I'm really sorry. I didn't want to put you in an awkward position. I just … wanted to give Sara a chance. I'm sorry. But you have to trust me on this."

Sgt. Seidel doesn't really give me much of a response to that, verbal or otherwise.

"Is Sara…" I swallow a hard lump. "Did you hear anything about her?"

"I'm sorry, Brown."

No.

"Jung didn't make it."

No.

"You're lying."

"Brown," she lets out a resigned breath, "I understand—"

"No, you're lying." I shake my head. "She's not dead. She can't be dead."

"The cure didn't work," Seidel says, "because it's not a cure."

"That's not true. It doesn't work on animals, but it could work on humans. It has to—"

"I know this is hard to process," she says.

"I want to see her. I want to see it for myself. Show me."

"I don't think that's wise, in the state that you're in," Sgt. Seidel says. "No one's allowed to see her."

"Why not?" I ask.

"There were some side effects with the injection they gave her. The research team has concluded that Jung's corpse is too much of a biohazard to allow anyone near it," she explains. "It could cause contamination."

"I don't care. You can get me permission. I have to see her with my own eyes. I have to know."

"And I said that's not happening, Private." Sgt. Seidel's voice is firm.

My jaw squares. There's no way Sara's dead. If she really turned and they had to put her down, there's no reason why they wouldn't let me see her. Seidel's lying. I know that she's lying. She has to be lying.

Please tell me she's lying...

"The bite was in a fatal part of the body, which you already knew," Sgt. Seidel says. "It's no one's fault. Not yours, either."

My throat is blocked up. My head feels both light and heavy at the same time, as if air is about to explode from it.

"Her corpse will be disposed of at the research team's discretion—"

"What?" My mouth falls. "Disposed of? What, we're not even going to bury her?"

"Like I said, there were complications," Sgt. Seidel repeats.

"Sir," I say. "You can't be serious. Sara was one of your top soldiers. How could you let them treat her like this? What the hell happened to what the lieutenant is constantly preaching? About how soldiers always deserve a proper burial? She deserves to be laid to rest next to all the soldiers who gave their lives for humanity. Just because she doesn't have a family doesn't mean she deserves any less. You don't dispose of heroes like you do garbage—"

"Brown." There's a clear shift in her tone, from compassionate to severe. "You've already put us in quite a predicament. Don't overstep, and don't forget you're talking to your squad leader. If there was anything I could do to make this loss easier for you, I would."

"How do you know that she's actually dead? Did you see her? Did anyone see her besides the research team?"

"Yes." Sgt. Seidel nods, confident, definite. "I saw her."

My heart breaks into a billion pieces.

"She's gone."

I want to scream, shout, punch, kick, but my body doesn't comply with any of that. It stands rigid. "I told her we could save her."

Sara can't be gone. *She can't be gone.* There's no way I don't get to see her one last time. I didn't even say goodb—No.

This is all a dream—a nightmare. It has to be. I'm not actually here. I was never in that building. I never saw the bite on Sara. We never met Nina. Maybe we died. Maybe I died. In Ground Zero. Maybe we never made it out. The infected got to us first. Or I got crushed under a big pile of debris and died on the spot. It's not like I would know what death feels like, right? So this has to be it.

This ... the way my chest feels like it's being ripped open with invisible, giant claws, sinking so deep and cutting up my heart and lungs. The way my throat squeezes as if a rope is wrapped around it, tightening by the second. The way my body's trembling incessantly and the whole room around me does a one-eighty. I turn away from Sgt. Seidel just before bile shoots up my throat. My soul almost explodes out of my mouth as my stomach clenches.

I vomit into a trashcan, emptying my already empty stomach. When I straighten, I'm clutching my abdomen with one hand, and passing the sleeve of my sweatshirt over my mouth with the other, wiping away the remains of the acid-y fluid.

"You can't save everyone." Sgt. Seidel places a hand on my back. I can't not hear those words in Sara's voice. Nina's voice. At this point, everyone should get together and sing the chorus to this song. "The most I can do is give you leave for two days. Take time to process the loss, and think really, really hard, about how you want to move forward."

My lips press together. Don't cry.

"This is only the start," Sgt. Seidel says. "You'll lose more comrades, and each loss is worse than the one before it. It doesn't get easy. You never get used to it. You just have to accept it. This is the life of a soldier."

A life none of us chose.

FORTY-NINE

I ARRIVE at the barracks building to my squad waiting for me in the yard.

Everyone's face is a slight variation of disturbed. Connor looks stressed, sitting on a bench and tapping his foot anxiously. He seems to have recovered since the last time I saw him, when he could barely walk. Lucille looks suspicious, leaning against a pole lamp with crossed arms. Stephen looks skeptical, pacing back and forth between the lamp and the bench. Cris looks conflicted, sitting next to Connor. Probably wondering if he should feel relieved that I'm alive, or sad about Sara. Dalal just looks sad while sitting on the bench across from the boys, like she's not completely there.

"Welcome back, Pinky." Connor stops the foot tapping and gets to his feet, slapping on a forced smile. "You had us crazy worried about you for a second there."

"You must be exhausted." Stephen abandons the back-and-forth pacing in favor of approaching me with a shoulder tap. He has a bruise on his left cheek. "Being stuck in the outside that long. You're a fighter."

"Don't you worry about her," Dalal says. All the sadness is gone from her face. She's bright and happy as she walks up to me. "She's gonna eat until she can't fit food in her stomach anymore."

I'd rather not. The mere thought of putting anything in my mouth right now makes me nauseous. Why the hell is everyone pretending all is okay? Why the hell do they think the right thing to do right now is smile and offer me food?

"Sure, Mirani, you can give her a whole menu to pick from," Lucille interrupts. Thank. God. Her usual calm and cool air are shifting to a stormy wind. She leaves the pole and walks up to me. "Now, if it's all the same to everyone here, I'd like to talk about the giant wave camped in the middle of the street."

"Lucille." Stephen turns to her. "Maybe now's not the time to—"

"How did it happen?" Lucille asks me. "How did she get bit?"

"Ashley, honey, you don't have to talk about this right now." Dalal looks to Lucille. "She doesn't have to talk about this—"

"Well, *you* don't have to listen if you don't want. But she owes us answers," Lucille insists. "Especially after putting everyone's lives at risk by taking an infected with us on the chopper."

Infected. That word stabs me in the chest. "You mean Sara," I correct.

"And this 'cure,'" Lucille says. "Is it real or did you just make it up?"

I don't know how to answer that. With all the trouble I got Haytham in, I probably shouldn't say anything.

"Hey, now." Cris glares in Lucille's direction. "Leave her be. She's been through enough already."

"He's right," Connor joins in. "I think Ashley needs rest right now, not an interrogation, which I'm sure Sergeant Seidel was all too happy to conduct already."

"Cry me a waterfall." Lucille throws her head back with an exasperated sigh. "What we need right now is answers, and she's the only one who can give them to us. But I think we all know what's really happening." When she holds my eyes again, the blame in them is loud, even if her voice isn't. "There is no cure. You just didn't want to deal with the loss that every single one of us has to deal with. But here is the reality: you couldn't protect your partner, and now she's gone. None of the ones before her came back. And she's not going to, either."

"How do you know she's lying?" Dalal says. "What if there *is* a cure?"

"Mirani, come on now." Lucille turns to her. "Not you, too."

"She's got a point," Connor says. "How many things did the

higher-ups keep from us before? You really think it's that unlikely that they might be keeping a cure from us too?"

"Sure, but I don't know that we should take the word of a traitor for it." Lucille gestures at me as if I'm a walking *Don't trust me* sign. "It's not like anyone here doesn't already know about her escape attempt. Just because Lieutenant Mansur chose her to be part of this platoon, doesn't mean she's trustworthy."

Ah... Is this why Lucille was so passive aggressive with me on my first day?

"Hey," Cris says. "Why don't you lay off her for a minute?"

"Or what, Rey?" Lucille sighs. "You're gonna punch me, too?"

"Lucille, grief is difficult enough as is," Dalal says. "We're all mourning Jayce still, and I know Sara was your friend—"

"A soldier like Sara deserved someone brave enough to end it for her before she turned," Lucille says.

"*But* consider that all of us are grieving, too," Dalal continues regardless. "And we should be supporting each other instead of tearing our comrades down."

"Whatever." Lucille shakes her head, shoulders dropping. She looks just about done with everything and everyone. "But I hope no one will be surprised when she runs off with her terrorist boyfriend and his freaky sister one day. In the meantime, I'll dig out my *I told you so* sweatshirt to prepare for the occasion."

"Ashley!" a voice shouts in the distance.

I hesitate before I turn.

Luke is sprinting toward us.

Oh, no.

Not Luke.

I don't want to.

"Ashley." He stops in front of me, bending over, hands clasped on his knees as he gasps for air. How long did he have to run? He straightens up to look at me. "Ashley, is it true?" he asks. "About Sara? Please tell me it's not."

I didn't even think about Luke's reaction, and seeing him now, I know exactly why I didn't think about it. I don't want to see it. I can't take the heartbreak in his eyes.

"Luke." Cris starts toward him. "Listen, we don't actually know what happened yet. We're still—"

"No," I finally manage. No point in giving him false hope. "Lucille's right."

Everyone's eyes fix on me now.

"Sergeant Seidel already told me," I say. "Sara didn't make it."

I half expect Lucille to yell at me, but not a sound comes out of her.

"I'm sorry," I say to Luke. It comes out in such a dull voice it doesn't even sound genuine.

Luke shakes his head. "How?"

"I didn't see it," I confess. "We were fighting the infected. And when the fight was over ... she was already..."

Tears well up in Luke's eyes, but he manages not to shed a single one. "She's not... Not that kind of person. She wouldn't let something like that happen. She's too careful. Too skilled. There must have been something. She must have been distracted. She told me she was dealing with something. I shouldn't have let her walk away. I should have insisted she tell me. I should have been there for her..."

Ah ... yes. Dealing with something.

With me.

With all the hurtful things I said to her.

All the blame I placed on her.

That's true.

He's right. Sara's too skilled to let something as stupid as a bite happen to her.

It's me. All me.

And I just stand there like a rock, while Luke finally breaks down.

Luke, the coolheaded, contained soldier is crying in front of me.

I open my mouth to try and comfort him, but there's nothing. I can't think of anything that would make him feel better.

Cris rests a hand on his back, and soon enough Luke turns to him for a hug. Connor and Stephen approach him, too. I don't know if they've ever spoken to Luke before. If they know anything about him and Sara, but nevertheless they try to comfort him because his pain is on full display. There's no hiding that Sara meant something to him. That Sara held a spot in his heart that nothing and no one is ever going to replace.

THOSE WHO FIGHT

Lucille is the only one who stands back, a hand clasped over her mouth. She can't comfort people right now. Just like I can't. Because neither of us knows how to comfort ourselves to start with.

Dalal rubs my arm gently and nods for me to come with her. I do.

FIFTY

I DON'T KNOW how I'm still standing.

How I drag myself to the bathroom. How I undress and step into the bathtub.

There's a sense of ... alienation when I turn on the faucet and the hot water rains over me from the showerhead.

Isn't it just absurd? That I'm standing here in a functioning shower with hot water, when water itself is a luxury? When sectors have timed water access and a limited amount that each person can have? And I'm wasting all this hot water just to shower? In a bathroom I only share with one person, when in Kadia we had to wait in lines. And the only reason I had any privacy back then is because I was privileged.

How did I get here? Why did I get here? Why is this just the norm for me now?

I can't stand for long, so I sit and let the water pour over me, wasted water, now running clean, going straight down the drain. Water people would fight for. Might even kill for. I sit here until I'm shaking. Until I'm breathing hard. Until my fingers are all wrinkly and I taste my salty tears mixed with the water running down my face.

"Ashley?" Dalal's voice on the other side of the door. "Are you okay? You've been there for a while. I mean, I get it. I'd shower for an eternity, too, after spending so long in the outside."

I don't answer her.

"I cooked us a nice, warm meal," Dalal says. "Will you come out and join me at the table?"

I bury my face in my knees and try my hardest to even my breaths. But I can't. I don't know how to breathe.

"Ashley?" Dalal calls.

Silence for one, two, three seconds. Then the door unlocks and Dalal rushes in.

"Ashley?" Dalal calls, voice shaken with worry, fear.

The water shuts off, and a hand rests on the top of my head to lift it up. She inspects me as if she's looking for something she can't find. I've never seen her without her headscarf. Her hair is so long and pretty.

Dalal moves her hand to my forehead. "You're really warm."

She gets up from the clean tile floor and grabs a neatly-folded towel from a nice wall shelf, then comes back and throws it over me.

"Come," she says. "You have a fever. You should be resting in bed."

I let her help me out of the bathtub, and I'm way too tired to care that she can see me naked. I lean against her for support, my arm around her shoulders, hers around my waist.

Dalal helps me get dressed in nice clothes I bought from a store in the Fifth Sector during the first week of AIT, then she helps me lie in a cozy, comfortable bed that can fit a whole other person next to me, under a thick, warm blanket. She leaves the room and gets a tray of food she cooked from scratch, because in Spheria we have this luxury. We have access to spices and vegetables and oils and milks and meats and all the things we only taste a canned version of in Kadia. I don't have the appetite, but she forces me to take a few bites regardless, even feeds me herself when my hands become too shaky.

I remember the days when I would get sick as a child, and my mom would take a day off work to take care of me. Sometimes I pretended to be still sick even when I started feeling better, just so she'd stay with me longer. And even though she could tell I was faking, she still stayed.

I'm right here, baby, Mom would say. *I'm not going anywhere.*

I miss those days.

I miss Mom.

I miss home.

"I miss my siblings," Dalal says. "I have four younger siblings back in Serco. Raised them myself, for the most part. You remind me so much of my youngest sister. She's five, but man does she have a personality."

"Is that why you're nice to me?" I ask. "Because I remind you of your sister? I'm not your sister."

"Oh, no." Dalal shakes her head. "That's not why. I mean, I didn't think I needed a reason to be nice to people."

I frown. Why can't I just be normal and say thank you? Why do I have to do this every single time?

"I think, if anything, I'd need a reason to be mean to someone." She smiles. "I think of kindness as a default, you know?"

"How do you have the heart?" I ask. "I just feel so ... dead inside."

Dalal frowns. "No. You don't."

"Yes, I do."

"No," she insists. "That's not true. You don't feel dead inside, because ultimately, you're feeling it, aren't you? You're feeling *something*. It's not a good feeling. It's not a feeling that you want to feel, but you feel it. And that's already proof that you're very much alive."

I blink, because somehow, I understand what she says.

"And you hate that feeling so much, because it reminds you of how miserable and powerless you are, so much so that you convince yourself you're not feeling anything. You reject that that feeling is valid, that it's real, that it's there constantly."

I look away from Dalal and at the tray of food instead. My heart racing.

"But you know what that feeling is? It's not emptiness. It's not deadness. It's the collection of all your negative feelings, building up one on top of the other, rising up in piles and mountains, clogging up every little bit of your heart, threatening to explode. And that feeling is the lid you're keeping over it all. The lid that's containing everything so that you don't explode. But the space in your heart will run out, sooner or later. And you can't stop yourself from exploding. I say, let it happen. So what? It's not the end, even if it feels like it."

Yes. I want to explode. Yet I can't.

I just can't.

"You know, my first partner... She died," Dalal starts. "Not from a bite. Not from infected tearing her apart. Not from an injury in training..."

I look up to meet her eyes again, listening.

"She ... killed herself," Dalal says.

Oh.

"She wasn't very…" Dalal sighs. "I mean, if you looked at her, you wouldn't really think that she would have done that. She was the one lifting our spirits all the time. The one making jokes all the time. The one taking things lightly, while I was terrified of everything, scared of dying, scared of fighting, scared of not seeing my family ever again. But then, sometimes, I'd catch her alone, curled up in a corner, crying to herself, so quietly like she didn't want anyone to know. I thought it was a tough-act type thing, you know? We're soldiers. We're not supposed to cry. She'd always slap on a smile and wipe her tears and act like nothing was wrong…"

"Time went by, eventually I forgot about it, but … I never forgot the last thing she said. When she was holding that M4 under her chin and I was trying so desperately to talk her down. And she told me: I just want to be free. I thought about that a lot, after. I couldn't ask her what she meant. What 'freedom' she was referring to, exactly. But it did get me thinking. That we are all restrained by something.

"In a way, I do owe my life to her. I wouldn't be the person I am now if I hadn't seen what happened to her. I wouldn't realize just how stupid I was for worrying about death when I was alive the whole time, and I wasted so much time not making my life count. She restored my faith, so to speak. I'm not happy that she took her life, and I would go back in a heartbeat to that night and snatch that M4 right out of her hands. But I'm happy that I won back my life, and I get to live it in a meaningful way."

"I…" I don't know what to say. "I'm sorry."

"When the reports came in a few months back about Lotiva and the conspiracy," Dalal continues, "she was the first thing I thought of. Her last words. A few investigations later, it turned out she was involved in the conspiracy. After she killed herself, her mother wanted to expose the colonel, but he threatened to kill her other kids, planted his men to keep an eye on her, so she stayed quiet, all this time, to protect her family. And I finally knew what my partner meant, when she said she wanted to be free.

"So when the general started putting together a task force to search for the fugitives, I volunteered. Begged the lieutenant to let me join. My partner was gone. There was nothing I could do to bring her back, but I thought … if I could save one person. If I could convince a single one of these fugitives that things could be better. That they're not alone. That we all *are* suffering together ... then..." Her shoulders drop. "I don't know. I just ... really don't want to see anyone else take their own life again. I don't want anyone to give up on themselves.

"Sometimes things feel hopeless. Sometimes it feels like there's no way out but death. Because life's too painful. Sometimes that pain lasts so long, we give up on believing that it could ever end. But I believe that ... if we just know that we have one person. Just one. Who believes in us, always. No matter how deep we fall. Sometimes that's all we need to climb out."

Yeah ... the lieutenant didn't close his eyes and pick people for the platoon at random. Everyone in the Renegades was chosen for a reason. Everyone is connected to the objective somehow. Everyone has a stake in this fight.

"Anyway." Dalal stands and picks up the tray. She slaps on a smile so fast, as if we weren't in the middle of the gloomiest conversation. Did she get that from her partner? "I'm glad you ate a little bit. I'll go drop by the infirmary and see if I can get you some medicine."

"Thank you," I say. *So much.*

FIFTY-ONE

THE FEVER BREAKS after two days of mostly bed rest. Or so I'm told.

I barely remember any of it. Dalal took care of me the whole time. Lucille also showed up, from the vague memories I have of her wandering into my room or hearing her chat with Dalal in the common area. She was probably lonely in her dorm by herself. Missing Sara.

Sara…

Sara is gone.

Gone for good.

Which doesn't make sense. At all.

I'm stepping out of a much-needed shower when voices reach me in the common area. Not Lucille. Someone else. And for a heartbeat it sounds like Sara. I don't know how I manage to get dressed before running out of the bathroom.

It's not Sara standing next to Dalal, though.

"Hey, Ash." It's Haze.

I don't wait another second. I run to her and plunge into her blonde curls, face first, clinging to her the way a soon-to-be amputee clings to their limb.

"I'm so sorry," she whispers to me, rubbing my back and holding me to her. "I came as soon as I heard from Cris."

"I missed you so much," I sob against her shoulder.

"I missed you, too," she murmurs. "I'm sorry I wasn't there when you left. We were sent to an outpost, and we didn't come back to Spheria until much later. You were already gone by then."

"I don't care. You're here now." That's all that matters. She's here and I can hold her and cry on her shoulder while she whispers comforting things to me.

We go to my room and lie in my bed, side by side, just like we used to when we were kids. Just like we used to up until we parted ways on the night of recruitment. But it feels the way it always has. Real. Raw.

"I'm going to ask you a really stupid question," she says. "How are you holding up?"

Somehow I manage a snicker at that. "That's not a stupid question. That's *the stupidest* question you could have asked me."

She smiles a sorry smile. "Well, even so. That doesn't mean the answer isn't important."

I've never been to therapy. I think partly because Haze has always been that kind of support for me. No wonder I was a wreck without her in Basic. Not that I'm not a wreck now. But I would probably be a bigger wreck. Like on a scale from the bombed street outside Spheria to the Pit.

How am I holding up?

"Barely," I answer. "Which is slightly better than not at all. Dalal's been taking care of me. But I'm still… I still don't believe it. We were together just a few days ago. Hardly spent any time apart. She was there. She was real, and now … I'm just waiting for all this to be a really long fever dream."

"Of course you are," Haze says. "She was your friend." No matter how many times I told Haze I was done with Sara, she always knew better. The same way she knew I had feelings for Cris long before I even realized it. "And Sara knew that, too. How much you cared about her. Only the people we care about can hurt us so much."

Even if Sara did know, that's not enough. Just because she knew, doesn't mean I couldn't have shown it better. Just because she knew, doesn't mean I shouldn't have been a better friend. Just because she knew, doesn't mean it's any easier to deal with losing her.

"God, Ash…" Haze places a hand on my cheek, bringing my focus back to her. "I was so scared for you. Really, I… When I heard that you went missing..." She breathes low. "I didn't know what to expect when Cris came to see me. I was preparing to hear the worst. Then he told me they found you... I know you may not feel like it, but I'm so damn happy you're here."

At least one of us is.

"I thought I lost you once. I don't know that I can do that a second time." Her eyes glisten with tears. "I wouldn't want to spend another second in this place without you."

I snort and nearly blow a load of snot into her face. "A few months ago, you'd have rather died than become a Spore. I thought you'd have come up with a new escape plan by now."

"I *still* would rather die than be a Spore," she says. "I haven't forgotten Mom or Liam, but..."

"But?"

"You're a Spore," she says. "And you made a choice to help people. You stood up to your superiors and insisted on doing the right thing."

My mouth falls. I had no idea that I'd played any part in changing Haze's mind. Not even a little bit.

"Running away ... that was to save *us*. But if we want to make sure others don't go through what we have, we have to be the ones to make the difference." Determination coats every one of her words. "We have to be that small percentage that stands up for others and doesn't stay quiet about injustice. And maybe that'll inspire more people to speak up. Fight for what's right. Otherwise, we're no different from the Spores who are in the system to look out for themselves and no one else. We're just part of another bad system."

I jerk my head back. "You're saying *I* inspired *you*?"

"It's a give and take kind of friendship."

Well, at least she's able to see the bright side in all of this. I've just been stumbling in the dark this whole time, looking for a way out.

"Hey," Haze says, "you tried to save her. You didn't give up on her. That's what she left with. She had someone fighting for her to the very end."

Yes, and now because of me, instead of being laid to rest next to Nathan, she's probably going to be thrown into a corpse dump and burned to a crisp with all the infected. My stomach churns at the mere image.

"Ash." Haze scoots closer to me. "If you wanna tell me to shut the hell up and let you cry about this—"

"Shut the hell up," I sniffle, "and let me cry about this."

"Okay."

FIFTY-TWO

THANKFULLY, Haze spends the night, and about ten minutes after she leaves the next day, my portor beeps—a message from Sgt. Seidel asking me to get dressed and meet her outside the barracks.

I practically sprint out of my dorm as soon as I finish putting on my boots. This has to be about Sara. She's gonna tell me there was a mistake—because there must have been. Sara didn't die. She woke up. The researchers made a mistake.

I run for the elevator, curse when it takes five long seconds to arrive, then I jump in it and push the button for the first floor repeatedly, hoping it'll transport me straight to Sgt. Seidel.

By the time I reach outside, I'm breathless and sweaty.

Sgt. Seidel eyes me with raised brows. "Brown, I thought you'd recovered from your fever."

"I did," I pant. "Sir, what's going on?"

"The general requested to see you," she says.

I've never felt so disappointed with an answer in my life.

"We need you to fill us in on some details," she says. "We were supposed to do that on the day you returned, but Mirani informed me you were sick, so we had to postpone."

"Right." I deflate. "Okay."

We take a vehicle to the Sphere building, and are dropped off just outside. There's some kind of setup going on in the front yard, vehicles parked and stacks of folded chairs and tables.

"What's happening?" I ask.

"They're preparing for the Pit's Memorial Day," Sgt. Seidel says. "December twenty-ninth will mark five years since Eukson's fall. The general is putting together an event to remember those who died."

That ... has to be one of the most egregious things I've heard in my life. "He's celebrating the day he bombed a sector?"

Sgt. Seidel lets out an exasperated sigh. "Not celebrating. *Remembering*. Mourning. Honoring. Not everyone who died in Eukson died in the bombing. You realize that, right?"

Sure. I also realize a lot fewer people would have died without the bombing, but I'm not in the mood to argue about this now. I follow her in silence. I can't remember if I've ever been inside the Sphere building before, but it's huge. We take the elevator to the top floor, then head down the hallway until we arrive at a conference room.

A large table takes up the center of the room, at which sits General Rodríguez along with the Division Commanders, whom I've only seen from afar since I joined training. Lt. Mansur is also at the table. As well as General Sears, who holds my gaze briefly with his one healthy eye.

"Sir," Sgt. Seidel holds a firm salute. I do the same. "This is Private Brown."

"Yes, I'm quite familiar with Private Brown." Rodríguez offers me a smile.

I haven't seen him since ... I graduated Basic? He looks different. Skinnier. His eyes tired. He must have had a rough few months.

"Let me introduce you to my Division Commanders..." He introduces me, one by one, and I'm thankful for the name patches everyone is wearing because there's no way I'm going to remember all their names—except for—

"Colonel Roxanne Decker," General Rodríguez gestures at the commander of the Spec Ops Division. Blonde woman. Cold, icy blue eyes... Almost an exact copy of Lucille, just ... older.

Is that her mom? Lucille is the daughter of a Division Commander?

Suddenly so much about her makes a lot more sense.

"And I'm sure former general of the Sector Protection Force, Howard Sears, requires no introduction." Rodríguez finishes.

"Uh, nice to meet everyone." I salute. It's odd, being in this close proximity with all the Division Commanders. And an older photocopy of Lucille. So uncanny.

"Sit down," General Rodríguez gestures at an empty chair.

"Yes, sir." I take a seat between Lt. Mansur and Sgt. Seidel, feeling so out of place among all these decorated soldiers.

"Brown, I requested your presence here because we're still trying to put the puzzle pieces together. The mission to Ground Zero left us with quite the number of casualties, and we came out with more questions than we had before. I've already read the reports, but I would like to hear more about what you and Specialist Jung found in the first basement level."

"I don't really know what we found," I say. "There were infected. A lot of infected. Sara said they looked like they were in stasis. They were connected to those tentacle things. On the ceiling. And there was this bright light. We followed it, and we found ... a giant blob, attached to the head of a corpse that belonged to a Spore. Sara and I thought it was from the expedition from five years ago."

"Can you describe the room you found it in?" Sears asks. "The position the corpse was in?"

"It looked like a lab, I guess. I'm not sure how to describe it any differently from most of the rooms in the building. The corpse was sitting on the floor, leaning against the wall. I figured if we destroyed the blob, or whatever it was that seemed to connect all the tentacles together that ... it might save everyone else."

"And did you do that?"

"I think so? We shot it. Sara used flame rounds on it. It started dissolving, but then ... the tentacles were shrinking and dying and that caused the building to start falling apart."

"By then we were already on our way back to the CCP," Lt. Mansur says. "We had to evacuate through the first floor."

"So..." I look at Sgt. Seidel and the lieutenant, "was it mission success? Did we get the data we were looking for?"

"Yes," the lieutenant says. No elaboration.

General Rodríguez looks expectantly toward Colonel Marchand, the head of the Research Division.

"We are still studying the samples we collected, sir," she says. "But this will surely help us advance in our research."

"What about the Active in our possession?" General Rodríguez asks. "Have you learned anything new?"

"All attempts to communicate with it are fruitless," she answers. They're talking about Melisa. "The Active is more intelligent than it seems, that's for certain. So far it has tried to manipulate us into thinking communication was possible, but as soon as anyone tries to make contact with it, it will attempt to attack with the purpose of reproduction, which seems to be its primary goal."

I try not to wince every time she refers to Melisa with "it."

"Other times, it will scream for an extended period of time. Like a wounded animal asking for help, as though it's trying to generate sympathy."

"Or it's actually trying to call for help," Colonel Steele of the Defense Division interjects. "Sir, if I may say, Spheria has seen an increase in the number of waves over the past few months. That number keeps going up—and has been ever since that Active was brought here. Knowing what we know, the Active is calling all these infected toward us, hoping they'll save it."

"That's impossible," Colonel Marchand counters. "The Active is locked in a secure compartment with soundproof walls. The only way the infected would hear it is if they were inside the compartment with it."

"That's assuming they need to hear it at all to know where to find it," Colonel Decker says. Her voice is thick, authoritative. Her chin is held high. Thin brows furrowed over hooded eyes that put the iciness in Lucille's to shame. "Let's face it, the infected are always one step ahead of us, sometimes more. We don't fully understand their method of communication. I have to second Colonel Steele here. Not only have the waves increased in frequency, but also in number and aggression."

"We need to think about what kind of threat this could pose to us in the future," Colonel Steele adds, nodding in agreement. "Sir, with all due respect, I think keeping an Active inside our military base, where our main force resides, is a huge mistake."

"And what are you suggesting we do, then?" Colonel Marchand gives them a forced smile, which, combined with the way her eyes pop wide open, make her look creepy. "Where else would we conduct this research? Spheria is the only place that is safe enough and has the necessary resources to help us learn as much as we can about the infected."

"I'm suggesting either we find a different place to conduct this research, or we don't conduct it at all because we're not prepared to face the dangers it would entail," Colonel Steele says.

"The safest option would be to kill the Active," Colonel Decker states it so matter-of-factly.

I hold back a gasp.

"Are you serious?" Colonel Marchand doesn't hold hers back. "I'm going to have to request that neither of you interfere with my work. It took us so long to get our hands on this subject. It will take us even longer to fully understand it. I am doing everything in my power, I assure you, as is my team, to find out as much as we can to help humanity and maybe even save it. Protecting the sectors, however, is your job. So perhaps that's where you should focus your concerns."

"At the rate my men are dying, I'm afraid we'll run out of people who can protect the sectors long before Colonel Marchand's research bears any substantial results." Colonel Decker's arms fold over her chest. "Then there'll be no one to keep this place running and your precious resources coming."

"I'm sure there are solutions for you to find," Colonel Marchand says.

"Like what?" Colonel Steele scoffs. "Lowering the recruitment age to five?"

"Might as well, if my own Division Commanders are behaving like five-year-olds themselves," General Rodríguez says. "Each and every one of you will maintain professionalism in my conference room."

Silence, then a collective, reluctant and disingenuous, "Yes, sir."

"Lieutenant Mansur," Rodríguez says. "I need that crawler ASAP. At this point, if a Tsunami were to hit any of our sectors again, we risk it being bigger than the first one, and more dangerous."

A Tsunami? Wait, what? Why are we talking about Tsunamis?

"Understood, sir." Lt. Mansur nods. "We've sent a team to the coordinates Private Brown provided. Assuming they're correct and that the crawler is there, it's going to be quite the journey. We're waiting to hear from them."

"Right now we're weak. Defenseless. But if we get the crawler, we might finally be able to communicate with the Active in our possession and facilitate Colonel Marchand's work. We may even gain control of the infected. The waves would no longer be a problem."

"Yes, sir," Lt. Mansur says.

Colonel Decker and Colonel Steele don't seem too pleased with this, though. They're exchanging skeptical, troubled looks with one another.

On the other hand, Colonel Marchand wears a smug smile. "Thank you, General. We will get the results we're looking for. We shouldn't lose hope now just because things are getting more difficult."

I don't know how to feel about any of this.

"As for your concerns, Colonel Decker, Colonel Steele." General Rodríguez turns to them now. "You may request backup from the sectors and transfer any units on reserve to Spheria. That should help our numbers in the meantime."

"Of course," Colonel Decker replies. "Thank you, General."

"Thank you for your cooperation, Private Brown," the general says. "Lieutenant Mansur and Sergeant Seidel can escort you out now."

"Uh, yes, sir." I push to my feet, giving everyone one more salute. "Pleasure to help."

"Best of luck to everyone," Lt. Mansur says, then nods for me and Sgt. Seidel to follow him out.

"Sir," I start, once we're outside, "why was the general talking about Tsunamis? Is something happening?"

"The team we sent to investigate the coordinates you gave us, they spotted infected—waves of infected, in separate locations, headed toward each other, about to converge," the lieutenant explains. "More units were sent to take care of them. Cleared them before that happened. And we've sent an all-out emergency call to the other sectors to do a sweep of the perimeters and make sure this isn't happening elsewhere."

"And?"

"And it is," Lt. Mansur says. "For some reason, the waves changed their activity pattern. At this rate, we'll run out of resources before we can wipe out all the infected. And if we don't find a way to control them, this phenomenon will likely result in a Tsunami. Only this time, there would be multiple ones at once and they would all be headed in the same direction."

"Why did their activity pattern change all of a sudden?"

"We don't know," Sgt. Seidel says. "We just know the waves have become more frequent everywhere. Spheria used to get one wave a week, maximum. Then it was two. Now it's three."

"Does it have anything to do with what happened in Ground Zero?" I ask. "With that strange growth?"

"We don't know," Lt. Mansur says.

"Do we know *anything*?"

"Brown." Sgt. Seidel shoots me a glare.

I huff. Okay. Well, it's their fault for bringing me here to their very top-secret meeting. Did they really expect me not to ask any questions?

"I'd like to see Melisa," I say.

Lt. Mansur raises his brows. "Who?"

"Melisa Elmore," I explain. "My comrade from Basic. She's the Active they were fighting about in there." I point behind me. "I want to see her."

"Brown, that's not—"

"I'll see what I can do," Lt. Mansur interrupts Seidel, who looks stunned.

I'm stunned, too. "Wait, really?"

He nods. "From what I heard in there, they're struggling to make progress with her. Perhaps seeing a familiar face can give us something."

"Uh ... yeah." I couldn't care less about their research development. I just want to see my friend. *You still have to be grateful, though, Ashley.* "Thank you, sir."

FIFTY-THREE

THAT MEETING not only drained me mentally, it also made me hungry.

So I head to the one place I missed most in Spheria: Vigor. One of the guards directs me to a path that's not blocked by the protests. The rest of the walk to the Fifth Sector is pretty lonely, quiet, until someone falls into step beside me.

"Hey, Ashley." Zack greets me with one of his signature flashy grins. I haven't seen him since Ground Zero. He must have resumed his AIT while we're off duty for the time being.

"Hey, Za—Egan." I catch myself before I slip. Gotta remember we're in public now.

"It has been a while, hasn't it? I wanted to come check on you, but I heard you were sick. How are you doing?"

"I'm better now, thanks."

And there goes his smile as his features contort into something more serious. I know exactly what he's about to say before he says it. "I'm sorry about Sarang."

Yep. Still don't know how to answer that. Still doesn't feel real. Still hate that everyone keeps reminding me of it.

Zack either notices my discomfort or doesn't like engaging in this sort of conversation for long. Either way, his tone switches to a more chipper and lighthearted one. "So ... when are we going to reschedule our dinner date?"

That's a very jarring jump in topics. Also, I ... completely forgot about that date. "Oh ... um, I..."

"It was never going to happen, was it?" No surprise. No disappointment. Zack's smile is easy, accepting "To be honest, I was surprised you said yes at all."

"I'm sorry," I say. "I don't know why I said—actually, I do know why. I was just trying to get someone's attention out of spite. It wasn't fair to you."

"For what it's worth," Zack says, "Cristian nearly lost his mind while you were out there. He and Stephen even got into a tussle at some point, when they were discussing calling off the search. It was pretty entertaining to watch. Connor and I broke them up before Seidel and the lieutenant caught wind of it. Lucille played the diplomat and made sure no one breathed a word about it."

Cris got into a fist fight with Stephen? That's ... so unlike him. I never would have imagined him punching someone—let alone someone of a higher rank—for my sake. I guess that explains that bruise on Stephen's cheek.

"Well," Zack says. "I'm sure he's been sleeping like a baby since you came back. He may lose those dark circles after all."

"You don't miss anything, do you?" I smile. He must have known this whole time. I guess only an idiot wouldn't notice. Cris and I aren't exactly subtle.

"I do like you," Zack admits. I will always admire how bold he is. "You stood up for me, on multiple occasions. You saved my people. You don't look at me like everyone else does. Not to mention, you're the daughter of the only Spore I respect. I find it hard *not* to like you. I'd be honored if I could simply call you a friend."

I actually manage a bigger smile this time when Zack bows in a courteous manner. Can't help a blush, too. "I think friend is good."

"So, you're headed to Vigor?" he asks. "We can go together. I'd still love to have dinner with a friend."

"Yeah," I say. "Sure. I can do that."

There's commotion outside when we arrive, like there normally is. Except that when we're about to walk in, an angry Mr. Tooley pushes Zack so hard he falls and hits concrete.

I'm stunned for a second, and in that same second Mr. Tooley jumps on Zack, one hand on his collar, and the other landing one punch after the other, so violent, so ruthless. I swear I can hear Zack's bones crack, and that's what snaps me out.

"Wait!" I start toward them. "Mr. Tooley, what are you—"

One of the other restaurant owners stops me and pulls me back. More of the owners come out to the street and surround the scene, but none of them try to stop what's happening. They just let Mr. Tooley beat Zack up repeatedly. Some of them even start cheering. I try to push past them, try to reach for Mr. Tooley to stop him, but he pushes me off with a force I never would have expected him to possess. I stumble and fall back, scraping my palms against the harsh concrete.

"I called you 'son'" Rage and disgust boil in Mr. Tooley's voice. He holds his fist up, bloody and bruised. "All this time. I treated you like family, when you're... You're the one who took her from me. You're the one who took my Zoe."

"Mr. Tooley," I scramble to him, "wait—"

"And you," Mr. Tooley turns to me, angry eyes filled with tears as he drops Zack, "you knew, didn't you? You kept this from me..."

"I..."

"Hey! Break it up!" Soldiers finally run up to the crowd and intervene. First with a warning, then by yanking people and pushing them off. A couple of them grab Mr. Tooley and pull him up. I want to tell them to take it easy. He's just an old man. But then I look at Zack on the ground. His bloody, swollen face, and I can't bring myself to say a word.

I crawl over to him, press the tips of my fingers to his neck just to make sure—he's got a pulse. If anything, his heart's beating too fast.

"Zack," I say, "I'm gonna get you up, okay?"

One of the Spores helps me get Zack to his feet, then leads me to a vehicle, and it's as we drive toward the hospital that I see him— Monty, standing a short distance from the crowd, eying the vehicle with a bone-chilling smirk. Of course it was him.

I stay with Zack the entire time as the medic tends to him. His left eye is swollen. His cheek all bruised up. Lip torn. Still, somehow, once the medic leaves and I walk up to him, he gives me a smile.

"I guess dinner's off the table," he says with evident struggle.

"Don't talk too much."

Zack stares up at the ceiling, exhaling. "I was an idiot, wasn't I?"

I'm not sure he actually wants me to answer that.

"I shouldn't have gotten involved with Lotiva. With Captain Hill," he says. "But to tell you the truth, I was desperate. *We* were desperate. Enough that it didn't matter what we'd have to do, who we'd have to hurt."

Zack told me about how, one day while he and some of the other kids were exploring, they came across a platoon from Lotiva. They saw an opportunity to get resources and took it, attacked them with Lori's help. Almost succeeded, but then the soldiers got the upper hand, found some of the kids and held them at gunpoint. Threatened to kill them unless Zack told them how he was able to control the infected.

Then Lori returned with a rescue party of chasers. The soldiers were nearly wiped out. Only one of them remained, begged for his life, said he'd give them three trucks of resources if they let him go. So they did. Then that soldier showed up at their rendezvous point with the trucks, and a whole platoon. That was when Zack met Captain Hill for the first time.

All the sick, starving kids got medicine and food. Rory, one of the kids I saw when I was in the Pit, could stand and run and play like never before. Hill left some of his troops to train them with firearms, even, so they could fight for themselves. Zack says he was operating on pure hatred, but I know it's a lie. I see it in the way his face softens whenever he remembers those kids. He took care of them, protected them as best he could. They were a family. He did what he did for his family. I don't think there's anything I wouldn't do for mine.

"I don't blame Mr. Tooley for what he did. I understand what he feels. I wanted to do the same thing to the man responsible for all I've been through. I'm sure Zoe was a nice girl. I'm sure she loved her dad and was thinking about him before she died. I was never after people like Mr. Tooley or his daughter."

"Do you … still want to make him pay?" I ask. "General Rodríguez?"

"Right now, all I want is to have Lori back," he answers. "That's all. I just want my sister back."

"I saw her," I tell him. I wasn't sure if I should, but … seeing how desperate he is, I can't help it. "When I was out there."

His eyes flash with endless questions.

"She wasn't in the best shape, but she was alive. I tried to tell her that you were alive. I think she understood."

"That's … good."

"I'm really sorry," I say. "Sara and I tried to get her. We tried to convince them to give her to us, and we did manage to convince some of them but … then the others decided to run off and take her with them."

"Yeah. Lori's too special to give up. I wouldn't give her up for the world," Zack says. "But it's okay. I know you would have tried everything you could."

"Have you ever met Vincent?" I ask. "Vincent Hayes."

Zack thinks on it for a moment. "It doesn't ring a bell."

"He's the one who has Lori right now," I say. "And he wants you to work with him."

Zack raises curious brows at that.

"He plans on keeping Lori, using her to build an army of infected to take down SPORE," I say. "And he wants to convince you to join him."

"Hmm," Zack says. "That sounds like a very tempting offer indeed. Did he tell you to relay this message to me?"

I shake my head.

"I know you're wondering if you can trust me," Zack says. "I know you're wondering about what'll happen. What I'll do, once we find Lori."

I can't even meet his eyes.

"It's okay. You should wonder," he says. "To be honest, I wonder about that myself."

I guess it's a good thing his mind's not made up yet?

"They wanted me to use you. The lieutenant and Sergeant Seidel. They thought that I could convince you to work for us. They thought I was the only one who could earn your trust because…"

"Because I like you?" Zack snorts. "It's true. If there was someone who could manipulate me, it'd probably be you."

"I don't want to manipulate anyone."

"You see," Zack says, "that is exactly what I like about you. You're genuine. I wish I could be this genuine all the time."

I place a hand on his. "We'll get Lori back."

I promise, I want to say, but I'm not sure I can actually promise him that.

FIFTY-FOUR

I PROCEED to the shooting range where I'd asked Cris to meet up.

"Hey." He's already waiting for me. "Glad you're doing okay."

"Do you have it?" I don't waste a breath.

He nods, casts a look around even though we're alone. Then he digs into his pocket and pulls out the radio, holding it to me. "Where'd you get this?" he whispers.

I take it and stuff it into my pocket, dodging his eyes.

"Ash," he steps closer, "why'd you ask me to hide it? Who are you contacting?"

"No one," I say. And it's the truth, even if he doesn't believe it. I'm not contacting anyone. Not now, anyway.

His brows knit together. He lifts my chin with his fingers. "You can tell me."

I push his hand away, gently, and step toward the stand. "Come on." I nod for him to join me. "It's been a while."

He lets out a low, worried sigh, then walks up to the stand next to me. Silence as we both put on our headpiece and start up the simulation.

I grab the M4 attached to the device, loading in a fake mag. "I saw Nina."

Cris turns to me, eyes big. "Is she the one who... How was she?"

"Alive." That's more than many of the fugitives can say. A deep inhale. "You remember that girl?" I ask "At the auto-parts store? The one I shot?"

The simulation loads into a first-person perspective of a soldier running through an urban terrain. Infected pop up on the screen, some hiding in windows, behind buildings, on rooftops, others marching down the streets.

"Yeah," Cris answers. He clears the first round of the simulation about five seconds after me.

You're supposed to kill all the infected on the screen before the soldier can proceed to the next area. Some of the targets are timed, only appearing for a short amount of time. The further you progress in the simulation, the harder it gets. In terms of the number of total targets in each round, how fast the targets move, and how long the timed targets stay on the screen.

"Her name was Chloe." I shoot a timed target that pops up behind the window of a building, "And she had a little sister called Mia."

There are a bunch of variants that affect the total score. There's the distance at which you hit a target (the further the target, the higher the score), how fast you clear a round, the body parts that you hit (headshots give the highest score), how many of the timed targets you get, and how much ammo you have left by the end of each round.

Cris is quiet. I don't know if it's because he doesn't know what to say, or because he's focused on the simulation.

"She was with Nina's group." I proceed to the next round in the simulation.

The simulation was programmed and designed by a team from the Engineering Division, and they keep improving it and adding things to it throughout the years. Apparently, one of them used to be a video-game developer, from before the outbreak.

"That must have been ... uncomfortable," Cris says.

Uncomfortable. Sure. That's not really the point, though.

"I've been thinking." My finger is growing sore. "What if you're right?"

"About what?" Cris discards a magazine and loads another one. He tends to go through his mags much faster than me. Though I'm impressed this is only his second mag.

"What's the end goal here?" I ask. "Killing each other? Until when? I mean, when you really think about it ... the people we're after, it's not like they had a choice in the matter. It's not like they chose to be where they are now. They're our enemies because ...

they have something that we want? Because they opposed a system that's pretty corrupt?"

"Ashley," he says. "Listen ... I know..." I can tell he's struggling to focus on both talking and going through the simulation. "Look, what I said before, it's not... I didn't mean to make you feel guilty. You did what you had to do. I know that. I understand that. You were trying to protect me. And back in Ground Zero, I should have listened to you. About that guy. I should have—"

"No." My own focus is wavering but I do my best, shooting the timed targets as soon as they pop up, because getting all of them will still boost my score enough that it won't matter if I don't hit the other targets from a distance. "I was just lucky that time, but I could have been wrong. Just like I could have been wrong about that boy, in the auto-parts store. I didn't know if he was actually going to shoot me. You were right. If I hadn't shot him, maybe Chloe—"

"Stop," Cris says. "You were right, too. What's done is done. No point wallowing about it now."

"But I am." I discard my mag when "No Ammo" pops up on the screen in blinking red letters. I load another mag. The text disappears. "I still think about Will, too. I still wonder if ... things could have played out differently. If I just hadn't—"

"Why are you doing this to yourself?" he asks.

"Because I'm tired," I admit. "Everything is so ... awful right now. And I'm going to see Melisa soon and I don't know if that's going to make things worse or better."

"Melisa?"

"I asked the lieutenant if I could see her."

"And he just ... said yes?" Cris lets out a low curse under his breath. I imagine one of the infected must have gotten a little too close.

"Yeah." It's starting to get a little overwhelming on my screen, too, but I headshot almost every single target.

"That's..." He doesn't know what to say, and neither do I. "How are you feeling?"

I've been wondering about that a lot. The truth is... "I don't know."

"I think ... I think Melisa will be happy to see you."

"She's an infected," I say.

"Well, I know, but…" Cris sighs. "Maybe you'll be happy to see her at least."

I pause to send a pointed glare at him. *"She's an infected."*

"I don't know, Ash." His voice strains. "Maybe you'll both feel awful about it. You're the one who wanted to see her."

"Gee, thanks, that makes me feel better."

"Sorry. Dammit—" He smacks a fist against the surface of the stand when the "You Are Dead" sound effect plays. I can't help a snicker. "I'm never going to beat this." Cris sets the M4 down, taking in a breath. "Sorry, I didn't mean to snap."

"No, it's fine, I'm just … venting. I didn't mean to drop all of this on you at once." There's just so much going on in my head. So much.

"It's okay," he says. "You can vent as much as you want. We didn't really get to talk all that much since you got back. I had things I wanted to say as well."

"Yeah?" I pause the simulation as soon as I finish the current round, then I give him my full attention. "What did you want to say?"

"Uh…" Cris's eyes fall from mine. I get the feeling he wishes we were still running the simulation so he'd have a distraction. "I just feel like we left things unfinished. Last time. Sergeant Seidel showed up and we … couldn't really keep talking."

"Well," I shrug, silently enjoying how flustered he's getting by the second, "we're talking now."

"Ash … you know what I mean."

Yes. I do. I just want to see his big brows arch in frustration. "You're gonna have to spell it out," I tease.

"You really are a bite on the back, you know that?"

"Yep."

"Fine." He inhales through his nose. "I like you. A lot. And yeah, I know, what a shocking revelation this is." Sarcasm. Then, not so sarcastically, "I've always liked you, and I never really stopped." A deep breath. "I've never confessed my feelings to a girl before, and this is really awkward and kind of uncomfortable, but I'm sure you're getting a hell of a kick out of it, so I guess it's fine. If making a fool out of myself means I get to see you smile the way you are right now, it's fine."

And that makes me smile more.

"I'd make you a list of all the things I like about you, but I don't think it can ever be long enough, so to summarize: I like you for who you are. Exactly as you are. I like you when you're being a menace just for the sake of it. I like you when you get passionate about something. I like you when you're vulnerable and raw. I like you when you're fighting viciously for those you care about. I..." He looks so deeply into my eyes I want to melt. "I just like you."

My smile stretches wider. I can't decide between laughing and crying.

"Okay, just in case none of that was clear," he says, "I'm asking you if you want to be my girlfriend."

I shake my head. "I think I should be the one asking you: do *you* want to be my boyfriend?"

He blinks. "What?"

"Do you *really* want to be my boyfriend? Are you actually prepared to subject yourself to that kind of torture?"

Cris's face relaxes into an easy grin. "You're right. Those *are* better questions."

"I know."

"Well, I guess there are some downsides to consider."

"Such as?"

"The most obvious downside is, quite literally ... that you're a shorty."

I narrow my eyes at him and give him a light kick to the shins. "I consider that an advantage."

He shakes his head sideways. "For you, maybe. But I have to bend way down to look you in the face. Eventually, that's gonna cause some serious back issues."

That's implying we'd be together long enough for that to happen. I like that implication.

"I have a lot of downsides to consider, too." I fold my arms in front of me. "Like the fact you get on my nerves all the time and I always want to punch you. That's not gonna do my blood pressure any good. But then again, you *would* make a great punching bag."

"I'd gladly be your punching bag." Cris takes a step closer to me and takes both my hands in his, holding them so gently. I love how warm his hands are. How warm they've always been. "Just as I'd gladly be your boyfriend."

My face isn't wide enough for a bigger smile. "Good luck, then," I whisper. "You'll need it."

A soft grin. He touches his forehead to mine, and my breath

catches. I love, love, *love* when he does that. We've come a long way from all the headbutting—most of which was my treat, to be fair.

But the longer I look into his eyes, the more lost I get in them. The closer he leans in, the harder it gets not to stare at his lips. So close. So tempting. So there. His breath practically touches my face, but guilt consumes me the second my nose brushes his.

I pull away from him with a conflicted sigh. "This feels wrong."

"What?"

"This." I gesture between us. "Us, being happy. I mean, Sara's dead and we're…"

Cris's shoulders drop. His smile gone, just like that. "You don't have to feel bad about not feeling bad all the time."

"I know," I say. "But I still feel bad."

"Yeah…" He frowns. "Me, too."

FIFTY-FIVE

LT. MANSUR and I take the elevator to the first basement level of the Sphere building.

We confirm visitation at reception, then proceed down the hallway to the familiar face waiting for us.

"Haytham?" I say. "You're working again?"

He shakes his head. "Not exactly. I... I'm just here to assist in minor tasks." He looks to Lt. Mansur with darkening cheeks. "Thanks again, Uncle—sir."

Lt. Mansur nods with a smile. "Don't mention it."

Ah, so the lieutenant must have intervened to lighten Haytham's punishment.

Haytham clears his throat. "I'm going to be your guide. So, if you would please follow me."

He leads us into a small scanner room. The door through which we pass closes as soon as all three of us are inside, then a red light scans us top to bottom and back. A green light blips, then the door across from us opens into the next section of the lab.

I've never been here before, but it looks exactly how I imagined it. Similar to the hospital, almost everything is white, if not whiter—the walls, the floor, the ceiling. I guess it's more needed here, underground, with the absence of natural light.

"How have you been?" I ask Haytham.

"Good, I guess." He lowers his voice. "People keep giving me side-eye because my uncle intervened to get me back in here, but I've learned to deal with it."

"You're good at your job, right?" I ask. "I'm sure they don't mind having you back."

"Someone who's good at their job understands the importance of confidentiality," he says. "And not revealing classified information to the public."

I want to say I'm sorry again, but apologizing isn't actually going to fix much at this point.

A few electric doors later, and a last one that requires a code he punches in, we enter a lab room. I stay with Haytham while Lt. Mansur heads over to talk to Colonel Marchand.

Chirping and chittering comes from a stack of cages containing different animals.

"What are those?" I ask.

"Our test subjects." Haytham swallows. "I told you we've been testing the cure and vaccine samples on animals."

Yeah. I don't know what I thought he meant when he said that, but I definitely didn't picture animals being kept in cages in an underground lab. "Where do you find all of these?"

"Some of them are raised here in Spheria or in Serco. Others are captured from the outside," he explains. "We need subjects that have been exposed to the virus and ones that haven't."

Of course. The hypothetical cure would only work on infected subjects. Vaccines on the other hand need uninfected ones. Inject the subject with it, then expose it to the virus and see what happens.

Haytham nods for me to come with him and follow him further into the room, behind that stack of cages. I come to a halt at the sight across from me.

Melisa's inside a cube-shaped compartment with transparent glass walls. There's a bed and a sink and a toilet inside, but none of them look used. Melisa looks almost exactly the same as I remember her. With that gorgeous curly hair of hers, even if it looks messier than usual. Her big, innocent, brown eyes wandering about the room. The only thing I don't recognize about her are the noises coming out of her mouth. Low, raspy moans. The ugly reminder she's no longer human.

"There she is." Haytham stands beside me, gesturing at the glass ... cage, is what I would call it.

"Does she get food?" I don't know why that's the first question that pops in my head.

"Yeah, she does," Haytham answers. "Some raw meat. She doesn't need to eat as often as we do, so it's easier to manage."

What kind of meat? I want to ask, but my vegetarian self is more than satisfied with this minimal information. "This is ... awful."

"I know," Haytham sighs. "Do you wanna talk to her?"

Did he just say *talk*? "Can I?"

"There's a mic." He points at a control panel on one of the glass walls. "We have built-in speakers in the compartment, so she can hear you."

Hesitant, I step toward the compartment, stopping in front of the panel. It feels like this cage was built more for humans than infected. Who else have they kept in here? What else did they use it for?

Haytham presses a button, then nods for me to go ahead.

"Hi, Mel..." I lean into the mic.

Melisa turns to me. Curious brown eyes. Mouth agape. Slow steps as she starts toward me.

"Do you remember me?" I place a hand against the glass. "It's Ashley... We trained together."

Her gaze fixes on my hand, studying, head tilted sideways. Then she lifts her own hand and places it over mine against the glass.

My breath catches. "Is this normal? Does she know who I am?"

"I think so." Haytham stands next to me. "The reason they allow me around her, despite the fact that I'm new, is that she seems to respond more to what I say. Our observations suggest that Actives do retain some level of memory."

A small flutter of hope in my stomach. I try to catch Melisa's eyes, leaning closer to the glass. "Mel," I call, and she looks up from my hand to my face. "I miss you so much. I'm so sorry that this happened to you."

I'm sorry we couldn't save you.

Her head tilts to the other side. She looks at me with a mix of curiosity and hollowness.

"Does she understand what I'm saying?"

Haytham shakes his head sideways. "It's hard to tell. I think sometimes she does. She still feels things."

"Feels things?" I turn to Haytham.

"Yeah, like right now, she's feeling pretty calm, relaxed. Maybe because she's in familiar company. Sometimes she'll be a little agitated. Other times she'll sit in the corner, hugging her knees, refusing to acknowledge anyone."

"Do you ever go inside?" I ask.

"Only if we need blood samples. And she has to be tranqed for that." He shakes his head. "Even if there is a part of her in there that's still the Melisa we knew, as soon as we try to attempt direct contact, she loses control to the—" He pauses, as if recalculating his words, then backtracks. "It's not possible."

"What were you gonna say just then? Loses control to what?"

"The parasite." Lt. Mansur joins us.

Color drains from Haytham's face. His eyes dart to where Colonel Marchand is standing, but she's not really paying us mind.

"Parasite?" I ask. Not sure I'm following.

Lt. Mansur nods. "Active is short for 'Active Host,' what we call current carriers of the parasite."

What in the world?

A hundred questions pop in my head at once, I don't know which one to ask first.

"Perhaps it's best if we show her, Haytham," Lt. Mansur says.

Haytham hesitates, looks again to Marchand, who doesn't protest. Then he nods and fetches a laptop, accesses some archives—files that look all-too familiar with their titling. Haytham double-clicks one of them, and it opens up a new tab that plays security footage.

I recognize the location immediately. It's the lab from Ground Zero, except ... this is the other side of that door we saw in the recording.

There's a cube-shaped glass compartment in the footage, suspiciously similar to the one Melisa's in. Inside is someone dressed in a white coat—a researcher, probably. Looks pretty young. Must have been a student?

There's someone standing outside that cage. The guy from the first footage. The one who was injured; except here, he's still fine.

The man inside the cage starts hitting his head violently against the glass. It doesn't look like the glass will break, but blood spatters all over. Then the guy drops. His mouth falls ajar like he's screaming, but there is no audio so I'm not sure. Something crawls out of his mouth. Small and slimy.

It looks familiar.

I've seen it before, during Fire Day duty, and again in Ground Zero, when I saved Stephen from that Active.

FIFTY-SIX

THE GUY on the outside panics. He unlocks the door to the compartment and rushes inside to check on the subject.

The subject who, seconds later, comes to and immediately attacks him, biting him in the neck. The researcher pushes him off and stumbles back. He closes the door and runs back out, bleeding, leaving the room.

I know the rest.

"That person, inside the glass cage... That's patient zero?" I ask. "And that thing that came out of it ... was the parasite?"

Lt. Mansur nods.

"But then that means ... patient zero was an Active?" My head is spinning. "So the virus is actually not a virus?"

"There is a virus," Haytham cuts in, "that's why Actives aren't like the other infected. Because there exists such a thing as a *former* host. So, for example, what you saw in that footage just now, if a parasite resides within a host for an extended period of time without food, and the body starts to become weaker, beyond the parasite's ability to maintain and feed off of it, the parasite will then detach itself from the body to search for another, more suitable host. The attachment process by itself causes irreparable damage to the host's body, and the detachment process even more. The parasite leaves a substance inside the host that can be spread via an exchange of bodily fluids."

The virus.

That makes sense, and yet I'm having a hard time wrapping my head around this new revelation. "How come we never heard of Actives until five years ago?"

"We didn't know about the parasite, originally," Lt. Mansur says. "It was the mission that Sears led to Ground Zero that revealed their existence. The lab in the science building was put on lockdown shortly after the outbreak. So, for all intents and purposes, patient zero, in our eyes, was a regular infected. But when Sears arrived at that lab and when they found that room, and all this footage, we learned that patient zero was originally an active host that had managed to separate the parasite from its body. That parasite you see there," he nods at the screen, "it was still in there when Sears's unit arrived."

"It survived?" I ask. "For fifteen years? Without a host?"

"Yes," Lt. Mansur confirms. "The parasite can survive without a host. What it can't do is reproduce. Sears's unit unleashed the parasite by accident when they unlocked the lab. And the parasite did what it was waiting to do all that time. It sought the nearest host it could find."

Luke's mom.

I turn away from the screen, back toward Melisa in that cage, who's lost interest in us and is just roaming around. "So ... then there is no chance that you can get rid of it and save her, is there?"

"Extracting the parasite," Haytham frowns, "will just turn her into any other infected."

"So, what have you learned?" I ask. "In the past months that you've had her here, what have you learned? If you couldn't even make a cure or vaccine using her blood. If you couldn't do anything to help humanity, what's the point of keeping her like this? Caged like an animal?"

"Ashley, that's not my call," Haytham says. "You think I like watching Melisa like this? You're only here today—I'm here every day. I have been for the past five months. Don't act like you're the only one hurt by this, okay? This doesn't bring me joy. It doesn't make me feel good about myself. Just because I'm not as vocal about it as you are, doesn't mean I don't have feelings, too."

No, maybe I don't know how Haytham feels, but I guess I'm not entirely done holding grudges after all. "This *was* your idea, wasn't it?" I nod to Melisa. "You're the one who wanted to do this to her."

And I know it's not fair. I know that, back then, he was trying to stop them from killing her on the spot. I was trying to stop them, too. But having seen her now? Maybe death would have been more merciful.

Not that any of us could have predicted that.

Sorrow clouds his gaze as it sits on Melisa. Then his head drops. "Yeah…" he sighs, "I guess I did."

And that's that.

"I'm ready to go," I tell the lieutenant.

He gives me a nod, offers Haytham a sympathetic smile before we start to the door. We go back the same way we came, through the reception hall, then the elevator.

"Do you regret it?" Lt. Mansur asks me when we arrive at the first floor. "Seeing your friend like that?"

I don't know. I don't really know how I feel about any of this.

And before I can figure out an answer, for myself or for him, the commotion in the main lobby draws our attention. There's a line of armed soldiers, the doors of the main entrance wide open, and then a familiar man with a missing eye and a long, graying beard walks through in handcuffs, surrounded by guards.

They've arrested General Sears.

FIFTY-SEVEN

THEY ARRESTED General Sears for the one crime he didn't commit.

After what happened outside Vigor, tensions rose between the two protesting parties, and those in favor of the Pit Survivors, according to what some guards told me and the lieutenant, vandalized Sears's home and office and assaulted him, all while operating under the belief this is the man who bombed Eukson, and why is he still walking around free, in a position of power, training new soldiers when he should be answering for his crimes?

So, Rodríguez ordered his arrest. The lieutenant suspects it's partially for Sears's safety, but the more obvious reason is because he wants to appease the civilians, sway them in his favor. I'm not sure if the public will be happy with the fact it took Rodríguez this long to take action. And of course, the only reason he never took any action is because Sears didn't even do what he's accused of.

I can only imagine how Luke is feeling about all of this.

My brain is mush by the time I get back to my dorm.

It's awfully quiet. Dalal's door is closed, lights out. She's probably asleep, even though it's not that late. Before I can head to my room, a knock on the door. I go to check. Lucille stands on the other side with a bunch of empty plastic containers and a box full of random things. Her hair has never been so disheveled. It's no longer tied up in a tight, neat ponytail, like it normally is. She has it loose, resting on either side of her shoulders, stray hairs sticking out, her fringe messy and swept to the side, revealing a bit of her forehead, and the scar that Dalal mentioned before.

"Hey, so..." Lucille's voice is subdued, as if she just woke up from a rough nap, "these are Dalal's. All clean." She hands me the containers.

I take them from her. "She's bringing you food, too?" Honestly, where does she find the time?

"Crazy, right? I told her I can cook just fine. But she thinks she's Jordan Randy or whatever his name was."

"Who?" I blink in confusion.

"Some master genius chef from like..." she waves a dismissive hand, "before."

Yeah. Still no clue who that is. I wonder if Jose would have known.

"Anyway," Lucille says. "I was clearing Sara's stuff... What she had in her room."

Oh.

"Thought you might want to have a look." She nods at the box. "See if there's anything you wanna take. For keepsakes. You can ask Dalal, too, when she comes back, wherever she is. She wasn't answering earlier."

"Uh..." I don't want to take it. I don't even want to look at it.

"You're gonna say no." Lucille's eyes are dull and heavy-lidded when they hold mine. "You're gonna tell me you don't want anything. That I can take it or throw it all away because you don't care. Because somewhere deep down, you still believe she's not gone."

So Lucille can read minds now?

"And then what's gonna happen is we're gonna flashforward a week from now—or a month, or even a year." Her shoulders slouch. She looks like the smallest blow of wind would send her flying across the hallway, and yet her words are heavy with grief. Remorse. "You're gonna be sitting on the floor crying, wishing you'd taken this box and had even a quick look. You're gonna be regretting for the rest of your life that you don't have anything to remember your friend by. Because you told yourself you'd never forget her."

I'm not going to forget.

"But guess what? That's not how humans work," Lucille continues. "You're going to forget, bit by bit. You'll forget what she looked like. What she smelled like. What she sounded like. You'll forget her ... and *then* she's really gone. For good. Because when you had the chance to take something that would keep a part of her alive with you, you said no, because you were an idiot."

I just stare at her in total bafflement. I don't know why she's telling me any of this. I don't know what to say to it, either.

"Don't be an idiot." She pushes the box against me forcefully. "Take the box."

I do. "Did you ... have a look already?"

"Yeah." She nods. "It's all yours."

"Okay." I breathe in. "Thanks."

Lucille's lips part as if she's about to say something else, then changes her mind, starts toward her dorm, changes her mind again and comes back to face me. "I know it's hard to tell sometimes, if people really care about you or if they're just ... using you, for one reason or another. Believe me, I've been there so many times."

I don't doubt it. Knowing who her mom is? I can only imagine how many people wanted to gain favor with a Division Commander's daughter.

"But she really did care." Lucille smiles—a sad smile that tells me she's remembering one too many heartfelt moments. "She cared about you. And she cared about me. That's just who she was."

Yeah... It is.

I shouldn't have doubted it. Not for a second.

Lucille goes back to her dorm. I kick the door shut and take the box to my room. I set it on the desk I have yet to decorate and give it a quick look.

I find an ID Tag. *Nathan Grant.* My heart squeezes. Sara told me she'd taken one of these, after his body was recovered—what was left of it. Nina had taken the other one.

There is a small hair band in there, with a few curly hairs stuck to it. Melisa's. Next to that is a compass, with initials carved on it: *J.B.*

I recognize that compass because I used to steal it from Dad's pocket every time he came back from an assignment. Haze and I would pick a direction, then follow the compass through the sector until we found a cool spot we'd never been before. I pick it up and flick the lid open, lips quivering. He must have given this to Sara, that day.

I set the compass aside to pick up what's underneath it: an envelope with photos inside. One of them is our squad photo from Basic, the same one I have. But this is special because it has a smudge on it, from when Sara gave me this photo to take, and I started crying as soon as I saw it. My tears fell on the photo, and when I tried to clean it, the pristine surface got all smudged. Sara then took this photo instead and gave me a new one. The next photo in the envelope is one of Dad. It looks like an ID photo, the kind that'd be attached to a file, and he looks so young in it I almost don't recognize him.

I take a deep breath as I place it aside and keep digging.

Then I see it.

A familiar, turtle snow globe with a turquoise base that reflects in the water and the glitter inside.

I take it out, hold it in both hands, and slide to the floor, breath hitching.

Hey, look! Sara had walked into my room, holding that globe in her hands. We'd been competing to win it at one of the game booths at Vigor. None of us managed to score high enough for it, though. Until she did. *I managed to win it!*

Good for you, I said flatly.

Well, actually. She toyed with the globe, tossing it in her hands. *I... I got it for you.*

I don't want it. I carefully removed my boot and rolled up my pants leg to reveal the bandage around my calf. I was still recovering from my injury during that one FTX.

Sara stood still for a moment, silent. She set the snow globe on my desk and walked closer. *Need help changing the bandages?*

No.

Do you want me to grab you some food?

No.

That was my second firm no, and still she refused to take the hint.

Do you need something? I asked.

How long are we gonna be doing this? Sara said. *Why is it that during training you can talk to me fine, but when we're in our dorm you can't even spare me more than one-syllable responses?*

Do you need something? I asked again.

Can you just look at me, please? Sara said. *Just look me in the eyes and tell me exactly how you feel.*

And I did as she wanted. I shot to my feet, looked her straight in the eyes, and I told her exactly how I felt.

Angry, I said. *I feel angry. Disgusted. At the thought I ever even considered you a friend.*

Go on. She gestured with her hands. *Don't stop there. Say all you got to say.*

You manipulated me. You pretended like you had no idea who I was, just so you could get close to me. You decided, all on your own, that we were going to be friends. You made that decision on both our behalfs. How do I know that any of it was real? That this—I motioned at her—*all of you wasn't just a lie you made up? How do I know that you're really who you are? How do I know that* we *are who we are?*

She didn't argue. She didn't defend herself. She just let me explode, and boy did I explode.

You know, when I got to Spheria... You have no idea how hard it was. To trust anyone again. To feel like I could belong. To believe that people could actually care about me. The pain of it all felt like a noose around my neck, tightening by the second. *But then I met you. I trusted you. Opened up to you. About everything. You made me believe you were actually there for me. You made me believe you actually cared about me, about how I felt. That you accepted me for who I was, just because. No matter how harsh or blunt or rude I may have been.*

Tears filled her eyes, just like they did mine, but unlike me, she didn't let hers fall.

I thought you were as genuine as you pretended to be. But you weren't acting out of genuineness. You were acting out of guilt. It was the least you could do to honor *him. That's what* you *said. You were trying to repay a debt you never even owed me.*

Her gaze fell to her feet. A hand wrapped around her free wrist, squeezing.

Even what I had with Nina was more real than what you and I ever had. At least she liked me for me. And not because she felt obligated to.

Her throat worked up and down. *Is there more?*

Yes, there is.

She nodded. *I'm listening.*

I just... I just can't understand why, I said—yelled. Sara's hurt eyes watched me, wide but not surprised. *Why you?*

I wish, she said, *that I could go back. Believe me, I do. Because I ask myself that question every day. Why me?*

I'm glad we agree, I said. *Are you happy now? You heard everything you wanted to hear?*

She stayed silent.

Good. So leave me the hell alone, I said. *And take that stupid snow globe with you.*

She sniffled, but still she didn't shed a single tear. *Okay.*

And that was the last time I saw Sara through the rest of AIT. She packed her things that night and left for the Renegades.

PART FIVE

FIFTY-EIGHT

LT. MANSUR CALLS a meeting inside a briefing room in the Spec Ops HQ for the pre-mission briefing.

Before we start, though, Sgt. Seidel pulls me aside, as is tradition. "When you gave me the coordinates, you said to keep them confidential. If there's a reason why, you should tell me now before the lieutenant makes a public announcement."

I should have known she wouldn't drop it. I'm still not going to tell her.

"Who is it?" Sgt. Seidel asks. "You have to tell me who it is you're protecting, Brown."

"No one," I lie.

She inhales a deep breath. "This can jeopardize our entire operation. The general isn't exactly happy with our progress, and considering how much worse things are now, we can't risk anything."

"We have forces stationed by the power plant, right? Keeping watch?" I try to keep a calm, unbothered voice. "Then we have nothing to worry about."

I can tell Sgt. Seidel's patience with me is running thin. She nods for me to go ahead and join the rest of the platoon while she goes to stand with the other staff sergeants.

The platoon looks different from the last time we did one of these briefings. So many new faces I don't recognize. It makes sense. We lost half of the Second Rifle Squad. I'm surprised they even managed to fill in all the empty spots.

When I stand in line, everything around me feels ... claustrophobic. The people are too close. The ground is too close. The air is too close.

"I would like to address first," the lieutenant starts, "the loss of one of our most brilliant soldiers yet. Specialist Sarang Jung, who joined us two months into our search for the sentient crawler, and who has fought alongside us with incredible strength and resilience, until the very end."

My throat tightens. I hold a breath in, close my burning eyes until the sensation dissipates and the tears inside drench my lashes. I open them again to a blur. The burning is worse.

Don't cry.

"Specialist Jung regrettably suffered a fatal bite in the outside, following an unfortunate encounter with the infected and while possessing very limited resources. We didn't get there in time to save her, but we did manage to bring back Private Brown, who is still with us today, and for that we are grateful. If you could all take a moment to remember Jung with a kind word."

Now's not the time to cry.

"Following up on casualties, let's welcome the two newest additions to the Renegades. Specialist Xael Parayno and Specialist Tyra Markell."

New additions. Meaning replacements.

They're replacing Sara already.

Is that how expendable we are? How unimportant?

I can't bring myself to look at Tyra. Because all I see is Sara. All I see is a reminder that she's gone.

"Now I know this may seem sudden to some of you, as we had kept things under wraps until we confirmed our intel for certain, but General Rodríguez has ordered an immediate ambush on the latest fugitive hideout we've located. The Yellow Cliff nuclear power plant in Zone Twenty. We had previously sent a scouting unit to investigate the coordinates. According to their observations, we believe that the sentient crawler is indeed at the power plant.

"We suspect the hideout was a strategic one, given that SPORE had been planning to restore that power plant as an energy source. We have also confirmed the identity of the three fugitives in possession of the crawler. Mia Sherwood, Justin Sullivan, and Vincent Hayes, who is presumably the leader." Lt. Mansur gestures at the screen behind him showing the profiles of the three fugitives. "With their identities confirmed, the general has taken their families into custody as a bargaining chip."

"Seriously?" Cris mutters under his breath, seemingly disturbed.

"Considering how vast the power plant is, and that we don't know where precisely the fugitives are hiding, we'll need to first establish three-sixty security and then assign assault units to each building to cover all potential hideouts.

"Each and every one of you will be equipped with a tranquilizer. We want the crawler alive. If you find yourself having to shoot it, do so to incapacitate and not kill."

My eyes immediately drift to Zack. He does not look pleased in the slightest with this.

"Once the objective is secured, we will make a full retreat. Assuming we're able to capture the crawler unharmed, we will attempt to get it to aid us with our retreat by ordering the infected to stand down. However, we need to be prepared for a worst-case scenario. Should we fail to capture the crawler, or should we capture it in a condition that doesn't allow it to cooperate with us, we will need as much firepower as possible to retreat successfully.

"These are the plans for the power plant." Lt. Mansur points at a map on the screen behind him. "Each one of you will have this blueprint sent to their portor. This power plant used to provide electricity to about a third of the country, and it continued running for a while after the outbreak, too. Now, this used to be a nuclear power plant, meaning there's risk of radiation. Assuming the fugitives are aware of this, likely they're staying away from the radioactive zones. This would leave us with a few key locations to infiltrate. That said, we can't exactly rule out other possibilities. As a safety measure, you will be given special equipment for scanning and measuring radioactivity.

"As for the fugitives, I'll say the same thing I said when the Renegades were formed; some of you who weren't present could stand to benefit from it. All life is precious, and our fight is for humanity. *All* of humanity. Some of you may struggle to see it, rightfully so, but our enemy is human, too. Let's remember that so that we may be able to remind *them*. We're in this fight together, and we're all suffering together. Let's extend a hand to our brothers and sisters. If they don't take it, at least we tried. Humanity suffers together."

"Humanity suffers together," everyone chants.

"Prepare for take-off in thirty minutes. We'll rendezvous with the backup from Kadia at our FOB. It gives us a chance to refuel, eat, and then continue from there," Lt. Mansur says. "May God protect us all. Dismissed."

The lieutenant approaches the new arrivals with a welcoming grin. A flash to my first day with the Renegades. Dalal's voice a whisper in my ear—*He personally comes to greet every new soldier that joins his unit.* Yeah. Anyone that joins. There was nothing special about me and Cris. We were just another replacement.

Is this how my squad felt on that day? When Cris and I joined them? Were they disappointed not to see their old comrades? The ones who were there before us? Did they feel all this resentment building up inside them? That their friends were being replaced so fast by some random people? And they're supposed to just welcome them with open arms? Were they thinking these new people could never replace the ones who are gone? Could never live up to them?

Because that's exactly what I'm thinking right now.

FIFTY-NINE

I FOLLOW as everyone starts for the armory, silently praying Sgt. Seidel doesn't pull me aside for a second round of interrogations.

Connor's walking a short distance from the group, hands in pockets.

I was really counting on Sara being here for this, maybe even doing the bulk of it. I don't know how I'm going to handle it without her, but I made a promise to Nina and I'm not going to break it.

"Hey, Connor." I catch up to him. "Can I talk to you for a sec?"

"Sure thing, Pinky." Connor slows to match my pace. "What's up?"

Maybe start casual first. Don't jump straight into it.

"You never told me Nina was your girlfriend." I still am curious about that either way. If I can't get the full story from Nina, might as well try the other trusted source. He tends to be chattier than she is.

He squints. "You saw Nina?" As if he doesn't already know that. I have to give it to him. He's good at pretending. Just as good as Nathan was. If this were the old times and people still made movies, he would have made a great actor.

"Uh-huh." I nod. "Sara and I ran into her and some other fugitives. They took us with them."

"I see." He blows a soft breath, eying me with raised brows. "What did she tell you?"

"Not much. She didn't even want to tell me why you broke up."

"That's because we didn't," Connor says. "Not officially. We just kind of ... drifted apart."

Huh. Interesting.

I sway side to side innocently and pray I'm not overstepping with this next one. "Aaaaand did the drifting happen before or after Lucille entered the equation?"

Connor's eyes bulge. Oops. Definitely overstepped.

"She was worried about you in Ground Zero," I explain. "Why would Lucille worry about someone she's repeatedly and publicly expressed her distrust for?"

"That's a good question." He snorts, but he's not denying anything either.

It always seemed like there was something more ... *personal* to it. The way Lucille talked about Connor. Like she was trying too hard to show just how much she hated him. Like she needed everyone around her to see that and *only* that. Like that was the only way she could convince herself.

"You think I'd still be alive if I'd cheated on Nina?" Connor gives me a side-eye. Yeah, probably not. "Lucille was after. We met when I finished AIT. Nina and I had been broken up for about eight months? Lucille and I dated for six, give or take. The highlight of our relationship, hands down, was when she accused me of treason, held a gun to my head, and threatened to blow my brains out."

Yeah ... but she wasn't entirely wrong for that, was she?

Now that I think about it, he may not seem like Nina's type, but I guess Connor himself has a type. Both Nina and Lucille have a bit of a ... flippant personality.

Anyway, I'm getting sidetracked. I was hoping for a seamless bridge, but time is precious. I may as well just make the jump. "Don't warn them."

Connor puffs up his cheeks, eyes narrowing with a question. "Don't warn who? About what?"

"Vincent," I say. "And his friends."

His hands fall out of his pockets and drop to his sides. "I don't know what you're—"

"I know you've been in contact with them," I cut him off. "Nina told me. The Raven. Is that what they call you?"

He lets out a nervous, conflicted chuckle. "Sounds badass, but nope. You got me confused with someone else, Pinky."

"I didn't tell anyone," I assure him. "I promise."

I don't think he believes me. God, Sara would have been way better at this.

"This is why you were asking me about Nina, isn't it?" I keep my voice low, even though the others are a good distance away from us. "You wanted to know how much I knew?"

"Wait," Connor looks at me, scrutinizing, "*Nina* told you? When?"

"After Vincent ran off," I answer. "He took the crawler and some resources and left."

"No." Connor shakes his head. "No. What is this? Who put you up to this?"

"No one—"

"I know what really happened." Connor's tone shifts from skepticism to accusation. "Vincent told me what you and Sara did. He told me you tried to steal the crawler and killed the others, including Nina—"

"Nina isn't dead," I say. "Nina helped me and Sara get away. Jed and Don are okay, too. Vincent lied to you, whatever he said."

"And why would he do that, huh? Why would Vincent leave Nina and the others behind? All they've got is each other out there."

"Because she wanted to give us the crawler," I say. "But Vincent didn't wanna give up Lori, so he, Justin and Mia decided to run off and leave the others behind."

Connor's eyes dart all over. There must be a billion thoughts running through his head right now.

Please don't let this backfire.

"Nina told me that someone was giving you orders, someone from within, but she didn't know who."

His whole posture shrinks. "I wasn't even involved, you know." The words come out shaky. "I wasn't part of this. The conspiracy. Not at first, anyway."

Wait, what?

"But a couple months back, all of a sudden my name was cleared, my family was released. I thought, finally, they realized I was actually innocent." A dry smile that dissolves into a frown. "But then ... someone contacted me anonymously. Told me that if I wanted to keep mine and my family's freedom, if I wanted to keep our name clear, that I should do as they asked. And if I refused, they'd plant 'evidence' to incriminate me and my family, and we'd all be exiled.

My siblings are four and nine. My mom is pregnant. What was I supposed to do?"

I see... They needed someone who wasn't involved to pick up where the others left off. Someone who was already thoroughly investigated, whose innocence was proven so that they wouldn't be suspected. But this means that someone somewhere is still pulling the strings.

"They gave me Vincent's contact ID," Connor says. "He'd contacted Lotiva, apparently, before SPORE arrived, and told them he'd gotten his hands on Lori. So they told him he had to keep the crawler as far away from Lotiva as possible, wait until someone contacted him and told him what to do. I was assigned to the Renegades to collect intel about their plans and relay that information. Make sure Vincent and the others didn't accidentally stumble across any of the patrols. Make sure they evacuated their hideouts before the Renegades got there."

"Who's your contact?" I ask. "Who is it you're relaying this information to?"

"I don't know." Connor shrugs in defeat. I don't think he's lying. "It could be anyone. They made sure I didn't know who they were. They couldn't risk their identity being compromised. And I can't risk my family's safety."

"What about all the other lives you're risking?" I ask. "By playing along. By working for this person. You think they'd resort to blackmail if they didn't have a hidden agenda?"

"They don't want Rodríguez to get the crawler. And neither do I," Connor says. "Why are you even talking to me? Why not just report me?"

"I'm not gonna do that."

"Why not?"

"Because Nina asked me not to," I say. "Because Nina seemed to believe that you would listen."

"Nina told you that to save herself. She ratted me out—"

"She told me that to save *you*," I counter. "They're both using you, Connor. Vincent's been using you to get intel himself. He doesn't plan on handing over Lori to your contact. He's acting on his own. He plans on keeping Lori, and using her to raise an army of infected to lead right to Spheria. So if ... Nina ever really meant anything to you, and if she knows you as much as she thinks she does, you won't say anything to Vincent."

"And then what? Just let Rodríguez have the crawler anyway?" He grimaces. "Give him yet another tool for fearmongering at his disposal?"

He's right. I don't know that the general should have Lori. I don't know that *anyone* should. And there's still the issue of Zack. He might have his own agenda. He could turn on us as soon as we find her. If Vincent manages to convince him, even worse.

"You're worried about your family, right?" I say. "If we tell Sergeant Seidel, maybe she can see to it that your family's safe."

"For all I know, she's the one blackmailing me." His eyes water, but he blinks the tears away. "I don't know who to trust. I don't know who to go to... I—"

"I don't think Sergeant Seidel would do that." And I mean it. "We can go to her together if you want. I'll argue your case."

He tilts his head to the side, uncertainty written all over his face.

"If not for Nina," I say, "then for Nathan."

That makes him freeze.

"You think he'd have wanted you to help someone who was happy to leave his sister to die?"

Connor looks down, shaking his head. He doesn't say another word. He just walks off to join up with the others.

SIXTY

MY BREATH CATCHES as we fly close to the overwhelmingly massive plant. How are we supposed to find three people and a crawler in this place?

"What are those?" I nod at three tower-like structures, hollowed out at the top.

"Cooling towers," Connor's voice is in my ears. "This is where water is cooled to then be reused. Like a cycle. If the plant were running, there would be steam coming out of those towers. Looks terrifying if you don't know what you're looking at."

"We're lucky to have a tour guide with us, then, aren't we?" Lucille's haughty taunt comes through my headset.

"You sure are," Connor teases.

All of Lucille's colorful commentary about Connor feels so ... jarring, knowing what I know. How soon would she toss him off the helicopter if she knew that he has, in fact, been helping the fugitives?

"Caves, while we're still in the air..." Sgt. Seidel says. "Can you pinpoint a potential location as to where Lori might be? Does the concentration of infected give any indication at all?"

"Not necessarily," Zack says, deadpan. "You see, Lori doesn't go around ordering infected. She communicates what needs to be communicated to other crawlers, and those crawlers will spread out and deliver the message. I highly doubt her kidnappers are allowing her to roam free, anyway. That wouldn't be too wise, would it?

It's like if SPORE had allowed Eukson's greenhouse produce to be public property. Can you imagine the chaos?"

Sgt. Seidel doesn't show it, but I can tell her patience is running thin. Unfortunately, everything Zack says is true, which is probably why she doesn't argue with him. That, or because she doesn't want to entertain him.

"You gotta watch that tongue of yours." Lucille sits with her arms and legs crossed. Stoic eyes caging Zack's across from her. At least someone *does* entertain him. "It's getting plenty slippery in there. One day it might just fall off. Like that."

What's also jarring is seeing Lucille back to her good old arrogant, pompous self after that unexpectedly heartfelt moment we had. But I get it. Can't let those barriers down forever.

"Oh, are you finally going to make good on your promise and bite it off?" Zack's lips draw into a sly grin while Lucille's press in boredom. "I have to say, getting threatened by pretty girls exhilarates me. Especially when said girls know just how valuable I am to them."

Lucille's cheeks flush with hot anger. Her legs unfold, arms fall, and she all but lunges out of her seat at him. I've never seen her lose her cool so fast. "Keep talking, and your tongue won't be the only thing I cut off."

"Give it a rest, you two," Sgt. Seidel scolds. "Or I'm throwing you both off the chopper as decoy."

Lucille leans back, grim-faced, muttering something that doesn't come through my headset.

"Zack," I tug at the sleeve of his shirt. "Please. We need to work together, now more than ever."

He turns to me with soft eyes. His grin molds into a tense smile. "Meaning, after this is over," his voice is clear as day in my ears—and everyone else's, I'm sure, but he still leans close to me, as if whispering a secret, "there'll be no need for us to work together, is that it?"

My mouth parts in a soundless response.

That's a valid point. What *do* they plan on doing with Zack and Lori once we get our hands on her? If somehow the higher-ups manage to get Lori to obey them, would they even need Zack after?

"I think," his gaze shifts from me to scan everyone around us, "the only reason anyone works with anyone is because they gain something from it. The real teamwork—the real trust—is proven once you've no use for each other, but still choose to fight together."

I take a mental note of the fact that no one tries to alleviate Zack's concerns. Is it because they expect him to turn on us? Take Lori and run? Leave us to die? And ... do I even blame any of them for thinking that?

Even looking at him, I can't decipher much. He's smiling like he's enjoying every little bit of the inner turmoil he's causing everybody as they shift uncomfortably in their seats and dodge his eyes. He's smiling like he's winning at a game we didn't know we were playing.

I breathe out and pray in silence for the best possible outcome, whatever the hell that's supposed to be.

Kadia's forces will establish security around the perimeter of the plant while our platoon is tasked with entering the buildings to search for the fugitives.

From the looks of it, there's only a few infected outside, most appear to be roamers. Our squad will enter from the security building, Bronson Squad from the turbine hall building, and Redfearn Squad from the fuel-handling bay.

We were briefed in more detail on the dangers of firepower inside this place, but it's still just as dangerous outside. We've been equipped with radiation detectors—an attachable device to the portor that monitors how much radiation is in the air. It'll warn us if the radiation reaches dangerous levels. It can also detect if we have been exposed to it and need to decon afterward. Given that the plant's been dead for years, left unattended, it's more than likely there will be radioactive zones. And the radiation monitors inside the building itself are useless when they don't have power to run.

On the bright side, we still have comms.

Leaving a fire support unit outside, we enter the security building from the first floor.

Unlike the science building in Ground Zero, which had more of a hospital-ish, administrative vibe, this has more of an industrial one. My flashlight shines on giant piping running around the place. Metal poles and shiny surfaces, some of which have been partially or fully consumed by rust. Instead of the plain neutrals in the science building, vibrant, refreshing yellows, blues and reds paint the dead equipment here.

We spread out in a wide formation, weapons pointing in various directions to cover as much as we can.

"Look at this place," Connor says. "It's huge."

"I can't believe it's still standing…" Stephen says. "I'd have imagined it would have been among the first places to go up in flames."

"There have been many accidents in the past, before the outbreak," Lt. Mansur answers, "that humanity has learned from. Many security measures were put in place to prevent catastrophic disasters like that from happening again. The mechanisms installed were designed to work even during total power outage. Although those weren't meant to last forever, either. They ran on on-site reserves until emergency-response teams could arrive to prevent the accident from escalating. Those reserves would have depleted eventually. But from what we saw above, the containment buildings seemed intact."

"What does that mean?" Cris asks.

"It means either there was a reactor meltdown and it was successfully contained, in one or all of the reactors. Or the plant workers managed to decommission the plant and prevent a reactor meltdown from ever happening," the lieutenant explains. "This doesn't mean the place isn't a radioactive zone still, just that it's not as bad as it could have really been."

We proceed through a turnstile entrance into Unit Zero.

So many sheets and clothes sprawled about the floor as makeshift mattresses, some bedrolls. All with layers of dust and grime on them. So reminiscent of Kadia, specifically the building where Haze and her family lived with other unprivileged. Haze always asked me to hide some of her stuff at my place. Otherwise, chances were if she kept them under her bed or anywhere in that building, they'd be gone by the time she came back. From a toy she may have scavenged during a work shift, to a necklace she couldn't tell whether it was made of real gold or not. People stole all the time.

"Guys," Tyra calls. "Look…" She points upward, at the piping.

Two faces peek at us.

SIXTY-ONE

THE CRAWLERS disperse as soon as we aim our weapons up.

"Could anyone identify the objective?" Lt. Mansur asks.

"Lori isn't one of them," Zack says.

I track one of the crawlers with my M4, as it leaps from one pipe to the next.

"Why aren't they attacking us?" Cris asks.

"Only one reason," Sgt. Seidel answers. "They know Caves is with us, and they want him alive. Is there a way the infected could identify you, Caves?"

Zack looks around at the two crawlers. "Lori could identify me by scent. I'm not sure how the other infected would, though, without having been around me before. But ... it's not impossible, I suppose."

"Then she may have instructed them not to attack anyone so as not to risk hurting you in the process," Sgt. Seidel theorizes.

"But that means..." Lucille's eyes dart to Zack. "The fugitives are after him?"

"Makes sense," Lt. Mansur says. "If they've been unsuccessful in taming the sentient crawler, getting the one person who's been able to is a logical next step."

"So, now what?" Lucille asks.

"They want us to follow them," I note. Each crawler is standing on a different pipe, a good distance from one another, peeking, making enough noise to get our attention.

"I think more accurately they want to split us up," Lucille comments.

"Which is clearly a trap," Stephen says.

"But what if one of them is trying to lead us to Lori?" Dalal asks. "That's possible, isn't it? If Lori knows her brother's here, then she could have asked the crawlers to lead him to her. The fugitives wouldn't necessarily be aware of that. Maybe she's acting on her own?"

"That doesn't make sense," Lucille says. "If they were trying to lead us to the sentient crawler, why would they be trying to split us up?"

"Decker's right," Lt. Mansur says, "though not impossible, that's too optimistic a thought, Mirani."

"Orders, sir?" Sgt. Seidel asks.

"Let's see what kind of traps they're leading us to," Lt. Mansur says. "Split into teams. Alpha, with me. Bravo, Caves, with Seidel."

"Yes, sir," we acknowledge.

Of our group, only Cris, Zack and I know what Lori looks like. We've tried to describe her as best we can, but honestly, it's still hard to distinguish her from other crawlers. I have the advantage of having seen her more recently, so that helps, but Zack is the only one who's ever been able to communicate with her successfully.

"Keep your eyes peeled," Lt. Mansur instructs. "The enemy might just be trying to confuse us, and the plant is likely full of crawlers."

"One could argue, the place is *crawling* with them," Connor interjects. "Right, guys?"

Tyra is the only one who laughs at the joke, though she's quick to stop herself.

"Well, glad someone has some sense of humor," he says.

"Connor, shut up," Lucille exhales.

I can't help but think of all the silly jokes Nathan would make at times like this. I never noticed how similar Connor and Nathan were until now.

Should I have said something? To Sgt. Seidel or the lieutenant? Or maybe Stephen? Cris?

But I don't know what any of them would have done to Connor. Nina didn't want him to get hurt. She told me to trust her on this, and I'm trying to. I want to. But trust is hard and people are ... people.

"May God protect us all," Lt. Mansur says.

We follow one of the crawlers down a hallway to the left, using a cross-cover technique.

Taking point are Lucille to the left, and the lieutenant to the right. Just behind Lucille is Dalal, assuming a position closer to the center of the hallway, and to her right is Tyra, behind the lieutenant. At the rear is me, and to my right is Private Aria in a mirroring position.

Curse how dark this place is. The lack of windows is also frustrating. Makes it feel isolating. Using our flashlights, we track the crawler.

There's a lot of fire doors. Warning signs all over the walls and said doors about radiation and toxic materials and all sorts of words I don't understand. Some scanning devices that clearly haven't worked in years. Control panels and storage cases.

We continue in a straight line, briefly peeking through any open door we pass by just to make sure we're not about to be ambushed. Most of the rooms are full of those makeshift beds and empty cans of food. A lot of papers and files, and old gear that I've no idea what purpose it serves. How many people lived here?

It's strange that the crawler hasn't tried to attack us but instead keeps jumping between pipes and making just enough noise for us to hear it, easily track it. Normally the crawlers can be quiet and sneaky. Fast. And pretty vicious. I still remember…

My chest tightens.

I still remember that time Sara and I got swarmed by them in the subway tunnel. It was terrifying. Back then, I was prepared to die on the spot with her. We held each other's hands, closed our eyes and—

"Sir," Private Aria says, holding her earpiece, "Redfearn Squad just spotted a fugitive. Female. Running in the direction of the reactor zone."

Crap. I really shouldn't get distracted. *Get it together, Ashley.*

"Capture her, if possible," Lt. Mansur orders. "See if she'll tell them where the crawler or the other fugitives are."

"Yes, sir," Private Aria says. "Redfearn, capture the fugitive if you can…"

"Approaching a three-way intersection," Lucille announces.

Private Aria and I slow our pace while the others proceed at the same speed. The crawler is continuing straight ahead.

"Decker," Lt. Mansur says. "I see movement on your side."

"Same on yours, Lieutenant," Lucille says.

"Get ready," the lieutenant warns.

Growls explode the moment they each reach their respective corners.

"Contact!" Lucille shouts, and the two leading parties open fire down the left and right hallways.

"Bravo to Alpha," Connor's voice in my ear. "We just walked into a trap. Group of infected waiting for us at the end of the hallway and now they got us surrounded."

"Would you believe we just walked into the exact same trap?" Dalal says.

Private Aria and I move to join them. I assume a position between Dalal and Lucille, who are both taking one side of the hallway. On one knee, taking aim, I shoot an infected, and another, and another. Their numbers stretch beyond what my eyes can see, and they seem to be filing out of rooms as well. Dammit. This *was* a trap.

I spare a glance in the direction of the third hallway, now to my right, where that crawler was. I can barely see its silhouette continuing ahead.

"We're gonna lose that crawler." I return my attention to the approaching wave ahead. Judging by their movements, these are all roamers. Where are the chasers?

"Brown, Aria," Lt. Mansur calls. "Take point and follow the crawler. We'll cover you from behind. Can't stop here."

"Sir," Tyra says, "permission to use an explosive round?"

"Negative, Markell," Lt. Mansur responds. "Dangerous enough as it is to use any amount of firepower in here. Let's not explode anything just yet."

"Yes, sir," Tyra says.

Aria and I take the lead down the third hallway, and I try to move fast so as not to lose the crawler.

"Sir," Aria says, "Redfearn lost the fugitive, and they seem to have been led to a trap. Reactor unit full of infected. They're surrounded."

"See if Bronson Squad can back them up." Lt. Mansur's voice is tense as he and the others keep on shooting the infected coming up behind us.

"Approaching a T-intersection." I nod for Private Aria to take the right side while I stick to the left, where the crawler is going. "Aria, movement on the right."

"Left seems clear for now." Private Aria comes to a stop at the right corner and I move further until the group of infected to the right comes into view. "More infected here!"

Private Aria hurriedly backs up to my side, and the two of us open fire on the infected. Lt. Mansur and the others come to a stop, still trying to clear the path we came from. But then the infected on our side move up and block them from advancing.

"Dammit," Lucille curses.

"We're going to have to cut through," the lieutenant says. "Check the rooms on your map. Find a way to go around. Aria, Brown, if you can get to a secure position—"

The infected split. Part of them come at me and Aria, and the rest go toward the lieutenant and the others. I'm split between helping Aria and keeping an eye on the hallway behind me, where the crawler is. Except, when I try to spot the crawler, it's nowhere to be found.

Crap.

A scream behind me—back to Aria—she's on the floor with a deep cut along her leg, and the crawler jumping back up and over to the pipes.

I rush to Aria, who's trying to crawl away, and drag her with me, firing one-handed at the infected—very inefficiently, but at least I score some shots on the infected's knees, causing them to fall and trip others behind them. I try to drag Aria to safety, her blood leaving a trail on the floor.

"Aria's down," I report. "Leg injury. Bleeding heavily."

"Roger, Brown," Lt. Mansur's voice. "We'll try to meet up with you. Stay on the defensive."

There's no way I can handle all these infected by myself, so I opt for the best option available. I drag Aria with me into the nearest empty room and barricade the door.

SIXTY-TWO

"I CAN'T MOVE MY LEG." Aria's voice trembles as I tear up the pants leg. "That crawler sliced it up. I'm infected, aren't I? I'm gonna have to lose the leg?"

"First." I bring my assault pack to my front, digging for a tourniquet. "Let's stop the bleeding."

The infected on the other side bang on the blocked door. I'd pushed a storage closet against it, and knocked another one over in front of it, but I'm not sure they'll hold for long.

We're in a room with a lot of black screens. So many control panels and color-coded equipment. Numbers and symbols that have no meaning to me whatsoever. Buttons and switches and levers I probably shouldn't touch, despite there not being any power. This must be the control room.

I apply the tourniquet to Aria's thigh as fast as possible. A scratch from a crawler can be just as bad as a bite. I take out an IBT and hold it against her thigh just to give her a few seconds to process. I push the sample button, she flinches when the needle pricks her skin, and then we wait for the device to analyze the blood while I dig out everything I need. Thirty seconds later, the IBT beeps and flashes a red light.

"Sorry," I whisper.

Aria puts on a brave face, holding back a sob.

I give her a numbing shot to help her with the pain, even if it won't kick in immediately, and get to it.

"Brown, watch out!" Aria points somewhere behind me.

I turn just as a crawler leaps out of a wall vent and jumps at me. I open fire at it, and it dodges away, landing somewhere behind a control panel and scattering some papers on the way. With a curse under my breath, I shoot to my feet.

"Cover me," I tell Aria, who retrieves her weapon from her side and aims up.

I reach into a pouch for a flashbang—crawlers are sensitive to bright lights. If I can incapacitate it for just a few moments, I can kill it fast. I bite off the safety pin and throw the grenade to where the crawler landed, taking cover behind one of the control panels and announcing "Flashbang," for Aria to take cover as well.

The bright and loud explosion is followed by a screech, which I trace somewhere on my left. I shoot up from my cover to see the crawler stumbling back, losing its balance. My sights are on it in a second. The crawler jumps away as I pull the trigger.

Clang, clang, clang as it jumps around, too fast for my eyes to track it.

"Dammit," I curse.

Aria drags herself across the floor, heading for better cover behind one of the control panels, watching for any sudden moves.

"Brown," Lt. Mansur's voice, "sitrep?"

"We're trapped with a crawler," I report. "Aria's incapacitated."

"We're on route to rendezvous with you, but we got infected blocking our path," Lt. Mansur says. "Soon as we clear them, we'll assist."

"No rush or anything." My eyes dart around in search of the dead-damn crawler.

Something moves just above my head. I find it latching onto the pipes upside down, and the second it jumps down, I throw myself to the opposite side, hitting a desk in the process. I roll off, land on the floor on one knee, then point my weapon at the crawler, but again, before I can shoot, it dodges.

Fighting crawlers, you have to be alert at all times. You can't let them get too close. You can't let them scratch even the surface of your skin. More importantly, you have to be as fast as they are—no, even faster. You have to predict their next move before they even know what it is.

I've done a lot of shooting practice over the past few months.

The normal shooting ranges have various but limited settings. But the simulated ones, those are insane. You can change a lot of settings, up the difficulty to your liking. The first few attempts are always a mess of trial and error, but then, once you get in the zone, once you're fully focused, once you're paying attention, the randomness isn't so random anymore. You start to notice the patterns. You start to memorize the order things happen in—because at the end of the day, the simulation is programmed. It may have different patterns, but sometimes those patterns will repeat.

It's the same thing here, with this crawler. The more it dodges. The more it tries to attack. The more it goes into hiding. I see the pattern it's following.

First, it draws my attention to somewhere safe, easily reachable, and it sits on the floor for just enough time for me to aim my weapon at it, make me think I'm going to score a shot. But the second it sees my fingers on the trigger twitch, it jumps away. It's not random where it jumps. It chooses the furthest and highest place from where it was sitting. So even if it was close to a wall, it won't climb up that particular wall. It'll instead opt for the opposite side, knowing that it'll take me more time to register the move in my brain—and by the time I do, it's already moved above me, ready to lunge at me again.

I switch out the M4 with the tranquilizer gun, momentarily losing track of the crawler. It may not be Lori, but it might still be a good idea to take a live sample home for research purposes. I follow its pattern, just the way it wants me to. I let it believe I'm as stupid as it thinks. But this time, I wait for it to land exactly where I want it to land. Once I trap its head in my sights, I wiggle my index finger just a little bit, enough to trick it into dodging. Before it's even there, I'm already aiming at the spot in the ceiling above me. A split second before the crawler jumps there, I pull the trigger.

The tranquilizing shot hits it right in the arm. I dodge when it lunges at me. This time, though, the crawler trips and falls on the floor. It tries to get away, whimpers upon seeing me approach, but we made sure the sedatives were strong enough that their effect would be immediate. It takes but a couple of seconds before the crawler lies motionless at my feet.

Carefully, I walk closer to the crawler, nudging it with the tip of my boot just to make sure it's not about to jump me. It doesn't.

A long sigh. "Aria," I call. "We're clear."

No response.

"Aria?" I call out again, but she doesn't answer. I follow the blood trail she left to where she crawled for cover.

Her decapitated corpse on the floor sends me stumbling back. I nearly fall.

Looking away, I close my eyes, hoping to will that sight away. When the hell did that happen?

A noise draws my attention somewhere behind me. The squeak of an old metal door as it opens.

I swap out the tranquilizer for my M4 and turn around, pointing in the direction of the noise, waiting for any blurry shadows to move past.

This could very well be another trap. But I still walk toward it.

I shine my flashlight around, and the light reflects off of the dead screens back to my eyes. The room looks fairly empty. The door is still blocked. But one of the storage units is open—I don't think it was when I walked in here earlier.

"Who's there?" I call. "Vincent? Is that you?"

I approach with careful steps, checking my corners. Some shuffling to my left. I turn to a stack of papers flittering in the air. Someone jumps me from the back. My M4 is knocked out of my hold as I'm slammed against the wall by someone taller than me. I push back against them, slamming them in turn against the closet they came out of. I rush to retrieve my weapon, but something grabs me by the ankle and I fall face first on the tile floor. My attacker scrambles toward my weapon. I take out my combat knife and stab his leg. He falls to his knees immediately, screaming in pain. When he makes to turn and attack me, I push myself up and dodge.

I grab the first thing I can from the desk to my right, which is a computer screen, and smash it on the guy's head. It incapacitates him long enough for me to jump over and finally grab my weapon again.

I turn around before he can get up, pointing the M4 at him, finger on the trigger, safety off.

"No, no, no! Please!" he begs. "Please don't kill me. Please."

I recognize him.

"Hello, Justin," I say. "I haven't seen you since..." I feign thoughtfulness, "oh right, since you tried to blow me to pieces."

"That was Vincent's idea!" Justin holds his hand up to cover his face, as if that could stop a bullet from blowing his brains out. "I told him we should just leave quietly, but he wouldn't listen. And if you hadn't tried to stop us, no one would have gotten hurt."

"Wow." My voice is flat. "I gotta hand it to you. You're a professional sellout."

"Please," Justin begs. "Please don't kill me. I don't wanna be out here anymore. I just wanna go home. My parents don't have anyone else. Please…"

Chloe's face flashes before me. Seconds before I shot her. Eyes red with unshed tears. And then another face. Mia's. Crying for her sister. Vengeful eyes boring into mine.

There's screeching, back at the door. I expect infected to barge in and I'm ready to open fire, but then—

"Don't shoot!" Dalal announces. "It's Mirani."

I exhale a little bit.

The rest of the team makes its way inside. The second Lucille spots Justin, she rushes to us, weapon aimed at him.

"Lucille, wait!" I shout.

"Sullivan," Lt. Mansur steps up beside her. He looks around. "Where's Aria?"

I shake my head. "She didn't make it."

"Oh, my God," Tyra gasps—she's standing where Aria's corpse is. "The crawler did this?"

The lieutenant takes in a deep breath. Then he crouches before Justin. "Your leg's not looking so good, son. How about in exchange for treating it, you tell us where the sentient crawler is?"

Justin swallows. His eyes dart between our faces, uncertain.

"He asked you a question," Lucille steps closer to him. We've got him surrounded. If he's smart, he won't try anything. I *really* hope he's smart.

"I don't know."

Lucille chuckles dryly. "Wrong answer—"

"No, wait!" he shouts. "Vincent has her locked up. He doesn't want anyone to find her so he's keeping her isolated."

"Your listening comprehension clearly sucks," Lucille says. "That *wasn't* the question."

"Okay, okay," Justin says upon feeling the tip of Lucille's M4 against the back of his head. "Vincent hid her somewhere. I'm not sure where. If I had to guess, I'd say in one of the reactor units, but I don't know which one."

"How can you not know?" I ask.

"Because he wouldn't tell me," Justin claims. "Listen. Vincent is ... he's cautious, you know? He's always preparing ahead. He assumed that if you guys were to catch me or Mia, we'd snitch on him, so he didn't tell us everything. Look, he ran off and left me here as soon as he heard the choppers coming."

"So convenient that you're still alive," Lucille says, "what with all the infected everywhere."

"Please, I'm not lying. Here," Justin tries to reach for his ruck, but Lucille snatches it from him before he can surprise us. "Just look inside. There's a radio. We found them here. And some batteries. They still work. You can talk to Vincent yourself."

Lucille tosses the ruck to me and nods for me to search it while she moves to face Justin with her M4, Dalal stays behind him. The lieutenant stands back up.

I'm prepared to have something explode in my face, but the radio is the first thing that greets me. I take it out and hold it to Justin. Because the radio could still explode in my face. "Why don't you call up your buddy for us?"

Justin shakes his head. "I'll press the button for you, if that's what you're asking, but please don't tell him about me. Don't tell him I gave you the radio. Tell him you killed me or something."

"Maybe we *should* kill you," Lucille says.

"No, wait." I place a hand on Lucille's weapon, urging her to lower it.

Lucille gives me a skeptical look. "Don't go soft on me, Brown. Not now."

"Let's just ... let's keep him around," I say. "He could be useful. Sir?" I turn to the lieutenant.

He gives an affirming nod.

Justin takes the radio with shaky hands. He holds the button on it and brings it closer to me.

"Hi, Vincent," I speak into the radio.

Silence, then static, then—

"Th-there's a voice I didn't think I'd hear again," Vincent says.

"I bet," I say. "You can thank Nina for that."

The way Lucille's eyes shoot to me gives me chills. I can think of more than one reason why Nina's name would piss her off.

"And let me g-guess," Vincent stutters. "She's the one who gave you the c-coordinates? I really sh-should have just killed you, huh?"

"So, we've got Justin here at gunpoint." I take the radio from Justin, straightening up. "If you want him to live, and, just in case you care about him as much as you cared about Nina, if you want your sister to live, how about you just surrender yourself?"

There's a long stretch of silence on his end.

"You want me t-to believe Rodríguez, after all the b-backlash he must already be facing, would toss out a sick, t-twelve-year-old girl just to punish me?"

"I know, right? It's just as unlikely as him dropping bombs on children," I deadpan. The lieutenant gives me a look at that, probably surprised I know about it at all. Good thing he doesn't know I told everyone else already.

More silence.

"Why d-don't you come see me in the reactor hall of Unit F-Four?" comes Vincent's reply. "Tenth story. We can t-talk there."

"See you in Unit Four, then." I release the button and lower the radio.

"We gotta decide what to do with him." Lucille nods at Justin. "Something about his eyes screams lying freak."

"I'm not lying," Justin says, "please…"

"Unfortunately," Lt. Mansur adds, "we can't take your word for it."

I know. I know that. I know that the safest option right now would probably be to kill Justin. Lori is here. There's no room for mistakes. No room for slip-ups. But I just … can't.

"I can keep watch on him," Dalal offers. "He's injured. He can't really do much like this. If we restrain him, then he won't really be a threat."

Lucille shakes her head at that, like—*This is a mistake.*

I really hope not.

Lt. Mansur lets out a resigned sigh. "Very well. Put a tourniquet on that leg, then take out the knife. Markell, grab Aria's portor. See if you can get in touch with Bronson and Redfearn. Tell them to meet up with us. Brown, inform Bravo."

I acknowledge with a nod and tap on my earpiece. "Alpha to Bravo. We found one of the fugitives. We also have Hayes's location. Can you rendezvous with us outside Unit Four?"

"Roger that, Brown," Sgt. Seidel replies. "We also got a bit of a situation over here."

SIXTY-THREE

WE FOLLOW the trail of infected corpses and regroup with Bravo in the radiological zone, on the first floor of Unit Four.

Bronson and Redfearn are also here ... or rather, what's left of them. Which isn't a lot. I can count about eight members in total.

"Lieutenant," Sgt. Bronson approaches us, "we didn't get there fast enough. Redfearn suffered too many casualties. We've got them all secured for the time being, but they'll need evac, fast, if we want any of them to survive. Sergeant Redfearn didn't make it."

"I see," Lt. Mansur says, always so calm. "Call in a unit from the Kadia backup. Have them Medevac the casualties. Send another one to the control room. There's a tranquilized crawler there. Collect it and prepare it for transport to Spheria."

"Yes, sir." Sgt. Bronson acknowledges.

"Seidel," Lt. Mansur says. "You said you got a situation?"

Sgt. Seidel gives a slow nod, then gestures to where the rest of our squad is.

Lucille pushes past me all of a sudden, hurrying toward them. I follow her—and that's when I see it.

Connor, sitting on the floor, hand pressed tight to his side, covered in blood. Beside him, Cris stands with the blankest expression.

"Hey, Silly, Pinky," Connor says in a strained voice, shooting us a weak smile. "Wanna join the debate about my fate? Right now, the votes are zero to four."

"What..." Lucille's stunned voice, "happened?"

"He got bit…" Cris's shoulders slouch. "The infected overwhelmed us and … I was reloading and I didn't see one coming up from the side…"

"Not your fault, Brawny," Connor tells him. "You'll just owe me one."

He protected him… Connor protected Cris. My heart almost stops, picturing that moment. A fraction of a second and Cris could have been the one sitting there right now.

Uncomfortable silence settles. Lucille's hands are shaking.

I walk over to Cris, placing one hand on his arm while the other searches for his. He doesn't look at me, but his fingers wrap tight around mine.

"Lucille." Stephen grabs her shoulder. "It's okay, I'll do it—"

"No!" She shrugs him off and turns, standing in front of Connor, shielding him from everyone else.

"Decker," Sgt. Seidel starts, "what do you think—"

"We can try," Lucille says. "Right? We can give him the cure?"

Oh no.

"Lucille," Stephen says, "you're not thinking straight. You said so yourself, there is no—"

"Just because it didn't work on Sara doesn't mean it won't work on him…" Lucille pleads.

"Decker," Lt. Mansur says, "we're a long way from Spheria. In the time it'll take us to finish here and take off, it would be too late."

"Well, in that case, I'll gladly handle it." She stands with her chin high. "I'll do it. I'll … shoot him myself." Not so confident when she says that last part.

"She's been wanting to do that for a while anyway—" Connor quips.

"But until then," Lucille cuts him off, "we can wait. Right? We can wait. We don't have to…"

Stephen shakes his head in disbelief. His eyes snap to mine, boiling, threatening. Something tells me he's about to yell at me, but he turns away, punching a wall instead. I dare a glance at Sgt. Seidel, who's communicating a very clear message to me through her hard jaw: *consequences of your actions.*

"Here," Connor clears his throat, "why don't I make this easy for you, Silly?"

"Connor, I swear to God," Lucille heaves a breath. "I don't wanna hear any of your dumb jokes right now—"

"I'd like to talk to Vincent," he says.

Lt. Mansur raises his brows at that. "Brooks?"

"He might listen to me," Connor says. "We're friends."

Lucille shakes her head, spinning around to face him. "You're also working for his enemy, genius—"

"No, I mean, we're friends," Connor explains. "Still. I *think*."

Lucille's jaw drops. Everyone falls silent. Sgt. Seidel's eyes close as realization settles. She's so done with me. She may have been contemplating scolding me a second ago. Now I think she might be contemplating my exile. Still, I don't regret keeping this from her.

"I've been in contact with him," Connor says, and he doesn't look at me, doesn't hint to anyone that I knew, "for a while now—"

The shock on Lucille's face is indescribable. As it is on everyone else's, especially Cris beside me. That's his second partner, now, who turned out to be a traitor. Maybe he has more reason to believe he's cursed than I thought.

"Does that sway your vote the other way?" Connor asks Lucille.

But she doesn't answer. She looks like she couldn't be more disappointed at having been right. Tears flood her eyes in one blink and fall down her face in the next. Crying. Lucille is crying. Not even trying to hide it this time like she did with Sara.

Did Sara know? About Lucille and Connor? Is that why Lucille always responded to Sara more than anyone else? Because Sara was the only one who truly understood her pain? Her reason for lashing out? Her lack of trust? Sara was good at that. I shouldn't be thinking about her right now. But Sara was good at getting people to open up to her.

"I can try and get him to negotiate—or, hell, just convince him to surrender." Connor looks at us one by one. "Please."

"Sir," Sgt. Seidel says, "if there is any chance of ending this peacefully, this might be our only one."

"We can give it a shot," Lt. Mansur says. "But we don't know what's waiting for us on that tenth floor and we have to be prepared for things to go south. Seidel Squad, you'll come with me. Bronson—" He turns to the sergeant.

"Yes, sir," Sgt. Bronson acknowledges.

"Take everyone left of yours and Redfearn's squad. Make your way to the spent-fuel bay of Unit Four, and stay there. Wait for my signal in case we need your assistance. You'll be our surprise element."

"Roger," Sgt. Bronson says.

"Now remember, our goal is to retrieve the crawler," Lt. Mansur says. "We'll try to talk first, and if we can't get anywhere, we'll resort to force."

"Hey, Lieutenant," Zack says, "now would be a good time to hand me a weapon, wouldn't you agree? There's no doubt I'll be one valuable target to the enemy. I have to protect myself."

"Brown will protect you," Lt. Mansur says.

"What if Brown and I get separated? How can she protect me then?"

"You'll just have to stick really close," Lt. Mansur says.

Zack smiles. The kind of smile that's more unnerving than anything else. "Yes, sir."

At Lt. Mansur's signal, we get moving.

COLD WEATHER UNIFORM
& OTHER GEAR

NIGHT VISION GOGGLES

GAS MASK

GLOVES

CANTEEN

ASSAULT PACK

FLASHBANG

SIXTY-FOUR

WE ARRIVE at the tenth floor and enter into an expanse of darkness.

My flashlight shines on unidentifiable objects and lights up the floor—but I can't find where the hall ends. I feel like I was submerged into absolute nothingness.

"Switch to your NVG," Lt. Mansur orders. "Spread out, line formation."

We comply. I fish out my night-vision goggles from a pouch and strap them on.

There's a somewhat circular shape on the ground ahead of us, with what looks like cuboid holes, as though whatever compartments were slotted in before have been removed.

"That's the pile cap of the reactor," Lt. Mansur informs us. "Should be all decommissioned but mind your steps."

My radiation detector makes a low, scratchy clicking noise as we proceed closer toward the top of the reactor. I stick to the side for the most part, watching my surroundings, careful not to bump into anything that could blow up the place or whatever.

"There's something up ahead." Sgt. Seidel comes to a gradual stop.

I look up straight. My goggles immediately highlight a line of bodies, stretching from one side of the hall to the other, at least two rows thick. Infected? It's like they're forming a barrier. But they're not really moving toward us. They're just standing there, swaying in place. Quiet.

"What do we do?" Cris asks. "Can we shoot them?"

"No," Lt. Mansur says. "Not here."

"I d-definitely wouldn't advise that," Vincent speaks up from somewhere across the hall, coming from above. He's standing on top of a catwalk, behind the infected barrier.

"Freeze!" Lucille shouts, her weapon aimed at him in a flash.

"I wouldn't advise that either," Vincent says. He, too, is equipped with NVGs.

"Yeah?" Lucille challenges. "Give me one good reason."

"Sure." Vincent holds up his left hand and points at the portor strapped around his wrist. "My p-portor is currently reading my vitals, and I just so happened to rig a set of exp-plosives strapped to none other than your precious c-crawler to go off the second my vital readings go flat."

That has us all nailed to our spots.

"He's bluffing..." Lucille whispers.

"Now you might think you can just incapacitate me so you can c-capture me and squeeze the details of the crawler's whereabouts out of me, but that would be p-putting too much faith in the fact that I would tell you anything to start with. Not t-to mention, those infected down there are waiting p-patiently for one of you to cross that line so they can finally have some fresh m-meat. But if you wanna open fire inside a reactor hall, b-be my guests."

"Sir," Connor whispers to the lieutenant again. "Please let me talk to him."

"He's going to kill you," Lucille tells him. "He's clearly unstable."

"Connor," Cris whispers to him, "I really don't think that's a good idea."

The lieutenant shakes his head at Connor, then looks toward Vincent again. "All right, Hayes, tell us what you want. You said you wanted to talk? Let's hear it."

"I have n-nothing to say to you," Vincent says. "But I have an offer for s-someone here."

My eyes drift warily to that someone on my right.

"Someone who actually d-deserves to see the crawler again," Vincent says. "Right, Zack?"

Zack doesn't respond.

"I'm sure you m-miss your sister," Vincent says. "I can relate. So I'm g-giving you the chance to join us. Those infected won't hurt you.

L-Lori instructed them accordingly. You can walk right past them and come over."

Everyone's eyes are turning to Zack, and he just stands there listening, unreadable as ever. Lucille looks ready to leap at him if he so much as twitches.

"I know you don't want to be over there. I know they forced you to c-cooperate, and I know they're holding your people hostage. I'm s-sorry about Captain Hill's lack of transparency with you. He let me down, too. But if we work together, we can make things right—"

"Vince!" Connor calls all of a sudden.

Lucille shakes her head at him, reaches over to grab his arm while he steps forward, but Connor shakes her off.

"Look, I'm putting my weapon down!" Connor places his M4 and grenade launcher on the ground then proceeds forward.

"Connor," Vincent says. "You're s-still alive. I was wondering why I haven't heard from you again."

So he didn't contact him. Then how did Vincent know that we were coming? Was he just anticipating an ambush? Did he foresee Connor betraying him?

"Look, buddy, I know you've been through a lot. Why don't we just take a moment to breathe, huh? We can work this out. I promise it'll be okay."

Vincent scoffs. "You promise? S-Sounds to me like someone struck a deal with the enemy. You're saving your family and d-dooming the rest of us?"

"It's not like that," Connor says. "And it doesn't have to be like that for you, either. Nina's alive. She made it. Her and the others. I know you must have been worried about them, but they're okay."

"And you got that information from Ashley?" Vincent says. "Then she must have told you what really happened."

"Well, I think it would be more fair to hear both sides of the story—"

"Sure, here's my side: I left her behind," Vincent says. "Nina wanted to hand the crawler over in exchange for our freedom. Nina's got n-nothing to lose anymore. Nathan's dead, so all she cares about now is herself. To hell with the rest of our families who are still stuck under S-SPORE's mercy. I couldn't have let her do that. Sabotage everything we worked for. But you're clearly n-no different."

"Come on, Vince, we can talk. It's me. How long have we known each other—"

"At the end of the day, people like you are p-part of the problem. People who accept oppression. People who only think about saving their skin, instead of f-fighting for everyone. People who forget where we came from. Forget what we had to end-dure."

"Vince..." Connor steps closer. The infected are starting to sway back and forth, ready to lunge.

"Connor, get back here," Lucille calls for him.

"People like you ... are actually *the* p-problem."

"Come on, man—"

Sgt. Seidel jumps at him in a heartbeat.

A pop.

Followed by a thud.

SIXTY-FIVE

SGT. SEIDEL DRAGS Connor behind some machinery, leaving a trail of blood.

Lucille sprints toward them, dropping to her knees as Seidel lays Connor on his back.

"Connor." Lucille presses her hands against the wound, but it's pretty bad. Blood drips from his mouth.

"Hey … now… Silly." He lifts a weak hand to place on her face. "Don't … cry."

My eyes snap to Vincent holstering his sidearm. He claps his hands, and just like that, the barrier of infected breaks as they all lunge at us. Vincent disappears through a door.

"Open fire!" Lt. Mansur orders.

We all join him, save for Lucille, who stays with Connor to wrap a bandage around his wound.

"We can't let Hayes get away." Stephen is about to charge across but the lieutenant stops him, grabbing him by the shoulder.

"There's too many infected," he says. "Markell, contact Bronson. They might be able to intercept Hayes from where they are."

"Yes, sir," Tyra responds.

"We have to retreat," Lt. Mansur says. "We'll meet up with Bronson and see about capturing Hayes." Then he turns to Justin. "Any idea where he might be headed? Must be where he's keeping the crawler."

"I don't know where he's keeping the crawler," Justin says. "I already told you that."

"He's useless," Lucille shouts, shooting up from Connor's side to stomp toward Justin, grabbing him by the collar. "Why the hell are we keeping you alive, huh?"

"Please," Justin cries. "Don't hurt me."

Dalal places a gentle hand on Lucille's, gesturing for her to let him go.

Lucille releases Justin and returns to Connor. He doesn't look too good.

"Where is Caves?" Sgt. Seidel asks. "Brown?"

I take a break from shooting to look around me. Crap. He's not here. He's not anywhere in my immediate vicinity. No one seems to be able to find him, either. When did he slip away?

I tap on my portor, looking for Zack, tracking his location—his dot is moving across the map. Somewhere on the upper level.

"He must have gone after Vincent," I say.

"Dammit!" Stephen says. "He took Connor's M4, too."

"I knew we shouldn't have trusted him," Lucille grumbles, frustrated.

"Sir," Tyra says. "Bronson Squad have been ambushed by a wave. They can't intercept Hayes."

The lieutenant curses under his breath. I've never heard him so frustrated before. "We have to retreat. Everyone! Move!"

I don't move. Instead, I scan the area. There's a lot of pipes to the left. If I climb them fast enough, I can jump to the platform and catch up to Zack.

"Brown..." Sgt. Seidel calls. "Move it!"

I ignore her and sprint for the pipes. I hoist myself up on the first one, climb to the next, then tread forward and make a jump at the railing.

I grab on as tight as I can as infected gather below me.

"Ash!" Cris's panicked voice. Gunshots. A few infected drop dead beneath me. "What are you doing?"

"I'll come back." I pull myself up and climb over the railing. "Just get out of here!"

I don't wait for him to respond. I sprint after Zack immediately.

I remove my NVG when I step into the hallway, where some light is coming in through windows, and tap my earpiece. "Zack," I say, "can you hear me? I'm on my way to you."

He doesn't answer, but on my map, he's still moving, so I keep following that, running as fast as I can to catch up, slowing at the faintest clang of footsteps, hiding behind a wall, waiting, before taking a peek—just in time to catch someone rounding the corner at the end of the hallway.

They're taking a flight of stairs down, and I'm right behind them, scanning every corner for infected.

"I'll be honest," Vincent's voice, "I didn't th-think you'd come with. I was p-prepared to blow my brains out if it came to that."

"You underestimate how much I despise SPORE," Zack says.

I try to walk slower when I step onto a metal catwalk, ducking behind the railing. There's some faint scratching, like nails against metal.

A pang somewhere above me. I look up to a crawler hanging to the pipes—no, wait, scratch that. Crawlers. Plural. Everywhere I look, standing with hunched backs on the platforms. On top of the machinery. Dangling out of vents. But they're not paying me any attention.

I peek from behind the railing to the floor below, where Zack and Vincent are, taking a short staircase onto a platform with some big machine.

Vincent bends over, removing a big metal plate from the machine to expose its interior—Lori lets out a loud shriek.

"Lori—" Zack's about to run to her, but Vincent blocks his path with his arm.

"Wait," Vincent says. "Like I said, she's rigged to the explosives. I wasn't bl-bluffing. I'm gonna have to take those off first."

Zack hangs back patiently while Lori whimpers. "So why don't you do that?"

I try to sneak down the stairs as quietly as possible. If I can just score a nonfatal shot on Vincent, render him immobile, then we can take both him and Lori and—

"F-First," Vincent says, "I need to make sure you're saying the truth. I can't j-just take your word for it. Especially considering how that went last time, with you lying to C-Captain Hill. The lack of transparency went both ways."

Zack hums in response. "That's very fair."

"Right," Vincent says. "So I figured, a good way to prove whose s-side you're on is to shoot her."

And I freeze in my place, for a moment thinking he means Lori, but then realization hits me. He means—

"Come out, Ashley," Vincent says. "We're not deaf. You might as well face your death with b-bravery."

Well, crap.

With a resigned sigh I step out of cover and stand facing the two.

"Nina told me you were the one who talked Zack into c-calling our deal off," Vincent says. "And I've been thinking since... If you had just kept your mouth shut, things would have played out as they were m-meant to. So, really, you sabotaged e-everything we worked so hard for."

"Yeah, sorry," I say. "There's just something about liars that *really* pisses me off."

My hands are shaking around my M4 as my eyes hold Zack's across from me. I always did hate how unreadable he was. How so infuriatingly unbothered he seemed by everything.

At the same time, I did grow to like that about him, more and more. I wish I could hide my emotions as well as he did.

"So?" Vincent looks to Zack. "Connor c-clearly didn't tell me everything, but he did tell me that you and Ashley got close. Too close. But you can't let her fool you. The S-Sparkles planted her by your side, told her to play nice. Gain your trust. Manipulate you. She thinks she can bat her lashes at you and you'd fall for it just like that."

Well, I don't know about that. I wasn't even trying to get Zack to like me.

"You k-kill her, and Lori's all yours," Vincent says. "We can get out of here immediately."

I know you're wondering if you can trust me. Zack's words come back to me. *I know you're wondering about what'll happen. What I'll do, once we find Lori.*

"Pity," Zack says. My throat is tight. "I always imagined a happier ending for us."

"Zack—" I start, but he holds up the stolen M4 and fires at me. I jump to cover just in time, unscathed.

"Honestly," Zack lets out an exhausted sigh. "Why am I even bothering with guns?" A pause, then, in a very casual yet authoritarian voice. "Lori."

One word. Just one. Followed by a very distinct shriek. And the entire hall explodes with growls. The crawlers finally start moving. And they're all headed in my direction.

SIXTY-SIX

I DON'T KNOW where to run, but I try anyway. I dodge, shoot, dodge again, but I can't really see a way through. They have me surrounded. The way back to the staircase is blocked, so is the doorway in front of me.

So I guess this is it then, huh?

I scramble behind a pole, back pressed to the concrete, take in a deep breath, release, and close my eyes. God, I wish I were holding Sara's hand. Or Cris's. Because now I have my answer to that question.

How do I want to die?

I don't care how, as long as I'm not alone.

And if I could just look in either one's eyes one last time. If I could just hear their voices. If Sara could give me one of her reassuring smiles. If Cris could whisper one of his comforting prayers to me. Everything would be okay.

The crawlers' growls wrap around me, inching closer and closer. Any moment now, one of them will slice up my neck, rip my head clean off my shoulders. At least it'll be a quick death, and I won't feel them munching through my flesh and bones—

The clattering of metallic objects startles me, followed by a loud thud of something heavy hitting the floor.

My eyes snap open. I take a peek behind the pole.

Vincent's on the floor, slowly picking himself up.

Zack is standing at the platform with Lori slowly climbing up his back and onto his shoulders. There's a device at Zack's feet, wires sticking out—the explosives?

It takes me another second to realize that the crawlers haven't attacked me yet. Not a single one tried to scratch me. And they absolutely could have. I can dodge one crawler at a time, but a dozen at once? I'd have to be a superhuman.

Zack's hand reaches up to stroke Lori's sunken cheek. A click of his tongue as he slowly makes his way down the stairs, off the platform.

Vincent props himself up on his elbows, turning to face Zack. Terror bleeding out of his eyes.

Lori jumps off of Zack's shoulder and lands next to Vincent, who startles, body shaking. He doesn't dare move.

"On second thought, I do remember you, Vincent." Zack makes his way toward him, slowly, reaching somewhere into his boot and fishing out a concealed blade. "I remember you hanging around Captain Hill, desperately waiting for your orders like a good obedient soldier."

Vincent's gaze darts between Lori and Zack.

"More importantly, I remember us fighting while you tried to steal Lori from me. And the very moment you gave me this." Zack lifts his shirt with the tip of the blade to reveal a scar on his abdomen. The stab wound. He lets his shirt fall back in place. "All this time I was hoping you'd been torn to shreds by the infected. But now I'm glad you weren't, because I can't tell you how happy I am, that I get to return the favor."

A sinister smile curves Zack's mouth as he kneels in front of Vincent and grabs him by the collar, pulling him into a seating position. Vincent grabs at Zack's hands, struggling to free himself. It's clear he's weak, though, just like the rest of the fugitives.

"You know, we and the infected may not share a lot, but we do share one thing. We both have blood running inside us." Zack stabs the blade into Vincent's stomach and drags it up, slicing his torso open. Vincent yelps. "Blood you can drain."

Zack releases Vincent's collar, and Vincent falls immediately. The blade comes out soaked in blood, and more of that blood is spilling all over, alongside guts. I want to vomit.

Zack tucks the blade away, looks to Lori and nods in Vincent's direction. "He's all yours."

Lori releases a shriek before jumping at Vincent and diving face first into his guts.

Finally, Zack turns to me. He walks toward me and stretches out a bloodied hand, reconsiders, then holds out his other hand to me.

I take it with a shaky one and he pulls me to my feet. My legs are so weak I lose my balance in an instant and stumble forward.

Zack holds me steady. The sinisterness is gone from his smile, replaced with something softer. The kind of softness I ever only see him display with me. "Be honest," he murmurs, "you thought I lied to you."

Guilty. As. Charged.

"I can see it in your eyes." His finger strokes my cheek. "It's okay."

My lips part to say something but I don't know what.

And I don't have to.

Because explosions rumble the place.

SIXTY-SEVEN

"WHAT THE HELL'S HAPPENING?" I look around us.

Lori jumps on Zack's shoulder and makes urgent chirping noises. Her mouth coated in Vincent's blood and flesh.

"We have to get out," Zack says.

"Not without the others," I tell him. "They need our help." I pull away from Zack and tap my earpiece. "Brown reporting. If anyone can copy, I'm with Caves. We have Lori with us. We can provide assistance."

"Affirmative!" Sgt. Seidel's voice. "What happened to Hayes?"

"He's dead," I say.

"That explains it, then," Sgt. Seidel says. "He must have rigged the entire place to his vitals. We're initiating retreat, but we've got infected on us. There are too many of them and too few of us. Get that crawler to the fuel-handling building, ASAP. We're going to the rooftop for evac."

"We're on our way," I say.

Zack takes the lead with Lori on his shoulders and the crawlers tagging along, though just as I'm about to follow, a shadow moves to my right. I turn quick, but there's nothing. I could have sworn—

"Ashley?" Zack calls. "Come on! Let's go."

We come out of the turbine hall with a pack of crawlers zooming above us.

They run ahead, growling menacingly at all the infected in our path, who back away, clearing the path for us—which is insane to watch. Insane that I can just run by these infected without them trying to eat me.

All this, thanks to Lori...

I've seen her in action before, but this is truly something else, and it doesn't stop amazing me for a second. Despite how sloppy she is, how much she's struggling to grab onto things and leap forward without losing her balance, she's still mind-blowingly fascinating. I can only imagine how much she must have missed being able to run around so freely.

"How did you do it?" I ask Zack. "How did you tell those crawlers not to hurt me? I didn't hear you give an order or anything... You just called Lori's name."

Zack looks at me from over his shoulder as we run. "Sign language."

"Sign language?"

"My mom was deaf," he says. "Dad taught me sign language growing up so I could communicate with her. I taught some of it to Lori."

I ... have never felt so impressed by someone in my life. Well, save for my dad, I guess.

"She's a quick learner," he says. "And I realized, pretty early, that we needed a way to communicate discreetly, if I wanted to keep her safe. It was just basic things, but enough for her to understand what I'm saying."

I knew Lori was unique—that's the whole reason why we've been after her all this time. But I never realized just *how* unique she is. I'm not so sure anyone other than Zack truly does.

We run past a few bodies crushed under debris—Bronson Squad? The explosions? My radiation detector clicks louder. This place is not safe anymore.

Gunshots echo up ahead. It takes us only a few seconds to arrive at the fuel-handling building. Big machines hang overhead, some look damaged and are dramatically bent or miraculously dangling. Catwalks all around, half intact, half falling apart. A large pool extends across the room, enclosed by metal railings.

And there everyone is, viciously fighting the infected pouring out from the containment building side while debris rains on the place.

Some people from Bronson Squad are here, too, assisting with the firepower. Others, among the casualties. My heart skips upon seeing

Cris, who's with Xael, escorting a couple of said casualties. Tyra, Stephen and the lieutenant are covering them, standing at the base of a staircase.

Lucille still has Connor leaning on her, though at this point she's dragging a corpse. Too many casualties and not enough people shooting.

The crawlers spread out all around, screeching at the infected. While some back down, others don't. They continue attacking.

"What's the problem?" I ask.

Zack shakes his head. "These infected were already aggravated. They're defending themselves, and Lori can't do much about that. It's the equivalent of walking up to someone, slapping them across the face, then asking them if they'd like to be friends."

Lori lets out a shriek that draws everyone's attention to her, and a second later the crawlers go from trying to scare the infected and keep them at bay to straight up attacking and slaughtering them. Infinitely better and more effective than firepower. Bodies drop. Heads and limbs fly.

"Brown, Caves!" Seidel hurries toward us, her face brightening up at the sight of Lori. "You did it."

"I think so," I say.

"Let's get out of here!" Sgt. Seidel gestures for us to regroup with them. "Go to the stairs!"

Zack leads the way with Lori. He takes out his blade again, and it seems to be more than enough with Lori's help. She's sticking close to him, probably lacking the energy to jump too far. The other crawlers are taking out infected at a fast rate, which gives everyone else time to actually retreat.

Dalal is struggling between shooting the infected and evacuating Justin. His hands are free—she must have cut his rope earlier so she can easily support him, but with his leg injury, he's still a liability. I rush toward them.

"Dalal!" I tell her. "I got him. Just keep moving."

"Hey, you!" Dalal beams at me. "You truly are a lifesaver. And here I thought we were all doomed. I was saying prayers and everything."

"Maybe hang on to those prayers until we make it to the rooftop." I move over to Justin. "Come on." I pull him up and throw his arm over my shoulders.

We head for the stairs. Dalal hangs in the back to shoot at the infected while I'm ahead of her with Justin, right behind Zack and Sgt. Seidel.

Justin grunts with each step. His eyes go between staring ahead then back at me. His face is pale. He bled too much. But it's not too late. We're almost out and—

A scream, way ahead. Lucille is stumbling sideways and falling. And Connor is biting right into her calf. She pushes him off of her, crawling away. He's about to jump her, when a bullet takes him out, courtesy of Stephen, who rushes to her help.

Dammit,␣Lucille, why did you have to—

A force pushes me hard to the right and smashes my head against the railing. I lose my balance and, just before I fall, Justin snatches my M4 from me and delivers yet another strike to my head with the butt of the weapon.

It all happens in broken beats. I blink once. Dalal's voice. Shouting at Justin to drop the weapon. Blink again. He's shooting her. Blink again. Sgt. Seidel and Zack are turning toward us. Blink. Blood explodes from Lori's head and she's falling off of Zack's shoulder. Blink. Justin's limp corpse drops before me. Blink. Zack's on his knees, sobbing beside Lori's lifeless body. Seidel is yelling at me to get up and yanking Zack with her.

The world stops spinning. My eyes are on Lori. Dead. Justin. Dead. Dalal…

I look behind me and scramble toward her. She's on the floor, shaking. Red pours out of her mouth, trailing the side of her face.

I place my hands on her lower abdomen but they're not big enough to cover all the holes. "Dalal."

Her body's twitching. Eyes staring up. Lips moving but I can't hear a word she's saying.

"I'm here," I tell her.

I'm sorry. I'm so sorry.

I remove one hand from her abdomen to hold her hand instead. Her fingers instantly curl around mine, squeezing tight, so tight, as if she's trying to grasp onto life as hard as she could.

Then she lets go.

"Please." I let go of her, tilt her head back, place both hands on her chest and press against her ribcage hard. "Come on. Not you, too. Please." I keep my eyes locked on her face, waiting for her mouth to open. Waiting for her to take a big gasp of air. Waiting for her body to move. My fingers are soaked in her blood, and she's not moving. "Please."

"Brown!" Seidel's voice.

I don't look at her.

I shouldn't have hesitated. Today of all deaddamn days, I shouldn't have doubted myself. I did this. To all of them. I did this.

"Brown." Seidel's at my side now, grabbing my arms. I pull out of her grasp and keep up with the useless chest compressions. "Brown, listen to me, we have to get out of here, or we'll die, too. You think Mirani would want that? You think she wants you to get yourself killed?"

No. No, she wouldn't. And she should tell me so herself. She should look me in the face and tell me to get up. Tell me we can both make it.

"Brown," Seidel insists.

"We take her with us," I say, slowly, reluctantly, stopping the compressions.

She has a family. Siblings. Parents. Waiting for her to come back. We can't leave her here. Not like Jose. I can't leave another friend to be buried under rubble.

"Get up," she tells me. "I'll carry her."

I get up. She carries her and starts toward the others. I hang back to shoot down some of the infected coming up behind us. Cris is on his way to us, probably worried when he realized we weren't with the group. Seidel tells him to turn around and keep going. We're both okay. I'm okay. We have to retreat.

Then a piece of debris falls between us, breaking the catwalk in half. Sgt. Seidel makes a fast leap forward, and Cris catches her.

I slip on Justin's blood and fall with him.

SIXTY-EIGHT

I'M LYING ON A PLATFORM. No. Not a platform, a crane. My radiation detector's clicking nonstop. There's a greenish-blue glow in the pool below me, mesmerizing to look at. I'm not sure what it is, though. There's no light source in there that I can see. That glow is coming out of those ... tray-looking things lining the bottom of the pool.

It's so ... pretty. One of the prettiest sights I've ever seen. Reminds me of the color of that snow globe Sara got for me. So much so, I'm tempted to roll around and jump into it. Drown in it.

Footsteps behind me.

I glance over my shoulder at Mia, kneeling beside Justin's corpse, sobbing quietly. That must have been her, earlier in the turbine hall. Following us.

She picks up my M4 and stands.

"You shouldn't have come here," Mia says. "You ruined everything."

I turn to lie on my back.

Mia points the weapon at me.

"Do it," I say. "You want to avenge your sister? Do it. I won't fight you."

Make it quick. Let it end. I can then get some proper sleep. Maybe forget, too. Everything. All the blood on my hands.

But she doesn't shoot me. She hesitates. Then she turns the weapon around and presses the muzzle under her chin.

Wait—

"Tell Mom and Dad..." she chokes on a cry, "tell them I'm so—"

Then a bullet pierces her head from behind. Blood explodes out of her forehead and spatters on my face. Her body falls limp on top of me, and I just lie there, still, until someone tosses her corpse to the side. Cris towers over me.

"Ash." He leans down and helps me sit. "Are you okay?"

My breathing is heavy, eyes foggy with tears. Mia's corpse lies beside me. Blood spills out of her head into a puddle.

"It's us or them, right?" Cris's voice brings my attention to him. His eyes are hard on me.

Oh.

Always learning, isn't he? First, I taught him how to idealize SPORE. Then I taught him how to shoot, and now I've taught him how to be a coldblooded killer. What a fantastic teacher I am.

"Get up," he tells me. A demand, not a request. "Fight. This isn't over yet."

I don't want to fight. I can't.

"What's the point?" I cry. That lid's finally coming off. There's nothing keeping it all bottled in anymore. Everything gushes out, a violent, incessant stream of pain. "Everyone's dead. Because of me."

"Not because of you."

"Yes, because of me," I sob. "You think you're cursed? Just look at how many people died around me." Their faces are there, always, every time I close my eyes. Regi, Ro, Will, Nathan, Melisa, Chloe, Henry, Jose, Sara and now ... Dalal and Lori. Even Mia. "If you're cursed, then I'm a deaddamn jinx. Every choice I make—it doesn't matter what—every choice I make backfires."

"Okay," Cris says. Hands on my face, bringing me close. "So, we're both cursed. You think the world will be better without us? Everyone will live if we're gone? Fine. Let's stay here, then. You and me. Let's stay here and save the world."

"Cris..." I shake my head at him. "You can't stay."

"What I can't do," he says, "is leave without you."

A flash of a memory. Of a night when I was stuck under a collapsed construction platform. Will's face, and the gutting words coming out of his mouth. *Let's go.* His back to me as he runs away, taking my best friend with him, and abandoning me for dead.

Sometimes that pain lasts so long, we give up on believing that it could ever end. Dalal's voice whispers in my ear. *But I believe that ... if we just know that we have one person. Just one. Who believes in us, always. No matter how deep we fall. Sometimes that's all we need to climb out.*

My tears dry. I place my hands over Cris's and give him a nod. "Let's go."

Not a second is wasted. He grabs my weapon off of Mia's corpse and hands it to me, then jumps up and pulls me with him, wraps his arm around my middle while I wrap mine around his shoulders, leaning on him for support. Something's wrong with my leg—it's the same leg that got caught under the rubble all those months back, in the Pit. Same one that got trapped under the collapsed construction platform. Same one that got hurt during that one FTX. I think that leg's a goner.

Cris shoots all the infected in our path. All of them. He doesn't miss a single one of his shots. I'm the one who can't get her aim straight. I'm the one who constantly wastes her bullets, so I save them up for him when he runs out of ammo.

"Rey? Brown?" Sgt. Seidel says in my ear. "Do you copy?"

"Copy, sir," Cris answers. "We're on our way back."

I lean into him as he guides us through the plant, making our way upstairs. Sgt. Seidel and Tyra meet us halfway and lead us the rest of the way. We make it to the rooftop, to the helicopter, and Cris helps me jump in.

Then we take off.

I glance around us. Dalal and Connor are dead. Lucille is unconscious. Lori's dead, Zack cradles her in his arms as he sobs.

We failed. All that work and we failed. It was for nothing. Everyone died for nothing.

"Chart a course for Kadia," Lt. Mansur says to the pilot. "We need urgent medical care for our wounded."

Kadia.

I exchange a tired look with Cris. Neither one of us is able to smile. My mouth twitches. Eyes sting. *Don't cry.* But I can't help it. I'm so tired and everything is coming back to me all at once. I explode into tears and Cris's arm drapes over my shoulders as he pulls me into a half-hug.

When the helicopter lands, a team of medics is already waiting for us. Cris and some others go to the regular decontamination station, while those of us injured, including myself, are taken by the medics to the casualty decontamination. I'm stripped of my clothes by a medic in a hazmat suit, doused in chemicals, then the medic dresses me in a patient robe before a couple others transport me on a new stretcher to the hospital.

My eyes dart about, scanning, taking in every detail. The fenced-in section of the helipads. The familiar SPORE HQ of Kadia. Flashes from Recruitment Day hit me in an instant. It feels like it's been years since I've been here. But it's only been a few months.

And there's ... commotion, just on the other side of the fence, outside the SPORE HQ. Civilians gathered with signs, chanting something. And Spores holding up a defensive perimeter, trying to keep them away. The protests. They're still going.

I'm trying to ask one of the medics about my mom, but I don't think she understands what I'm saying. I don't think *I* understand what I'm saying. My head hurts. A lot. And there's this annoying ringing sound in my ears.

I pass out on the way.

SIXTY-NINE

WAKING up in Kadia's hospital sure is becoming tradition at this point.

I wince as I try to sit up. My head is still a bit woozy, though my leg doesn't hurt as bad anymore. Thank you, painkillers.

Hushed voices draw my attention to two people standing close to the treatment room's entrance.

Stephen is talking to his mom—Monica. She reaches to hug him, but he backs up and walks off toward one of the cots, where an unconscious Lucille is lying. The covers flatten where half of her left leg should be. But she's breathing. She made it. Stephen sits beside her and takes her hand, brushing a gentle thumb on it.

Monica stands with her palm to her chest, watching her son with tear-filled eyes. I want to reach over and shake Stephen hard. His mom clearly loves him, and she always seemed friendly to me. What happened to make him so cold and distant with her?

There was a time when I was ready to run away and forget all about my mom, too, but now that I've spent months without her, I don't know how I thought I could ever erase her from my life. I wish she'd walk right through the door and come hug me, just like the last time I was here. But I would have woken up to her face if she were here. I can only pray she's okay out there.

I prop myself up. "How is she?" I ask Stephen.

He looks so lost when he turns to me. "Brown ... you're awake."

He doesn't answer my question, though, just looks back at Lucille with a frown.

Not that I'm the right person to comfort anyone in grief right now. Far from it. But I can't help remembering what Sara told me. About everyone. She cared about them. If she were here, she'd try to comfort him. Once again, he had to kill a friend to save a friend.

"Stephen," I say, "I'm sure it wasn't easy for you, with Connor—"

"Don't," he says, voice stern, sharp. A warning. "Don't talk to me about Connor."

"I was just—"

"Lucille hesitated. She never hesitated before." His words come out bitter. "And it's all because of—"

Me? I can see it in his eyes, clear as day. He blames *me*.

"You planted the thought in her head that there is a way to save them," he says. "She thought she could save Connor. But you and I both know that wasn't possible. We all knew, and yet—"

"She's alive," I say. "That still counts for something."

"She's alive, but she lost everything she built her life for," Stephen says. "The thing about Lucille is…" he breathes, frustrated, "she's hardened. I'm sure to someone like you, she might have even seemed heartless. But the truth is she cares, a lot. And she hurts a lot. I can't even tell you how many of our comrades she put down. She shouldered that pain all on her own, and she took it off me more times than I can count. The only thing that gave her strength to do it, over and over, was the belief that killing them was the only option. But if you told her there was a cure, if you told her there was a way we could have saved all those we couldn't save, it's like telling her she killed all our comrades for nothing."

"I don't think it was because of me." I clear my dry throat. "I think Lucille couldn't do it to Connor because she still loved him. What I said about the cure was just her excuse to hold onto him a little longer."

His eyes go wide, but I don't think it's shock at the news. Maybe more at the fact that I know about it at all.

"They were together before," I say. "You knew that, right? Sara did, too?"

He doesn't answer.

"Are you upset because she could have died, or because of who she was going to die for? Both?" I ask, noting the hardness in his jaw, the heartbreak in his gaze. "Do you have feelings for her?"

He doesn't answer that, either, which in itself is an answer.

"Oh, you're up." A medic walks into the treatment room and straight toward me. Stephen gets up and leaves in a hurry. "How are you feeling? Any nausea?"

"No." I keep still as she examines my eyes, then follows up with a set of standard assessments of concussion, which I pass.

"Not bad, not bad."

"Hey, uh," I say, "There's a patient here ... Juan Rey? Do you know which room he's in? I'd like to see him."

"You, honey, should do one thing, and that is stay in bed," the medic tells me. "You suffered a mild concussion. Rest is your friend. We have to make sure your symptoms don't get worse."

"Please. He's ... my grandpa," I lie.

The medic gives me an offended look and lets out a disapproving sigh. "You think I don't know who you are? *Ashley Brown*."

Well. It was worth a shot. "Okay, so if you know who I am, can't you just do me a favor and tell me how he is?"

"I don't know," she says. "I'll have to check and get back to you."

"No need." It's Monica who answers. "Mr. Rey isn't here anymore." I hold my breath, bracing myself before the rest of her words come. "He passed a few days ago."

SEVENTY

I'M quick to get changed out of the patient robe and into my semi-dry uniform. Then I head out.

My leg doesn't hurt as bad but that's probably thanks to the painkillers they gave me. I still can't walk properly on it, but I don't care.

Even after so long, the walk is familiar. I'm almost at Cris's place—or, well, the place he used to live with a bunch of others, like his friends, Sam and June.

The streets are as I remember them, littered with piles of trash and cardboard boxes. Dumpsters filled to the brim and spilling out. Walking through this part of the sector, curious eyes follow me. Eyes always followed me in Kadia for one reason or another. But I recognize this look on people's faces instantly. It's the one I used to give the Spores who walked the streets. The Spores I blamed for Dad's death and the miserable mess that my life turned into. Turns out my medicine doesn't taste so good.

I arrive at the building in a few minutes, but I hesitate to knock on the door. If he's in there, he probably needs some time alone. At the same time, I want ... I want to be there for him. Comfort him.

"The hell's a Spore doing here?" a guy in janitor clothes says from my right. He leans against a broom. "You're not from here, are you? What's that say on your uniform? Spheria?"

"I *am* from here, actually," I say. "I'm ... here to visit a friend."

"Visit a friend? Is that what you call making random arrests these days?"

"Arrests? No, I'm not here to arrest anyone."

"No, I recognize her," someone to my left says. A woman in a maintenance jumper. "She's that girl. The bootlicker. Remember? The one who got Li exiled."

"And the Porters!" the janitor gasps with realization.

Oh boy...

"Look at you." The woman steps closer. "Sure moved up the ladder real fast. Is that what it takes to get you a nice comfy life over there? Sell out your people?"

I frown. "Please stand back."

"Is that a threat?" The janitor cackles. "Think we're scared of the likes of you? You got any idea how many of you we sent to the hospital just last week?"

My body tenses. I doubt they'd be this bold if I were armed. And although I'm confident I have more hand-to-hand experience than both of them combined, I'm not in top shape right now. Not to mention, I don't actually want to hurt civilians. That defeats the whole purpose of the uniform I'm wearing.

"Way it's looking, you people won't stay on top of the food chain long." The woman stands in front of me, flicking a strand of my hair with her finger. "You can't keep us quiet anymore—"

"Is that Ashley?" a familiar voice calls.

The woman steps aside and I spot June, approaching in a wheelchair. Sam in the back pushing him. The sleeve of his shirt flapping back and forth where his arm was amputated—where *I* amputated it.

"June." I smile, relief slowly returning to me. "Sam."

"I'd recognize that pink hair anywhere!" June grins.

"Is there a problem, Bennie?" Sam asks. "Frank?"

The pair exchange a few looks. Then Bennie shakes her head. "Not yet."

"Good," June says. "Don't you have work to do? Frank, these streets aren't gonna sweep themselves, buddy."

"No, they're not." Frank clicks his tongue and backs away. Bennie follows him.

Well, it sure pays to save some lives.

"Hey, Ashley." June looks up at me. "You shouldn't have come here alone. Things in Kadia aren't so good. The Spores are … well, I'll spare you the gory details."

I snicker. "Gore is basically what I've been living off of for the past seven months."

"It's just that things have been rough over here," Sam adds. "Ever since word about the Pit got out."

"If you thought people hated Spores before, boy you're in for a surprise," June says. "It's too dangerous to walk around here by yourself. Unarmed, even."

"I think I can handle it, but thanks."

"We heard that Cris came back." Sam's face brightens up. "But this is a lovely surprise, too. How have you been?"

"I'm … good," I lie. "How are you guys?"

"Alive," June says. "Which is all that matters, I guess. I get to impress girls all the time with the story about how I fought off not one, but two infected, *and* survived."

"They pity him," Sam interjects.

"They think I'm badass," June argues. "You should see their faces. They're all in love with me."

"Anyway," Sam cuts him off. "It's nice seeing you again."

"You, too." I smile. At least not *everything* is awful.

"You're here to see Cris?" Sam asks.

"Yeah." I nod. "Yeah, I heard about his grandpa."

June frowns. Sam gives me a nod. "Let's go inside."

Sam opens the door and goes in with June, and I follow the two of them hesitantly.

I've never actually been here before. The place is run-down. Dusty, dark, and old. Sam leads us down the tight hallway and toward a door. He knocks.

The door opens and a woman stands on the other side. Cris's mom. I recognize her because I've seen her before, part of the maintenance crew.

"Hey Mrs. Rey," Sam says. "Sorry to disturb you. We just wanted to see Cris. If that's okay."

Mrs. Rey scans the boys before stepping aside and allowing them in. Then her eyes settle on me. A grimace.

"She's with us, too," Sam tells her.

"Hi Mrs. Rey," I say. "I'm Ashley—"

"I know who you are." She nods for me to come inside, and I ever so uncomfortably do.

There are a couple other people inside that I don't recognize, I assume the people that Cris and his family share the apartment with. They don't really pay us much attention.

"Look who's here," Mr. Rey walks up to us. "Cris! You're gonna want to see this."

Cris walks up behind his dad soon enough. His eyes are swollen and red. "Sam? June?"

"Hey, buddy!"

Cris doesn't waste a second to hug Sam, then moves on to hug June. "I missed you guys so much."

"And you're Ashley, right?" Mr. Rey walks over to me, holding a hand. "I'm Manuel."

I shake his hand. "Nice to meet you, Mr. Rey. I'm so sorry for your loss."

Manuel's frown settles in quick, but he tries to mask it behind a smile. "Thank you."

I walk over to Cris next. Cris who just stands there with half a smile and half a frown. I can tell just how heartbroken he is that he wasn't here. How much he wanted to see his grandpa alive one last time.

"Cris…" I rest a hand on his arm, but he pulls me into a hug instead. A tight one. His arms surround me and his face hides in my shoulder. I hold him while he sniffles. Sam approaches from behind to pat his back. June watches from his chair with furrowed brows. "I'm so sorry," I whisper to him.

"Yeah," he murmurs, voice muffled against my shirt. He should have been there. It was all for nothing in the end. We didn't even get Lori and Cris should have been there with his grandpa. He pulls from me to look over at his dad. "I … think I'm ready. To see his grave."

Mr. Rey nods. "I'll take you. Come on."

I step to the side, allowing Cris to pass. Sam and June follow him as well. His mom doesn't budge, though. She stands far from the rest of us, by the window. Her eyes are glued to Cris as he heads for the door, and there's something about the way she's looking at him… A mixture of scrutiny and longing. For a moment there, I swear, there are tears in her eyes. Tears that dry as soon as her gaze meets mine, before she turns away from me.

"Ashley," Sam calls. He's the last one at the door. "You coming?"
"Uh… You guys go on ahead," I say. "I'll be right behind you."

SEVENTY-ONE

I FIDDLE with my hands and turn to Cris's mom.

"What do you want?" she snaps. Once she finishes not-so-discreetly wiping away her tears, she faces me. Her eyes are pointed and grim.

My hands fall to my sides. "Mrs. Rey, I was just wondering if there was anything I could do to help?"

"Help with what?" Her arms fold in front of her.

"Anything," I say. "I just thought you seemed tired—"

"Do I?" She lets out a wry laugh. "You're very perceptive."

I'm not sure why she's so hostile toward me. Is it just grief, or something else?

"Cris really wanted to be there for his grandpa," I say. "He was gonna come home as soon as we finished AIT, but then we got reassigned at the last minute."

She doesn't react to that. She just stands there, contemplating whatever it is she's contemplating. "Last I remember, you two couldn't stand each other," she says. "But that was one intimate hug just then, wasn't it? You're seeing my son? Now you're here because what? You want my blessings?"

Well, this is awkward.

I didn't think I'd have to do this part alone. Figured it'd be Cris who'd introduce me as his girlfriend. What the hell am I supposed to say now? I already got on my ex's dad's bad side.

"We didn't get along before," I pinch the tip of my index finger, "but things change. Especially when you're out there. So many things start looking silly in hindsight."

"Mhm." Mrs. Rey walks away from the window and toward the fireplace. She opens a metal box on the mantle and gets out what looks like a cigarette I've seen a few soldiers smoke before. A rarity.

She fishes out a light from her pocket, takes the cigarette in her mouth before lighting it. A long drag, then she blows the smoke through her mouth.

"I get it, you know? You're young and passionate, and most importantly, hormonal. Boys especially, they see a girl and their brains stop functioning just like that." She demonstrates with a snap of her fingers. "They don't think. My big brother was like that."

"You have a brother?" Cris never mentioned an uncle.

"Had," she corrects. Ah. That's why. "We used to live in a big house. Bigger than you could imagine. My room was double the size of this sad living room. I had a bathroom all to myself, with a bathtub and everything."

Wow. Even my parents didn't live like that before the outbreak. Dad grew up in an apartment, and Mom told me her family moved often, always renting.

"Then the world went to hell and nothing mattered anymore." Mrs. Rey takes another drag. "All those useless dreams I had of going to college, becoming a reporter, traveling around the world, finding my prince charming, proposal, shopping for a wedding dress, planning the party, buying a house... None of it mattered."

Yeah... So many people had to give up everything they'd built their lives for. My parents were just lucky their jobs were more important than ever after the outbreak. They still gave up a lot. Mom told me that to this day, she's still haunted by the fact she'll never know what happened to her parents and siblings.

"So, there I was, a dumb girl with no more dreams, throwing herself at a boy whose brain stopped functioning," she says. That takes me aback. "I was eighteen, just a few years older than you, when I found out I was pregnant."

I ... didn't know this. Does Cris know this? I guess his parents do look pretty young, but I always attributed it to great genetics.

"You're probably thinking what the hell is this woman on about?" Correct. "But you see, even us smart girls can be stupid sometimes.

We make mistakes that we can't take back, and then we have to live with them for the rest of our lives."

I try not to flinch at the insinuation that Cris is a mistake. "Oh, I don't even think I'm smart enough to make a baby by accident, so don't worry about it. Plus, the kinds of mistakes I make are more likely to kill babies than anything."

That gets a small chuckle out of her. I don't know if she's insulted or amused by my audacity. "It's not so hard to see what he likes about you. You're quick-witted, pretty, and you got the name and status that turn heads wherever you walk. But what do *you* see in *him*, truly?"

"Clearly I see more than you do," I bite back. "For starters, I see the way he puts his life at risk every single day so that he can give you and his dad a better one."

"He's wasting his time. Manuel has been trying to do just that for the past seventeen years—pointlessly," she says. "He could never give me the life that I wanted. I already had that, and it's rotting out there with everything else." Another drag from the cigarette. "But maybe it'll be different for you. Who knows? If you're lucky, you may even die together, in each other's arms. That's the happiest ending you can hope for today. No more fairytale, happy-ever-afters."

And I thought I was a pessimist. Holy crap.

"Be glad you never knew life before. Both of you. It makes it easier to immerse yourselves in this illusion of an existence. You forget all about being *their* property."

And those words. Those words sting most of all, because those are the kind of words I used to say myself. Somewhere down the line, I forgot. I forgot just how chained we all are.

I storm out of the apartment and head straight to the cemetery, where I find Cris with his dad, June and Sam, by his grandpa's gravestone. I join them in silence, sitting beside Cris while they say a prayer and recall memories. Eventually, Cris's dad excuses himself to get back to work, then June and Sam claim they also have work to do, though the way they keep snickering and smacking each other playfully on their way tells me they just wanted to leave me and Cris alone.

I'm more than grateful for the privacy. I rub Cris's arm with one hand, link our fingers with the other, and lean against him. "Are you gonna be okay?"

"In time, I'm sure I will be." Cris rests his head on mine. His voice is dry and groggy. "Dad says he was there, so ... at least Grandpa wasn't alone."

When I heard my dad died, I was shouting and screaming and crying nonstop. I lashed out at anyone who tried to approach me, Mom included. But Cris is so ... quiet about all this. So calm.

"You're allowed to be upset." I pull back to look him in the eyes. "You're allowed to be angry and grieve. You don't have to be tough all the time. Not around me anyway."

His lips quiver, and his head falls, along with tears. "I feel like I should be grateful, you know? After everything we've seen out there, all the horrible ways people can die, passing away in a hospital bed at seventy isn't the worst way to go. And Grandpa knew that. He always told me he's one of the lucky ones, getting to live as long as he did." He swallows a lump, voice cracking. "But it's just... I wanted to be there, too. He's all I had."

I shift from his side to sit facing him instead, and take his face in both my hands, nudging him to look up, but he can't hold my eyes straight. I release his face to wrap my arms around his shoulders instead, and he pulls me tightly against him, his arms firm around my waist, face nuzzled deep in my neck. I run my fingers through his hair in soothing strokes, plant a kiss close to his ear, and let him cry in silence as long as he wants.

It's already dark by the time we pick ourselves up to leave the cemetery, walking hand in hand.

"Dad did give me this." Cris tugs out a cross necklace from under his shirt. "It was Grandpa's."

I give him a tender smile. He has something to remember him by. That's good. And a grave to visit as well.

"Thanks for coming with me. It means a lot."

He comes to a slow stop and turns to me, leans in until our foreheads touch. His hand is a mix of gentle and firm around mine. Good thing we don't have to worry about Sgt. Seidel showing up out of nowhere and yelling at us.

"Of course," I say. "What kind of girlfriend would I be if I didn't?"

And there, that faint, albeit broken, smile is slowly curving his lips. "*Girlfriend* does have a nice ring to it, doesn't it?" He breathes the words in my face.

The knot in my stomach has never been tighter. The shiver that runs through me renders me both speechless and motionless. I fight between looking into his gorgeous eyes and his stupidly close, tempting, inviting lips. It would probably be inappropriate to kiss him now, huh?

"Hey, uh…" I toy with the buttons of his shirt with my free hand and squeeze his in the other, "I was thinking, maybe you'd like to come over to my—"

But then his lips are on mine and I already forgot what I was going to say. Oh, my God. My eyes close on instinct. A burst of heat has my body melting in seconds—no, really. My knees wobble like the bones in my legs have dissolved. For how warm his hands are, his lips are hot times infinity. I all but freeze to death when he pulls away in the next heartbeat. *Why?*

"Sorry…" His shaky breath fans my skin. I open my eyes to shy brown ones gazing into mine. "I-I should have asked first, shouldn't I?"

"Yeah. You should have."

I can talk? Oh, thank God I can talk. Even though now I want to do anything *but*. I hold his face and bring him in for another kiss. Short. Sweet.

"There," I whisper against his mouth. "Now we're even."

His cheeks flush, and the chuckle he lets out twists my insides on themselves. "Let's start over, then." The tip of his nose flirts with mine. His throat works up. "Can I kiss you?"

"Please do." I can't even hide how desperate I am.

Our third first kiss is even hotter and sweeter than the previous two. Slow and soft, until that careful discovery of the new turns familiar. Then the eagerness takes over and my mouth gets a mind of its own. A mind occupied by the sole need to taste every little inch of Cris's lips. He meets me with a matching, if untried, passion. The saltiness of his dry tears soon washes out and makes room for some sweetness in the mixture. The kind I can only describe as his. I float on my toes so my arms can fly over his shoulders while his steal me by the waist, nearly lifting me off the ground. Our bodies press together and the fire in the pit of my stomach burns wilder.

This is my new oxygen and I'm taking it all in—

The squeal of metal and leaves rustling.

Cris and I jump away from each other and turn to none other than June and Sam, hiding not so discreetly behind some bushes. By the looks of it, they were in the process of quietly leaving the scene upon realizing they overstayed their welcome. So much for Sgt. Seidel's lack of interruptions.

The heat boiling inside me sizzles down. I try to catch my breath.

"Guys, what the hell?!" Cris's brows furrow. "Are you spying on us?"

"Dude, don't swear in a cemetery. That's so disrespectful." June gives a disapproving shake of his head.

"Also, don't kiss your girlfriend in a cemetery, that's even more disrespectful." Sam frowns in feigned disappointment.

Cris turns to me with apologetic eyes, lips perfectly swollen. "I'm so sorry. They're idiots."

I take his hand and hold it firmly, bringing it up in front of us. "Oh, my God!" I fake-gasp. "I can't believe you're holding my hand in a cemetery. *That's so disrespectful.*"

A smile cracks his features. In the not-so-far distance, June and Sam whistle and cheer.

"Okay, seriously, who's being disrespectful now?" Cris scolds as we start toward them.

Neither one gives it a rest, though. Seems like they opted for distractions and jokes to help Cris cope, and I'm glad they did, because I want Cris to wear that heartstopping smile forever.

SEVENTY-TWO

THE SMELL of home hits me with an overwhelming wave of nostalgia. Nothing like that good old mix of humidity, ancient wood, and suffocating dust.

After sharing a meal in the cafeteria, I left Cris with his friends so they could conduct the uncensored version of their interrogation. I'm sure they'll find the stories of all our secret hand-holding and forehead touches equally thrilling and scandalous. They invited him to spend the night at their place, which ... thank God for that. Otherwise, I was going to invite him here. There's no way I'd have let him spend the night at his. If his mom was comfortable saying all those things to me, God knows what she might say to him.

Then again, he probably heard it all over the fifteen years he lived with her. I can only hope his parents are the 'opposites attract' sort of couple.

I stand in the middle of the living room, scanning the chipped walls, the fancy, cheap-looking furniture—of which, according to my parents, ninety-nine percent was already here, including the big, broken plasma TV fixed to the wall. Our small kitchen that we rarely used. The dining area that was more Mom's workspace than anything, and occasionally where Haze and I sat to do homework.

When I go in my bedroom, nothing is different, save for the fact that everything is neatly in place. My bed is made. My desk is organized. No leftover sheets on the floor from that makeshift rope I made on the night of recruitment.

There's a stack of my old sketchbooks on my desk, where I used to doodle random things that fascinated me, mostly infected, clouds, and buildings.

Home feels ... exactly the same and yet entirely different. It's the same, because everything looks the same. Mom's not here, and she rarely was. It's different, because it's like no one even lives here anymore. Even my own stuff is covered in a thin layer of dust.

I'm exhausted, so I go sit on my bed, and sink right into the hard frame. God, I forgot how flat this mattress is. I definitely did not miss *this*.

Still, when I lie down, I fall asleep on it all the same, soothed by the ghost feeling of Cris's lips on mine.

The morning comes. I dig through my closet to change out of my uniform before heading out again. Surprisingly, I struggle to fit into my old clothes. And I'm positive I heard something somewhere rip on the shirt, so I throw on the only baggy jacket I have to cover any potential holes.

A quick drop by the hospital, though I only make a stop by reception to ask about Zack. I'm told he checked out earlier to go to the orphanage. So that's where I head. I haven't seen him since the power plant, and I can't imagine he's doing too well right now.

I attract far less attention this time around. Well, for the most part. My pink tips still draw *some* attention, and eventually I do pull the hood of my jacket over my head.

Arriving at the orphanage is so jarring. I used to come here a lot to visit Ro or pick her up. She used to sneak out on her own and that always got her in trouble, so I became her unofficial chaperone. Mrs. Gordon trusted me to look after her.

Just like Ro trusted me to look after her.

I stand there, frozen, as the front door opens and her ghost runs at me excitedly, ready to jump me with a hug. Then she's falling from a construction platform into a horde of hungry infected. Her screams loud and guttural.

Shaking my head, I snap out of it. There's a little girl sitting on the steps, trying to put on a pair of shoes, struggling to make a knot.

I climb up to her and kneel in front of her. "Do you need help?"

The girl brings the shoes to her chest and covers them protectively. Intense brown eyes bore into mine.

"Hey, it's okay. I just want to show you how to tie the laces." I offer her a smile. "My name's Ashley. What's yours?"

"I know who you are," she says, tone accusatory. "You're that girl who took Rowen to the outside and let the monsters eat her."

Those words rip through me like a barrage of bullets.

"You're the one who got Mrs. Gordon kicked out," she says. "And now, because of you, they brought Mr. Harold and he's awful and hates me."

My mouth opens to say something, defend myself from the accusations but ... there's nothing. Absolutely nothing. This little girl is right. I did get Ro killed. I did get Mrs. Gordon kicked out.

"You're just another stinky Spore and I hate you!" the girl shouts in my face before shooting up and running away from me.

I stay still, letting those words sink in.

"It changes you, doesn't it?" Captain Malhotra's voice says behind me, "being a soldier."

I stand and turn to face him. He looks almost the same way he did the last time I saw him, maybe with a slightly longer beard and extra gray hair.

"Did it hurt?" I frown. "When I looked at you the same way that girl just looked at me?"

Malhotra looks down. "You had your reasons."

Yes. I did. He failed my dad. He was his partner. He was supposed to be there for him. I never considered the guilt he must have already felt, without me reminding him all the time. I never understood it until now. Sara's face flashes before me. Jose's. Dalal's. Melisa's. Nathan's. My heart is in pieces.

And I'm sure he sees it, because it's the kind of pain only those of us who have been through it can see, because he takes me in a hug. One my dad would probably give me if he were here.

"I'm glad you're okay, kiddo," he says.

I wrap my arms around him. "Do you ever forget? Those who are gone? Those you can't bring back?"

"Never."

"So what's the point?"

"The point *isn't* that they're gone, or that we can't bring them back." Malhotra draws back, meeting my eyes. "The point is that they were here. We wouldn't be who we are now without them. No one lives forever. That doesn't mean our life, limited as it is, is meaningless. Whether it's for a few seconds or a few decades. We always leave a mark. Even in just one person's life."

I guess, even knowing all of that, it doesn't really make it any easier to deal with the loss.

"How is Mom?" I change the subject, blinking away the tears.

"She's good," he says. "She can shoot a sidearm now. Very impressive."

I still wish she didn't have to.

"You'll see her soon," Malhotra assures. "She was invited to the Pit's Memorial Day. We'll both be there."

Oh. Right. I almost forgot about that whole thing...

I look into Malhotra's eyes, and pay extra attention to his expression when I ask, "Did you know that Rodríguez ordered the bombing on Eukson?"

His soft smile vanishes. "Where did you hear that?"

"Did you, or did you not?" I ask again.

"No." He shakes his head. "But I can't say, hearing it now, that it's shocking."

"How well do you know him?" I ask. "He told me that he trained with Dad in Basic. That Dad was a hell of a rival. You trained with Dad, too. Were you friends?"

"Well..." Malhotra arches his brows, shaking his head sideways. "The two of them were friends, yeah. They went to high school together, and I'm sure they served in the same unit for a while, too. I didn't work closely with Joseph until we were stationed in Kadia."

"Dad never talked about him." That's what I find so strange about it all.

"Yeah." Malhotra nods. "I don't think they stayed close after the outbreak. But I don't know the details of their fallout. It was one of those things your dad kept to himself."

And now Dad's not around to tell me about it, either. Does Mom know more? Maybe I can ask her. She has to know. If no one else, surely Dad told *her*.

"I don't wanna keep you if you have work to do. I was about to go see a friend." I nod toward the orphanage.

"All right." He gives me another, quicker hug. "It's good to see you again, Ashley. Look after yourself, okay?"

"You, too," I say. "Take care of Mom."

"Always."

I offer him a smile, then take the stairs and head inside.

Zack is coming out of a room with a bunch of kids tagging along behind him and grabbing onto him. One sitting on his shoulders and playing with his hair, the others pulling at his shirt and fighting to hold his hands. Jordan—another Pit survivor, and also Haze's boyfriend, is there, too. He acknowledges me with a nod.

He and Haze made it official shortly after coming to Spheria. Fortunately, or unfortunately, Jordan's anemia disqualified him from the training program. He was sent here to work at the orphanage instead.

"Will you come see us again, please?" one of the kids says. I recognize him. He was one of those two kids I saw in the Pit, who came running into the hall just before things went south.

"I'll try, I promise." Zack smiles. Then his eyes meet mine. "Ashley…"

"Hey." I walk up to him. "Look at you…"

"Uh-huh." He grins. "It's good to be among friends."

"Did you … run into any trouble on your way?" I ask.

"What, you mean the protests?" Zack raises a brow. He sets the kid on his shoulders down. A nod from him signals for Jordan to keep the kids with him while the two of us walk a short distance away. "No, I didn't get into trouble. And I'm pretty sure the crowd is angrier with the general than they are with me. The man who's supposed to protect them and keep them safe is bringing dangerous killers aboard."

"Zack—"

"It's okay," he says. "I've done horrible things in retaliation to the horrible things that were done to me. I've killed people who had nothing to do with what happened to mine. I can admit that. But the truth is I didn't start any of this. The general did, the day he decided to drop bombs on innocents. Do you think *he* has any regrets about that? Do you think he regrets leaving these kids behind? He thought burying us under the rubble of our own sector would silence us forever. But people will always rise up against injustice. That's what these protests are for. That's what my parents stood for. Justice."

I don't know how General Rodríguez feels about anything, to be fair, but I can't imagine he's happy with these protests. After he arrested Sears, I'm not sure where things are headed, here or in Spheria, but probably nowhere good, if the Pit is anything to go by.

"I'm really sorry about Lori," I say. "I shouldn't have—"

"You're not the one who shot her," he cuts me off, "so as far as I'm concerned, it wasn't your fault, and you don't have anything to apologize for."

I still feel guilty.

"You fought for me harder than anyone else," he says. "And between us, we both know Lori would have ended up in another cage, anyway. I don't think that would have been any better." He sounds calm, but the redness in his eyes betrays him. He runs his sleeve over his face before the tears drop. "Now they won't even let me bury her because they think her body might be valuable for research…"

"I think she was really happy to see you again." I rub his arm for what little comfort I can provide, if any. "And fight beside you. Even if it was for a little while."

"Yeah." He lets out a broken chuckle. "We were one hell of a duo."

PART SIX

SEVENTY-THREE

BEING BACK in Spheria is weird.

It's almost like coming home, which doesn't sound right. Doesn't *feel* right. How do I feel more at home here than I did back ... home? I thought being in Kadia, I wouldn't want to leave again. That being there, I would be happy. At peace. But I felt none of that.

Maybe if I'd been able to see Mom, I wouldn't feel like I no longer belonged. But everything that made my life what it was is no longer there. Regi, Ro, Will... They're gone. Cris and Haze are here. For now, at least. And Mom's off with Spec Ops.

We spent until noon there, had lunch, then packed up to leave. As soon as we landed here, a research team was already waiting to retrieve Lori's body. Zack was escorted by his AIT sergeant and two guards.

Lt. Mansur called for one last meeting for the Renegades at the Spec Ops HQ, and that's where we're headed. Now that our objective is obsolete, I don't know what's next.

Cris is ahead, walking with Stephen, Xael, and a few of the boys from the other squads. Tyra's walking next to me with the other girls. Lucille is still hospitalized.

"Jose was your friend, right?" Tyra asks.

That question takes me aback.

"It didn't really register immediately when we met in Ground Zero, but you're *the* Ashley Brown," she says. "She talked about you a lot."

"What could she have possibly had to say about me?" I ask.

I was nothing short of distant the whole time. We only hung out so much because Sara dragged me with her at the start of AIT, before things turned sour between us. And after she left, Jose and I hung out more because of habit than anything else. She was always the one asking if I wanted to go out. Always the one asking if I wanted to grab food together. Always the one reminding me I had to eat and rest and relax and watch a movie or two with her till we fell asleep. Live a little because it's not just about work.

"A lot of things," Tyra says. "She said you were brilliant on the battlefield—a sharp shot, a great medic, so determined and so resilient. She said you saved her life more times than she could count. That she could only dream to repay you for some of it by treating you to strawberry milkshake and inviting you to watch movies with her."

I feel like someone slapped me so hard my face turned in a direction I didn't even know existed. All that praise is ... unnecessary. I did what I had to. What I was supposed to. What I vowed to do. But even if I hadn't vowed to protect my comrades ... I would have still done it. Because I wanted to. Because I couldn't watch her die. But I never expected her to repay me. Never once thought she owed me.

"She said it's thanks to you she actually got to go home and bring her grandma all those movies she's been collecting for months," Tyra says. "That if she were to die now, she'd die happy."

I need Tyra to stop talking because every word she says hits me with a flash of an unpleasant instant where I snapped at Jose for one reason or another—most of which were unrelated to her. I need her to stop talking because I'm going to suffocate for holding my breath too long to stop myself from crying right now.

"I like to think it all happened as it was meant to," Tyra says. "And you saved me that day so that I could tell you on her behalf, how much you meant to her."

Okay. I'm suffocating.

"Brown," Sgt. Seidel calls for me, and God I've never been so thankful for anything in my life.

I leave Tyra's side as she proceeds to the briefing room and walk over to Seidel. Trying my best to slap on a totally-not-having-a-meltdown expression.

"Mirani's corpse was sent to Serco," she says.

Oh, great! Just the other thing I wanted to talk about. I hate my life so much. I should have told Cris yes to staying behind. I should have just let us get buried there. Then I could just float here as a ghost and laugh at everyone's misery.

"Her family will lay her to rest there and have a grave to visit. They were grateful for that."

"Yeah, okay." I shrug. "I'm sure they would have been more grateful to receive her alive."

"You can't save everyone, Brown," she says.

Yeah, I got that. Loud and clear. The universe is making sure I know this particular fact very well. I'm not contesting it.

Sgt. Seidel doesn't say anything for a very uncomfortable moment.

"Is there anything else?" I ask.

"I wanted to ask how you're holding up," she says.

Oh. Okay.

"Fine," I lie. "Thanks."

"Sure you are," she sighs. "Loss is hard. Consecutive loss is harder. I'm no therapist, but it's part of my job to hear out my soldiers."

"It's a good thing we're disbanding, then," I say. "Means I no longer fall under the umbrella of your authority. So you got nothing to worry about."

She gives me a stern look. *This is not the time for your deflective humor.* My bad.

"If you need to talk, you should. Take it from someone who's been in your shoes on multiple accounts. It's difficult. Hell, probably more difficult than solo-fighting a wave. But it gets easier the more you do it. The only way to keep yourself sane, is by learning that everyone around you is losing it, too. You're not in this alone. You don't have to be in it alone."

I was almost out of it when it happened, but those glimpses I caught are still vivid. If I had acted a little faster. If I had tried to snatch my M4 back from Justin. Or even stood between him and Dalal... If, if, if, if. Endless ifs.

"How do you know?" I ask. "You've been doing this for a while now, so how do you make the difference? Between those you can trust and those you can't? Those who deserve mercy and those who don't?"

I used to think I couldn't take any chances. That it's us or them.

Then I thought maybe it didn't have to be like that. Maybe Cris was right and peace was possible. But no matter what decision I made, it was the wrong one. Someone somewhere got hurt regardless of what I chose.

"You want the simple truth, Brown?" Sgt. Seidel says, "you can never know for sure."

That's not a satisfying answer.

"Humans are unpredictable," she says. "Things can change in a heartbeat. A friend may suddenly become your foe—and a foe, your friend. You listen to your gut and your brain. You try to analyze the situation as fast and rationally as you can, to determine what the right course of action is. But you can't read the other person's mind. You get better at reading situations, and you get better at listening to your gut, but you can never be a hundred percent certain about the outcome. You can never be a hundred percent certain of what the other person will do."

Because this totally needed to get more complicated than it already was. God, I shouldn't have asked.

"The only thing that's set in stone," Sgt. Seidel continues, "is the past. And you shouldn't beat yourself up over that. We soldiers have to prepare for the absolute worst, and hope for the bare-minimum best."

Tell me about it. Actually, no thank you. I don't want to hear any more about it because I'm not sure my sanity levels can go any lower —and no, universe, I'm not asking you to prove me wrong. Kindly, butt off.

"Talk," she insists. "It doesn't have to be to me—but talk to someone. Talk to Rey. If you don't talk to the people you're close to, you're as good as alone."

How pathetic do I look right now that Sgt. Seidel is practically begging me to throw myself at Cris after spending so long ensuring we stood no less than an arm's length from one another? Which, obviously, didn't work. Can I count that as one fight I actually won?

"Okay, I will." I look down to dodge her eyes. My gaze lands on her left hand, the metallic band on her ring finger. Was that always there? "You're married?"

She looks down at her hand, then at me. "Yes, Brown, I'm married. I have two kids as well. Believe it or not, my life doesn't *only* revolve around being your sergeant."

"But you're so young." I probably shouldn't have said that out loud. Well, too late.

"I'm twenty-five," she says. "Twenty years ago, when humans weren't on the brink of extinction, yes, that was too young. Today, we survive to fight, so we can fight to survive."

SEVENTY-FOUR

"RENEGADES," Lt. Mansur starts, "I'll cut straight to the chase and say this is not the outcome any of us hoped for. A speech is easy when you have something to point to and say: this is what it was all for. A simple 'good job, you did it. Now go and celebrate' suffices. It's not as easy, however, to motivate after failure.

"Some of you may be questioning what we fought for all this time, if it was all for naught, if all the deaths we witnessed, all the comrades we lost were in vain. If all the sweat and blood we shed meant nothing. Believe me, I'm no different.

"At times like this, it's almost impossible to see the one good apple dangling in a tree of rotten fruit. But failure isn't the end. Failure is a stop on the way. Failure means we're on the right track. We just have to keep going. If humankind is known for one thing, it's for its persistence. Strength is nothing without weakness. Nor is courage without fear. And success without failure.

"With hardship, comes ease," he says. "We failed. It wasn't one person's fault, or one person's responsibility. We failed together. And when we win, we'll win together. But the fight continues, and we do that together, too.

"I want to thank you all for your service. May we reunite again under better circumstances. I leave you now in God's care."

Despite the gloominess coating the entire room, people still manage to clap and cheer, and I force myself to do the same. Then the one-on-one goodbyes ensue. I resort to mere handshakes and forced smiles for the most part, before retreating to the back for what little lonesomeness I can get.

"Ash," Cris says as he walks up to me. "The lieutenant wants to speak to us in his office."

So much for lonesomeness. "About what?"

He shrugs. "Don't know. Let's go find out."

We leave the briefing room and follow the lieutenant to his office. Which is ... really empty, save for the cardboard boxes on the floor, stacked with papers and files and other objects.

"Sir..." Cris starts, "are you leaving Spheria?"

"Yes." He's rummaging through a stack of papers on his desk. "I'm returning to Serco. My home." He keeps looking for another few seconds, then checks a different stack of papers. "There they are."

He grabs a couple of files, then hands them over to us. I take one of them and Cris takes the other. It's a request-of-reassignment form.

"Sir?" Cris looks up from the paper with big eyes.

"I'm sure," the lieutenant says, "that short visit to Kadia wasn't enough. You can each fill out those forms, and I will personally sign off on your reassignment. You served the Renegades well in the short time you've been with us, and the least I can do is let you both go home."

"Uh ... sir," I say. "That may be doable for Cris, but in my case, Colonel Sergei—"

"I'm aware." Lt. Mansur smiles. "I've been in touch with Captain Malhotra, and he told me about the situation. I spoke to Colonel Sergei myself when we were in Kadia. She won't interfere with this. She acknowledges you've proven your loyalty, and even she can't deny how remarkable a soldier you are. We need those today, more than ever."

I don't believe it.

"You have my word, Brown," he assures. "And if anyone does try to interfere with this, you let me or Sergeant Seidel know, and we'll handle it."

Cris beams at me. Joy shining in his face. I wish I could feel it, too.

"Get these forms to me as soon as possible," the lieutenant says, "and I will see to it that you'll be back home in a week or two, max."

"Yes, sir," Cris answers for both of us, excited. He snaps into a hard salute, and I follow his lead. "Thank you, sir. We appreciate this. A lot."

"My pleasure." Lt. Mansur salutes back. "All right, Privates. Dismissed."

Cris barely wastes a breath. The moment we step out of the office and the door closes behind us, he swipes me in his arms and lifts me up, swirling me around.

"We're going home." He places me down before we attract more attention than the flitting gazes of guards passing by. His grin is wide. I've never seen him this happy before. Ever.

"Yeah…" I can't really match his enthusiasm. "We're going home."

"See?" Cris waves the form at me. "I told you it was temporary."

"You sure did." I stare at the empty form in my hand.

"Ash," he takes my free hand in his, "I know you're still worried about Sergei, but you heard what the lieutenant said. He'll vouch for you. Your file will speak for itself. Sergei would be mad not to let you back. It's going to be okay."

"Yeah, it probably will be." I nod.

It's not really about that, though, is it?

"We should start packing," Cris leans down and presses a soft kiss to the top of my head. It would make me melt if my body wasn't stubbornly icy right now. "Call me when you're done filling out your form. We can hand them in together?"

"Sure."

"Great," he says, impatiently backing away. "I'll see you soon, okay?"

"See ya." I start to wave, but he's turning and running off already. And I am so, so, so jealous of him right now. So jealous of his excitement and eagerness and enthusiasm.

Because I feel absolutely nothing.

―――

I'm not feeling *nothing* nothing.

That's what Dalal would say anyway. I'm not feeling what I'd like to be feeling. I'm not feeling what I *should* be feeling. Or maybe it's not even that. Maybe I don't want to feel happy or excited, because I shouldn't, because I don't have the right, because there is so much to be upset about, so much to mourn. Why do I get to go home when so many others don't? Why do I deserve to be happy when others aren't?

Or maybe it's not that I don't want or deserve to be happy. Maybe

I'm just scared of being happy. Scared of embracing this joy, only for it to be short-lived. Because, come tomorrow, something else will go wrong.

So, I'm not feeling *nothing*. I just don't know *what* I'm feeling.

As I leave the Spec Ops HQ, I run into Haytham at the bottom of the stairs, some papers in his hand.

He stops in his tracks upon seeing me. "Hey, Ashley," he greets.

"Hey." I force a smile. "What are you up to?"

"I just need Uncle Zaid—Lieutenant Mansur to fill out some forms," he says. "For ... the crawler."

That sours my mood even more. "I bet you're excited to have a new test subject."

He lets out a nervous chuckle. "Uh ... I don't know if excited is the word. And we were really hoping we'd get the crawler alive, so..."

"But you can still do something with her, right?" I ask. "Her corpse is still valuable? It wasn't *all* for nothing?"

"I don't know, maybe. It's too early to tell." His eyes dart between me and the papers in his hands. Right. He probably can't tell me anyway. "I'm sorry."

"What are you sorry for?" The question comes out flatter than I mean it to.

His grip tightens, almost crumpling the forms. He looks down to his feet, chewing his lip. "I'm sorry ... you failed your mission. I heard the Renegades are disbanding."

"Yeah." I heave a tired sigh, then start on my way. I have to pack. "Good luck, Hayth."

"She's not dead." It's a whisper behind me. So low I almost miss it.

I spin around back to him. "What did you say?"

He looks up, lips twitching, and takes a few steps toward me. "She's not dead."

"Lori?" I blink. It takes a second. Another. A third. Then it hits me. No, not Lori. "Who?" I need him to say it. I need to hear it.

"Sara's still alive."

SEVENTY-FIVE

HIS WORDS MAKE no sense at all.

"What do you mean she's still alive?" My head tilts to the side. The tightness in my chest makes the smallest inhale a challenge. "She was infected. The cure worked?"

"No," he says. "It *didn't* and it *did*."

That doesn't make sense either. "Explain."

"She didn't turn." Haytham fumbles with his hands. "But the cure... It didn't eliminate the virus. It just stopped it from spreading further in her body."

"And?" I urge him, my voice sharpening. He's killing me with these half-answers.

"And..." Haytham swallows hard. "She's not an infected, technically, but ... she's not entirely human either. It's hard to explain. But we're keeping her in the lab to try and figure out what happened."

Keeping her in the lab.

"You mean you're experimenting on her?" My guts twist at the mere thought. Repulsion burns my throat. "Is she ... aware? Can she speak?"

"Like I said." Haytham's timid, guilt-filled gaze evades mine. "She didn't turn."

My heart skips. Despite the disgust crawling through every inch of me, a spark of hope lights up at the pit of my stomach. "You've spoken to her?"

"I... Y-yes, a little bit," Haytham stutters. "They don't really let me talk to her much. Conflict of interest and all that—"

"I need to see her." I take a step closer, demanding he look at me. "Haytham, I have to see her."

"I can't." He shakes his head, stepping back. "I can't. I'm not even supposed to tell you this."

My fists clutch around his collar. Rage scrunches up my face and shoots through my voice. "Then why the hell did you tell me?"

His trembling hands struggle to unfold my fists. "Because I can't ... bear the sight of it. Of her. She's in pain. And I just ... I had to tell someone." Every word builds up the reserve of tears in his eyes. "I feel like I'm going to explode. I wanted to help humanity. I wanted to help find a cure, but all I've done is watch my friends suffer. Melisa... Sara. Who's next?"

My fists loosen around him, allowing him back some personal space. I stand still, a whirlwind of emotions spinning through me.

"There's been talk ... about what to do with Melisa. Some of the Division Commanders want to kill her. They think it's too dangerous to keep an Active alive in Spheria, especially now that we lost the sentient crawler and any possibility to communicate with her." He swallows a cry. "Dr. Marchand wants to keep her alive."

Yeah. I was there in that meeting. I heard it all.

"I don't know how long I can keep doing this. It's one thing if we experiment on those who are already gone. That's what I told myself about Melisa. She's dead. She's not really here anymore. But experimenting on the living?" He sniffles. "And for what? We don't even know that it will amount to anything. We don't even know that it will save anyone. I thought I had it in me. I thought, maybe I'm too weak for the battlefield, but this is a fight I can endure. A fight I can be a part of. But I can't..." His head falls, and so do his tears, one drop after the other, dotting his boots. "I can't be a part of this anymore."

"Then don't be," I tell him. "You're privileged. Your family's name is big. Use it. Put a stop to this."

"I can't." Haytham looks up at me with streams on his face. "If I say anything, my family's name won't matter. General Rodríguez would take away our status in a flash. He'll label me a traitor and probably sentence me to exile."

"So what?" I scoff. "At least it'll be for a good cause."

"What do you mean, *so what*?" His brows pinch. "I'm not like you, Ashley. Not the kind of person who sabotages everyone else for my own personal whims. I can't destroy all the work my parents and family have dedicated their whole lives to just because I feel bad about myself. Life is good in Serco. Privileged or unprivileged, life is good for everyone, because my dad can make sure that it is. I can't risk taking away what little influence my family actually has, all the good that they're doing, just because I don't have the stomach for the work I do."

My nails dig into my palms. Haytham's face has never looked so punchable. "You're a coward."

"Yes, I am." Haytham doesn't even flinch at the insult. His tears dry up fast with renewed acceptance. "I know that already. But if you're so brave, then why don't *you* do something about it? Why don't *you* try to stop it?"

Despite the unquenchable anger constricting my throat, I still manage a confident, "I will."

Haytham's jaw slacks. He sucks in a shaky breath. "*Ya Allah*! Ashley, you can't be serious—what do you think you can do on your own? You'll get yourself killed."

Now he wants to talk me out of it? I swear … if I didn't think I'd actually break his face…

"If I had just let them kill Melisa in the Pit," I cut him off, "you wouldn't have taken her as a test subject. You wouldn't have made those cure samples. You wouldn't have told me about it, and I wouldn't have used that as an excuse to stall Sara's fate. She wouldn't be where she is right now…" If it weren't because of me.

"You can't take the blame for all of that," Haytham says. So does everyone keep telling me, but really, I don't believe those words one bit.

"It doesn't matter now. It is what it is." My eyes burn, and yet they've never been dryer. Neither has my voice. "I'm going to get Sara out of there, with or without your help."

SEVENTY-SIX

I FIND Haze at one of the workshops she's usually at, fixing up some vehicle.

Part of me wants to turn back, think this through once again. But the other part of me knows my mind's already made up, even without a plan, so I walk into the workshop and knock on the side of the car she's hunched over.

"Hey!" Haze beams at me. She wipes her hands on a dirty apron before greeting me with a tight hug. "You're back!"

"Yep." I return the hug. She smells like gasoline and grease, but I want to bury my face in her hair forever.

Haze pulls away. "How are..." Pause, probably trying to figure out which question to ask first. "Is it true what they're saying? Was Lori really...?"

I nod.

"Oh, my God." She frowns. "Poor Zack. How is he doing?"

Shrug. "He's good. At pretending he's good."

"That's Zack." She leans on the car beside me. "I'm gonna have to find him later. Do you know what's gonna happen next? What are they going to do with him? Will they let him finish training?"

"I have no idea." To be honest, I don't think I'll have time to worry about that. "How about you? What's new?"

"Well, I filed a request of reassignment to Kadia," she says. "I don't know that Colonel Sergei will be too excited about having me back, but Sergeant Clint said he'll write me a personalized recommendation. So hopefully it's just a matter of time before I see Jordan again. I miss him so much."

Wow. Talk about timing.

"The Renegades have been disbanded." I let that sit, because I don't want to give her the false hope I'm about to. "Cris and I ... will be sent to Kadia."

"Really?" Her eyes brighten up again. She pushes away from the car to stand facing me, taking my hands in hers. "Ash, that's amazing!"

"Yeah..." The smile I give her hangs by a thread, and falls with the next breath I release.

"What's wrong?" Haze doesn't miss it. "Don't tell me... You don't wanna go back anymore?"

It doesn't really matter if I do or don't want to go back. I'm not going back, period. So at least I don't have to worry about not knowing what to feel.

"Ash?" Haze leans close, soft blue eyes searching mine. Her hold on my hands tightens. "What's going on?"

And I tell her. "Sara's alive."

The way she backs up at those words, the way she looks at me screams, *oh no, she finally snapped*. A nervous smile, like she's not sure what kind of face to put on to brave through whatever I'll say next. "What?"

"She's alive." I repeat. I also had to say that to myself over and over before it finally sank in. I don't think it actually has yet. "Haytham told me. After they gave her the cure, she wasn't cured but ... she didn't turn, either."

"What does that mean?" Haze's brows furrow. Her hands let go of mine.

"It means she's a perfect test subject," I say. "Lab rat. That's what it means. And I can't ... let this happen to Sara. I just can't."

"You can't let this happen..." Haze casts me a skeptical look. "So, what are you gonna do exactly?"

"I'm gonna break her out."

Haze's mouth falls open, then closes, then opens again. "Break her out of where? The lab?"

"Spheria." I state it as the simple fact that it is.

"Okay." Haze nods, but her voice shakes with doubt. "And then what?"

"We find a place," I say. "We lay low—"

"Ash," Haze cuts in. "I'm sorry but … we've tried that before, remember? Look how well it turned out for all of us." She gestures vaguely around us.

"It doesn't have to end the same way this time," I argue. *Please don't let it end the same way.*

"Do you realize what you'll be putting at risk?" she asks. "You'll jeopardize everything. Your chance of going home again—"

"Yes, I know."

"I'm not sure you do," she says.

"Are you calling me an idiot?" I snap.

"You're not an idiot, you're reckless," she corrects. "It's not the same thing, but it's still bad."

"I'm doing this, Haze." I shrug, a mix of determined and indifferent. "You're not talking me out of it. So, uh … we can say goodbye. That's all I'm here for."

Haze frowns. "Did you tell Cris?"

I was hoping she wouldn't ask. "No."

She exhales through her nose. "Are you *going* to tell him?"

I swallow. "No."

Her eyes close, head shaking in disapproval. "Why not?"

"Because…" I bite my lip, trying to focus on anything but the growing pain in my chest. "I'm scared of what he'll say," I confess. "I'm scared that he'll try to stop me, and we both know he can't stop me. So that'll be the end of that. The end of us, before we even had the chance to *be* us."

Haze's frown deepens, but she doesn't interrupt me.

"I don't want to break his heart, and I know for a fact that this would break his heart. It would break mine, too." I sniffle. "But I'm also scared that he won't try to stop me. I'm scared that he'll try to help and … and that'll ruin everything he worked for. Everything he risked his life for. Everything he's ever wanted. To help his family. I can't take that away from him. I can't … ask him to give everything up for me. I don't want to put him in a position where he has to choose. I don't want to be the reason he can't go home."

He was ready to stay with me in the power plant, leave everything behind, just because I decided I couldn't fight anymore. Just because I decided I didn't want to live. I can't make him do that.

Haze watches me with the saddest face. Yeah, I'm a pathetic mess,

I know. The pinch in her brows already tells me she's so not on board with any of this. I don't blame her. I didn't expect her to be, but it would have hurt to leave without telling anyone. If she knows, then at least she can tell Cris for me, when I'm gone, because there's no way I can face him myself. She can tell Mom, too.

"Okay." Haze holds my face with warm hands, lifting my head so she can meet my eyes. "So let *me* help you."

"What? Haze—"

"I want to help you." For all her doubt moments ago, she sounds confident. "I owe you that much."

"You don't owe me anything." I push her hands away from my face, shaking my head. "I didn't tell you this to guilt-trip you into helping me. I don't want to jeopardize what you have either. We've been over this already. And I meant what I said before. I forgive—"

"But I don't." She cuts me off. "I know you forgave me, but ... I can't forgive myself." She shifts her weight to one foot. "Sure, at the time, it felt like the right thing to do, because surviving was what mattered most. And I guess it all turned out okay in the end. Maybe if things had gone differently that night, you and I wouldn't even be alive today. But I swore to myself, I'd never abandon you again. Ever. And if this is what you want. If you're *sure* this is what you want. If Sara's worth taking this big risk for, then ... I'll be there. Right where you need me. It's the *least* I can do."

And that, well, crap, now I'm sobbing a waterfall. Haze takes me in a hug tighter than the first. I hold her in my arms and whisper against her shoulder, "Thank you."

SEVENTY-SEVEN

HAZE and I meet up with Haytham in the Fifth Sector, then he leads us to where we're supposed to be having our secret meeting. Some fancy, two-story house in the privileged part of the neighborhood. We pooled our lunch breaks to make this happen, so we only really have a limited time.

"Hey." Luke is the one who opens the door.

My jaw drops. I look to Haytham. "You told Luke?"

"And you told Hazel." Haytham shrugs. "Look, I'm trying to make sure you don't get yourself killed with this ... insane idea of yours. Luke can help us a lot."

I ... guess that's fair.

The inside of the house is a bit of a mess, the kind of mess that could only be the result of vandalism. Some broken windows. Broken chairs. A coffee table missing half its legs. What was it like for Luke to come back home that day? What has it been like for him since? He didn't even have the time or mind to clean up.

Four maps are sprawled on the dining table. One is of Spheria's layout, another one is a general map of the territory that SPORE occupies, including sectors and outposts, the third one is of the blueprint of the first floor of the Sphere building, and the last one is the blueprint of the lab layout located under the Sphere building.

"Okay," Haytham says, "the lab can only be accessed through two points. There's the elevator in the east wing of the Sphere building. That's the main entrance. And there's a second one located in the parking garage, south-west of the Sphere building. That one is mostly used for emergencies, and is normally locked, but the lock can be overridden.

"Only lab staff and high-level personnel are normally allowed to go in through the main entrance. The front desk checks everyone that comes to the lab, even if they're regular staff. IDs have to be double-checked, and people usually log their activity when they arrive and again when they leave."

"So how the hell am I supposed to get down there?" I ask.

"One thing I did think of is the BSC Program—Blood Sample Collection," Haytham suggests. "Normally there are specific days during which some staff will organize a blood-donation station. We're always in need of more blood samples for our research. But people can still donate on any given day. I was thinking we could sign you up for that. That would grant you temporary Level A clearance. You'll go through reception and then be allowed into Section A of the lab.

"Obviously, you're not actually going to donate blood. Once a medic checks that you're okay, they'll likely leave you alone and check in every now and again to make sure you didn't pass out. We usually keep Sara in Section D. That's where the ... uh," he falters, "the rooms where we keep the live subjects are when they're not needed for studies. But I think our best chance is to set up your BSC appointment around the time when Sara's in Section C."

"And when is that?" I ask.

"Sara has regular checkups every day. We move her from Section D to a treatment room in Section C, just around the corner from where we have Melisa. We take a blood sample, do some brain scans and the sort. She'll be there for about an hour or more. Staff filter in and out, but she'll be alone anywhere from five to ten minutes. That would be your window to get in and out."

"I missed the part where I get the clearance to Section C." I squint at the map.

Haytham turns to Luke expectantly.

Luke reaches into his pocket and digs something out. A keycard. "It's Level C clearance." He sets it on the table and slides it across to me. "My dad's. It should still work. As I understand, once you get through initial security at the entrance, you should be able to use this card freely. Its activity will be logged, and it can be traced back to my dad. Considering he's locked up in a cell now, they'll assume someone stole it when they broke in here. You'll still have enough time to get wherever you want. You'll just have to be sneaky. Don't let anyone take a close look at the card."

"Is that gonna be enough?" I ask. "Don't they have like, handprint scans or codes?"

"The treatment room Sara will be in doesn't have a code, no," Haytham explains. "You'll only need the section clearance. However ... there is one issue."

"Which is?"

"You won't be able to take the same way out. As soon as you get Sara, you really can't be seen by anyone. You'll have to take the emergency exit. And before that ... you'll have to go through the scanner. We have multiple scanners throughout the lab located at exit points. You step inside this small room, it locks up and scans for any infected individuals."

Right, I remember. We went through one of those during our visit to the lab.

"Are you saying—"

"It will detect Sara as an infected," Haytham confirms.

"And how do we bypass that?"

"You can't bypass the scan, but the lock can be overridden. It has to be done manually, either via a computer or via a control panel located on the outside of the scanner room."

That sounds risky. "Is there any other way? Any button I can push on the inside?"

"No." Haytham frowns. "It was designed specifically to contain infection in case any test subjects managed to escape. We had a few cases before with some of the animals."

"Can *you* unlock the door, then?" I ask.

Haytham shakes his head. "Ashley, I'm sorry. I'm helping you as best I can but ... getting involved at all, helping with the execution of this plan ... I can't do that. I'm already risking so much just by giving you all this information."

Of course. Don't get greedy, Ashley. Be thankful your friends even agreed to support this crazy idea.

"You'll have to pass first," Haytham says. "Get scanned. Cross to the other side, and then, once it's Sara's turn for the scan, you'll have to punch in the code to unlock the room. The code will be displayed on the control panel on the wall. Those codes expire, so you have to enter it fast, and before someone unlocks the door on the other side. It's usually a five- to ten-digit number. Random each time. Just pay attention and be quick."

"Pay attention and be quick. Got it." This is becoming more and more stressful by the minute. "And what about the emergency exit? You said it's locked?"

"Yes, but as I said, the lock can be overridden with clearance, which you should have." Haytham nods at the keycard in front of me. "Level C clearance should help you get through most of the lab with ease. That card solves half of our problems. You just have to not get caught."

"Okay." Easier said than done.

"The alarms will be going off at this point. So chances are you'll run into security in the parking garage. You'll either have to hide, or sneak out of there as fast as possible. Cameras are all over the place, and they'll be able to find you if they have to."

I nod, though my heart races so fast I can almost hear it.

"And the lab isn't our only problem," Haytham adds, gesturing to the map. "Even if you and Sara manage to get out of it, you still need a way to get out of Spheria."

"That's where I come in," Haze says. "There's this APC we've been trying to fix. It's almost ready but it's not in top shape just yet. I think I can get it running in time. I'll put more juice in it and it should be good to go."

I perk up at her. "That sounds promising."

"This is where it is right now. Workshop A2." Haze points at a building on the map of Spheria, a few blocks south of the Sphere building. "I can try to time my shift that day accordingly so that I can be there. Do you think you can make it all the way to the garage?"

"I think so?" I say. "Depends on how much security will be on me—"

"It'll be a lot," Luke says. "You'll have to stay out of sight or find someplace to lay low until the Spores have dispersed enough, but I wouldn't recommend that. The longer it takes, the tighter security will get and the harder it'll be for you to get anywhere. The watchposts will likely have two guards posted at all times. Security at the gates and checkpoints will triple. They won't rest until they've searched every inch of Spheria to find you. You have one shot to make this happen. One shot. You screw it up, it's all gone."

"No pressure or anything." I let out a nervous chuckle. "So, what are you suggesting?"

"Haze will have to drive the vehicle to you," Luke says. "You have to drive out as soon as you get out of the lab. Don't waste a second."

Haze's eyes pop. "I... I'm not... I'm not allowed to drive outside of our practice runs."

"Sure, because this whole plan we're working on relies so much on what we're allowed to do, right?" Luke deadpans. "We're all breaking one rule or another. Either we all commit to make it work, or we don't, and it falls apart."

Haze doesn't say anything, but I know what she's thinking. I told her she could help me discreetly, without risking getting caught in the process, so that she may still have a chance to go home.

"No," I say. "I don't want Haze to do it. I don't want any of you to get in trouble or get caught for helping me."

"Ash, we're all gonna get in trouble sooner or later." Luke raps his fingers against the table, leaning back against the chair. "It's about how long we can delay getting in said trouble."

"I can get to the workshop with Sara," I say it more confidently than I feel it. "I'll do it. We'll be sneaky and fast and we'll make it there in time."

Luke sighs, shaking his head. "If you're so sure."

"Now tell me about the gate," I say.

Luke shifts to lean over the table. "You remember the Double Wave Attack? We went out through the southeastern gate." He points to it on the map. "That's the one. The roads outside are pretty clear. Only problem is, there's an outpost here—" He points at a spot on the SPORE territory map, further southeast. "They'll be alerted to your escape by the time you get there, so my advice is to ditch the car somewhere and go on foot. You'll have to run as far as you can and hide. Wait it out if you have to."

"Okay." I nod. Drive, ditch the car, run and hide. "Okay. Thanks."

"So, I guess," Haze says, "all that's left to decide is ... when?"

"I think we should do it on the Pit's Memorial Day," Luke says.

"Why's that?" I ask.

"Because there'll be a big gathering outside the Sphere Building. Sounds counterproductive, but there'll be a lot of civilians there, not just Spores. Considering the protests, they'll have to tighten security, both at the memorial service, and the Fifth Sector. Meaning it will thin out everywhere else, and if the alarm does sound once you and Sara break out, there'll still be a lot of commotion, with the civilians needing to be evacuated. It could be a good way for you to just … blend in, if you have to. Use it to your advantage."

"Does that mean we skip the celebrations?" I ask.

"I think it would be smarter to attend for a little bit, just so people see you're there," Haytham says. "I can schedule your appointment accordingly."

"Okay." I should be excited that we figured something out. And yet … I'm about to explode from nervousness. All it takes is one mistake. Just one. It all blows up.

"Guys…" Haytham says. "I know you all know this already, but I feel like someone has to voice it: this is *insane*. Thinking we can pull this off? Just the four of us? Technically, just one, because Ashley is the only one really executing the plan. It's insane. The odds of it succeeding are … so minimal that I can't even give you an estimate. We're not just infiltrating a lab, we're … betraying SPORE."

I know. Haze and Luke know that, too, but that's not the point.

"We have to try," I say, determined. "Even if we're doomed to fail, we have to try."

And on that, we all agree.

Haze and Haytham have to run shortly after. I stick around to help Luke gather the maps and fold them up. We haven't talked since he came to the Spec Ops barracks, since he found out about Sara. I didn't really have it in me to see him again.

"I'm really sorry about your dad," I say.

Luke spares me one glance. "Thanks."

"Do you know what Rodríguez plans to do with him?"

He shakes his head. Huffing, tired. "Rodríguez will do whatever needs to be done to maintain his position." He meets my eyes with determination. "Don't worry about my dad. Worry about Sara. That's all. You just … get her out of there. Get her somewhere safe."

"I'll do my best," I promise. Then I look down at my portor, and remember one important detail. "Luke … think you can help me with something?"

"What's up?"

SEVENTY-EIGHT

AS I PREPARE for the journey ahead, I feel like I'm back in my room in Kadia, packing for the night of recruitment, trying to decide what to make space for and what to leave behind.

I dig through the box of Sara's things that Lucille brought me. I take the snow globe I should have taken from the beginning. Dad's picture. The compass. Nathan's tag. Melisa's hairband. Then I go into Dalal's room. I had already started packing her things, separating them into what will be sent to her family and what will be returned to SPORE. I grab one of her headscarves and wrap it around my neck.

I leave the personal box at Lucille's door and take the other down to the reception desk. I drop off my ruck with Haze, then I go to the one place I've been dodging for months.

"Hey, Dad..." I stand by the memorial, a hand resting next to his carved name on the rock. "I'm sorry, it's been a while..." It feels as stupid as it did the first time. Talking to a deaddamn rock. "You're probably wondering why Sara hasn't been here, either. I know she visited you a lot."

I let silence fall, waiting, as if the rock will answer me.

"You always said that you and your partner either make it together or die together." My head drops. Eyes sting. "But I can't really say I found that to be the case at all."

The rock keeps ignoring me. *Jerk.*

"I wish I could say I'll be visiting you more often from now on but ... I'm here to say goodbye. For good. Because I probably won't be able to come here again. I probably won't be able to go to Kadia again either." I try not to dwell on that fact for too long, so my feet don't get cold. "There was a time when all I wanted was to be a soldier just like you, but, man, it *sucks*. Why did you never tell me that? Why did you never tell me how hard it actually is?"

No answer.

"Is it because you didn't want me to know how much it actually hurt? Or was it really so different for you? Was it really as easy as you made it seem?" My hand curls into a fist. I wish I could look him in the eye right now. "You once risked it all to save a little girl. You were ready to give your life to make sure she survived, and you did it knowing it meant you might never see me or Mom again. And I'm ... going to do just that. I'm going to give it my all to save that girl again, because I know that if you were here, you'd do the same thing. Right, Dad? You wouldn't leave her in that lab. You wouldn't let her be someone's experiment. No matter what it cost."

I want the rock—I want my dad—to say something. Tell me it's true, that he wouldn't let that happen. Tell me I'm doing the right thing. Tell me I'm risking everything for something—someone who's worth it. Tell me I'm not making a mistake by throwing away this life I have and leaving everyone else I love. I want him to manifest before me and wrap me in his embrace and tell me it won't hurt like this forever.

But he doesn't.

He doesn't.

The memorial service is set up in the big field at the front of the Sphere building. The place looks vastly different from how it normally does. A huge platform is put together with a podium on it, separated from the seating by barricades and guards. Visitors and civilians have their own seating, while the rest of us Spherian Spores are confined to the bleachers on the sides of the platform.

There are buffet and dining tables in the back—it reminds me a bit of the setup from my graduation in Basic, except that was indoors. They have a tent installed to shield from any potential rain or snow. Some ribbons and lanterns and potted plants. Light-strips dangling from the tent ceiling and spread over the tables. Such a cozy atmosphere for a miserable occasion.

The attendees form a line to have their IDs checked before they're allowed to sit. Apparently, protestors were trying to hijack the event. The Fifth Sector, just like Luke said, has been under strict supervision since the incident in Vigor. People now need authorization to cross over to the military base section.

I scan the visitors for two particular faces, but it's hard to distinguish anyone, and before I can dive into the crowd, a guard stops me and waves me off, tells me I'm supposed to be taking my seat on the bleachers, and this is a civilian-seating area only. I want to argue with him, but that could get me in trouble, and I'm not trying to get in trouble sooner than I need to. I thought I could say goodbye to Mom and Malhotra but ... maybe I can at least catch their faces from the bleachers.

I head over to the bleachers and climb up, taking a seat next to Zack. His two bodyguards, who've been assigned to him since he was attacked, are behind us.

Cris sits to my left. Haze and Luke aren't here, and neither is Haytham. Sgt. Seidel is with other squad leaders on the bleachers across from us, but I don't see Lt. Mansur. He must have already left for Serco.

I look over to Cris, who meets my eyes with an unsuspecting smile. I give him a guilty one in return.

I haven't really said goodbye to him. I don't know how, and I'm worried that if I say anything, he'll figure out I'm up to something. So my only choice is to ... say nothing.

General Rodríguez stands by the podium, his sergeant to his right. The Division Commanders line up behind him as usual, though I think one of them is missing. My gaze drifts to the Sphere building behind the platform.

In a few minutes, I'm gonna go in there. Get into that lab. Find Sara. Then get her out.

Without getting us killed in the process.

SPORE UPPER COMMAND CHAIN

GENERAL RAPHAEL RODRÍGUEZ
GENERAL OF THE SECTOR PROTECTION FORCE

- SERGEANT MAJOR BILLY HENDERSON — SENIOR ENLISTED ADVISOR

DIVISION COMMANDERS

- COL. ROXANNE DECKER — SPEC OPS
- COL. DARIUS STEELE — DEFENSE
- COL. JIYA GANESH — COMMUNICATIONS
- COL. PERCY LEECH — ENGINEERING
- COL. LINDA MARCHAND — RESEARCH
- COL. DAVIN ROSS — MEDICAL

SECTOR COMMANDERS

- LTCOL. MIKAELA SERGEI — KADIA
- LTCOL. JAMAL MANSUR — SERCO
- LTCOL. ERIK WINTER — LOTIVA (CURRENTLY)
- LTCOL. EMILIA LORIS EUKSON* — (DECEASED)
- LTCOL. BJORN EDSTRÖM — (FORMERLY, DECEASED)

*THIS POSITION NO LONGER EXISTS.

DUE TO LACK OF MANPOWER AND RESOURCES, CERTAIN RANKS AND ROLES HAVE BEEN REMOVED, SKIPPED, OR MERGED WITH OTHERS FOR MORE EFFICIENCY.

UP TO YEAR 15 A.O., DIVISION COMMANDERS HELD THE RANK OF CAPTAIN, AND USED TO ANSWER TO SECTOR COMMANDERS. SINCE THE PIT'S BOMBING, INCLUDED IN THE LAW REGULATIONS WAS THE PROMOTION OF THE DIVISION COMMANDERS TO THE RANK OF COLONEL, WHICH PLACED THEM ABOVE THE SECTOR COMMANDERS ON THE COMMAND CHAIN, AND RESERVED THEIR AUTHORITY TO OVERSEE AND DETERMINE MANPOWER DISTRIBUTION FOR EACH SECTOR.

SEVENTY-NINE

MY HEART RACES. My palms sweat. That giant sphere sitting at the top of the building is the first thing I ever saw when we flew into Spheria. I don't know why I'm nostalgic, but I am. It glints under the night sky as the moon comes out from behind the clouds for a brief moment, and in that brief moment shadows move at the base of the Sphere: a couple of people. Probably Spores.

Luke really wasn't kidding about security. They're likely snipers, and I'll bet there's many more of them all around the place. How many undercover Spores did Rodríguez plant with the civilians, too?

"Thank you for being here for the Pit's Memorial Service." The words bring silence in seconds, and the general waits until the crowd settles down before he continues, "To honor our fallen heroes is a duty we each carry in our heart. To remember the dead is the least any of us can do to repay their sacrifices. Today we remember the great losses that humanity suffered five years ago, and the unprecedented threat we faced and survived against all odds. Every year we make it without another Tsunami at our doorstep, we're grateful for the sacrifices that granted us this chance to be alive today."

Zack snorts audibly at that. Everyone around us gives him a questioning side-eye.

"Oh, come on! I can't be the only one who finds this funny," he says.

"Not to be that guy," Cris leans over me to Zack, "but shut up."

"Cristian, I do wonder," Zack leans over me and whispers back, "has anyone ever told you that you actually *are* that guy?"

I roll my eyes hard. "Can you two have this conversation anywhere else that isn't in my face? Thanks."

That seems to do it. They both retreat to their seats.

"Let's make this a reminder that when humanity unites, we stand powerful," the general continues. "When conflict arises among us, we need not let our differences divide us. We need instead to find all that binds us together. That makes us one."

I hold up my portor to check the time. My appointment is in about thirty minutes.

My gaze uncontrollably drifts to Cris, and he probably feels me staring because he turns to me, too, gives me a soft smile. My hand slowly sneaks over to steal his, and he squeezes it in a tight hold, our fingers linked. I'm going to miss how warm his hands are. I'm going to miss his scent. His voice. And the way he looks at me. I'll miss our bickering. I'll miss our shooting practice. I'll miss feeling his hands on my face. Listening to his prayers and...

I'll miss *him*.

Stop it, Ashley. Don't think about it. Don't think about him.

"Perhaps in the days leading up to the Tsunami," the general says, "humanity wasn't at its most united. Civilians and soldiers alike forgot what it was that humankind fought for. In the five years since the fall of Eukson, we've hit some rough patches, and perhaps today we're facing the roughest one yet."

"Are you crying?" Cris's question makes me realize that, yes, I am crying.

I let go of his hand and wipe away the tears. "No."

"What's going on?" he asks.

"Nothing," I lie.

What's going on is, I'm not going to see you, for a long time, probably ever again. What's going on is, I'm leaving you. How about that? I'm leaving you, not even a month into our relationship, if we can even call it that.

Cris knows I'm lying. He reaches up to wipe away another tear, then takes my hand again, firmly. "Let's go somewhere. We don't have to listen to this if you don't want."

"No." I can't go anywhere. Especially with him. I can't be alone with him. I'll change my mind, and I don't want to change my mind.

I don't want to tell him I'm going to run away, *again*. I don't want to see the heartbreak in his eyes when he realizes he can't talk me out of it this time, either.

Zack watches me from the corner of his eye, skeptical. I don't look at him for long, though, lest he can actually read my mind and figure out what's happening.

"Ash," Cris murmurs, "clearly something is wrong—"

"Yes, I'm on my period and my hormones are a mess and I'm crying for no reason," I blurt. Under different circumstances, the embarrassment would have killed me, but I couldn't care less right now.

That shuts him up. Still he doesn't let go of my hand, so I hold it while I can.

"We conquer the roadblocks as one. We find ways to cross over to the other side—or take these obstacles down together. What happened with Lotiva should not determine our destination. It is never too late to fix what others have broken—"

The speech is cut by loud buzzing coming from what I think are the loudspeakers set up all around the grounds. Technical issues?

More crackling. Someone on the platform hurries to check what's up. Everyone in the audience looks confused. The general is trying to say something into the mic, but it's not working.

Then a voice comes through the loudspeakers: distorted, robotic, unidentifiable.

"How nice of our general to see the rain through the storm," the distorted voice says. I can't tell if it's a man or woman. Can't really link it to anyone around, either. "But I speak for everyone when I say we're sick of the lies. Sick of the pretend games. The world deserves to see what kind of man speaks for humanity. The time has come for SPORE to take accountability for the failure that it is."

The voice cuts. Some more buzzing, then—

"This is Lieutenant Joseph Brown."

My heart stops.

EIGHTY

"REPORTING from the school building in Eukson..."

Dad... Dad's voice? A recording?

"I need evac." He sounds tired, out of breath, out of strength. I haven't heard his voice in years and yet ... it's almost like I was just listening to him yesterday. "I have children here with me. No one's bit, but many are injured and need urgent medical care."

Tears fog up my vision. A jumble of emotions explodes through me. Shock. Confusion. Pain. Longing. Whispers and conspiratorial chatter surround me. No one knows what's happening.

"Sir..." Another voice comes through the loudspeakers. A woman's. Panicked. "Lieutenant Brown. Says he's with some kids. Requesting evac—"

Silence for a while. Even from this far, I can see the blood drain from the general's face. He's looking around him, as are the Division Commanders. More soldiers are rushing off the platform—I imagine trying to stop the recording or turn off the speakers.

"Joseph," that's General Rodríguez's voice now coming through the loudspeakers. "How are you holding up, brother?"

"Raph?" Dad sounds surprised. "I'm hanging in there. Listen. I don't know what the hell is going on over there. I need at least two choppers to pick up these kids. I contacted Kadia, but they said the evac operations have been halted—"

"Joseph," General Rodríguez says, "we deployed fighters, about an hour ago. They'll be there momentarily."

"Fighters?" Dad grunts. "What is Sears thinking? He can't bomb the sector. There are still people to save."

"Given the extreme losses our forces sustained, we can't afford to lose more manpower in pointless rescue efforts. The other sectors stand at risk if we don't stop the infected." A pause, then Rodríguez adds, "Kadia would be next, Joseph."

"Then we evacuate Kadia, too!" Dad shouts. His voice rings with a desperation that creeps into my bones. "Spheria's got more than enough room. Serco and Lotiva can afford more people, too. We get a head start. But we can't—"

"I'm sorry." And yet there isn't a hint of regret in his voice. "It's done."

"Raphael," Dad begs, "they're *children*. Just talk to the general. Tell him ... some of them are his son's age. Most of them younger. Would he do this if it were his son?"

"Sears is no longer in charge," Rodríguez declares.

"What?"

"I led a coup."

"Then you can order the fighters to stop!"

"No," Rodríguez says. "I can't, because I sent them. Someone has to make the tough calls here. Someone has to do what Sears couldn't. In order for humanity to prevail, we must be willing to sacrifice the few to save the many."

"Raph, listen to yourself!" Dad mutters. "This isn't you—"

"Do you want to say anything?" Rodríguez says. "For Stacy and Ashley? A message you want them to hear?"

My breath hitches. I don't want to hear this. I can't stop listening to this. Cris's hand around mine tightens.

A grunt on Dad's end. "I don't want my wife and ten-year-old daughter to listen to me as I'm about to die. I don't want that to be the last thing they remember of me."

"Are you sure? They'll want answers."

"Yes, I'm sure. Stacy and I talked about it," Dad says. "Tell them you lost contact with me. I turned off my comms. You didn't hear from me again. They both know I love them very much."

"May God forgive us," Rodríguez sighs. "Joseph, those kids... Take care of them. Before the fighters do."

The recording ends there.

"Oh," Zack says with a low exhale, "to reap what you sow."

I turn to him, noting the amused smile on his face. I have about a billion things I want to ask him. "Zack... That recording..."

He holds my gaze as though he can read my mind. "You never asked me, so I never brought it up."

Because I wasn't ready. I was barely ready to hear what Sara had to say. I could no longer remember Dad's face with all its details, but that? That I could picture so vividly because it's what I saw every day. His warm skin turning a cold blue. His green eyes going hollow. His lips a dark purple. If not the blood loss, I could picture him torn to shreds by the infected he could no longer fight off. Bits of him scattered all over, rotting between leftovers of buildings.

If not the infected, then the virus in his body, because the amputation was too late. Eventually he'd drop dead, seize just like Melisa, then rise again, the man he once was gone forever, or worse, locked away deep inside, never to be free again. He'd roam the streets, same as all infected, searching for food instead of home. He might have even killed a few animals and people before someone did it to him. The bombs or someone who miraculously survived.

Like Zack.

I want to throw up just thinking about it.

"He took us to the subway tunnels, when he learned rescue wasn't coming," Zack says. "Even helped carry some of us. With one arm. I don't believe in heroes but ... there's no other word I can think of to describe him."

My lips press together. I try not to choke on my tears, so I can finally ask. The one thing I've been dreading to ask.

"Do you know if he ... if he was infected? If he..."

"Turned?" Zack finishes.

I nod. Cris squeezes my hand to comfort.

"He had an IBT on him," Zack says. "When he felt himself starting to slip away, he used it, to check. He told me he didn't want to use it before, just in case it came out positive. Easier to believe he still had time to help us. But then he had to worry about whether or not he'd be a threat to us in a few minutes."

"And?"

"It came out negative," Zack says. "I'm guessing ... chopping his arm did save him from the infection. But obviously, the blood loss..."

The tightness in my throat releases. I can't explain the relief that washes over me.

"I was there with him," Zack says, "to the end. I'm sorry I couldn't bury him. We had a room, where we kept the bodies. Away from where we stayed. We laid him to rest with everyone who didn't make it."

I nod. That makes sense, and yet ... as relieved as I am to learn that my dad didn't turn, something else seeps into me. Anger. Rage.

Because in the end, and after it all, I was right. My dad *was* abandoned. Not by his comrades, not by his partner, no. Worse. He was abandoned by his friend.

All that rage fills me with determination. Because I now know for certain, there is no world where I'd abandon my own friend.

The echo of a pop draws my attention back to the platform.

One of the Division Commanders falls over. The others scramble. General Rodríguez turns behind him in shock. Gasps among the audience.

Pop-pop-pop.

Two more of the Division Commanders drop next—The sergeant major tackles Rodríguez and the two of them fall. Blood pools on the platform as the remaining commanders scatter among the guards, who are also dropping one by one.

The crowd rises, as do all of us on the bleachers.

"Jesus," Cris says from my side. "What the hell is going on?"

An explosion rumbles the place all of a sudden. For a second, I can't trace it, until the screech of metal reaches me. I look to the top of the Sphere building...

And the globe tumbling down.

EIGHTY-ONE

THE SPHERE ROLLS to the edge of the rooftop, destroying the ledge as it tips and falls, sending a rain of debris with it. It destroys a few balconies on its way down, and as soon as it hits the ground, it rolls off the stairs and straight toward the platform, crushing some soldiers in the process.

"Evacuate the area! Now!" someone shouts.

Panicked people leave their seats and run in chaotic directions.

Someone is escorting the general away while the bodies of the sergeant major and three Division Commanders lie still in a pool of blood. The globe buries them under the wreck of the platform as it rolls over them and continues to the crowded seating area.

A grim realization slaps me.

"Mom!" I let go of Cris, about to run down the bleachers when a firm grip wraps around my wrist.

"She's okay," Zack whispers in my ear, then points to the distance, where my mom and Malhotra stand away from where everyone was seated with a Spore that I don't recognize.

My chest hurts. I haven't seen Mom in months, but even from this far, the horror on her face is evident, and I can tell, just by the way she's struggling to come back, that she's worried about me. I want to run to her and hug her—

"Now's our chance," Zack says. "Let's get moving."

"What—"

Zack's hand remains on my wrist as he drags me along with him, pushing past people trying to leave the bleachers.

Cris calls after me, but when I turn, I lose him in the jumble of bodies.

I wish I could meet Zack's eyes now. I wish I could read his mind so I know exactly what's happening.

We make it down the bleachers to the ground and Zack continues to push past those rushing to help the casualties and straight toward the Sphere building. Alarms blare inside. Red lights blink through the windows and doors and the crevices in the walls.

Parts of the top floors have been destroyed. Walls collapsed. Bodies on the floor, stairs and ground. My head is spinning.

"Zack..." I call, and when he doesn't answer, I stop and force my hand out of his grip.

If there is one thing you should trust about me, Zack told me, that day we spoke about Vincent and Lori, just as I was getting up to leave, *it's that I ... have a really hard time ... letting go of grudges. In fact, that might just be my biggest weakness. Or greatest strength. Depending on your perspective.*

He turns to me. "We don't have time to waste—"

"Zack," I say, firmly, and look behind us. The sphere is still rolling. The path it took is flattened and lifeless while everywhere else is buzzing with panic. I turn back to Zack bending over and fetching a pistol from one of the Spore corpses.

"You want to save Sarang or not?" Zack asks.

My throat constricts. My body is shaking. How does he know about that? "Haze told you?"

"Hey, you!" a voice calls behind me. I don't have to turn to know it's the bodyguards that have been following Zack. "Stop right there!"

"Wait!" I turn to them, holding my hands up, but an arm wraps around me and pulls me back. My body slams against Zack's. The tip of the pistol presses to my head. My breath catches.

"If I were you, I'd stay back." Zack backs away and pulls me with him.

The guards point their weapons at us. I can't tell if they're aiming at him or me or both of us. They hesitate to follow, though, and in a second the pressure against my head is gone and Zack's arm stretches out. A bullet shoots through the pistol and pierces a guard's head. The second one follows suit, but it wasn't Zack who shot him. Snipers?

"Ash!" Cris runs up in our direction, unarmed. The shock on his face kills me when he sees the dead guards and traces his gaze to me and Zack.

"Wait!" I call out. "Stop. Don't come any closer!"

He stops, conflict clear as day on his face. "What the hell is going on?"

"Sorry, Cristian." Zack releases me and throws me behind him before holding the pistol to me. "I wish we had time to chat, but Ashley and I have somewhere else to be."

I take the pistol with shaky hands. My throat is all clogged up. I look behind me, to the building, and try to spot the snipers. But I can't see anything.

"Now back up." Zack starts toward the guards' bodies. Cris stands still.

"Cris," I plead with him, "please don't do anything stupid. Just step back."

The look he gives me breaks my heart. Full of betrayal and hurt. He doesn't back up, but he doesn't come closer either. He just watches while Zack takes the guards' weapons and hurries back, keeping one and tossing the other M4 to me. I catch it and sling it over my shoulders.

I'm so sorry, I mouth to the stunned Cris, before Zack takes my hand and drags me with him.

There's a big flow of people coming out of the Sphere building: staff, injured soldiers, civilians. But instead of going in, we run to the back side, toward the parking garage. There are people coming out of there, too, some wearing lab coats. Zack pulls me to hide behind a vehicle.

I take a moment to breathe, gather my thoughts.

"You *really* should have told your boyfriend what you'd be up to." Zack is calm, collected—and observing our surroundings. "He probably thinks we're eloping. Which, admittedly, I do find pretty amusing."

"Zack," I snap. This is so not the time for jokes. "What's happening?"

"What's happening is we're going to save Sarang and get the hell out of here," he says. "We're taking the emergency entrance."

That doesn't answer *anything*.

"Let's get moving." Zack takes my hand again and guides me with him, using the parked vehicles as cover as we approach the emergency exit. Two more people come out of there, and once they pass, we run to the door.

It's unlocked.

We go down a set of steps, reaching the basement level. The door opens to an armed Spore.

I almost jump to cover, but the Spore instead stands to the side, clearing the path for us. "We've cleared this floor, but reinforcements will be here soon. You have to be quick."

What. The hell. Is happening?

Zack gives a nod to the Spore then proceeds inside. I tag along behind him into a long hallway. Just like the top floors, emergency lights are on here as well, and the alarm is blaring from the speakers on the walls.

"How many people are in on this?" I ask.

"Not enough," Zack says. "So, like he said: we have to be quick."

"Emergency. Emergency," the voice on the speaker says. "All personnel proceed to the nearest exit and evacuate immediately."

Zack and I run down the hallway and make a right turn—there are corpses. One sprawled on the floor, another one pressed against the wall in a seating position. Blood sprayed all about.

My stomach flips. I come to a forced stop and turn away, eyes shut. "This isn't... This wasn't part of the plan. No one was supposed to get hurt. I didn't..."

"This has nothing to do with your plan," Zack says. "You're here to save Sarang. That's all you have to do."

"But—"

"People were going to get hurt, regardless," he says. "These guards would have shot us both. You would have had to defend yourself. You would have had to kill them. Now you don't have to. But we do need to get moving, Ashley. We can't just stand here. You get Sarang. We go. Then you can cry all you want about these dead Spores."

How do I always end up with more than I bargained for? First Haze planning to meet up with Zack and his people behind our backs, and now this? I take a deep breath and turn around, pointedly ignoring the bodies. If I don't look at them, I can't think about them. Ahead of us are four doors, two on the right and two on the left, marked from letters A-D.

I take out the keycard from my pocket and run it through the reader for Section C. The doors glide open into the scanner room.

Once we step inside, the doors close and a beam of light manifests and moves up and down our bodies, scanning. The light above the opposite door turns green, then the doors open to a messy hallway. Staff running left and right between rooms, some screaming. More corpses. God.

"Okay," Zack says. "Come on. We're looking for a treatment room, right? Let's go. I'll take one side, you take the other."

I'd memorized the schematics of the lab from that blueprint Haytham brought us. He didn't specify the exact treatment room because it's random each time, so we'll have to check all of them.

The first room is not it. Second one is not it. Third is not it. I look to Zack—he shakes his head. So I continue and make a turn around the hallway.

As I'm about to check the first room to my right, the door flings open. A researcher rushes to the room across. Just before the door closes, I catch sight of someone lying on a stretcher. Dark strands of hair sprawled under her head. Pale skin.

My heart jumps.

I peek through the window of the door into the room. No other researchers in sight.

So I open the door.

I step inside.

Then I freeze.

There she is, lying on a hospital bed, her wrists, ankles and waist restrained. A device hovering over her head. Tubes and needles connected to her body. And it's only when I note the rise and fall of her chest that it hits me.

She's breathing.

EIGHTY-TWO

I PUSH a tool cart against the door and approach her, whispering, "Sara..." as I unbuckle the restraints on her wrists and waist and carefully remove the needles stuck in her.

Her tired eyes open slowly. A pinch in her brows upon seeing me. "Ashley?"

Hearing her voice—hearing her say my name—it sends me into a spiral. I can't believe what I'm seeing. I can't believe she's here. I can't believe I'm here.

I scan her top to bottom. She's dressed in a patient robe, looking paler than usual. The skin under her eyes somewhat blue. But she's breathing. She's looking at me. She said my name.

"You're really alive," I say.

"Why are you—" She sits up with evident struggle. Panic is clear in her hoarse voice. There's a scar on her shoulder. Is that the bite? "You shouldn't be here."

I take her in a tight hug, squeeze her in my arms. Her body is frail against me, like she can barely hold herself together. They were probably pumping her with drugs.

She struggles against me, pushing away. "Stop. You can't ... be here. You can't be inside with me—you're not even wearing a mask. It's—"

"You're not a threat." I pull back, gripping her shoulders, looking her dead in the eyes. "You're my friend."

She shakes her head, shrugging off my hands and leaning away from me. "No. You don't know what you're talking about. How did you even—" Her brows pinch when she spots the cart blocking the door. She looks at me again. "Ashley, why are you here?"

"To get you out."

"Out," she repeats, "out where?"

"Anywhere but here."

"No. I can't go anywhere. Not like this—" She grunts and lies back down, coughing, hands clinging to her chest. "You have to leave."

"Sara." I place a hand on hers. "What did they do to you?"

"Nothing. They're trying to help me," she says. "Trying to understand what happened to me."

"They're experimenting on you," I correct. "They told me you'd died. They told me they'd disposed of you—"

"What else were they supposed to do?" she snaps.

"But you're fine." I gesture at her. "Look at you. You can talk. You recognize me. You know who you are. You're fine."

"I am … *so* not fine."

"They can't keep you down here like this." I squeeze her hand. "You're not an infected."

"Ashley, please." Sara fights to free her hand from mine. "If they catch you here, you're gonna get in so much trouble."

"Then tell me." I punch a fist next to her head, forcing her eyes back to me. "Tell me you wanna stay here. Tell me you're really okay down here."

She swallows. I count all five seconds it takes her to give me an answer. "I need you to leave."

"No." It's firm, definite, and without another word I undo the restraints on her ankles. "Come on," I urge her. "We have about five minutes to get out."

"Ashley." Sara sits up again. Tears on the verge of falling. "You can't save every—"

"I'm not trying to save everyone!" I'm sick of people telling me this over and over, as if I don't know it. "I'm trying to save *one* person. I'm trying to save *you*, so shut the hell up and let me do that."

Her lips quiver. She doesn't fight me.

"Sara…" I rest a hand on hers. "I'm not letting go."

"God, I so regret telling you that," she says in a tone that tells me she so doesn't.

"Hey!" A man in a white coat rushes into the room. The same one who ran out earlier. "What are you doing here? This is a—"

I don't even think, I lunge at him and slam him against the wall, then wrap a tight arm around his neck and squeeze.

"Ashley!" Sara stumbles out of the bed, falling to her knees in the process. "Stop!"

I don't stop. I squeeze until his muscles relax, then I drop him on the floor, unconscious. I strip him of his coat and shoes then walk back to Sara. "Put these on. It'll make it easier for us to walk out."

She takes them with shaky hands, and I help her with the shoes as she throws the coat on. I pull her to her feet, balance her for a moment before releasing her. I would support her all the way through, but I'll probably need both hands in case we run into trouble.

When we come out to the hallway again, Zack's just exiting the room across from us.

"Sarang." He grins. "Good to see you again."

"Zack, no time to chat," I tell him.

"Right. Let's go." Zack leads us back from the way we came. Only, as soon as we turn the corner, a group of Spores runs in. Judging by the way Zack retreats and pulls us with him, they're not on our side.

"That's the reinforcements. You'll have to take the elevator." Zack looks at me with confident resolve. "I'll hold them off."

"What do you mean you'll hold them—"

Zack reaches around the corner and opens fire randomly into the hallway. Screams and shouts follow.

"Go!" He gives me a gentle push and nods for me to run the opposite way. "There should be more Revolters waiting on that side, keeping the path clear. For a while anyway."

Revolters. How long have they been planning this for? Who exactly is involved? So many questions. No time to find out. But I guess this was a long time coming, wasn't it?

I squeeze Zack's arm. "Don't get killed."

He flashes me one of his charming grins. "Anything for those pretty eyes."

I give his shoulder a light punch and turn around. Sara's hand in mine, we retrace our steps back to the hallway of treatment rooms, then turn left to another hallway.

One of the staff spots us and instantly drops to the floor, hands over his head, shaking in fear. "Please," he cries, "please don't shoot me!"

"Ashley." Behind me, Sara comes to a stop.

"Sara, we don't have time—"

"No." She points at a room to our right. "We have to go in there. Please. We have to take her with us."

I recognize the room she's standing at. That's where they're keeping Melisa.

"We can't take Melisa with us." I take her hand again and try to pull her along.

"But she wants to come with us," Sara says. "She wants us to get her out."

"That's not Mel, Sara," I say. "It's not her. It's ... something else."

"She's calling to me." Sara's eyes are glued to the door, as if she's entranced. "She's been calling to me this whole time."

She's been calling to her? I shudder at the unsettling revelation. Is that the same effect an Active has on other infected? Is it manifesting differently on Sara because she's not entirely an infected?

"Do they know?" I ask her. "The researchers. Do they know that you can feel Melisa? That you can communicate with her?"

She shrugs.

If they know that… If that's the case, then ... they probably won't kill Melisa. If they know Sara can communicate with her, they'll keep her alive, and they'll have more reasons to hold onto Sara. Even without Lori.

"Please," Sara begs. "We can't leave her here."

No. No, we can't.

I turn to the researcher on the floor, who's crawling away, and yank him up by the collar of his lab coat.

He shrinks, eyes squeezed shut. "Please! I'm not a soldier like the others. I'm a civilian. I can't hurt you."

I place him in front of the locked door. "Open it."

"I can't," he cries. "Only personnel with clearance—"

I press the muzzle of my weapon against the back of his head. "Open it, or I'll find someone else who will."

"Okay! Okay!" He holds his shaky hands up briefly before reaching for the control panel on the side of the door. He punches in some numbers.

Beep. The door unlocks.

"Sara," I say. "I have a handgun tucked in the back. Grab it."

Sara complies, fetching the sidearm from me, then we proceed inside. I drag the researcher with me.

Two more researchers turn to us with confused faces. Then, not so confused when they catch on. These two carry themselves much more confidently. One of them sticks to the back, the other one steps toward us. Colonel Marchand.

"Private Brown." Her gaze shifts between me and Sara. "Do you realize you're holding a civilian hostage right now?"

"Yes," I say, "so you best tell your friend over there not to grab whatever he's grabbing if he doesn't want anyone to get hurt."

The other researcher comes to a stop. He looks to Marchand questioningly, and she gives him a nod before holding my gaze again, raising her hands in the air to show they're empty.

"You're so lucky that you're down here in your lab, so safe." I take a few more steps further into the room, walking around a desk to get a proper view of her and her partner. "The other Division Commanders weren't so lucky. I wonder how many of them are dead by now."

"Are you accusing me of something, Private?" Marchand's brows arch daringly. "You think you're in any position to point fingers right now?"

I move closer, Sara at my side, keeping the sidearm trained on the other researcher.

"I see you're with Jung," she notes. "Will you let me explain why this is a mistake?"

"No, thanks." I force a smile. "I don't have time to listen to lies."

"I doubt you have time for much either way," she says. "So why are you here?"

I nod at the reinforced glass compartment behind her, where Melisa is. "I want you to open it."

Marchand shoots one glance over her shoulder before turning back to me, snorting. "Come on, Private. I know I don't need to explain to you why that would be an even bigger mistake."

God, I really don't have time for this.

"Do you know the code?" I ask the researcher I'm holding.

He stiffens. "Uh... I..."

Marchand's eyes scream *don't* at him.

Gunshots explode past my ear. For a second there I think I'm hurt, then the researcher in the back drops to his knees, screaming in pain.

I turn to Sara, finger on the trigger of the handgun. She points it at Marchand next, who is standing still, unflinching.

"Open it," Sara demands.

"Okay!" the researcher in my hold cries. "Okay, I'll open it. Just please don't hurt me."

I release him, keeping my weapon trained on him as I follow him toward the compartment. I nod for Marchand to step further back, away from us. Sara keeps her handgun aimed on the woman as well, sticking close to me.

"You have absolutely no idea what you're doing, do you?" Marchand says. Of course. She thinks she can talk me out of this. If my own boyfriend couldn't have talked me out of this, she never stood a chance. "You think you're doing the right thing? You think you're saving your friends? These aren't your friends anymore. They're not the people you used to know, as much as you'd like to believe they are."

I ignore her. She may as well be shouting nonsense. The researcher, through tears and with a shaky hand, punches in the code for the compartment then immediately jumps away, scared.

The door slides open. Melisa doesn't lunge at me. She just stands there, watching me with a hollow yet simultaneously piercing stare. Has she been waiting for this moment?

"I'm so sorry, Mel. So sorry I did this to you." I suck in a sharp breath and point my M4 at her. To think, I fought so hard to stop the others from doing this to her, only to end up having to do it myself.

"Wait!" Marchand's panicked voice. "Don't—"

I shoot a bullet through Melisa's head just as she starts to shriek.

Sara leaps from her spot and lunges at Marchand, tackling her on the floor. The cages behind me rattle as the animals are suddenly alert. Growling and hissing and releasing all sorts of threatening noises.

"Sara!" I run toward them, pulling Sara off of Marchand, who's backing away under a desk, holding her arm. "What are you doing?"

She stumbles back, nearly falls as she holds her head, squinting. "My head…"

"We have to go." I steady her, then start for the door.

EIGHTY-THREE

THE SECOND WE GET OUT, we're met with a group of Spores to our left, fighting amongst themselves. So Sara and I run right.

A turn and then a long run down another hallway. God there are so many hallways here it's like a maze. I use the keycard again to unlock the Section C door leading to Section A, and from there I take the main hallway toward reception.

"Freeze!" someone shouts behind me, and I glance over my shoulder at two Spores—judging by the weapons they have aimed at me and Sara, it's safe to assume they're not with the Revolters.

I have no choice. I push both me and Sara into the scanner room. The door closes just before one of the Spores fires. It's only when the doors are fully shut that I remember I had a second option: shoot to kill.

My breathing is hard as the scanner runs. The strip of light goes up and down. Beside me, Sara's lost eyes dart around us.

"How did you get in here? In the lab?" She looks at me now. Her lips are so colorless. "Where did you get that card from?"

"Luke gave it to me," I say. "Zack helped me get in here. Haze is getting a car ready for us."

Her mouth falls. "You did ... all this—" she gestures around the scanner room but I know what she means extends beyond these walls "—for me?"

Red lights flash. A second alarm starts blaring. On the other side, the clacking of combat boots approaches. Gunfire. Some shouting. Is that Zack's voice? Thank God he's still alive.

I turn to the other door, the one that's supposed to take us to the reception hall. I pointlessly try to pry it open with my bare hands. I kick it and punch it and kick it again, hoping if I break something, it'll magically open the doors. There's no button anywhere. No control panel. And these walls look too thick. I can't do anything. Zack's not going to hold them off forever, even with backup.

I deliver one last desperate kick to the door, but nothing happens. It can't end here. Not like this. I haven't even gotten her out of the lab yet. I haven't even—

"Ashley." Sara's hand rests on my shoulder. I look at her from the corner of my eye. She's smiling. Why the hell is she smiling? There is nothing to smile about. This is so scuffed. We're screwed. "It's okay," she says. The audacity to lie to my face. This is not okay. "I can't leave here anyway. I appreciate—"

The blaring stops and the lights return to normal. The door in front of us opens with a metallic hiss. A breathless Haytham stands on the other side.

"Hurry," he says. "The elevator is clear."

"Hayth—"

"Just go!" he yells.

I give him an appreciative smile, nudging Sara forward as we both bolt for the elevator. As soon as we get in and I punch the button for the first floor, the second door in the scanner room opens to a group of Spores running at us. I catch sight of Zack on the floor, not moving. My heart sinks. The elevator closes before they get to us.

My portor beeps with a call. I hurriedly fetch my earpiece from my pocket and put it on, pressing the button.

"Ashley, do you copy?" Luke's voice says in my ear. He'd established a private comm channel for us earlier.

"Luke," I say. Sara perks up at that. "What's up?"

"There's a problem," he grumbles. "Protesters blocked most of the roads in the southeast parts. You won't be able to get through there unless you're willing to run over a lot of civilians."

"That's not good." I smother a gasp. "What do I do?"

"You'll have to take the southwestern gate," he says. "But I'm not gonna make it there in time. I might be able to get in touch with some of my buddies, though."

"Okay..." Don't panic. Do not panic.

"Otherwise, you'll have to just ... drive through." He's out of breath, like he's been running for an hour. "If you drive fast enough, the APC can probably break through the gate."

Everything's going wrong. Everything.

"All right," I say anyway, because what choice do I have? We're here and we're doing this and we have to go all the way. "Thanks, Luke."

The elevator doors open and I step out first, check my corners. I lead Sara with me to the back exit of the Sphere building. We hide when Spores pass by—and once they're out of sight we continue until we're outside. Now we just have to sneak all the way to the workshops—

"Drop your weapon." A Spore comes out of the parking garage. He taps on his earpiece. "I've got eyes on the fugitives. South exit of the Sphere."

Screeching tires draw our attention to the road on the right. I'm prepared for a backup squad, except the car drives straight at the guard. He's probably just as confused as I am because it takes him too long to react, and the car rams into him and sends him flying across the backyard.

In the driver's seat sits Haze.

"Ash, get in!" She unbuckles her seatbelt and gets out of the car.

"Haze?" I rush down the stairs toward her. "What are you doing here? I thought I was supposed—"

"Zack called me," she explains. "Told me you won't make it. So I came." She opens the back door of the vehicle, allowing Sara to go in. Then she circles around to the passenger seat. "You drive."

I don't argue. I jump into the driver's seat, lock the doors, and once everyone's buckled up, I turn on the vehicle radio and drive.

"... Two fugitives, teens, female," a voice on the general comms channel announces. "Sarang Jung. Asian; dark hair, brown eyes, dressed in lab attire. Ashley Brown. White; brown and pink hair, green eyes, formerly with the Renegades. Last seen south of the Sphere building. I repeat, we've got two fugitives..."

"Ash." Haze takes out a beanie from inside my rucksack and leans over to put it on my head, tucking my hair under it.

"Thanks."

She then takes out a Spore uniform and passes it over to Sara in the back. "Here. You should get changed. Sorry if it doesn't fit you."

I try to focus on driving, despite the distracting comms chatter. So many reports coming in. Something about armed mutineers invading homes in the Fifth Sector and targeting privileged families, taking hostages and murdering others. Protesters attacking soldiers and stealing their weapons. The echoes of gunfire that surround us emphasize the chaos. What in the world is happening?

I follow the map on the nav system of the APC, heading southwest like Luke said.

"Did you know?" I ask Haze.

"Know what?" she asks.

"About all this! The explosion?" I slam the steering wheel for emphasis. "The assassination attempt? They tried to kill the general. They shot some of the Division Commanders and blew up the Sphere."

I catch Haze's puzzled reflection in the rearview mirror. "Of course I didn't know."

"Don't lie to me."

"I'm not!" Haze says.

"Zack knew. You told him about our plan," I say. "You told him I was going to save Sara."

"I didn't," Haze says.

"Then how the hell did he find out?"

"*I don't know*," Haze says, frustrated. "I thought maybe *you* told him. He just contacted me and told me to drive the car to the Sphere building because you wouldn't make it in time."

As I drive down the road, some of the protestors start to gather here as well. I curse under my breath.

Speeding up, I punch the horn, hoping that'll be enough to warn them to move. They don't budge, though. They stand stubborn blocking the road. Some of them pick up rocks and throw them at us. At the last minute, I swerve and drive up on the sidewalk, narrowly missing the crowd, but I still hit someone. Their body bumps against the windshield before rolling over to the side. Dammit.

"Ash, don't stop!" Haze shouts.

The angry protesters chase after us. The rock-throwing intensifies.

I drive faster, taking a sharp turn to the right and continuing in a straight line, faster and faster, until the protesters disappear.

"What's happening?" Sara's reflection peeks at me in the rearview mirror. She's put on the uniform Haze gave her.

"I don't know," I say. "It doesn't matter."

It takes a few minutes before the gate looms into view. Some guards are stationed there already, so I slow to a stop, unsure.

Luke told me to drive straight.

"Hey, you!" A guard stomps toward us from my left. "Where are you going with that vehicle?"

I can't think of anything fast enough, and my lack of response seems to alarm him.

He taps his earpiece. "I got an APC here at the southwestern gate. Two females. Please advise—"

Someone runs at the guard and tackles him. The two fall on the ground with a hard thud, sending up a cloud of dirt. The assailant sits up and delivers one punch after the other to the guard's face until he blacks out.

Luke rises to his feet and turns to me.

"Luke?" I gasp.

Sara leans over my seat to look outside the window.

Luke is stunned the moment he sees her. Shock. Surprise. Disbelief. But more importantly, longing. And no time to process any of it. He swallows a lump, eyes back on me. "Where is Zack?"

"He didn't—" The sudden realization cuts me off. "Wait... *You* told Zack?"

Luke doesn't answer me. He walks up to the car and smacks the door urgently. "Go." His conflicted gaze moves between me and Sara. "Drive. Get out of here. Go as far as you can."

I wish I could let him and Sara say goodbye, but we don't have time to waste. "Thank you."

He gives me a nod and backs up. I start driving again. The guards at the gate are forming a line, weapons up, but it's clear they can't decide between shooting or getting out of the way.

I don't stop. I don't slow down. The guards jump aside before I run them over. I drive at the gate hard and fast, busting it open in the process. I duck my head when bullets hit the back of the vehicle, but I don't stop driving. I can't stop driving.

"Ashley..." Sara's tired voice behind me. She's clinging to the driver's seat. "Where are we going?"

"Away," I tell her.

The comms chatter continues, orders to deploy a search party after us. Something about a resistance force sent to the Fifth Sector. Within minutes, a helicopter flies up behind us.

"They're going to kill you," Sara says. "Both of you."

She's right. They don't have any use for me or Haze. As soon as they get their hands on Sara, they'll have no reason to spare us. Not after this. So it's pretty simple: they won't catch us. I won't let that happen.

A wince draws my attention to Sara. Her reflection in the rearview mirror—hunched over, a hand clutched around her hair.

"Sara?" I call. "What's wrong? Do you need some water?"

Not a second later, she looks up with a grim expression and lunges at me with bared teeth.

"Sara, what're you—" I struggle to keep her off, but she fights me, her mouth wide open as she tries to bite into me. Haze tries to push her away, too. A hard shove knocks Sara over.

"Ashley! Watch out!" Haze shouts, and I look ahead at a vehicle blocking the road.

I swerve the car just in time to dive down a hill and slam into a tree.

EIGHTY-FOUR

I SHAKE MY HEAD, dizzy. It takes me a moment to orient myself. Rotors whir above us. Engines rumble in the distance. Incoherent chatter buzzes through the radio.

"Ash…" Haze calls in a broken voice. "You okay?"

"I'm … fine." I undo my seatbelt and stumble out of the car. "Sara." I walk with unsteady steps toward the backdoor and open it. Sara nearly falls out. I catch her and help her stand.

"You have to leave me." Sara uses the vehicle for balance. "Both of you. It's too dangerous."

"No," I say. "I'm not leaving you. Let's get moving."

I'm about to start walking but … Haze still hasn't gotten out yet.

"Ash," Haze's shaky voice calls.

I run back to the front of the vehicle. "What's up?"

"It's my leg." She gestures to the smashed-up side of the car where it hit the tree. There's blood. "I don't think I can run."

"No." I shake my head and circle around to the other side. "No, no, no, no. I can get you out."

"You have to go," she grunts.

"No." I fight the door to get it open and snatch her hand. "Come on, you gotta help me out here."

"Take Sara and go." She sits still, fighting to free her hand from my hold. "Even if you manage to get me out, I'll slow you down."

"Haze, we're not doing this, okay?" My grip firms up around her hand and I pull hard.

"Let them find me," she says, pulling back. "You don't have to worry about me. You need to run. I can stall for you, send them in the wrong direction, if they'll believe me."

"Haze..." I choke on a sob.

"We can't stop now." She passes the rucksack to me. I take it in one hand. "Keep going. Get her to safety."

I nearly choke on a sob, grip loosening bit by bit. "I'm so sorry."

"It's okay." She smiles as her hand slips out of mine. "It's okay, Ash. I'm *asking* you to leave me."

Fighting tears, I leave her with Sara's pistol, then we dive into the woods. The helicopter won't be able to spot us easily like this, but the ground troops will be upon us in minutes, if not seconds.

I can use the darkness to my advantage. But not for very long, because I trip on something and then slip and fall down a slope. I drag Sara with me, all the way down, until I hit something hard. A tree or a log or a rock. I can't tell immediately.

Moans surround us in seconds. I scramble to sit, take out the M4, looking around to spot the infected. Footsteps to my right. I turn, but the figure isn't walking toward me. It's ... it's walking right past me. As is every other infected. There's enough to account for an entire wave.

"They're ... ignoring us?"

"They're ignoring *me*." Sara sits to my left, rubbing at her arm. "They can ... sense me. Just like I can sense them."

I don't know what the hell that means, nor am I waiting around to figure it out. This is our chance.

Shooting to my feet, I help Sara up, then we continue straight ahead, past the infected, who don't even look in our direction. I don't know why being with Sara makes me invisible to them, but I'll take it.

We emerge on the other side of the woods onto a road, buildings ahead. We've been walking and running for God knows how long, I'm starting to feel it. The crash and the fall didn't help my legs, either.

I guide us to one of the buildings. An old pharmacy, from what I can tell. Thankfully, the inside is clear. I leave Sara's side to push the counter against the door and block the entrance. Just in case.

"Ash," Sara calls.

"What's up?" I pant as I push. I'm so tired and this counter is heavier than it looks.

"Where are we going?" she asks.

I suck in a deep breath and turn to her. "Nina gave me this radio. I have it in the ruck. She told me I can use it to find her. We can meet up with her. Join her and the others at the *Red Queen*?"

Sara nods. Her lips draw into a line. "I can't go with you."

"Sara, stop it." I take a step toward her. "There's no going back."

"I don't wanna go back," she confesses, "but I can't stay with you either."

"Yes, you can." Another step. I hold her by the shoulders. "You can fight this."

"I can't." Tears fill up her eyes. "Ash, you don't get it. I'm not ... me. I mean, I am right now, but sometimes... Sometimes I lose ... sense of myself. I don't know who I am, where I am, or what I'm doing. What happened in the car will happen again. You're gonna have to go without me."

"No." I shake my head. "I already left Haze. I'm not leaving you, too."

"Ash, I know you think this is your fault, but I want you to know, I don't resent you."

"You should, though," I argue, hands falling to my sides. "I was... I've been a terrible friend. It's all because of me that this happened to you."

"It's not. It just happened," she assures me. "And you're not a terrible friend. Ash, you're the *best* friend I've ever had. You infiltrated Spheria's lab and turned all of SPORE on you *just* to save me. Which is arguably stupid and reckless, and will probably end with us both dead or captured, anyway, but ... I appreciate it," she says. "I appreciate *you*."

Yeah. That's great. It's great that she appreciates the helpless mess that I am.

"I know you want to hold on. I know that's what I told you to do, and thank you for taking my words to heart but..." Sara breathes in. "I don't want to hurt you. Ever. So *I* have to let go."

"Please," I beg. Don't leave me, too. "Where are you even gonna go?"

"I'll figure it out," she murmurs. "I'm so sorry, for everything."

I stand there for a heartbeat. Two. Three. And before she leaves, I blurt, "I'm gonna lure them away."

She faces me again, a question in her eyes.

"It's you they're after. I'm not important. So you're gonna run, and I'm gonna lead them away from here."

"That's too dangerous."

"I can handle it." I have to. "Sara … all of this… I did all of this for you. So you could get away, and I'm not letting it all go to waste."

She frowns. "You're sure?"

"I am." I nod. "I won't try to fight them. I won't try to shoot anyone. I'll just try to get them to follow me."

"Okay." Sara nods, but she doesn't move. She stands there, staring at me.

A beat, then we both go for a hug. Her arms wrap tight around me, and mine around her. I savor the moment while it lasts.

"Take care of yourself," she whispers.

"You, too," I whisper back, then pull away with a sniffle before I have any second thoughts.

She leaves through a back door, then I'm left alone in the middle of the pharmacy.

"Goodbye," I whisper to no one, "partner."

EPILOGUE

I DON'T KNOW how long I've been running for. How much longer I can keep going. My legs are starting to give.

I stop for a minute, lean against a wall and suck the air in big gulps. God this was a mistake. Every inch of me hurts and the fact I'm not running anymore makes the throbbing pain shooting through my leg the center of my attention.

Tap-tap-tap. Footsteps. I bolt into a sprint again.

I decided, like an idiot, to run toward the gunfire after Sara and I separated, just briefly to let them spot me, so I could lure them in the wrong direction. But I got a little distracted, of course, when I spotted Cris among the search party, and took a second too long to bolt. One advantage I have is that I'm able to squeeze into places most of them can't, but still, I haven't managed to lose them since, and I don't know that I will.

"Ash!" the voice that calls out makes my heart leap out of my chest and back. "Wait!"

I don't wait. I can't wait. I keep running. I don't turn around. I don't want to see his face again.

Then a chaser jumps out of a building up ahead and runs at me. I come to a forced stop, shaky hands, weapon up. A bullet zooms past me before I can steady my aim, and the chaser drops dead in the next second. Another corpse falls off the top of a truck to my left. A third *thuds* behind me.

"Wow," I pant as I turn around, lungs on fire, skin drenched in hot sweat. "Look at you…" Pant. "Didn't even miss a single one."

Cris stops a few paces away from me. He lowers his weapon just as I reach for mine. Can't tell if I'm about to join those chasers in the very near future.

"Unless," I say. "You *did* miss all three of your shots."

"You know, if anyone should worry about getting shot, it's me." His words sting. A flash of Will's face passes me by, and a few other unlucky ones. I could've done without this specific déjà vu. "Why can't we ever see eye to eye? You and me? Is it just force of habit? Or are we really that different?"

"Opposites do attract," I tease. Ill-timed, I know, especially for someone who abandoned her boyfriend.

It gets a small chuckle out of him, though, before he puts his serious face back on. "There's no reason we can't talk."

I stay quiet.

Humans are unpredictable, Seidel said. But this is Cris. He wouldn't want to hurt me.

"Remember what you said to me before?" He approaches. "That out here, it's either the people we love, or the people they love? Us or them?"

I swallow a lump. I hate when people throw my words back in my face.

"But I doubt you ever considered the possibility," he says, "that there'd be no *them*. It's just *us*."

Humans are unpredictable. It's Cris. He doesn't break the rules. He won't hurt me but he will detain me.

My hands shake. I squeeze my weapon tighter, safety's still on. Despite my aching heart, I aim it at him, if only to deter him from coming closer.

Is this how Nina felt that day in the Pit? Was she also trying to decide whether she could trust me or not? I don't have to kill him. I can just incapacitate him. That's what he'd say, right?

Except I don't want to do either. Give me something. Anything.

"You know," his tone drops to a soft murmur, "I wasn't going to report you. On the night of recruitment." What the hell is he on about now? "I was really hoping to convince you, but at the same time, I could see it in your eyes. Just how much you wanted to go. And I thought … if that's what you want, who am I to stop you?"

My shoulders drop. There's this side of him, too. The side of him that stays behind to save children. The side of him that's willing to kill to protect me. The side that takes my hand and strokes my face and hugs and holds me in spite of what the rules say.

"The only reason I reported you, is because I heard about the wave," Cris says. "And I worried you'd run into it, and I thought ... if there was even the smallest chance that reporting you could save your life, and I didn't do it ... I would never forgive myself. And I knew you'd hate me even more, but I was willing to risk that if it meant you got to survive."

Yeah, I did hate him for reporting me, temporarily anyway. He saved my life, and I appreciate it. But... "Then you of all people should understand," I say, "that I also had to try to save her, no matter what it cost. No matter who it pissed off."

Muffled comms chatter seeps through Cris's earpiece. I'd turned off my portor altogether and disabled my tracker earlier—I'd asked Luke to show me how—so I don't know what's been going on in Spheria or out here. I can only hope they didn't find Sara.

"Rey?" a muffled voice calls repeatedly. "Status report."

He could have called this in. He could have reported to the others that he found me. But he didn't.

Or maybe he did. Maybe he's just biding time by talking to me while they surround the area.

"Ash," he says in that soft voice of his and holds his hands up as a sign of surrender. "Shoot me if you want. If that's what you think you have to do to protect yourself and get away. But I haven't changed my mind. I believe in other options. Just ... *please*, talk to me."

I believe... Dalal's voice whispers to me, *we humans have more choices than we think, at any given moment.*

"Rey?" the voice continues. "Status report. Is everything okay?"

"What are the other options?" I ask. "I surrender? You arrest me and take me back to Spheria?"

He nods. "That's one option."

"What's another one?" I ask, head tilting to the side, searching his eyes.

Cris hesitates, the voice in his earpiece persisting. Then he takes out the earpiece and throws it away. "I come with you."

Did... Did I hear that right?

"Wherever you wanna go," he says, stepping closer. "I go with you, and we do this together."

"Don't be an idiot." I shake my head at him, backing away. "You can't leave SPORE. That'll just make you another target."

"I don't care." His shoulders drop. "I told you this before, but maybe you forgot. I don't ever wanna be the kind of person who stands aside and watches his friends die. No matter which side those friends are on."

My lips twitch. I fight the burning in my eyes. Here we are. Exactly where I didn't want us to end up. A fork in the road.

"You're supposed to be returning to Kadia," I remind him. "Don't risk that just for me."

"Home isn't home, without those who make it so," he says, as if reading my mind. "Grandpa's gone. And my parents ... well, they won't really miss me much. I wanted *us* to go. Together. I still do. Even if it's not Kadia."

"What about you? Your life. Your privilege. Your safety," I sniffle. "Would... You would ... abandon all of that? For me?"

"In a heartbeat," he answers. Another step. "You just ask. Say you want me to."

My voice cracks. "That would be really selfish of me."

"It would be just as selfish of me to go back without you," he says.

"I don't..." My breath hitches. I lower my weapon at last. "I don't wanna be alone."

"You don't have to be." Cris takes a few more steps and closes the distance. "I'm here." He offers me his hand. I take it.

A click of boots startles us. We both turn to it.

Stephen comes out from behind a building, weapon in hand, pointed down. Cris doesn't waste a breath to point his M4 at Stephen, but I smack it down before he shoots. He gives me an unsure look.

I step in front of him, looking over at Stephen, whose stern eyes are on Cris, before they move to me. He doesn't raise his weapon. A silent nod of acknowledgment, then he taps his earpiece. "No sign of Rey or Jung," he says. "But I see Brown running north. I'm right behind her."

And that's mine and Cris's cue to run south.

We run until we can't breathe anymore. Until we can't stand. Until the night is swept away by day and faint streaks of light pierce the cloudy sky. Until we're tripping and falling and helping each other up and dragging ourselves as far away as we can.

It's on the rooftop of an abandoned building that we stand. The sun rises in the distance. The infected roam the streets below, their moans echoing.

"I can't believe Stephen helped us." Cris slides down to the floor with his back against the parapet.

I can.

"He owed me." And he also now knows ... I wasn't lying about Sara or the cure.

"Owed you?" Cris asks.

"It doesn't matter." I sit beside him, scooting close until our arms touch. Because I'm cold and he's warm. And I need warm.

"You wanna tell me what happened with Sara?" he asks.

"She's gone," I say. "Doesn't want to be found."

He breathes out. "You okay?"

"Yeah." I lean my head on him. My eyes fight to stay open. Cris drapes his arm around my shoulders and pulls me closer. He smells like the one place I want to be right now. "I just ... really wanted to go home."

"I know." The weight of his head rests on mine. "Me, too."

ACKNOWLEDGMENTS

It's been roughly nine months since *Those Who Survive* came out as I'm writing this, which is as insane as when I learned from my agent in 2023 that we have a two-book deal.

Getting to share a *second* book with the world is an unbelievable honor. Even more so because, for a long time, my only audience was my best friend, Naila. She'd read three-months' worth of summer vacation writing in a week, and always ask me to write more. She always wanted to read *more*. A few weeks ago, I got to hand her a physical copy of my first ever published book. The joy in her eyes, the pride, the excitement—it's unforgettable! Wherever I am by the time this one comes out, I'll always be grateful to have had you in my life. I can't wait to see you again and give you a copy of this one as well.

My mom's and siblings' joy was just as heart-melting when I handed them the fruit of my work after months of them seeing it through a screen, and before that, years of me writing in repurposed school notebooks that my mom is still storing for me. And I don't know where I'd be without my husband, who sat with me through the endless moments of self-doubt as I worked on this book. You all reminded me that I should be as proud of myself as you are of me. You all reminded me of what's been regrettably easy to forget amidst the chaos and stress: I realized my childhood dream, and that by itself is a worthwhile achievement.

This achievement couldn't have been possible without my agent, Laura Bennett, guiding me through, and sometimes even taking the lead in, this uncharted territory. It couldn't have been possible without my editors, Ajebowale Roberts, who got me and my story through first barriers, before handing the torch over to Rosie Best, who's keeping the light shining ahead while this book makes its way to the end of the tunnel. Thank you to Charlotte, Sofia, and everyone at OMC for holding the doors open for this story. To Gavin Reece (@gavinreece62 on IG) for illustrating another out-of-this-world cover, which has become my new obsession. To Ashleigh Haddad (@ashleigh.haddad on IG) for giving voice to my characters and allowing me to experience my story in a way I never imagined.

And I wouldn't have made it this far without those of you who believed in my work in its messiest stages. My critique partners: Luke Garcha, who pushed me to challenge myself and do better, all the while cheering me on. Fellow author Scott M. Sargent, who gave me pointers on the military bits I inevitably got wrong, and gave me different perspectives and options to consider. My beta readers: Adele Leech, Amelia Yates, Andréanne, Aria Crane, Cat Balteanu, Gaeten Nelson, Kirsty Southwell, Nasrina Zahra (or Beyonce, as she wanted to be called), and Warisha Tabassum. More thank yous to Yasmin K. for giving me pointers with some of the medical stuff, and Edward Nelson III for providing extra feedback on the military shenanigans.

Endless gratitude to the lovely reviewers who supported me in my debut year, and even helped me spread the word about this book. Andréanne (@andreanne.p_booksta on IG—yes, I'm mentioning you twice!), Emily Jane (@emilyjane_theworrierprincess on IG), Kirsti Ferguson (@mrsfegfiction on IG), and Rachael Wharmby (@books.with.rachael on IG). To all you lovely people I've spoken to on social media, and everyone else who took the time to read, rate and review my book. You give me reason to try harder, push further, and do better.

Lastly, I'd like to thank my agency and publishing sister Sophia Vahdati, author of *The Girl with the Fierce Eyes*, for cheering me on since my book came out. Best of luck with writing your second book. I can't wait to read it!

Working on *Those Who Fight* was a challenge for many reasons, from dealing with health issues to imposter syndrome. At times it was hard not to tunnel-vision on the bitter parts. All of you reminded me that the sweet parts were there too. I hope I managed to deliver something worthwhile to those who loved the first book, and I hope I can continue to deliver.

The author and One More Chapter would like to thank everyone who contributed to the publication of this story...

Analytics
Imogen Wolstencroft

Audio
Fionnuala Barrett
Ciara Briggs

Design
Lucy Bennett
Fiona Greenway
Liane Payne
Dean Russell

Digital Sales
Laura Daley
Lydia Grainge
Hannah Lismore

eCommerce
Laura Carpenter
Madeline ODonovan
Charlotte Stevens
Christina Storey
Rachel Ward

Editorial
Rosie Best
Kara Daniel
Charlotte Ledger
Jennie Rothwell
Hana Rowlands
Sofia Salazar Studer
Caroline Scott-Bowden
Emily Thomas
Helen Williams

Harper360
Emily Gerbner
Ariana Juarez
Jean Marie Kelly
emma sullivan
Sophia Wilhelm

International Sales
Ruth Burrow
Bethan Moore
Colleen Simpson

Inventory
Sarah Callaghan
Kirsty Norman

Marketing & Publicity
Occy Carr
Chloe Cummings
Grace Edwards
Katie Sadler

Operations
Melissa Okusanya
Vanessa Coubrough

Production
Denis Manson
Simon Moore
Francesca Tuzzeo

Rights
Ashton Mucha
Alisah Saghir
Zoe Shine
Aisling Smyth

Trade Marketing
Ben Hurd
Eleanor Slater

The HarperCollins Contracts Team

The HarperCollins Distribution Team

The HarperCollins Finance & Royalties Team

The HarperCollins Legal Team

The HarperCollins Technology Team

UK Sales
Isabel Coburn
Jay Cochrane
Leah Woods

And every other essential link in the chain from delivery drivers to booksellers to librarians and beyond!

One More Chapter is an award-winning global division of HarperCollins.

Subscribe to our newsletter to get our latest eBook deals and stay up to date with all our new releases!

signup.harpercollins.co.uk/join/signup-omc

Meet the team at
www.onemorechapter.com

Follow us!

@onemorechapterhc

Do you write unputdownable fiction? We love to hear from new voices. Find out how to submit your novel at
www.onemorechapter.com/submissions